SHADOWS ON THE FLAG

A Don Carling Mystery

Russ Graham

RUSS GRAHAM

Shadows on the Flag: A Don Carling Mystery

This is a work of fiction. All of the characters, organizations, and events portrayed in the novel are either products of the author's imagination or used fictitiously. Any resemblance to actual persons, living or dead, is purely coincidental.

Published by Wheatmark®
610 East Delano Street, Suite 104
Tucson, Arizona 85705 U.S.A.
www.wheatmark.com

International Standard Book Number: 978-1-60494-599-7
Library of Congress Control Number: 2011930638

For my wife Patricia,

our daughter, Valerie, and son, Ken,

the three most important people in my life

The author wishes to sincerely thank those who generously spent time to proofread the manuscript or contributed in other ways to the final draft. They include: Pamela Claridge, Bryan Proctor, Marion & Ron Rathwell, Karen & Russ Anderson, Dr. Wilf "Andy" Anderson [no relation], and Patricia, of course.

I also want to offer a belated "thank you" to Roger Burgess-Webb for his help with my first novel, DEADLY DIVERSIONS..

The professional team at WHEATMARK were a pleasure to work with in getting SHADOWS ON THE FLAG into print, and for that I am also most grateful.

Prologue

Even before the euphoria generated among radical Islamists by the deadly suicide flights on New York City and Washington on September 11, 2001 had waned, the men behind it were looking to strike again. Their efforts intensified after the US-led incursions into Afghanistan and Iraq. al-Qaeda leaders, hiding out in the mountains of northwest Pakistan, let it be known that they would finance any viable plot to attack the United States again. A plan submitted by a French Muslim caught their attention immediately. His idea to punish the American public if it re-elected the Bush administration this coming November, the reviled warmongers behind the occupation of the two Islamic countries, was exactly what they envisioned. A plot to cause a nationwide panic, resulting in catastrophic damage to the US economy.

"Praise be to Allah! The great visionaries behind al-Qaeda World have approved my plan. We will launch the next victorious attack on America!"

Three men were meeting in a chalet above the small village of Bois-sur-Mont in the secluded Bruelle Valley. The chalet, 120 kilometers north of the port city of Marseille, had originally been built for the Amara brothers and their families.

Nasir Amara, 69, and his brother, Jabaar, 67, were natives of Algeria, the former French colony on the African shore of the Mediterranean Sea. Another brother, Rashad, had died 30 years ago. The speaker was Carlos Amara, 32, son of Nasir.

The elder Amaras' were not strong advocates of Jihad, or Holy War, as espoused by Osama bin Laden and his circle of advisers, and cringed inwardly every time Carlos spoke of 'we' when discussing his plan. Only Carlos felt passionately that the West was the hated enemy of Islam. The elders had only agreed to use their resources and contacts to help Carlos in exchange for financial gain.

They listened without comment while Carlos brought them up to date on his plans. When he finished, his Uncle Jaabar asked, "Are you sure your cousin is capable of the task? His lack of training in these matters still bothers me, you know."

"Yes, uncle," Carlos replied confidently. "Francois, is fully aware of his limits, but living in Canada means he is well-placed for the job. I thought I made that clear after I returned from Toronto last December. Now that we are going ahead, I will meet with him again very soon."

A short and heated discussion followed about the nephew's suitability. It ended abruptly when the younger man slammed his fist on the table. "Enough! The decision has been made. There will be no change! Francois is *the person we need. The other members of my cell have the operational skills needed. Francois's role is only as a facilitator …he will not be involved in the attack itself. Trust me, at the end of the day we will cast a dark and demoralizing shadow over the flag these infidels so brazenly fly in the countries of our worthy brethren!"*

PRIVATE INVESTIGATOR DON CARLING SHRUGGED. "Sure, I'd be glad to take it on," he said. "But let's see if I've got it straight. All you want me to do is follow your husband around Paris for a few days. Why? Do you suspect him of some sort of illegal activity?"

His question was directed at Ms. Danielle Clyde, president and CEO of Empire North Minerals, a private company with vast holdings in the Canadian North. They were meeting in her large yet comfortably appointed office on the thirty-second floor of the building bearing the company name.

"No, I'm keeping an open mind," she answered. "After all, I have no proof that he's committed any crime. That's where you come in."

"Where is he now?"

"Probably playing tennis or at his condo. He leaves for Europe tomorrow night."

"*His* condo?"

"Yes. Our personal arrangements needn't concern you. Nor should they interfere with your investigation." She slid a bulky envelope across her desk towards him.

Don sat back in the soft leather chair, fingering the envelope. "You used the phrase 'after he disappears' when we spoke the other day. What did you mean by that?"

Ms. Clyde made a steeple of her well-manicured fingers, leaned forward and rested her chin on them. She eyed him for long seconds before replying. "Mister Carling, I..."

"Don, call me Don, please," he interrupted.

"...Don." Her intonation told him that she wasn't used to dealing with someone she'd just met on a first-name basis. "Frank is listed as our firm's art consultant. You may have noticed the paintings and sculptures on display in the ground floor reception area when you arrived. It's a multi-million dollar collection." He hadn't, but nodded anyway. "Frank travels to exhibitions in Europe and the United States to acquire properties for the collection. Basically, it gives him something to do, other than play tennis."

"I see. But you suspect that he's not just looking for paintings on these trips."

"That's correct. On his last buying trip, for instance, we couldn't contact him."

"And where was he supposed to have been?"

"In Zurich. Not that I keep track of his every movement, but a Swiss gallery that he'd dealt with previously wanted to speak to him. My personal secretary couldn't reach him. But..." she sighed.

"But what?"

"The thing is, he hadn't checked out of his hotel, and we didn't hear from him all the time he was away. He did fly home as planned, though. All his travel arrangements are made by our staff and the agency we use exclusively, you see."

Carling asked the logical question. "Did you challenge him on his uhh... *disappearing act*, when he returned?"

"No," she replied, abruptly. "That's not how I work, and that's why I called you. If he leaves Paris on this trip, I want to know where he goes and who he sees. I'm sure I don't have to spell it all out for you. His flight information and your ticket are in that envelope, along with the cash you requested."

Don didn't like her tone, that of a boss speaking to an uninformed underling. He briefly considered telling her to find someone else for the job, but the hefty fee he'd be charging more than made up for his bruised ego. Instead, he opened the envelope she had pushed across her desk.

The itinerary for Mr. Frank Archer had him departing Toronto at 8 p.m., June 1st, on a flight to Paris. A room was reserved for him at the Hotel Nouveau Monde for seven nights. His return flight left Paris at noon on the 9th. He was booked in business class. A separate sheet of paper listed details for Don's travel. He was booked on the same flights and his assigned seat was 36A. Three color photographs of a rather handsome man were attached to the itinerary. Don figured Archer to be in his late thirties. He either had a great tan or he was a native of a country bordering the Mediterranean Sea. His full head of dark hair could only be described as shaggy. He certainly didn't look to be as old as his wife, who Don figured to be in her mid-forties

"Are these recent photos?"

Danielle shrugged. "Yes, all within the past few years, I believe."

Don looked at them again before asking, "Where is he from?"

"Ah yes, his appearance. You're thinking it doesn't match his name, aren't you?" Don gave a non-committal shrug. "He was born in France. His father was from Algeria and his mother was French. His name was Francois Amara until he had it changed legally last year."

"Why?"

"He had a few problems travelling after the terrorist attacks in New York."

"You're referring to 9/11?"

"Yes, and the 'no fly' lists the Americans drew up as a result. Apparently 'Amara' is a common surname in Algeria, and someone with that name is on the list."

4

"Does he have Canadian citizenship?

"Yes."

"What about his status with France? Does he have dual citizenship?"

"I'm not sure."

"Has he ever lived in Algeria?"

"Oh, no. He grew up in southern France, near Marseille." After a pause she added, somewhat reluctantly, "We met in Paris. He was working there."

Don waited to see if she was going to offer any other details, but none were forthcoming. Instead she indicated the envelope and asked if he was satisfied.

"Not really," he replied. He handed her the sheet of paper with his flight bookings. "I don't travel in economy."

She gave him a rather whimsical look, almost a smile. "Of course. I will have my personal assistant re-book you immediately. Anything else?"

"Nope, I'll have a full report for you the day after I return."

He rose and extended his hand, which she shook without warmth. As he turned to go, she said, "Just one more thing..."

"Yes?"

"Don't come back and tell me he's seeing other women. I'll already know that."

Surprise, surprise, he thought as he left her office.

TWENTY MINUTES AFTER EXITING THE parking garage under the Empire North building, Don accelerated onto the westbound Gardiner Expressway. He was heading back to his office near Pearson International Airport, twenty miles from the city centre.

At fifty-two years of age, Don Carling was content with life. KayRoy Investigations, the company he'd started fifteen years ago after giving up his job as an airline pilot, was busy and profitable. After a slow start, he had gained a reputation as a discreet and reliable investigator. The cases he took on during those first lean years dealt mainly with insurance fraud and divorces. The list of lawyers retaining him grew progressively larger, thanks to referrals and his reasonable rates. His big break came when an undercover operation he'd set up played a major role in exposing a drug smuggling ring operating at Toronto's Pearson International Airport. Most of those involved ended up in jail, and his firm became increasingly busier as a result of the favorable publicity . He now had ten investigators on his staff, three full time and the others available for short term assignments.

He was pondering how he could learn more about Archer before leaving for Paris. He'd had a vague knowledge of Danielle Clyde before she'd called him last Friday. The mining corporation she headed was mentioned frequently in the financial pages and on the business news network, but little was ever printed about the lady herself. An Internet search hadn't added much to what he already knew. An idea struck him...

Using his car's state-of-the-art communications set up, he called his office and asked Joanne, his secretary, to look up a number. As he repeated the number he was also voice-dialing it. A pleasant voice answered after two rings.

" Marion Teller."

"Hi Marion, it's Don Carling. How're you doing?"

"Well, hi Don! I'm just fine, thank you. What's up? Have you finally convinced that stubborn cousin of mine to marry you?"

Don let out a loud chuckle. "No such luck! But hey, it took me years to get Yvonne to move in with me, so progress is being made!"

"Well, don't give up," Marion laughed. "So what can I do for you?" Marion was the society page editor for a Toronto daily newspaper. Don told her he was hoping she could enlighten him about Danielle Clyde and her husband.

"Ahh, 'The Steel Lady'. That's an interesting request, Don."

"Is that what they call her?" he chuckled. "Anyway it's business, Marion. Can I leave it that way for now?"

"Sure, no problem. Can you give me half an hour? I've got to get a piece down to the editing desk. Like about ten minutes ago."

"Oh sure. I'm on my way back to the office. Just give me a buzz at your convenience. Thanks, Marion."

2

TUESDAY NIGHT, JUNE 1

Don arrived at the airport well before departure time and checked in. Rather than take the courteous agent's suggestion that he head for the airline's lounge, he moved to a position from which he could watch other passengers check in. Frank Archer rushed up to the counter forty-five minutes before departure, followed by a sky cap wheeling a cart holding two large suitcases. Archer had a carry-on bag over his shoulder.

Archer was easy to identify. The photos his client had given him left no doubt that he had the right man. Archer was dressed casually in tailored jeans, a white dress shirt open at the collar, and black patent leather loafers. He was shorter than Don had envisioned. No taller than five foot eight, he guessed, and with a definite European 'play boy' look about him. A gold chain around his neck completed the picture. After they had both passed through the security screening process, Archer headed directly to the business class lounge. Don bypassed it and continued towards the departure gate. So far, Archer hadn't shown any indication of checking for a tail. But the fewer opportunities I give him to notice me, the better, Don reasoned. He stopped at a bar near the gate and ordered a beer. He had just finished it when the flight was called over the PA system.

The business class cabin was filling up as Don settled into his window seat in the last row. He figured Archer would remain in the lounge as long as possible, and he was right. Archer appeared moments before the door closed and the in-charge flight attendant began his pre-flight announcement. His seat was on the aisle, five rows ahead of Don.

As the Airbus 340 slowly taxied towards the runway for take-off, Don wondered if the relationship between Frank Archer and his wife was a classic case of 'opposites attract'. On the surface, that's definitely what it looked like. But the information that Marion Teller relayed to him yesterday afternoon told a different story.

Danielle Clyde was an only child, born in 1958 to Canadian mining magnate Wilfred Clyde and his wife Michelle, a Quebec native. After graduating from high school graduation in Montreal, she had spent a year at a finishing school in Switzerland. She then obtained an arts degree from the Sorbonne in Paris before returning to Montreal to study business administration at McGill University.

She was 28 in 1986 when she joined her father's firm. Three years later, a tragic boating accident claimed the lives of both parents and she was thrust into the CEO's position at the private company overnight. For the next six years, Danielle immersed herself in Empire North, a regimen that seemingly left her no time for a social life. She was called the Steel Lady because she was perceived as lacking a sense of humor and had rarely been photographed wearing a smile.

In May 1995, in France, she married Francois Amara, seven years her junior. The surprise wedding didn't become public knowledge in Canada until two months later. Danielle gave birth to her daughter, Gabrielle Marie Clyde, on Christmas Day the same year. There had been no public notice of the child's birth. She lived with her mother, according to Marion's information, and had been privately-schooled since an early age.

The girl's father had moved into condo on the Toronto waterfront shortly after arriving in Canada. Danielle maintained a secluded home in the city's upscale Forest Hill neighborhood, and a penthouse apartment atop the Empire North building. On the rare occasions Francois had been photographed with his wife, it was usually while acting as her escort at a social function: charity events, opening nights, and once at a reception for the president of a South American country where Empire North operated a massive copper mine.

Their relationship was indeed a strange one, Don thought. Perhaps Danielle—in place of her dead father—had held the proverbial shotgun to Frank's head once she realized she was pregnant. Not that he would have objected. After all, it seemed, he led a rather cozy life, presumably with his wife's company picking up the tab. He had plenty of time to pursue his passion for tennis, in exchange for escort duties. His 'job' as an art consultant didn't sound too onerous, either.

Where do I apply? Don mused. *Substitute golf for tennis and I'm your man!*

PARIS, WEDNESDAY, JUNE 2

Don didn't try to follow Archer after they landed. He knew where he was headed, and his reservation was at the same hotel. It was large enough, he reasoned, 300 or so rooms, two restaurants and three bars, that the chances of his coming face-to-face with Archer were minimal. He left the airport in a taxi ten minutes after he'd seen the one carrying Archer pull away.

His caution was rewarded when he arrived at the hotel forty-five minutes later. Archer was just disappearing into an elevator as Don crossed the lobby towards the reception desk. Before he could speak, the clerk excused himself and turned away in response to a summons from someone in the office behind the desk. Don noticed a registration card in plain view on the counter. Reading upside down, he saw it was Archer's. But he'd registered in his birth name of Francois Amara. Don noted his room number: 842.

The young man was back in thirty seconds, apologized once again, and quickly had Don registered. His room number was 512, which, Don assumed, would be three levels below Amara's. He paused to look around before heading for the elevators.

The lobby of the Hotel Nouveau Monde seemed to be more North American in style than most of the European hotels that Don had stayed in previously. It was large and open, with plenty of comfortable-looking sofas and chairs placed in nicely arranged clusters. The large floor to ceiling windows offered patrons a clear view of the street outside. According to the hotel website, the building had opened for business five years ago. It was designed to attract overseas tour groups requiring large blocks of rooms. There was even a separate check-in desk for group travel, Don noticed.

He also noted the two restaurants, one at each end of the spacious lobby. The entrance to the bar was just past the bank of four elevators. Room 512 was on the second level of guest rooms. The first two floors above the lobby were taken up with meeting and banquet rooms and another bar. Don's room and its furnishings were nothing special, he decided, as he unpacked: a double bed, one not-very-comfortable-looking armchair, and a small screen television set. He wouldn't be throwing any parties in the cramped bathroom, either. The daily rate in Euros, equivalent to $275 CDN, would rate at least a modest suite in comparable hotels in North America.

But what the hell, I'm not paying, he thought. The hotel was in a great location, though. The Arc de Triomphe was only three or four blocks away, and its top was visible from Don's window.

He also noticed a door which, he presumed, led to the adjoining room. He'd seen this layout before: it was designed to turn two rooms into a mini-suite, allowing guests to access each other's space without having to use the hallway. The rooms could only be shared if the doors in both rooms were opened. The doorknob was the 'push-and-turn-to-lock' type. Don opened it, pushed against the other door to ensure that it was locked, and then closed and re-locked his. The door on his side hadn't been used very often, he realized. He'd had to give it a good tug to pull it over the nap of the carpet.

After a quick shower, Don headed down to the lobby, to watch for Archer. He sank into a sofa and opened the complimentary copy of USA Today he'd picked up when he checked in. His vantage point gave him an unobstructed view of the elevators. If Archer had just dropped off his luggage and left the hotel immediately, Don would have missed him. He didn't think that likely, though.

Twenty-five minutes later, his assumption proved correct. Frank stepped out of the nearest elevator with his carryall bag over his shoulder. Without so much as a glance around, he moved towards the concierge's desk, pausing briefly to take a brochure from a display rack adjacent to it. Don was too far away to make out what the stand was advertising. He watched over his newspaper while Archer and the uniformed concierge held a brief discussion, a phone call was made, and Archer was handed a slip of paper and turned towards the hotel entrance.

Casually Don rose, folded his newspaper, and strolled towards the display stand. When he was close enough to read the poster, he knew exactly where his man was headed. The poster was an advertisement for the French Open tennis tournament, and the brochure listed match times and prices.

"May I help you, m'sieu?" asked the concierge.

"Uhh... maybe. I thought I might go and watch some tennis this afternoon, but I've never been to the matches here," Don said. "Do you think there would still be seats available?"

"Perhaps, I just booked one for another guest, but there were only a few seats available for matches at centre court. They are the most expensive seats," he added, indicating the seat section and price in the brochure he showed Don. "Would you like me to check for you?"

Don mentally converted the euros to dollars. The cost per ticket was almost three hundred bucks Canadian. "Ah, no, I'm not that big a fan, actually. That's a bit steep for me!" he answered, smiling sheepishly.

"Eh, bien. But you could always go out to the stadium and try the ticket office. I'm sure there will be tickets available for matches on the lesser courts."

Don thanked him and walked away. Now that he knew where Archer was going to be—probably for most of the afternoon—he could decide on how best to keep tabs on him...

3

IT WAS IDEAL WEATHER FOR outdoor sports with clear skies, a light breeze, and the temperature hovering around 25C. By 1:30 p.m., Don was mingling with the large crowds inside the Stade Roland Garros, home of the French Open. His fifty euro ticket allowed him inside the spread-out complex that comprised the courts, food stalls, souvenir stands and corporate tents. Don had never attended a major tennis event, but the atmosphere reminded him of the day he'd spent at Canadian Open golf tournament last September.

He purchased a sun visor with the Open's logo on the brim to go along with his sunglasses. He'd brought along his binoculars and digital camera as well. His ticket was good for all matches other than those played at centre court. He didn't plan to watch any, though. Archer's reservation, on the other hand, was for the headline matches in the largest stadium. Just as Don reached one of its entrances, a loud roar and prolonged cheering erupted from within. He guessed that a match must have just ended. Sure enough, seconds later the exits were awash with spectators flowing out of the stadium. An electronic signboard announced that the next match would begin in thirty minutes.

An idea struck him as the animated fans passed him. Once the rush subsided, Don approached the bored-looking young man guarding the turnstile.

Could he go inside and look around for a few minutes? Just to take a photo to show friends back home? The guard shook his head. "Pas possible, m'sieu, je regrette."

He had a change of heart when Don slipped him a ten euro note. Don thanked him profusely and promised him he would only be inside for a few minutes. The private investigator climbed the stairs up to the ramp between the third and fourth tiers of seats. Two players, who he assumed were to be adversaries in the next match, were already warming up. Using his binoculars, he scanned down to the courtside seats. Most of them were still occupied, and it took Don a minute before he spotted Archer's yellow polo shirt.

Archer's back was towards Don and he was now wearing a white cap. Archer was studying his program and appeared to be alone. The seats to his left were still vacant, and a grey-haired couple occupied the two seats to his right. They were chatting with each other, but not with Archer. The stadium was beginning to fill up again and Don had to move away from the top of the ramp. He briefly considered trying to find an empty seat when play began, but decided not to. His presence had been noticed, and a female usher was casually making her way towards him. Rather than risk being asked for his ticket, he retraced his path back down to the exit.

Now that he had located Archer, he had time to kill. He joined a lineup at a beverage kiosk, bought a bottle of beer and sought out a table in the nearby seating area.

Well, this isn't the most unpleasant stakeout I've ever undertaken, he thought, taking a large sip. *I wonder how long he'll watch tennis? All afternoon? So far he's been true to form. Just an avid tennis junky getting his fix at one of the game's most famous tournaments. With his wife footing the bill...*

FRIDAY, JUNE 4

Archer had followed the same routine yesterday. Don had been staked out in the lobby when he appeared a few minutes after 10: A.M and entered the coffeeshop. An hour later he emerged, had the concierge order him a ticket, and spent the afternoon watching tennis.

Archer appeared earlier this morning and had finished breakfast by 9:30. He struck off on foot towards the Arc de Triomphe, Don trailing him from the opposite side of the street. Once Archer reached the Champs Elysees, Don fell in behind him, using the now-heavy flow of pedestrians as a screen. His target veered off onto rue Washington and turned right at the next corner. He had never looked behind, and Don was still ten yards back when Archer entered a building. He crossed to the opposite side of the narrow street and glanced at the store front as he passed it. He wasn't surprised to see that it was an art gallery.

The Canadian PI slipped into a 'bar tabac' a few yards past the gallery and ordered a café crème. From a stand-up table just inside the café's front entrance, he had an unobstructed view of the gallery's all-glass facade. Archer re-emerged forty minutes later, carrying three packages wrapped in brown paper. He began to retrace his route towards the hotel, Don a discreet distance behind. Archer seemed to be having difficulty handling his packages, however, and just before he reached the Champs Elysees, he stopped and flagged down a taxi. Don could only watch as Archer bundled the packages into the back seat and got in himself.

Shit! I hope I haven't lost the bugger, he thought. It took Don ten minutes of waving at passing taxis before a vacant one stopped for him. He returned to their hotel, hoping to pick up Archer's trail again. There was no sign of Archer, and Don realized his only option was to settle down and wait. He'd assumed Archer would have taken the taxi back here, but if he hadn't, he was out of luck.

Well, I can only hope he came back to drop off the packages before going out again, probably to the tennis stadium.

Fifteen minutes passed, then twenty. His coffee intake had worked its way to his bladder, leaving him no choice but to make a hurried trip to the men's room at the far end of the lobby. Five minutes later, and feeling much better, he returned to the lobby, praying he hadn't missed Archer.

He sighed with relief when his target appeared seconds after he sat down again, approached the concierge desk, and went through the same procedure as on previous days. Three minutes after Archer's taxi pulled away, Don hailed the next one in line. As his driver manoeuvred his way through the five lanes of traffic circling the Arc de Triomphe, he was beginning to think that he might be on a wild goose chase. Since they had arrived in Paris, there had been no hint of ulterior motives in Archer's movements.

But that was about to change…

Don followed the same routine as he had on Wednesday and Thursday afternoon. He sought out a shaded table in the food court area, an ideal location in more ways than one. The scenery was most definitely easy on his eyes, a seemingly endless parade of attractive females whose attire ranged from 'short shorts' and halter tops to the latest summer fashions. *Vive La France!* Most of the passing attractions didn't appear to be have any interest in tennis, but then again, neither did he.

On both days, Archer left the stadium between 5:30 and 6 p.m. and took a taxi back to the hotel. Don had also returned by taxi, and watched from a corner of the lobby as Archer entered the more upscale of the hotel's two restaurants. He had ended his surveillance each night after Archer finished eating and took an elevator up to the eighth floor, presumably to spend the rest of the night in his room.

The temperature had been inching up daily, and the heat and inactivity was giving Don the yawns. It was only three o'clock, and he didn't expect Archer to exit the main stadium for another two hours or so. He stood and stretched, and cast an eye towards the main stadium for the umpteenth time. *Maybe a beer will help,* he thought.

He headed for the nearest kiosk and bought a bottle of Kronenbourg beer and a 'jambon et fromage baguette'. The sandwich consisted of a minuscule amount of ham and cheese wrapped in a hard, crusty roll, designed no doubt to wreak havoc on the consumer's gums. He had just made it back to his table when a flash of red appeared in his peripheral vision: Archer was on the move. Don had no choice but to drop his beer and sandwich on the nearest table and take off after him. Archer's red shirt made it easy for Don to keep him in sight as he strode purposely towards the exit gate. A huge crowd was milling about outside, and Don lost him momentarily. He pushed through the mob just in time to spot Archer opening the rear passenger door of a dark blue sedan. The vehicle pulled smartly away from the curb as soon as Archer was inside. Its tinted windows prevented Don from seeing if there was anyone other than the driver in it. The vehicle sped around a corner before he could get his binoculars focused on the licence plate.

He turned anxiously towards the taxi rank, only to see that at least 20 passengers were waiting in line. "*Goddamn it!*" he muttered aloud, startling an elderly man passing behind him.

4

SUNDAY, JUNE 6

Carling spent Friday night, most of Saturday, and Sunday morning prowling around the hotel looking for any sign of Archer, but to no avail.

He slumped into a chair at the far end of the lobby, and once more rehashed the possibilities about where Archer might have disappeared to and why. One thing he was certain of: the pick up outside the stadium had been planned. Don had checked the large electronic clock outside the gate just as the car pulled away. The numerals had just clicked over to 3:00. A pre-arranged meeting time? Probably. He couldn't perceive another explanation for Archer's sudden move...

Was Archer—or someone connected to him—aware that he was being followed? What about the driver? Could it have been a woman?

Archer's wife was thousands of miles away, and apparently didn't care if he was seeing other women. Surely he knew that. He'd walked by room 842 late Friday night and every few hours yesterday. A *'DO NOT DISTURB'* sign hung from the door handle each time. It was still there at eleven o'clock this morning.

Maybe he's been holed up with a woman all this time, living off the fruits of passion, as it were, that and room service. But that didn't make much sense, either. Don leaned back in the chair and let out a frustrated sigh.

He had to find out if Archer was in his room, and accomplish it without giving himself away. An idea struck him. It would be a bit risky, but just might work. He headed for the elevators and pushed the UP button. Seconds later the muted chime for the elevator behind him announced its arrival. Don turned around and his heart skipped a beat. Stepping out as the doors parted was a breath-taking double of Frank Archer. A female Frank Archer...

With barely a glance at Don, the woman turned towards the lobby. The startled detective stared after her, making mental notes of this unexpected apparition. Taller than Frank, but probably because she was wearing spike heels. Her hair—not quite as dark as her brother's—was short, accenting the back of her elegant neckline. Her shapely figure was attractively outlined in a silky, floral-patterned dress that said 'Paris fashion house' to Don. He moved further into the lobby, following her progress towards the main entrance. He watched as she reached into her large, leather handbag for sunglasses and then nodded to the doorman. Seconds later she folded her legs into the back seat of the taxi he'd summoned. She slipped the doorman a folded note as he closed the door, acknowledged by a tip of his cap as the taxi pulled away.

First set to you, Archer, or Amara, you sly bastard, he muttered to himself.

DON DIDN'T OFFER AN APOLOGY to Danielle Clyde for phoning her at 7 a.m. Toronto time on a Sunday morning, even though her annoyance was evident when she finally answered.

"I suppose you knew that your husband had a twin sister," he said without preamble.

"Yes...Francoise. I met her a few times in Paris before we were married. She still lives in France, I believe. Why do you ask?"

"Because it appears that she is the F. Amara' that's been staying in the room reserved for Frank for the past three nights. He registered using that name, so obviously he's still carrying a French passport."

"And Frank is—"

"Missing," Don interrupted, "at least for the time being. Have you heard from him?"

"No, but then we rarely do when he's traveling."

"Not even if he changes his itinerary?"

"Not that I recall. Perhaps he has made such changes, but my personal assistant would have dealt with him," she explained. "Is there anything else?"

"Does he have other family here in France?"

" Not that I'm aware of. Both parents are dead, and his sister is his only close relative. At least that's what he told me."

"Right, thanks. I'll be in touch next week. I'll find him before then."

"Good. That's what I'm paying you for."

DON WAS GLAD HE'D COOLED off before calling Danielle Clyde. His first inclination after he'd bumped into Amara's sister was to chew her out for not mentioning her existence. But he realized her reaction would probably have been a caustic *'you didn't ask'*. Lesson learned, though, and he vowed not to be put on the spot by her again.

Before calling Canada, he had dialed room 842 using the hotel's room-to-room calling feature. When no one answered, a computer-generated voice invited him to leave a message. He hung up without doing so, now almost positive that Frank was no long staying in the hotel.

DON HAD CONTACTED PAUL BOUTIN, head of Agence Boutin, a Paris-based private detective agency, the day after he'd arrived. He'd consulted with Boutin before leaving Toronto and asked the Frenchman to find out all he could about Francois Amara. After the surprise appearance of the twin sister, Don had called Boutin's private number, apologized for intruding on his Sunday, and made a few more requests of him.

"Not a problem for me, Don. I'll see what I can turn up on her. Perhaps we could meet tomorrow, say about eleven o'clock?"

"Definitely! Just tell me where to find you. Thanks, Paul."

MONDAY, JUNE 7

"Oui, Don, you were correct," Paul informed him. "A *Francoise* Amara is staying in room 842. My source told me the original reservation was for a Francois Amara, obviously a male name."

"Yes, that's what I thought. I had a peek at his registration form just after he checked in. But it was changed to her name, you say."

Boutin nodded. "Yes, sometime Saturday, apparently."

They were sitting outside a brasserie near Boutin's office. The brasserie was on a busy side street a block from the Place de L'Opera. It was another sunny day with the temperature in the low twenties. The small, round table they were seated at was shaded by a brightly-colored umbrella advertising Kronenbourg beer.

Boutin had ordered an expresso, a coffee so dark and thick-looking that Don thought he might need help stirring it. He opted for an 'un demi', a small glass of draft beer. He took a large swallow before replying.

"Hmm...I wonder what he's up to," said Boutin, after Don told him about Amara's sudden and seemingly calculated departure from Stade Roland Garros on Friday afternoon. "And his return flight to Canada is booked for Wednesday, you say?"

"Yeah, unless he's changed it."

"So, where he has disappeared to and why presents a big problem for you, n'est-ce pas?"

"Definitely," shrugged Don. " I don't think he was on to me, though. But the way he left suggests otherwise."

"Perhaps someone he's associated with spotted you," offered Boutin, raising an eyebrow.

"Yeah, that makes more sense," Don nodded. "From what I've seen of Archer so far, he hasn't displayed any traits of a covert operative."

Boutin was about to speak when his cell phone emitted a muted buzzing . "Excusez-moi, Don," he said. He stood up and turned away, covering one ear to block out traffic noise.

The break gave Don a chance to have a good look at his new colleague. He and Boutin were about the same height, but the Frenchman's build was noticeably slimmer. Probably weighs about 160, 165, he figured. He was wearing a custom-fitted, light grey business suit, and a darker grey shirt and navy tie. His glossily-polished black oxfords would have drawn praise from a drill sergeant. What little hair he had left was neatly-trimmed and topped off the image of a former military man. Age-wise, Don guessed mid-fifties. And unlike the dozen or so males seated around them, Boutin appeared to be a non-smoker.

He sat down again after finishing his call. "So, that was my office calling. We're still pulling information together on the Amara clan."

"Clan? I was told that he didn't have many relatives."

"That may be true. His family name, though, has...hmm, how shall I say it," he frowned, searching for the right word in English, "...some *notoriety* attached to it."

"No kidding!"

"Yes, but I don't know yet if they are related to your man." He reached for his coffee and took a sip. "Do know much about Algeria, Don?"

"Not really. Algeria was a French colony at one time, wasn't it?" Don asked. "Seems to me I watched a documentary a few years ago about the Algerian war."

"Very good. Actually it wasn't until quite recently, 1999 in fact, that our government acknowledged the term 'war'. Up until then it had always been officially referred to as a 'public order operation'."

"Ahh, and when did all this take place?"

"From the mid-fifties until 1962. The end result was independence for Algeria, thanks in large part to President De Gaulle realizing it was inevitable and throwing his government's support behind the move."

"And the Amara name was involved in some way?"

"So it seems. More than one male with that name served a prison sentence during the struggle, probably for activities on behalf of the insurrectionists. Most were released after the war, though. The name surfaced again in and around Marseille. A Nasir Amara was alleged to have been the head of a crime syndicate operating from that port city."

"When was this?"

"In the seventies and early eighties, before the authorities finally cracked down on the ring. Two men named Amara were among those jailed for their crimes. Nasir and Jabbar, probably brothers, were paroled in 1990. But you think the father of this Francois Amara you're after is dead?"

"That's what I was told, yes."

"Well then, he could be the Rashad Amara who married Gabrielle Lauzon in August,1967, in Arles. That's near Marseille. We have a copy of their marriage certificate. Not only that, but the birth of triplets to the same—"

"Triplets?" interrupted Don.

"Yes, Madame Gabrielle Amara gave birth to two boys and a girl in June of 1968. Francois, Francoise, and Rene."

"And if the father and brother are dead, presumably their death certificates would be on file somewhere?"

"*If* they died in France. I expect to have more information for you later today, tomorrow at the latest."

"Okay, that would be a big help, Paul. Also anything you can dig up on the sister, too."

"Mais oui, I put one of my operatives on to her first thing this morning."

They watched the passersby for a few minutes while they finished their beverages. Don broke the silence, politely asking Paul how he'd made a living before becoming a private detective.

After college, Boutin had joined the army, graduated from Officers Candidate School, and trained as a military police officer. He'd switched to the intelligence branch after ten years, and retired in 1998 with the rank of colonel, having served a total of twenty-five years. He'd taken a year off to sail around the Mediterranean Sea with his wife before opening his agency, in early 2000.

Don reciprocated with a summary of his career before Boutin signaled for the bill.

"Well," sighed Don. "I wonder if he'll show up again in Paris before Wednesday?" It was more rhetorical thinking out loud than a question, and Boutin's only reaction was a Gallic shrug.

5

TUESDAY, JUNE 8

Don was still without a lead to Archer's whereabouts or why his sister was staying in the hotel. The last remnants of a hangover, a painful spike embedded in the back of his right eyeball, didn't help his disposition, either. His last sighting of Francoise was last night. Don had been staked out in the lobby when she appeared, casually dressed in slacks, a roomy sweater, and sandals and spent an hour in the smaller of the two restaurants. She'd been alone, and was still unaccompanied when she came out of the restaurant, bought a magazine in the gift shop, and took the elevator upstairs.

Don's patience ran out when she hadn't reappeared an hour later. He asked the doorman to recommend an American-style bar. By 9:40 he was on his second Crown Royal and water, holding down the end bar stool in Reggie's Tavern, one street over from the hotel.

The drinks were about fifteen dollars each. But what the hell, he was charging his client a grand a day for his services, so cost wasn't an issue. Even if the 'Steel Lady' fired him when he got home, he'd be money ahead. *Damned frustrating so far, though, to say the least.* He signaled for another drink. *But there isn't much else I can do at the moment, is there?*

Don nodded his thanks to the bartender when the fresh drink arrived and added the sales chit to the others tucked under the corner of the damp coaster. He took a sip before pushing the glass a foot away, as if the extra distance would somehow make it last longer. He leaned back on the stool and crossed his arms, determined to put the questions tumbling around in his head into some semblance of order before the Canadian whisky shut down his brain for the night. He still didn't have a clue as to where Archer was, or why he had resorted to his furtive getaway. And he hadn't figured out why his sister had been staying in the hotel, either.

Was her presence just a ploy to throw him off? Make him think that Archer himself was still in Paris? He shook his head again in frustration and reached for his drink. *All I know for certain is that Archer didn't just come to France to watch tennis and buy paintings. And I damn well hope I can find some answers before I leave.*

Paul Boutin's reference to the Amara name in a criminal context also raised disturbing questions. Hopefully he'd know more about the family after Boutin got back to him. A profile that would either eliminate or confirm that the present generation of Amara's, Francois and his sister, were involved in criminal doings. It might also shed light on his parents and brother, specifically when they died, or their whereabouts if they were still alive.

One avenue he could explore on his own would have to wait until he returned to Toronto. What *did* his wife suspect Frank of? She'd made it clear she wasn't concerned with his infidelity, so it must be something else. But what? If she wasn't prepared to come clean with him he might just tell her he was finished. He hoped it didn't come to that. He had never resorted to throwing in the towel on a case before and didn't plan to start now. He leaned back on his barstool again, reached for his drink, and drained it.

Close the hangar doors, buddy, he pricked himself. *Have another drink and think good thoughts. The sun's going to come up tomorrow, anyway.*

The pep talk cheered him up and he stayed for two more drinks. He nursed them through the next hour, chatting amiably with Chet, from Kansas City, the twenty-six-year-old nephew of Reggie, the American expatriate whose name adorned the dimly-lit and not-very-busy-on-a-Monday-at-midnight tavern. Reggie, Chet informed him, had made a small fortune scavenging for treasure from seventeenth and eighteenth century shipwrecks in the Caribbean. Why he picked Paris to fulfil his dream of owning a bar so far away from his Gulf Coast roots, Chet didn't know. Or at least Don didn't remember this morning if he did. However, he did remember munching his way through a hell of a lot of peanuts in the shell.

Why? You don't even like peanuts, you big dummy. And you're not that crazy about rye whisky, either.

His phone rang, ending his self-debriefing. Paul Boutin was on the line. Could they get together later? He told Don he had more information on the Amara family.

"Yeah, but it will have to be today, or tonight at the latest," Don said. "I'm still planning to fly home tomorrow, remember?"

"Not a problem, Don," Boutin assured him. I'll come to your hotel at six o'clock. We'll have dinner at an excellent restaurant nearby. One that isn't found in any tourist books, my friend!"

"Sounds terrific...and expensive!" laughed Don. "But dinner will be on me anyway!"

Hope he isn't a Crown Royal fan, Don thought, after he hung up.

BOUTIN POURED HIS GUEST A glass of the wine he'd ordered for a pre-dinner libation, and urged him to try it. "Well, what do you make of it, Don?"

"Mmm...I like it. Has a bit of a tang compared to most whites I've had before. What is it?"

"It's a Gewurztraminer, from Alsace, the province where I was born and raised. Have you ever visited eastern France?"

"No, no I haven't. Right on the German border, isn't it?"

"Yes, and Strasbourg is the region's main city. There are plenty of vineyards along the banks of the Rhine. This particular vintage comes from a small winery not far from my family home. And you're quite right, Gewurztraminers as a rule have a more...ahh..." the Frenchman paused, searching for an English word. "A more *sharper* taste than most whites. Is that a good word?"

"Yeah, that's a good way to describe it."

They chatted about wine while savoring a second glass. Boutin did most of the talking, Don content to listen and learn from a man so obviously well-versed about one of his country's main industries. He didn't think it was the time nor place to mention that he and Yvonne had started their first batch of *'do-it-yourself'* wine last month.

The visitor looked around the quaint interior of the Auberge des Alpes while Paul and the waiter discussed the menu. It resembled the interior of a chalet that one might find in the mountains: plenty of dark wood paneling, heavy tables, and sturdy, thatch-backed chairs. The room wasn't that large, though, and Don thought the wall murals depicting panoramic mountain slopes in different seasons made it appear even smaller. He counted only eight tables, and they were all occupied, mostly by men in business suits. He turned his attention back to his host when the waiter left.

"I hope you are hungry, mon ami. I have selected dishes that you might not have tried before. A fitting repas for your last night in Paris," Paul said. "Sante!"

"Yes, Cheers!" Don responded, touching Paul's raised glass with his own. "So what am I going to be eating? Nothing alive, I hope!" he chuckled.

"No, no, nothing still moving," replied Paul. "I thought we'd start with a pâté, one of the chef's own concoctions. Not too spicy, but not bland, either. They serve some admirable soups here, but they are best taken in the fall and winter, in my opinion."

"Couldn't agree more. I usually devour too much bread with soup, anyway! Especially French bread." The third glass of wine on an empty stomach was giving Don a warm buzz, and he had almost forgotten why they were meeting.

Paul nodded. "I'll tell you about the rest of the meal as it is served. But let's get business out of the way first."

During the twenty minutes or so it took them to nibble their way through the pâté and bread, Paul outlined the new information that he and his operatives had dug up on the Amaras'. When he finished, he removed a slightly bulky envelope from his breast pocket of his jacket. "It's all in here, including some old photos," he said, sliding it across the table.

"Thanks a lot. I'll read through this later. Still no indication as to his present whereabouts, I guess."

"Unfortunately not. I'm sure he'll turn up, though. As you've said, you have no reason to believe he won't be catching his return flight to Canada."

Their deliberations were interrupted while the waiter served the main course: slender strips of venison that had been simmered in a red wine sauce. It was also one of the chef's personal creations, and Don had never heard the name he gave it before. The only words he recognized while the young man was describing the dishes he was spooning onto their plates were 'legume' and 'pommes de terre'. But he didn't need to be fluent in French to enjoy the vegetables and sauce that complemented the meat.

The 1997 burgundy his host had ordered to drink with the main course led Don to remark that he couldn't remember having tasted a better red wine. And he wasn't exaggerating. Paul gave a modest wave of thanks and refilled their glasses.

"This is fabulous, Paul," said Don, after he'd finished, "but I thought that wild game was only served in Europe during the fall hunting season."

"Ahh, well, that was once the case. And probably still is in regions where the animals are hunted. But deer are now farmed extensively to satisfy demand. Traditionalists probably abhor the thought of it, but city dwellers aren't so discriminating," he explained. "Personally, I think it's the sauce that most game is prepared in that makes or breaks it as far as taste."

"Yeah, that's a good point," answered Don. "I've eaten deer and moose meat back home that might have tasted a lot better if it had been cooked like this. Ketchup didn't help, I assure you!"

BY THE TIME THEY HAD polished off dessert—both opting for crème brûlé—they had finished their theorizing as to what Amara might be up to.

"So there was still no sign that he had returned to the hotel today?"

"Uhh, no, at least not before you picked me up," said Don. "I haven't laid eyes on him since he jumped into the car outside the tennis stadium. And he didn't have any luggage with him then, just his carryall. It didn't exactly give me the impression he was heading off to parts unknown forever."

"True, but it's possible, is it not, that his luggage may have already been in that car. Perhaps his sister or someone else had seen to it," offered Paul.

The Canadian let out a long sigh. "Yeah, that's definitely a possibility. I'll probably never know," he added, shaking his head.

They dropped the subject and passed the rest of the evening in convivial conversation, two new acquaintances swapping backgrounds and tales of cases they had worked on. By the time they ordered coffee, all the other diners had left, giving the owner/chef, Emile Leclair, an old friend of Paul's, a chance to join them. He was carrying a bottle of Calvados and three brandy snifters. After he was introduced to Don, Emile poured three full measures. "Sante!" he said, raising his glass.

Don returned the toast, and took a sip of the apple-flavored liqueur, feigning enthusiasm for the added alcoholic intake. *When in Paris*, he mused, settling back in his chair as the two Frenchmen began an animated conversation. Paul tried to include Don, but Emile, obviously not comfortable speaking English, kept reverting to his native tongue. Eventually, Paul shrugged an apology and Don nodded his understanding.

It was another forty-five minutes before they were able to call it quits, settle the bill and make their exit, much to the disappointment of the chef, who had already signaled his waiter for another bottle of brandy.

Back in his room, Don undressed, used the toilet and brushed his teeth. He fumbled two aspirins out of the bottle and washed them down with a large glass of tap water, hoping to ward off the headache he usually suffered after drinking too much red wine. Even excellent vintages of the stuff. As he left the bathroom, he stumbled over a shoe and put a hand on the door to the adjoining room to steady himself. The door clicked shut. Puzzled, he stood looking dumbly at it.

Why was that ajar? I'm sure it was closed before I went out...

He couldn't think of a plausible explanation and forgot about it as soon as his head hit the pillow. There was something he'd planned to do after dinner, but his brain was already in shutdown mode. It came to him just as he dropped off.

6

WEDNESDAY, JUNE 9

Don awoke slowly, the beeping sound emanating from the unfamiliar alarm not getting through to him immediately.

Paris, Seven a.m., Wednesday, departure day. Must call Yvonne. The information registered sequentially, surprising Don at how sharp he felt considering his alcohol intake last night.

Call Yvonne, that's what I forgot to do! He'd left a message on her cell phone before heading out to dinner, saying he would try again when he returned. Too late now. It was the middle of the night in Toronto. *That leaves me two options: call later from the airport, or e-mail her. Maybe both. Yes, an e-mail this morning to her work address, and a phone call after he'd checked in.*

Twenty minutes after the alarm had roused him, Don had showered and shaved and was fully awake. He was surprised to find that he was quite hungry, given the filling meal he'd enjoyed last night. Rather than ordering from room service, he decided to go down to the coffee shop and take advantage of the breakfast buffet. He checked the time as he waited for the elevator. It was only 7:45, leaving him plenty of time to eat, pack his suitcase and check out. The concierge had arranged for a car at half past nine for the trip to the airport.

A quick check of the lobby and main restaurant for a possible sighting of either Frank or his sister proved negative, as did a glance around the coffee shop before he entered. He returned to his room at 8:40 and began packing. The phone rang while he was closing his suitcase

"Bonjour, Don. Paul ici. How are you feeling this morning?"

"Quite well now, but it took a couple of strong coffees to get me going. How about you?"

"Ah, très bien, aussi. I'm glad we were able to get together."

"Well, I sure enjoyed everything you ordered. A fine example of your national reputation as connoisseurs!"

"You're too kind," the Frenchman replied. "Don, the Amara woman left the hotel a few minutes ago."

"How did you …"

"I had a man watching for her. She may be a blind alley, but worth pursuing. In any event, he is following her taxi. She lives in a suburb on the Seine and I wouldn't be surprised if that's where she is heading. If you can call me before your flight departs, I'll confirm that."

"Uh, yeah, I'll try to. Thanks again for your able assistance, Paul."

CHARLES DE GAULLE AIRPORT, 11:30 A.M.

After checking in, the agent advised him that his flight had just posted a twenty minute delay due to the late arrival of the inbound aircraft. He headed to the business class lounge that along with other amenities had Internet access. He dashed off a short e-mail to Yvonne before calling Paul Boutin's office. His new colleague picked up immediately and told him that Francoise Amara had indeed returned to her apartment, and he was dropping surveillance of her for now.

"We can get back to her if it will help your investigation, just let me know," said Boutin. "There is some personal information about her in that report I gave you."

"Good, I haven't had a chance to go through it yet, but I'll read it on the flight."

WITH BOARDING NOT DUE TO start for another fifteen minutes, Don got himself a small bottle of orange juice and found an empty chair. His thoughts turned to Yvonne. The past week was the longest time they had been apart since she'd moved in with him three months ago. Now it suddenly dawned on him how anxious he was to see her. Before, in their 'on again, off again' relationship, he would call her a day or so after returning from a trip. This time it would be different: Yvonne would be waiting for him.

Don had lost count of the number of times he'd asked her to marry him, but still hadn't been able to overcome her reluctance to say 'yes'.

How long would it take before she changed her mind? Six months? A year? Maybe longer...

It didn't matter: he was prepared to go along with their present arrangement, until she finally agreed to become Mrs. Carling.

He was still thinking about her when Frank Archer slipped into the lounge. Without so much as a glance around, the man with two names dropped his carry-on bag on an empty table and headed for the food and drink table. Even though Don had been half expecting Archer to show up, his sudden reappearance still came as a shock. The Canadian's heartbeat returned to normal as he watched Archer fill a plate, grab a bottle of water, and return to the table .

The frustration Don had been living with since Archer's disappearance began to ease. Relieved that he hadn't completely fumbled his assignment, Don started planning his next moves. A thorough study of Boutin's report was the first step. Hopefully that would provide him with a fuller picture of Archer's background. In Toronto, he'd put someone on Archer's tail to find out how he spent his time, including whom besides his mistresses he might be associating with.

. *Whatever you're up to Mister Archer, or Amara, or whoever you are, I'm going to find out*, Don psyched himself. He was already heading for the exit when the lounge hostess announced that Flight 875 to Toronto was ready for boarding.

DON FOUND THE FIRST CLUE to where Archer may have been soon after their flight landed. He was standing near the skycap Archer had summoned to handle his luggage. When his first bag arrived, he pulled it off the carousel, and shoved it towards the porter. Don sidled close enough to read its tag. Beneath YYZ, the code for Toronto, was another three-letter identifier, CNN. This, Don knew, was the code for Cannes. Archer had taken a connecting flight from that city on the French Riviera to Paris. It was info that Paul Boutin might be able to use, and he made a mental note to mention the next time he spoke to him.

TORONTO, THURSDAY, JUNE 10

Don had left a message for Danielle Clyde's last night, telling her he would see her this morning. "No need to reply," he'd said. "I'll be at your office at 9 o'clock."

He entered her PA's office at exactly one minute before the hour. Ms. Clyde herself opened the door to her office and showed him in. He could tell be her frosty look that she didn't appreciate his impertinence in setting her schedule. But he wasn't going to apologize, and declined her offer for coffee.

"Who did you have following Frank before you hired me?"

The question took Danielle completely off guard. I...I didn't...How did you know?"

"Just answer my questions first, please."

"She shot him another icy look before answering. "It was some time last fall, I believe."

Don calculated quickly. "Less than a year ago, then." She nodded, and Don continued. "Did you use another private detective?"

"No, no, at least I don't think one was involved. My firm has a director of security. He has a small staff, mainly to oversee operations at our mine locations. I asked him to check on Frank. He confirmed what I had already suspected about the other women."

"Women? More than one, you mean."

She shrugged. "Oh yes, more than one. Not that the number is important."

"And this, ah, *surveillance*. Was that just here in Toronto?" She answered with a nod. "So Frank wasn't followed on any of his trips out of town before you hired me."

"...No," she answered slowly, suggesting she knew what was coming next.

"But something's changed since then, hasn't it?" Don said. Danielle swiveled her chair around and stared out the window. "Obviously you're not concerned about other women when he's away. So it must be something else. Do you suspect him of stealing from the company? Or fraud of some sort? Maybe on behalf of contacts in Europe?"

"No, no, nothing like that. There is no evidence of financial misdoing. Our books are in good shape," she replied.

"Then what is it?"

Danielle let out a long sigh and turned to face him again. "I can't explain it really, but he's changed from just going along with what our relationship allows him. A job, if you can call it that, one that basically gives him leave to do what he wants and when he wants, with no time constraints, a reasonable income, and a generous expense account. Quite a cosy set up when you think about it."

"Couldn't agree more," said Don. "But what made you aware of this change? I was under the impression that you didn't see each other that often."

"Yes, it's true that we live apart, and have done so since shortly after the wedding. He is my escort at various functions I have to attend, for instance."

"So you maintain this, ahh, *public facade*, if you will, strictly for appearances?"

"Yes," she replied tersely, and when it was obvious she wasn't going to elaborate Don took another tack.

"Let's get back to when and why you noticed this change, and why you think he's up to something other than tennis and art collecting. Does he take an interest in politics, for instance?"

"Not that I'm aware of. At least he'd never expressed any political opinions in my presence."

Don started to speak but she held up her hand. "No, let me finish. I know what you're thinking, and you're quite right. We don't spend much time together so I can't be sure of what he's thinking most of the time. What happened was so out of character for him, and that's about the time I think he got involved with whatever he's up to now."

Don gave her his full attention while she explained what had happened last August. She and Frank were attending a reception for mining industry executives. They were chatting with four men, all management types or board members, and the discussion had turned to the recent American-led invasion of Iraq. One outspoken American, head of a New York-based investment banking firm, was expounding at length about why it had been necessary, et cetera, et cetera, even insisting that the Muslim world's backing and elation after the suicide attacks on the World Trade Center in September 11th, 2001 justified his president's decision.

Frank, who was normally quite content to linger at Danielle's elbow, making small talk when necessary, jumped all over the man, accusing him and his ilk of being the cause of the unrest in Muslim countries; all but suggesting America had it coming; that 9/11 was peanuts compared to the suffering the Palestinians had endured because of Israel. He'd stomped out at this point leaving his wife and the others speechless.

Danielle had called him the next morning and voiced her displeasure for his outburst. Frank had apologized for embarrassing her, but not for his remarks. He'd also told her he wouldn't be escorting her to any future events if the guest list included Americans.

"And this was the first time he'd expressed such anti-Jewish sentiments, or maybe pro-Muslim sympathies in your presence, I take it."

"Exactly. Even though his father was a Muslim, he was brought up in the Catholic Church. We were married by a priest, in fact."

Don let it rest there. He knew there were plenty of others opposed to the American presence in Iraq, not just Muslim nations. Many politicians, columnists, talk show hosts and individuals in Europe as well as in the US were becoming increasingly vocal in their opposition to the war.

Had Danielle's husband taken his anti-US feelings beyond the talking stage? Don didn't have any proof to support this sudden thought yet, but it was definitely an avenue worth exploring.

Danielle quickly agreed when Don suggested he was willing to continue his surveillance of Frank Archer. Money was no object, she told him, but that wasn't his primary concern. What intrigued him now was why a so-called 'art consultant' was acting like a secret agent.

IT TOOK DON A FEW calls to track down Chuck Todd, Empire North's head of security. Todd maintained an office at the company's Toronto headquarters, but spent most of his time at far-flung mine sites. Don reached him at a northern British Columbia location. After explaining who he was and why he was calling, Don was surprised to learn that they had a common background: both men had once served with the Royal Canadian Mounted Police. Todd had joined the Mounties a few years before Don, and their paths had never crossed. But it did put their ensuing conversation on a comfortable level.

Fifteen minutes later Don had only one question left for Todd. "So, other than this man he picked up at the airport, the rest of the people he comes in contact with—including the women he bangs—all live in the Toronto area, right?"

"Yes, sir, and there aren't that many of them, as I said. Mostly other members of the tennis club."

"Okay, Chuck. Thanks for all this. Call me when you're back in town. Beers will be on me."

"Hey, now you're talkin' my language! Gotta go."

DON REPLAYED THE TAPE OF their conversation and made notes. Todd had given him the names of three women Frank Archer was involved with. Two were married. Robin Tyrell played tennis two or three mornings a week. Todd trailed them twice to a motel near the club. He figured she was just a bored housewife tired of her husband. The same description fit the second woman. Elizabeth Wood was also a conquest of Archer's at the club. Their trysts took place at the same motel.

"Maybe he has a loyalty card for the place!" Don had joked.

Todd laughed. "Nah, it's a 'no name' motel good for an 'afternooner', that's about all!"

The third relationship was different. Jill McNeil was an attractive blonde, younger than Frank, and single. She usually stayed overnight at his condo on the evenings they had dinner together, twice a week on average. Jill worked at the travel agency that Empire North used for employee travel bookings. Todd surmised that Frank had probably first met her while picking up a ticket.

The mention of the male visitor intrigued Don. They were either related or old friends, according to Todd. Frank had greeted him with a hug and a kiss on both cheeks. He appeared to be about Frank's age, and stayed overnight at the Airport Hilton. Frank spent the afternoon and evening with him on the day he arrived, and met his visitor again the next morning. After a two-hour breakfast, Frank drove him to the airport. The dates, according to Todd's notes, were December 12th and 13th.

Todd hadn't been able to identify the visitor, because Frank Archer had booked the room in his name. Information he'd learned by slipping the head bellman twenty dollars.

7

....

FRIDAY, JUNE 11

Don was a few steps from the glass doors when he noticed Joanne urgently beckoning to him. He was on his way back from working out at his health club, conveniently located in a strip mall less than a hundred yards north of the KayRoy offices.

"Please hold on, sir. He's just walked in," he heard Joanne telling the caller as he opened the door. She placed her hand over the handset and said, "It's from Paris, a Mister Boutin. He says it's important he speak to you."

Don pointed to his office behind the reception area. "I'll take it in there, thanks, Jo."

He closed the door behind him, settled into his chair and picked up the phone. His desk clock read 10:30, late afternoon in Paris. "Bonjour, Paul, what's happened?"

"A bit of a problem here that I thought you should know about, Don."

"Go ahead, I'm listening."

"I've just heard that a woman's body has been found at the Hotel Nouveau Monde. Apparently she'd been murdered."

"And why is that a problem for me?"

"Well, perhaps 'problem' is too strong a word, Don. Her body was found in a room on the same floor as yours. The police will no doubt want to talk to guests that were staying in the area, especially men on their own."

"I see your point. But I checked out Wednesday, more than forty-eight hours ago. I don't see why I would be on their list of suspects."

"And perhaps you're not. Do you remember some rooms near yours that had been blocked off?"

"Yeah, now that you mention it. The rooms at the end of the hall-way were roped off. The maid told me there had been a big water leak in one of the bathrooms, and all the carpeting in those rooms had to be replaced."

"Ah, I see. Well her body had been left in one of them, and wasn't found until this morning. Apparently the repairmen had to wait a few days for something to set or dry, and it was only when they returned to finish the work that they found her."

"Ahh, so the police think she was probably killed while I was still there. Is that it?"

"Yes, that would account for their interest in you. But I know a detective who works out of the precinct handling the investigation," explained Boutin. "If you have no objection, I'll speak to him, mention our connection, and tell him how we spent the evening together before you left for home. I won't mention why you were in Paris, though."

"Yeah, okay. Sounds like a good idea, Paul."

"That's what I'll do, then. But they will probably want to interview you no matter what I tell them."

"Sure, I have nothing to hide. Keep me updated, my friend."

WHO WAS SHE? DON WONDERED, *and how did she die? He hadn't heard any commotion after he'd returned to his room. But then again, it would have taken a hell of a racket to rouse me after I had hit the sack.* An ominous thought crept into his mind. *Could this murder have something to do with my investigation of Archer?* Don slammed his fist on the desk. *Ahh, Jeezus! What the hell am I mixed up in?*

Seconds later his secretary cracked his door open and peered in.

"Are you all right, boss?"

"Yes, sorry about that, Joanne. Didn't mean to startle you. Would you look up Tom Allman's number, please?"

"Sure thing. I'll have it for you 'toot de sweet'," she replied with a smile. "That's French for 'like now', boss!"

"Yeah, yeah, just do it," he said, returning her smile.

TOM ALLMAN'S MESSAGE MACHINE PICKED up and Don was just starting to speak when a live voice cut in.

"Hang on, Don...I hear ya'! Gimme a sec' to turn this damned thing off." The tape continued, accompanied by more cussing before it was silenced. "That's better. How're you doin', pardner! It's been a while."

"Hey, I'm just fine, Tom," replied Don. "Keeping busy, making a buck or two, you know."

Allman, 41, was an ex-US Army Special Forces Ranger, known as the Green Berets. His expertise was explosives. Don had run into him five years ago when he was wrapping up an investigation at a diamond mine in the Northwest Territories. Always on the look out for possible operatives, he had recruited the American for occasional undercover work.

"Same here, what's up?"

"Well, if you available, I've got a job for you. One that'll take a couple of months, maybe longer."

"This is your lucky day, my man! I've justa' 'bout had enough of blowin' big holes in the ground for a while. Just finished a six-month contract last week."

"Where was that?"

"Oh, still up Fort Mac way. This tar sands thing is gonna be real big before it's over, ain't no doubt about it!"

Fort McMurray, approximately 400 kilometers [250 miles] northeast of Edmonton, Alberta, was the center of the massive new industry extracting oil from the bitumen-like sand that abounded in the region. It was only a few feet below the surface in places. Allman's specialty had led him north, that and a feisty redheaded nurse he'd met on the beach in Hawaii shortly after his discharge from the army. The relationship had ended a few years ago, but the high wages had encouraged Allman to stay on. He leased a one-bedroom apartment in Edmonton to use when he wasn't working.

Don gave Allman a brief rundown on the Archer investigation. A more detailed briefing could wait until he arrived in Toronto, he told him.

"Great! Count me in. Set me up to fly down next Monday," enthused Allman.

"Will do, Tom. Joanne will email you that info later today. Thanks, buddy."

"One more thing, Don."

"Yeah?"

"Will I get to shoot somebody this time?" Allman's hearty laugh boomed over the line.

Don laughed along with him. "No, but it'll help if you know your way around a tennis court!"

Don was still chuckling as he hung up. Allman had joked more than once that what he missed about his Ranger career was not getting to handle firearms any more. The highlight of his army years had been skulking around behind enemy lines in the first Gulf War. He hadn't instigated talk about his experiences, but Don had been enthralled with tales of his team's exploits when he did get him to open up, usually after they'd downed a few drinks.

By the time 4:30 rolled around, the private investigator had fully recovered from the uneasy feeling Boutin's call had brought on. He was confident now that he would quickly be cleared of having any connection to the killing, although he had no doubt he would be considered a suspect. If someone was trying to set him up, though, he'd have to be wary, and the sooner he figured out what Francois Amara/ Frank Archer, was involved in, the sooner he could stop worrying about this unknown enemy.

He resolved to leave the case on the shelf over the weekend. He debated making dinner reservations, but settled on a better plan. The warm weather was ideal for a barbeque, so he'd pick up a couple of good-sized steaks on his way home. In Paul Boutin's honor, he thought, he might even spring for an expensive bottle of French wine.

8

SATURDAY, JUNE 12

Frank stared out of his seventeenth floor window at the waterfront below. Sailboats dotted the surface, drifting in all directions as their helmsmen searched for what little wind was blowing on this late spring morning.

Jill had just left, albeit unwillingly. She hadn't bought his weak excuse that he had too much to do after his trip to spend the morning in bed. It would soon be time to tell her *'Ciao baby'* for good. He'd enjoyed their passionate sex last night as much as ever, but there was no way he was going to commit to a more permanent relationship, in spite of her continued hints that she would welcome one. Earlier this morning she'd brought it up again, while trying to arouse him. He'd pushed her hand away brusquely, visibly upsetting her.

No, for the next few months he needed to focus on the mission, not on the horny Jill. He might need her a bit longer, however. It was her casual remark that Empire North had booked a second ticket to and from Paris—and on the same flights as his—that had alerted him to a possible tail. He had never heard of the man, and he hadn't noticed anyone paying attention to him before his flight or after arriving in Paris. But then again, how would he know if he was being followed? He'd never had any training along those lines. But Carlos had, and as soon as Frank mentioned that a man named Carling held a similar flight itinerary, he canceled their planned meetings in Paris. Instead, he'd arranged for Frank's sudden departure and had his sister, Francoise, move into the hotel. They had taken different flights to Cannes, and Carlos had briefed him there on his upcoming role in the cell's plot.

Not for the first time, he was having second thoughts about working for Carlos. He had never held any strong views concerning world politics. Even the 9/11 attacks on the US hadn't fostered any particularly strong feelings, even though he had rather agreed with some of the editorials published in Muslim-dominated countries that America had it coming. Not the innocent victims who died, but their almighty 'we are the greatest', chest-beating government. Still, he'd been hesitant when Carlos came to Toronto last December hoping to recruit him.

He had never considered converting to Islam, in spite of pressure to do so by his uncles when he was in his teens. He thought he'd heard the end of it after his marriage and his move to Canada that followed. Not so. His cousin's sudden appearance in Toronto had changed that.

Carlos had harped on the family honor aspect at first. The family had looked after his mother after his father was killed, he told him. The triplets had only been six years old at the time. Apparently his uncles sent her money regularly, money she relied on to bring up her three young children. His mother had never mentioned this and he'd grown up none the wiser. In hindsight, Frank realized the money probably came from her brothers-in-law's criminal dealings.

Your own brother, Rene, died in the Algerian Civil War, fighting un-der the banner of the Islamic Salvation Front, Carlos had reminded him. Frank hadn't forgotten, but why Rene had volunteered in the first place had always mystified him. He was sure his uncles had been the instigators, an opinion confirmed by his mother shortly before she died in 1993. His mother never talked about her husband's death, stifling any talk of it, even as he and his siblings got older.

He'd spent a restless night before making up his mind, and Carlos had been overjoyed when he reluctantly agreed to join his cell. However, fam-ily loyalty had nothing to do with his decision. He had two better reasons.

The US-led incursion into Afghanistan, followed a year later by the unprovoked invasion of Iraq, stirred a deep sense of outrage in him for President Bush and his supporters. The vitriolic anti-Muslim rant spouted by the ill-informed American banker at the reception last year only added to his anger. The second reason was of a more personal nature. He real-ized soon after coming to Canada that his stay wasn't going to last forever. His bitch of a wife made that perfectly clear via a legal document she'd had prepared shortly after the birth of their daughter.

FRANK HAD NOT BEEN PRESENT when Gabrielle was born. She was placed in the care of a nanny when she was three months old, and that was the last time he saw her. When she was old enough, Gabrielle was to be told that her father had died soon after her birth. They would be di-vorced at a time of Danielle's choosing, but no later than 2007. He would receive a million dollar settlement at that time, but only if he left Canada for good. All these clauses were included in the document she'd had her lawyers draw up. He'd swallowed his pride and signed it.

I'll still be in my early forties when it's over, and I'll have enough money to set up my own art gallery, he reasoned. Along with the large sum he'd been promised for cooperating with Carlos, he would be financially se-cure after they divorced.

He also had an ace up his sleeve that just might get him the settle-ment from his loveless wife sooner than planned. He hadn't had sex with her since their week long fling on the Riviera that resulted in her pregnancy. And that was almost nine years ago. *Had she been leading a life of celibacy ever since?* He'd never really given her private life much consideration until recently.

That's when he first heard rumblings that Danielle might be involved with the head of a well-known investment firm. An affair that would no doubt do enormous damage to both their reputations if it became public. He came by this information quite out of the blue. Gerald Tupman, a mid-level manager at Empire North, had incurred the wrath of Danielle Clyde, undeservedly in his opinion, and was looking to hurt her in return. He had button-holed Frank in the washroom at the company Christmas party last December. Even though Tupman was half-smashed at the time, Frank quickly realized that his assertion that Danielle was involved with a married man might be worth knowing more about and gave Tupman his card.

Tupman had sworn his discretion and promised to let Archer know if and when he could provide irrefutable proof, proof that Frank could use to his advantage.

He poured himself another coffee and took it over to the computer desk. From a pile of magazines in one of its drawers, he pulled out a glossy Sotheby's catalogue from an auction he'd attended three years ago in New York. Inside the back cover, he had hidden a two-page missive Carlos had given it to him before he left France. He had heard it referred to more than once during his briefings in Cannes.

The document, written in French, was the updated mission plan for the cell headed by Carlos. He reread the opening paragraphs of the document, obviously intended to inspire cell members. Frank didn't know who the others were yet, or where they were located. Carlos told him that information was best kept secret for the time being.

'*Our task is to wreak havoc inside America if their anti-Islam president is re-elected this coming November. An Armageddon to cause widespread panic and fear to the populace at large. One that will bring the country to a shocked standstill, much like the aftermath of September 11, 2001.*

Those attacks by our martyrs were a great success and brought joy to our Muslim brethren around the world. Joy that we must rekindle anew, by striking back at the warmongers for their murderous attacks on Islam in Afghanistan and now Iraq.

The next great attack on their homeland will come from within: by recruiting their own greedy and criminal element to help us carry out the plan.'

Frank thought the rhetoric a bit over the top. No doubt it was designed with younger and more impressionable recruits in mind. *Who knows?* he thought. *It probably works.*

The document was supposedly written by one of the secretive leaders behind the al-Qaeda World network: the increasingly-active organization that was funding the plot conceived by Carlos. There were others, his cousin had intimated, all working on plans to attack America and her interests around the globe. He'd smiled inwardly when Carlos told him that in future correspondence—either by email or phone—code names would be used. Frank would be referred to as GROWER, and Carlos as BREEDER. No name was mentioned for the operation itself. His rationale for using such names was that they might attract less attention from possible electronic surveillance by US watchdogs than something with an Islamic or Arabian reference in it.

"Let's hope it works," he'd said to Carlos, "I don't want to spend the rest of my life in an American prison."

His cousin had made light of his concerns. "Your part is not dangerous, cousin. We will be taking all the risks." He wouldn't divulge who he meant by 'we', either. "Just do what I ask of you for now, and it will all fall into place at the proper time."

Frank had pressed him about what would happen if the president wasn't re-elected. "That will be decided by others after the election. It's possible that the mission will aborted in that case," said Carlos.

Frank reached over, fed the pages into the shredder, and picked up the weekend edition of the *Globe and Mail* newspaper. He thumbed throught it until he found the article he was looking for.

The latest CNN/USA TODAY/GALLUP poll of likely voters had President Bush leading any of the potential Democratic contenders, it read.

DON ROLLED ONTO HIS BACK and let out a satisfied post-coital sigh.

"Whew! You're too much, hon'... The second half of the doubleheader was even better than the first, I must say!"

"Smartass," exclaimed Yvonne, boxing his ears playfully. "Why do always think of our love-making as a sporting event?"

"Well, why not?" he chuckled. "It's good exercise, you know. And the more we exercise, the fitter we'll be in our dotage. I just read that somewhere."

Yvonne curled upright. "Dotage? When did you start thinking like that? Trust me, big fella, if you ever go dotty, or loopy—"

"Loopy?" interrupted Don, pushing himself to a sitting position beside her. "Now I'm going to go loopy, am I?"

"Whatever... loopy, dotty, take your choice. At the first sign you're off to a home!"

"Nice talk. I suppose you want that in writing, too."

"Definitely! You can put the coffee on first, though."

"And you'll make breakfast, right?"

"Not a chance, I'm too tired," she said, throwing her arms around his neck. "Last night's game was a winner, too, remember?"

Don nuzzled her throat. "Want to go a few extra innings?"

TWO HOURS LATER THEY WERE browsing the brunch buffet at Brenda's Bistro, the popular eatery on the main street in Orangeville, twenty minutes from Don's country home. They had toured the Saturday Farmers' market first, and Yvonne had bought three trays of colorful bedding plants for her garden.

After they returned to their table and ordered wine, Don told her about his trip to Paris. Yvonne had taken an interest in his investigations ever since they'd started dating eight years ago. He trusted her discretion, and therefore felt comfortable telling her about his work.

"That sounds scary. Especially if he is somehow connected to terrorists," said Yvonne after he'd finished.

"Well... yeah, but I stress *possible*. I say that only because of the history of some of his relatives, stuff that Boutin dug up," said Don.

He had read the report twice on the flight home. Archer's father, Rashad, had been suspected by French authorities of supplying arms to rebels during the Algerian insurrection in 1961 and '62. He was never arrested, though. After Algerian independence, Amara senior and his two brothers, Nasir and Jabaar, turned to major crime. Marseille was their base, and Rashad was gunned down in the city's port area in 1974. Rumors suggested that the French Secret Service was behind the hit. The remaining brothers continued to run the lucrative syndicate until they were finally arrested in 1980. After a long trial, they were found guilty on heroin distribution charges and sentenced to twelve years in prison. They were paroled in 1989. Nasir was 54 and Jabaar 52 at the time. Frank, age 21, was at university in Lyons.

Here Boutin's report ran out of hard facts. It suggested that Frank's brother, Rene, the third triplet, was killed fighting for the Islamic Salvation Front in 1992 or '93. Were his uncles supplying arms to the ISF at the time? By all accounts they were devout Muslims.

And what about Frank's cousins? Apparently there were two approximately his age, but the report gave no details about them. Francoise, his twin sister, was mentioned, but only briefly. She was apparently still single and worked as a model. But Boutin didn't think she would have been directly involved in any criminal activities run by the male members of the Amara clan.

"She was just acting as a decoy, then, by staying in the hotel," Yvonne summed up.

"...Yeah, that's what it looked like to me."

"Well, it all sounds rather alarming," said Yvonne, her concern showing. "Please be careful. I shudder to think that you could become a target for terrorists."

"Ahh, it won't come to that, hon," smiled Don, placing his hand over hers. "I think it'll turn out to be something simpler...smuggling or fraud, maybe."

It would only be a matter of weeks before Carling would discover just how disastrously wrong he was...

LAST NIGHT AND ALL MORNING Don had been able to push thoughts about the dead woman to the back of his mind. Now though, on the drive home, the possible ramifications for him surfaced again. Yvonne couldn't help but notice. "You're frowning, Don, What's the matter?"

He turned to her, forcing a smile. "Ahh, nothing really. Just had a thought about the case. Something that'll keep until Tom gets here on Monday," he lied. "Should we barbeque again tonight?" he asked, changing the subject.

9

MONDAY, JUNE 14

Don rose to greet the fit-looking, prematurely grey-haired man entering his office.

"Hello, Tom. Welcome back to Toronto!"

"Hey man, great to see you!"

Tom Allman had come directly to the KayRoy offices after flying in from Edmonton. Don indicated the sofa in his large office. "Take a load off, Tom, make yourself at home. Want a coffee?" asked Don, settling into a chair across from Allman.

"No more coffee for me today, pard, but thanks." To the ex-special forces warrant officer, everyone was 'pard', or pardner.

"Well, it'll be Happy Hour soon enough, and I'm buying. That's if you haven't been converted by one of those prairie bible thumpers!"

Allman let out a loud guffaw. "Too late for my salvation, I'm afraid! But I must admit I've slowed down a bit since I hit the big 'four oh'," he offered, patting his stomach. "You're lookin' good yourself, pard. That purty li'l miss must be takin' good care of you."

Allman had been met Yvonne a few years ago at a party Don had hosted for his small team of investigators.

"Thanks, she feeds me too well, though. Gotta get to the health club most days," Don replied.

After exchanging a few more pleasantries, Don briefed the American on the assignment he'd brought him to Toronto for. He provided him with the latest information he had on Frank Archer: photos, address and phone number, names of women he was seeing , and the location of the fitness and tennis club he belonged to. When he'd finished, Don handed Allman a copy of Paul Boutin's report.

"Take this with you, and once you've looked it over, destroy it," Don directed. "You're set up with a small apartment downtown. Should make a good base for you. You'll find a cell phone there and a list of pertinent numbers. And your rental car is right out front. Any questions?"

Allman riffled through the report before replying. "Yeah... how come you're still lissen'n to this gawd awful music?" A CD playing on the office entertainment system was just loud enough to be audible in Don's office. "Whose that moaning away? Red Bovine? No, don't tell me. It's Lefty Frazzle, right?"

Tom had pulled Don's leg before about his liking for country music. "I see you haven't changed with the times," he chuckled. "And it was Red Sovine, with an 'S', and Lefty Frizzell. They both died years ago. You listening to what they call 'new country'... that's a Garth Brooks tape."

"It still sounds like 'cryin' and dyin' music to me, pard," said Allman, getting in the last word.

TUESDAY, JUNE 15

By three o'clock Allman had been fully briefed. Don had picked him up at nine, and set out to familiarize him with the locations most frequented by Frank Archer. The tour included the building on Lakeshore Boulevard where he lived, his club three miles away, and the motel he used for his afternoon trysts with two different women. They also stopped by the Empire North office complex a few blocks from Bay Street, heart of the city's financial district.

The art collection that Danielle Clyde was so proud of covered the walls surrounding the bank of elevators huddled in the center of the ground floor. The exhibition was open to the public at no cost. On his two previous visits to see the CEO of Empire North, Don had only glanced at the display as he passed through the lobby. Now he and Tom made a slow circuit, stopping at a wall that displayed large and colorful action paintings of cowboys, cattle drives, and native Indians in ceremonial dress. The corner held bronze castings of animals that once roamed the western mountains and plains.

Was Archer responsible for acquiring these works, too? And if so, where would he have purchased them, Don wondered. He excused himself and used his cell phone to dial Danielle Clyde's private number.

She answered after the fourth ring with a curt 'hello'.

"Don Carling here, Danielle, with a question for you. Who selected the paintings and castings for the western exhibit in the lobby?"

"Why Frank, of course. It's all from the American southwest. Why do you ask?"

"So his buying trips aren't necessarily confined to Europe," said Don.

"No. The company owns a vacation home in Scottsdale, Arizona. Frank spends time there, usually in the winter. Apparently it's another place to indulge his tennis addiction. Have you ever been to Scottsdale?"

"Nope, can't say that I have."

"It has many galleries that carry such art. Frank suggested a selection would make an attractive addition to our gallery and I went along with it."

"Yes, well, I'd say you made a good decision. That's all I wanted to know, Danielle. Thanks. And I'll expect a call from your PA as soon as Frank has firmed up his plans for London." He closed his phone before she could reply.

"What did you find out?" asked Allman.

"It seems our boy spends time in Arizona, combining tennis with art collecting. Stays at company digs in Scottsdale."

"Scottsdale...'up market' area, man," offered Allman.

"So she told me. Anyway, that's where this stuff came from. He goes there in the winter, supposedly to play tennis."

"But you think that his tennis playing is just a front for whatever he's involved in," Allman said, "which is also the impression I got from reading the French guy's report."

"Yeah, I'm leaning that way. Although he's been playing tennis ever since he moved here, according to his wife." They were moving slowly towards the exit doors while they talked. "But my gut instinct tells me that it's only recently that travel and tennis have become a convenient cover for him." Don added.

The heat and humidity hit them as soon as they passed through the revolving doors. "Jeez, it never gets this bad in Alberta!" remarked Allman.

"Can't have you melting away, then," said Don. "Let's go grab a beer and make sure we've covered all bases before you go after him."

FORTY-FIVE MINUTES AND A PITCHER of beer later, Don and his investigator were ready to call it a day. As Don signaled for the tab, his cell phone rang. Paul Boutin was on the line from Paris.

"I expect you will be hearing from the French police, probably in the next few days," Boutin advised him. "I have provided them with your office number, Don, but none others."

Boutin had met with his police contact and given him details, including the time frame, of their evening together the night before Don flew home. When asked why the Canadian had been in France, and what they had been working on, Boutin had stretched the truth. He'd suggested that Carling was investigating a man suspected of fraud by his Canadian employer. The inspector in charge had been cooperative, agreeing with Boutin that there was no need at present to make Don's name public. The hotel, not wanting any adverse publicity, had refused comment, referring all queries to the police. The murder made headlines for a few days, but there hadn't been any mention of it in newspapers since Saturday, according to Boutin.

'Thanks, Paul, and I'll get back to you if I do get a call from your police."

So far Don hadn't mentioned the murder in Paris to Allman. While they stood in the building's shade, he told him about the woman's body found in a room near his, and his suspicion that it had something to do with his investigation.

Allman muttered a subdued 'wow' when he finished. "Just adds to the mystery surrounding this guy, doesn't it? They can't extradite you merely as a suspect, can they?"

"Don't think so," Don replied, shaking his head. "But I should probably check with my lawyer. It could affect a trip I might want to take to England next month."

According to Danielle Clyde, her husband flew to London every summer for the matches at Wimbledon. Just as in Paris, checking out art galleries when he wasn't watching tennis meant the firm could write off his trip as a business expense.

Don dropped Allman off at his new apartment and headed back to his office. Allman would begin his surveillance of Archer tomorrow. Calls between them were to made at night to or from Don's home number. Two other KayRoy investigators—a husband and wife team—were available if Allman needed help.

They had discussed at length how Tom might work his way into Archer's confidence. The result was a cover story, one they felt would hold up if it was questioned. A ploy that they hoped would lead to a bond between Allman and the Frenchman based on his apparent loathing of the US government.

Little did Don know that his casual suggestion would be the key to the American becoming an insider in the convoluted plot designed to wreak havoc once more on a still-jittery and innocent American population...

DON HAD MORE THAN ONE problem on his mind as he drove home. Dealing with the French cops was obviously a big unknown. Could it be taken of care by phone? Probably not. If they needed his fingerprints, he was sure that could be arranged. What about DNA? A person's personal signature was a common tool police relied on nowadays to confirm or eliminate suspects. Could he provide a sample here that would be accepted in France? He wasn't sure, but made a mental note to check with a contact in the RCMP who would know.

Another thought had been bugging him ever since Archer pulled his disappearing act in Paris. *How did his cover get blown so early?* Maybe Archer's actions weren't those of a trained agent, but someone must have made him. He would have to steer clear of Archer for now, and give Tom Allman time to come with some answers.

If we don't find any hard evidence about what Archer is up to in the next few weeks, then I'll go after him in London, Don thought. *But I'll have to close a few possible loopholes first…*

10

Don was still on his first coffee of the day when Joanne buzzed him. "An Inspector Monet calling from Paris, boss. Line two." "Got it. Thanks, Jo."

Monet identified himself, apologized for his English, and politely inquired if Monsieur Carling had any objection to answering his questions. Don assured him that his English was certainly better than his fractured French, which drew a chuckle from Monet. Don reached over and punched a button to record the call.

Monet began by telling Don that he was not a suspect in the woman's death. The police were just following normal procedure, which meant checking out male guests who had been staying at the hotel around the time of the murder.

"I understand completely, Inspector. Fire away."

Monet had already spoken to Paul Boutin. He asked Don to confirm the time frame of their evening together, which he did. Satisfied, Monet moved onto Don's actions after returning to his room. Had he heard any sounds or voices from the adjoining rooms either that night or the next morning? A commotion of any sort, perhaps?

Don's answered 'no' to both questions. He'd heard muted voices from the adjoining room over the weekend, but nothing during the two days before he'd checked out, he told Monet.

Monet asked him if he had opened his side of the connecting doors at any time during his stay.

"Uhh...well, I did, now that you mention it. I opened it the morning I checked in. You know, just to make sure the other side was closed."

"And was it?"

"Yeah, there's no handle of course, but I did put pressure on it to ensure it was locked."

"And did you have occasion to open it again?"

Don detected a slight change in the inspector's tone of voice. 'Less casual' was his impression, causing him to wonder where he was heading. He paused for a moment, deciding if he should mention that he thought his adjoining door had been slightly ajar that night, and only closed when he stumbled against it. Right or wrong, he decided not to.

"Uhh, no...I don't think I touched it again. Had no reason to, I guess."

"Very good, monsieur. I just have one request of you. Once again, just routine, you understand."

Don had anticipated Monet's request for his fingerprints. He told Monet they were on file, probably with the national police registry in Ottawa. His prints had been taken years ago when he joined the RCMP, and more recently when he applied for his private investigator's licence. He had objection to the French authorities requesting them, he told Monet.

"I'm sure you'll find my prints all over the room, perhaps even still on the doorknob."

"Yes, the room you stayed in and others nearby were sealed as soon as the body was discovered, and we have dusted it for prints," Monet said. "Thank you for your cooperation, Monsieur Carling. I shouldn't think we'll need to bother you again."

"Well, you know how to reach me if you do," Don said. "Cheers!"

INSPECTOR MONET HAD BEEN TIGHT-LIPPED when Don asked a few questions of his own. He did name the victim, but wouldn't give any details about how she died, or if she'd been sexually assaulted.

Don leaned back with his hands behind his head, and listened to the playback of the call. The emphasis on the questions about the connecting doors intrigued him, but he couldn't figure out why. Again, he had a vague recollection of stumbling into the door and hearing it click shut. But had that actually happened? Or had he just imagined it?

Not much I can do about it now. Time to get to work. Don rose and turned off the recorder. *At least the subject of DNA never came up, but I should check out just what it entails in case they do request a sample.*

The French police had wasted little time processing a request for his fingerprints. It wasn't the call from Ottawa that surprised him, but who was calling. Brian Roberts was an old friend.

"Can't you just stay home and investigate wayward husbands or wives, Don? What the hell were you doing in Paris?"

Roberts was now an Inspector in the RCMP, commonly referred to as the Mounties. He'd moved up the ranks quickly and was now the number two man in the counterterrorism division. Their paths had crossed twice in the last ten years. Initially during a drug smuggling investigation at Pearson International Airport, and a few years later when Don was investigating the suspicious deaths of four airline pilots in Europe. They'd got on well, and Brian had urged the private detective to call him any time.

"I've got a team now that takes care of the 'peep and shoot' cases, Brian," Don said, referring to the practice of gathering incriminating photos to be used as evidence in contested divorce cases. "Save myself for the more intriguing jobs." Don wondered how the request for his fingerprints ended up in Brian's office.

"Well, it didn't come directly to me, Don. But an officer in the section that handles such matters remembered you from the drug case we worked on with you and gave me a 'heads up'," Roberts explained.

Don quickly filled in the gaps for the Mountie about his Paris trip, and why the French police were seeking his cooperation. "So, as I have nothing to hide, I agreed to waive any legal hoops that might have delayed their request. Won't be a problem, will it?" asked Don.

"No, no, and it will definitely expedite the process," said Roberts. "By the way, have you mentioned this to your lawyer?"

"... No, but I get the impression you think I should, eh?"

"That would be the prudent thing to do, yes. Just to cover all bases down the road, you know."

"Okay, I'll call him," said Don. "May as well run a few other things by you if you've got a few minutes."

"Go ahead. What's on your mind?"

Don asked about DNA testing and extradition, if, hypothetically, the subjects arose.

"DNA would have to be done in person, Don, it probably wouldn't be allowed as evidence if someone here in Canada took your sample and sent it to France. They'd probably send someone over to take the sample from you. Unless you went there, of course."

Don grunted. "I guess I'd want to know why they were asking for it before making that decision, wouldn't I?"

Roberts agreed, and then paused before addressing the extradition scenario. "Hmm, these requests are a bit more complicated. Depends on the charges." Roberts explained that as neither Canada nor France had the death penalty, a murder charge could lead to a suspect being extradited. "Don't quote me, though. That's one for the 'legal beagles'."

"I see. Well thanks for the info, Brian. I won't keep you any longer."

"Not so fast, my friend," said Roberts. "Want to tell me why these issues are on your mind?"

"Yeah, I guess so. It's probably just my suspicious nature at work, but..."

Don explained why he was a suspect in the Paris murder. Although Inspector Monet hadn't said in so many words, Don got the impression that the crime had been committed in the room next to his and the body moved afterwards. The thought kept crossing his mind that it may have been an attempt to frame him by whomever Archer was working with. Especially in light of the disappearing act Archer pulled while Don was following him.

"Could be just a coincidence, Don."

"Yes, but too many factors tell me it wasn't."

"Tell you what. I'll have my people run a check on him. You said this Amara fellow was born in France, right?"

"That's what I've been told. And from what I've learned about the family so far, I'm sure you'll find references to them in Interpol's files."

"I'll put someone on it today and let you know what turns up. Cheers!"

11

MONDAY, JUNE 28

Don's overnight flight from Toronto landed at Heathrow at 10:30 a.m. Frank Archer wasn't due to arrive until Wednesday morning. He'd only got word of Archer's impending trip from Danielle Clyde last week. As usual, his itinerary had been booked by agency where his girlfriend, Jill McNeil, worked.

Just to be on the safe side Don had made his own flight arrangements. He hadn't informed anyone at Empire North, including Danielle Clyde, that he would be in London at the same time as Archer. According to Danielle, only a few company employees were involved with her husband's trips. Still, the fewer who knew of his own plans, the better. Someone had tipped Archer off about Carling's trip to Paris. It didn't matter where the leak came from: he wasn't taking any chances this time around. He'd even briefed Joanne to tell anyone calling for him to say he was vacationing in Northern Ontario.

In fact it was only on Saturday that Don booked his trip. He'd made his decision after getting Tom Allman's update. They now had a better picture of Archer's daily routine, but no hard proof of any illegal activities. Tom confirmed that Archer was still having a weekly tryst with a lady he played tennis with.

"Her name is Elizabeth Woods, late thirties or early forties, married to a senior partner in a bond trading firm. They live in Oakville, big place on the lakeshore. Probably worth close to a million bucks. Two children, both in their early teens. They go to private schools. You can fill in the blanks yourself, pard," Tom said.

"Got it. Besides their afternoon romps, does he have any other contact with her?"

"Nope. As to the other married gal mentioned, she seems to have been dropped from his play list. She's at the club a couple of times a week but they don't seem to be on speaking terms."

"And the regular girlfriend, Jill McNeil?"

"They don't seem to be hitting it off too well, either, according to the Walters." Doug and Liz Walters were part-time KayRoy operatives. As a couple, they were less likely to be noticed when following people to restaurants, for instance. "The McNeil woman, a real knockout, by the way, stomped out of a bistro last Saturday night, after an apparent quarrel and before they had finished eating," Tom reported.

DON WAS TIRED AFTER HIS flight, having managed only a few hours of restless sleep en route. He didn't argue when his host suggested he grab a few hours sleep after they got back from Heathrow. Rod and Kate Weathers lived in the small village of Milnes Marsh south of London. Rod was a Boeing 777 captain with British Global Airlines. They had been friends since the mid-1980's when Don was still a pilot himself. The welcome mat was always out for the Canadian whenever he came to London. Don asked Rod to wake him in two hours, and retired to the guest room.

Staying at the Weathers home wasn't always convenient for Don—Milnes Marsh was twenty-five miles from central London—but this time it wouldn't matter. Archer would be staying in a private flat situated on a cul-de-sac near Wimbledon, which was much closer to Milnes Marsh. It would still be difficult, if not impossible, for Don to watch Archer's flat without the risk of being noticed. Rather than take chance, he had come up with an alternate plan to keep track of his quarry.

James Coates, a retired British Intelligence agent, still lived in London. In 1997, James's expertise and enthusiasm had proved invaluable in helping Don unravel the mystery surrounding the death of an American airline pilot in London. Don had phoned him before leaving Toronto, and James had immediately agreed to help.

Another Londoner had been closely involved with that investigation seven years ago, and Don was hoping he could count on him again as well.

I'll call Derek after my nap, Don thought, just before he drifted off. If he could join them for lunch tomorrow, he'd be able to brief both of them at the same time.

TUESDAY, JUNE 29

Carling was the first to arrive at the restaurant and was looking over the short menu when Derek Houghton walked in. Don waved to him and rose to take his outstretched hand.

"Hi Derek, really glad you could make it on short notice," he told the handsome British police officer. "You look amazingly good for someone who's just hit the big 'five-oh'!"

Derek chuckled. "Ahh... I'll bet Rod couldn't wait to tell you that!"

Houghton was Rod's brother-in-law. He had joined the Metropolitan Police when he was twenty-two. When Don phoned him last evening, he'd readily agreed to come along and hear about Don's present case.

"Rod also told me that you're toying with retirement. Any decision on that yet?" Don asked after Derek sat down opposite him.

Houghton sighed and shook his head. "No, haven't made up my mind yet. I've been offered a few tempting positions in the City, jobs that would pay rather handsomely, but..." Derek paused and shrugged. "But I feel I'd be letting the side down if I left now."

Detective Superintendent Houghton was second-in-command of Scotland Yard's counterterrorism division. He was in charge of police efforts to identify and track down members of the homegrown terrorist cells thought to be planning attacks in Britain. He painted a disturbing picture for Don of how young British Muslims were being recruited vigorously for the Jihad, and the manpower necessary to keeps tabs on them and known radicals.

"Helluva job, Derek," Don offered quietly when he finished. "And I can understand why you want to see it through. But hey, look on the bright side. I'm sure you'll still be in demand when you're ready to pack it in."

Their chat was interrupted when James Coates arrived. Don greeted him with a warm hug, and James and Derek shook hands. Don knew that James was in his late seventies now, but other than a few more creases in his closely-shaved face, he wore his age well. As always, he was attired in jacket and tie, neatly pressed trousers, and shoes that looked as new as the day he'd bought them.

"James, I can't thank you enough for offering to help me out again," Don said.

"Not at all, Donald. After all, we can't have you prowling around our fair city alone. You need someone to watch your backside, old chap! Am I right, Superintendent?"

"Couldn't have put it better myself, James!"

"Well, as before, I'm grateful that my uhh... *backside*... is in such good hands," smiled Don.

THE CORNER TABLE DON HAD chosen left them in relative privacy. The modest Greek restaurant on a quiet street off Knightsbridge was less busy at lunchtime than in the evening. James had recommended it for that very reason. While they were eating, Don related all that had transpired since he'd taken on the Archer case. Now, forty-five minutes later, he'd answered most of their questions. They paused while the waiter served their post-lunch beverages: tea for James, coffee for the two younger men.

When the waiter was out of earshot again, Derek asked, "It would seem that your client hasn't come completely clean with you as to why she wanted this chap investigated. You say she'd had him watched before?"

Don had mentioned the surveillance handled by Chuck Todd, Empire North's chief of security. "That's right," he answered. "All he turned up was the fact that Archer's had numerous sexual partners. Revelations that didn't bother his wife, apparently."

"But you suspect that she's concerned about possible fraud, or corporate espionage, for instance. Something her company would be hurt by if it became public knowledge," said James.

Don shrugged. "Yeah, that was my first inclination, but—"

"But his actions in Paris made you think otherwise," summed up James.

They had already covered this ground, but Don understood why they wanted to go over it again. From his previous experience with these men, he knew they were just making sure that they had a complete picture before getting involved.

Derek offered to help, to the limit his present duties allowed. For starters, he would have the Amara name run through the Scotland Yard data base. "These days, any possible thread to terrorist organizations past or present is worth looking into," he said.

James, a widower, had no such restraints on his time. Before parting they had agreed on tactics to keep watch on Archer after he arrived. James would be the point man at Wimbledon. They would communicate via mobile phone and Don would try to keep track of him when he was on the move. His buddy, Rod, had the next four days off and would serve as his driver.

"WHAT DO YOU THINK, DEREK? Has our Canadian friend got caught up in another improbable case with a local twist or two?"

The police officer shrugged. "Certainly a possibility," he answered. "I'm curious now to see what, if anything, we have in our files on this man or his family. If we do get a hit, I'll see you get the 'gen' straight off."

They were walking south towards the Thames River. Carling had turned the other way after leaving the restaurant, heading for Knightsbridge. Derek had suggested an agency near Harrod's where he'd be able to acquire a daily pass to Wimbledon for James.

DS Houghton had known James Coates for going on twenty years. They had met shortly after Coates retired from the Secret Service, in fact. The former spy had taken on a number of temporary undercover assignments for Scotland Yard since then. The job might be as innocuous as watching to see if a certain person appeared at a particular establishment on a certain date, a bank or a train station, for instance. He'd also helped out snapping photos of individuals of interest at large rallies when the police resources were stretched too thin to spare the needed manpower.

They had reached Derek's vehicle, parked alongside the riverbank. James declined Derek's offer of a lift home. He had moved into a modern flat on the south bank of the Thames last year after selling his spacious home in north London. "Lovely afternoon for a stroll!" he said, setting off towards Vauxhall Bridge.

12

WEDNESDAY, JUNE 30

Frank Archer was in a foul mood as waited for his flight to board. A number of factors contributed to his displeasure. He'd had to get up at the ungodly hour of 6 a.m. for his morning flight to London, only to be told when he checked in that the flight was delayed for an hour.

"Maintenance problem, sir," the agent told him, smiling sympathetically.

"Nothing to smile about, "he'd muttered as he turned away. The lukewarm and tasteless coffee in the first class departure lounge didn't help, either.

The newscast airing on the large screen television was running graphic footage shot in a Baghdad suburb of civilian casualties being whisked off to hospitals, supposedly victims of a bomb dropped by a US jet that had missed its intended target. It was recurring scenes like this that made him forget his initial reluctance to join his cousin's cause. The bloodshed was also front page news in the paper he picked up. He tossed it aside disgustedly after reading the first few paragraphs, drawing a questioning look from the traveler seated the chair next to his.

Last night's break up with Jill was still rankling him, too.

Maybe I'll never understand these Canadian women, he told himself, shaking his head. He thought he'd made it perfectly clear, right from the first time they'd slept together, that she shouldn't ever entertain any ideas about a permanent relationship. And he'd reinforced that as gently as he could each time she hinted at it. At least he thought he had. But the silly bitch still didn't get the message. After he'd phoned her last night to tell her it was over, she had shown up at his condo and caused a scene in the lobby, buzzing him repeatedly until he relented and let her in.

It took him over an hour to settle her down. Eventually she realized nothing she could say or do was going to change his mind. Their affair was over. She'd left quietly, dabbing at her tear-stained cheeks.

He shut her out of his mind once his flight was called. It was time to focus on what awaited him in England...

FRANK NOTICED THE FLASHING LIGHT on the answering machine when he entered his rented flat. The message was from Carlos, and left a number for him to call. From the first four digits, he knew it was a London number. Frank didn't think Carlos was living in Britain, but figured other members of his cell did. E-mails to him from BREEDER always came from a UK address, 'yahoo.co.uk.' His cousin hadn't explained why, but he thought it was probably a security precaution. Maybe he would find out tomorrow who was relaying the messages.

THURSDAY, JULY 1

He was no further ahead after making the call this morning, though. A voice with a English accent gave him a street address and its city location and told him to come there by taxi tonight between eight and eight-thirty. That was the extent of the message. He lazed around for most of the morning before leaving for Wimbledon.

Don and Rod had been watching the building and fell in behind Archer's taxi as he left the cul-de-sac. A few blocks on, it was apparent he was heading towards Wimbledon, and Don called James Coates to let him know Archer was on the move. The retired spy was already in position in front of the tennis stadium. Ten minutes later, Don called him again to report Archer's imminent arrival. When Archer got out of the taxi thirty seconds later, Don called James a third time to describe what he was wearing, notably a long-sleeved, navy blue sweater.

Almost immediately Coates replied. "Got him, Donald. I'll take it from here," he said as he folded his phone and slipped it into his jacket pocket.

AFTER ARCHER ENTERED THE CENTER court stadium, Coates employed the same tactic Carling had used in Paris. He found a row of benches from which he could observe both gates on the side Archer had entered, and settled down to wait for his reappearance. The benches were in constant use, and Coates changed his position every thirty minutes. He was in his element, and, after an hour of watching the crowds coming and going around him, he was confident that he himself was not under surveillance.

Inside the stadium, Archer checked his watch again: it was only 3:30. He'd lost interest in the one-sided tennis match between two female quarter-finalists. A men's match was to follow but wouldn't begin until 5 p.m. He rose from his fifth row seat, left the stadium, and wandered towards the food stalls, undecided whether to stick around or head back to the flat and take a nap. For some reason he hadn't slept well last night. Normally arriving at night let his body clock adjust immediately to the time change. Then again, all he usually had on his mind when he got to London was tennis and art dealers, not what he was now irreversibly caught up in.

Coates had just moved again and unfolded the daily program he'd been idly perusing when he spotted Archer approaching. Archer passed within five yards of him without so much as a glance and continued towards the nearby food court. When he reached it, he stopped in front an open-air café. After appearing to study the menu for a minute or so, Archer abruptly turned and headed for the exit gates. James pulled out his mobile phone and hit the speed dial button. "He's on the move now. I'll follow him out and let you know what he does next. Stay on the line," he instructed.

Don acknowledged and alerted Rod, who had been dozing with the driver's seat tilted back. They were parked on a corner three blocks away on the main route back to central London.

Two minutes elapsed before James spoke again. "He's in a maroon minicab just pulling away. The vehicle has advertising on its bonnet in bright yellow. Can't make out the logo, unfortunately."

"No problem, James. We'll pick him up as he passes. Check with you later. Thanks!"

Three black taxis passed, heading towards the city, before the minicab carrying Archer stopped for the traffic light at the corner. Don trained his binoculars on it and confirmed that the lone passenger was Archer. At his first opportunity, Rod turned into the stream of cars behind the taxi. Five cars and a delivery van separated them, and the narrow roadway limited the speed at which traffic was moving.

"He's probably headed back to his apartment, Rod," said Don, as he studied the street map. "If so, they'll be taking a right turn at Crest Lane. Remember being on that earlier?"

"I do, its roughly another mile. Should be able to spot the cab when it makes the turn. If not, we'll be able to close the gap when they reach the four-lane stretch just past there. Can't see them now because of the bloody van, " Rod replied.

Five minutes later Don spotted the maroon vehicle signaling a right turn. Rod followed and reached the entrance to Maple Crescent, the name of the cul-de-sac, just as Archer entered the apartment building.

"GREAT JOB OF DRIVING, BUDDY! Thought we'd lost him a few times, didn't you?" said Don. It was a few minutes past 8 p.m.

Rod rounded a corner a block past the house where the taxi had dropped Archer off. He switched off the engine and let out a nervous sigh. "Yes, especially when they turned off the flyover onto Edgware Road. Good thing it's still daylight and traffic is fairly light."

After trailing Archer back to his rented flat earlier, they had set up watch again. They'd taken turns to grab a quick bite at a pizza shop on the nearby corner with the main road. They had just about decided to call it quits for the day when a taxi entered the cul-de-sac, stopped in front of Archer's building, and pulled away with him in it moments later.

They were now parked on a side street a half mile past the point where Maida Vale became Kilburn High Road. From this vantage point, they had a clear view of passing traffic on the High Road. They had been watching the busy pedestrian flow for almost ten minutes when Don commented, "Lots of Arab types, eh? I thought Kilburn was an Irish area."

"Still is, as far as I know," Rod replied. "But plenty of Muslim immigrants have been moving in, a trend that started around the time of the first Gulf War."

"Oh yeah? That would've been during the early 1990's then."

Rod agreed, and mentioned the problems that a few radical leaders and their minions had been causing British authorities.

"Betcha' it gets worse. At least until the strife in Iraq and other Mideast trouble spots gets settled. Fat chance of that happening soon, though," mused Don.

Waiting around for an indeterminate time for Archer to appear again wouldn't be a smart move, they soon decided. For one thing, Don didn't want to risk being noticed by anyone who might be watching Archer's back. And with darkness less than an hour away, any further attempt to follow him tonight, assuming he did reappear, would probably be very difficult, if not impossible. Not only that, they were both yawning more often.

"Let's try this before we head for home, he said, getting Rod's attention. After outlining his plan, Don got out of the vehicle. He reckoned they had about half an hour of daylight left. He walked to a newsagent's shop at the corner and bought a newspaper. He crossed to the opposite side of the street from the house Archer had entered and strolled towards it. While pretending to be engrossed in the paper, he noted the dwelling's number as he passed. Number 118 was the second in a row of six brick houses. There no lights showing inside yet and no figures visible through the large first floor window, but he was sure he had the right house. A chador-clad woman, with three chattering youngsters in trail, turned into number 120 next door as Don passed. Although the row houses were old, built in the 1930s, according to one visible marker, most appeared to be well-kept. No broken windows, overturned rubbish bins, or discarded furniture on front stoops prevalent in other older areas of the city. Don covered another hundred yards before Rod pulled up alongside him and pushed the passenger door open. Forty-five minutes later they were back in Milnes Marsh.

"Nightcap, Don?"

"Thought you'd never ask!"

13

FRIDAY MORNING, JULY 2

"How did you come by that address, Don?"

The PI had left a brief message for DS Derek Houghton about Archer's movements yesterday.

"Uhh…that's where Frank Archer went last night. We followed him. That was just after eight o'clock. When we left the area about 9:30 he was still inside."

"Where are you now?" Derek's tone was all business.

"Well, we're heading towards his flat, hoping to see what he's up to today," Don said. "James will be watching for him at Wimbledon. Play isn't scheduled to start until ten o'clock, and Archer doesn't always take in early matches. Is something wrong?"

"No, but I want you to back off. The Kilburn address is known to us. That's all I'm at liberty to say at this point. Consequently we'll take over surveillance of Archer while he's in the UK. I've two of my officers heading for Wimbledon as we speak. Give me the address of the flat he's using, please."

After Houghton had the address, and the numbers for the mobile phones Don and James were using, he rang off. Don was to call him if Archer moved before his men got to the area. If he hadn't, they would arrange a rendezvous. Once that had been accomplished they were to clear off.

An hour later, Don and Rod met with the plainclothes officers in a Tesco's parking lot half a mile from Maple Crescent. Archer hadn't shown his face yet this morning. In fact, Don told them, he couldn't be certain that Archer had returned to the flat last night. He'd shown them a photo of Archer, and added his own observations on his appearance.

James had called at ten o'clock from the gates at Wimbledon. Scattered showers were crossing the area and the opening matches were on hold, he reported. Don told him about the police taking over. Derek hadn't voiced any objection to James's role, at least for today. He agreed to remain at Wimbledon to see if the rain stopped and play began.

"Just like having your bags packed, done all the pre-flight duties, and then having your flight canceled minutes before departure time, right Rod?"

The English pilot gave a short chuckle. "Spot on, Don. That's exactly how I feel right now."

They were on their way back to Milnes Marsh, having failed to come up with an alternative. "Let's stop at that favorite pub of yours and I'll buy you lunch," Don said as they approached the outskirts of Reigate.

Five minutes later he wheeled into the parking lot at the Highwayman pub. They had just settled at a table with pints of bitter when Don's phone rang. It was definitely not a call he was expecting. Paul Boutin was on the line from Paris.

"Godammit," Don muttered disgustedly after ringing off.

"Now what?" asked Rod, who had quietly been sipping his beer while he listened to Don's side of the conversation.

Don took a long swallow. "The French police are probably going to ask me for a DNA sample. For some reason I'm still on their list of suspects in that woman's murder."

He told Rod about the latest developments. The victim was believed to have been a prostitute, age nineteen, and only recently arrived in Paris from a small town near Bordeaux.

"Really!" Rod said. "Not that I've had any personal experience, mind you, but I'd of thought the ahh... *ladies* working the big hotels would be somewhat older, wouldn't you?"

"Yeah, Paul mentioned that aspect, too. She wasn't known to the police, and they haven't been able to trace her pimp. Not too many try to freelance, apparently, but it's a possibility. Paul thought she was probably new to the game. How or when she came to be in the hotel is still a mystery. Someone must have summoned her, though."

"And they think that call might have been from you?"

"Well, they haven't come right out and said that, but they're probably thinking along those lines. Apparently the concierge on duty denied any knowledge of her. So far the police haven't divulged those details. Maybe they don't know yet."

"Do they know you're in London?"

"No, I don't think so. I'll have to call my office. Maybe they've called there." Don checked his wristwatch. "Still too early in Toronto, though. Better check with my lawyer, too"

IN HIS FLAT, FRANK ARCHER was watching the weather report on BBC 2. He was still in his nightshirt and barefoot, and on his third coffee. With play delayed, he was in no hurry to get tidied up. In fact, if the rain didn't stop before noon he was going to forgo Wimbledon today. It was the final matches he really wanted to see and they were scheduled for Saturday and Sunday.

He yawned and stretched. It was after midnight when he'd returned from the meeting last night. His cousin Carlos hadn't arrived until 10:30. The two men who had sat with him during the wait had offered no explanation for the delay. One was a young Englishman, a recent convert to Islam, dressed more like an opulent sheik than a modest believer.

He pegged the other man as an Indian or Pakistani. His name was Saahir Kayani, and he told Frank that the house belonged to his parents. Conversation was limited and time dragged while they waited for Carlos to show up. All very secretive, Frank thought, but he wasn't surprised. It had been the same during his trip to France in June. Meetings never started at the times he'd been given. On one occasion he'd been summoned to a rendezvous three hours before Carlos appeared.

When Carlos finally showed up, he greeted Frank warmly, but offered no reason or apology for his tardy arrival. Carlos wasn't alone. The second man with him was a dark-skinned Arab named Omar. Saahir's mother appeared silently from the kitchen with tea and a plate of sweets for the newcomers, then left them alone again. Frank studied Omar, trying carefully not to stare, as he drank his tea. Omar was about six feet tall and slim, and had strikingly black eyes. His beard was black and unkempt, and Frank guessed him to be between thirty-five and forty years old. He spoke French with very little accent, suggesting to Frank that he was either a native of a French-speaking North African country or had been well schooled in the language. According to Carlos, Omar would be joining the operation in the US closer to the planned date. Frank was to be his guide when he arrived, but no other information concerning his role was mentioned.

"That will be conveyed to you in due course, cousin," Carlos said, putting an end to his questions.

I'll certainly recognize him when I see him, Frank thought, during the taxi ride back to his flat. But he'd better change his appearance before coming to the US or he'll stand out like an orthodox Jew selling newspapers in front of a mosque on Friday.

Carlos switched the subject to the American Frank had met recently. A man whose expressed animosity towards his own government led Frank to believe he might be the recruit they'd been looking for. His name was Tom Allman.

The others listened carefully to Frank's explanation of how they had met at his club, and overheard him bitterly expressing his treatment by the army to anyone who'd listen. "Apparently he'd been accused of misconduct regarding prisoners in Iraq during the first Gulf War, explained Frank. "He'd strongly disagreed with the report, but resigned from the army rather than face a court martial."

Carlos pushed back from the table they were sitting around and stood up. "Interesting. I agree he might be a candidate worth pursuing, especially because of his experience with explosives. As you know, our people in New York have already been in contact with a few disaffected Americans—greedy men with similar sentiments—but this man could be a better bet," offered Carlos. He'd quizzed Frank about everything he knew about the ex-Green Beret, questions designed to ensure this man was what he purported to be and not a possible undercover agent.

Carlos had been pacing about the room as he peppered Frank with the questions. When he finished, he sat down again and studied his hands, deep in thought. Eventually he looked up and said, "Okay, you should proceed with your relationship with this infidel. But be very careful, my brother. We have sources that may be able to confirm this man's background. Do not make any offer to him until we check him out. Just continue to observe him and nurture his friendship. Understood?" Carlos had looked him straight in the eye as he spoke.

Frank nodded. I won't make any overture to him until you give me the go-ahead."

"Anything else?" Carlos asked him.

"Yes, cousin," replied Frank. "You never explained why you rushed me out of Paris last month."

"Ahh, that was strictly a precaution, but in hindsight it was the right move." Frank's frown indicated his puzzlement. "You recall the name you gave us? The man booked on the same flights as you?"

"I remember..." Jill McNeil had given him Carling's name a few nights before he flew to Paris.

"This man Carling is a private detective. Coincidence? We don't believe in them."

"Well, I'm sorry, but I know nothing about him. Or why he'd be following me."

"What about your wife? Have you given her any reason to hire him? I presume you haven't discussed our operation with her."

Carlos knew all about his cousin's marital situation, because he had thoroughly questioned him about it when he flew to Toronto last year. A meeting that convinced him that Frank's loveless marriage, and freedom to come and go as he pleased, made him an ideal recruit for their cause.

Frank shook his head. "No, no, nothing has changed."

"Good. If you ever have any inkling that you are being watched, let me know immediately. We will do some further checking on this man in the mean time."

Before Carlos dismissed him, he asked about the latest news concerning the presidential campaign in the US. "The polls show the race is still very close. The Republicans are playing on the public's fear of terrorism in their ad campaigns, and there are signs it is working. Perhaps he will be re-elected after all," Frank told him.

"If he is, their fears will be justified. We will see to that! Trust me, cousin," vowed Carlos, his eyes ablaze.

After Frank left, Omar said to Carlos, "This man does not worship Allah?"

Carlos shook his head. "He was raised in his mother's faith, but that is not important."

"How can you be so sure he is committed to our cause, then?"

"Money, pure and simple. He has lived in North America for a long time, which means he is better qualified to do what is required there to ensure the success of our plan. You will realize that once you arrive there. I myself felt very uncomfortable during my short trip to Canada last fall. We stand out, you see, and he does not."

Omar persisted. "Has he been to a training camp? Perhaps he might not be up to the task when we need him most."

Carlos was becoming annoyed at Omar, and his reply let him know that he didn't want to discuss it further. "No, time-wise, it was not feasible to send him for training. I briefed him thoroughly last month in France. His role is that of a facilitator, and, as I have already made clear, he is the best person available to us. And we need him to help you when the time comes."

14

DOVER, SUNDAY, JULY 4

Inspector Jean-Luc Monet extended his hand to Don. "Monsieur Carling, let me thank you personally for your quick cooperation, and apologize once again for having to ask you to provide your DNA," he said.

Carling shook his hand, and offered a half-hearted smile. "Well, it's a nice day for a trip to the seaside, if nothing else."

Don and Rod had driven down to the English Channel city, arriving at 1 p.m. After the call from Boutin on Friday, Don had phoned Toronto and asked his lawyer. Clay Simmons saw no reason to refuse the request for DNA. Make them come to you, though, Simmons had suggested, rather than chance being detained in France for whatever reason. When he phoned his office after speaking with Simmons, Joanne told him that Monet had called and asked that Don get in touch 'at his earliest convenience'.

Monet had been surprised to hear from Carling yesterday morning, Saturday. "I'll only be in England until Monday, so if you can set it up, I'll be happy to give a sample before I leave," he'd told the inspector.

Within two hours Monet called back. He and his team would take the Eurostar to England Sunday morning. The express passenger train passed under the English Channel via the Chunnel, as it was affectionately known, and drastically cut the travel time between Paris and London.

They had reserved a room in a hotel near the famous white cliffs. Monet had brought a lab technician and another officer with him. With typical Gallic hospitality, they'd had a lunch buffet delivered to the room. Monet invited Don and Rod to partake of it after he'd made the introductions.

"Let's get business over with first, Inspector," said Don.

The technician suggested it would more convenient if he could set up in the bathroom, and Don shrugged his agreement. After he'd swabbed the inside Don's cheeks for saliva samples, the technician drew a vial of his blood. "You might find traces of Newcastle Brown Ale in that, you know," he joked.

Don came back to the sitting room holding a cotton patch to the inside of his arm.

"Eh bien, Monsieur Carling! Now please enjoy some cheese and a glass of wine," smiled Monet. "Or perhaps you prefer a beer?"

Don dabbed at the needle mark. "No, wine will do for me. A glass of the red, please," he replied, his flat tone suggesting he wasn't buying the Frenchman's attempt to turn the meeting into a social occasion. "Now how about telling me why I'm a suspect in your murder investigation."

"Please, *suspect* is too strong a word, monsieur. I believe the English police would use the term 'helping with inquiries', and I hope you will see it in that light. After all, we have taken DNA from many persons during our investigation."

"Such as?"

The inspector reached for the bottle and refilled his wine glass. "This is a most complex case, you see, and at this stage we are simply eliminating many of the guests who were in the hotel at the time. So…"

Don jumped in when he paused. "Including hotel employees, I hope. Isn't it possible she had inside help to get into the hotel in the first place?"

"Of course. Very possible. Rest assured we are checking out all such scenarios."

Inspector Monet still wouldn't say how she died or when. Nor, when Don asked, would he say if she'd had intercourse before being killed. Instead, he had a question for Don.

"By the way, did you make any phone calls from your room on your last night at the hotel? Or did anyone call you?"

The questions were unexpected, and Don had to think for a moment before he replied. The last call he remembered was the call from Paul Boutin inviting him to dinner. "But that was earlier in the day," he explained. "I was going to call home after I got back from the restaurant, but having consumed a fair bit of your country's excellent wine, you know, well it just slipped my mind until morning," Don smiled. "Why do you ask?"

Monet ignored the question and changed the subject. He asked Don to explain why he'd been in Paris at the time. His tone was still casual, not aggressive.

Again, Carling paused before replying. He knew Paul Boutin had informed the police that he had been in Paris on business, but hadn't offered any details. And Monet hadn't brought the subject up when he'd called Carling about providing his fingerprints.

Had they learned anything about Don's investigation of Archer/Amara since then? He didn't think so, or Monet would have brought it up already. Rather than leave Monet with the impression that he had something to hide, Don gave him a complete account of his investigation of Archer..

"I can't offer any hard proof, yet," Don shrugged, "but I think the prostitute's murder may have been a foolhardy attempt to incriminate me. Not that I think this guy I'm after was directly involved, but other family members may have been behind it."

When Monet asked him what he meant by 'family members', Don told him what Paul Boutin had learned about the Amara clan's criminal history.

Monet wasn't familiar with the Amara name, he'd admitted, but agreed it was an angle worth pursuing. They'd parted on amicable terms, with the Frenchman assuring Don that he would contact him personally once analysis of his DNA cleared him. He'd thanked Don again as their meeting ended.

During the drive back to Milnes Marsh, Don was thinking out loud about the seemingly lack of progress by the police in finding the killer. "I mean, if she'd pissed off a drunken or dissatisfied 'john', and he'd strangled her in a fit of rage, or whatever, you'd think the police would've been able to find him by now. That type of killer usually leaves an easy trail to follow."

Ironically, the man who had orchestrated the killing was seated in the same car Inspector Monet was riding in, as the bullet-shaped train sped across the French countryside that evening. Carlos Amara, head of the French cell of al-Qaeda World, was on his way back to Paris after meeting Frank Archer in London. He was wearing a business suit and went unnoticed by Monet when he passed him on his path to the toilet.

Omar had also left the British capital today, on a flight to Cairo. His final destination was unknown to Carlos, and future communication between them was to be via phone or email.

MONDAY, JULY 5

The winner of the men's final at Wimbledon had been decided while Rod and Don were on their way back from Dover yesterday. Roger Federer, the Swiss sensation, had won his second title in a row, defeating the American, Andy Roddick. Frank Archer had been on hand for both the Sunday match and the women's final on Saturday, according to Superintendent Derek Houghton. He had called Don last night to update him on Archer's activities since the police took over surveillance of him.

Not that Don learned much from Houghton. It was more of a courtesy call, with the British officer almost apologizing for having to keep some details from Don.

Had Archer returned to the house in Kilburn? Had he met with anyone else? Had he acted like a man trying to throw off a tail? Don had asked. Derek had politely quashed any discussion along those lines.

"You must've found some links to the Amara clan, then, I'm thinking," offered Don lightly. Derek hesitated. "...Let me just say that you should be most careful in your investigation. This Archer chap may not be someone to fear, but those he's involved with are a different matter."

He was thinking about Derek's words of warning as Rod Weathers was driving him to Heathrow Airport. It was the second time he'd been cautioned. Paul Boutin had basically delivered a similar warning the last time they spoke. Don realized their concerns were probably based on Frank Archer's connection to his relatives in France, and vowed to take them seriously.

15

TORONTO, WEDNESDAY, JULY 7

Frank cursed when he opened his living room drapes and looked outside. Rain showers, heavy at times, were beating against the window. A layer of solid grey stratus cloud stretched unbroken to the southern horizon. The top of the CN tower half a mile away was obscured by wisps of mist swooping down from the cloud base.

He hated mornings like this. With no reason to head for his club—the outdoor courts would be too wet to play on and the two indoor courts were reserved for a youth clinic—he was left with little to do, except think again about what his cousin had inveigled him into. The two meetings in London had done little to ease his nagging misgivings about the mission. He still didn't know exactly how the operation was to end. When he'd finally had a chance to speak to Carlos alone, he'd told him again that he didn't want to be part of any plan that would result in civilian deaths. And once again Carlos had assured him that would not happen. Yet he still had doubts. Mainly because there were still times when Carlos came across as the impassioned radical, ranting abut revenge for the American presence in Iraq and Afghanistan.

Where will it end? Will Iran or North Africa be the next targets? He'd thrown rhetorical questions like these at Frank every time they'd talked, it seemed.

Still, the positives outweighed the negatives as far as he was concerned. If it meant bringing an end to his meaningless marriage sooner rather than later, he was willing to continue.

He erased his cousin's harangues from his mind for the moment and refilled his coffee cup. Time to move on. Carlos had called yesterday and given him the green light to recruit Tom Allman. Or at least to try.

The American was 'clean', according to sources that Carlos didn't elaborate on, and the next step was up to Frank. He and Tom had played together twice last week, and while they had been cooling down afterwards over coffee, he'd casually drawn Allman out about his army experiences. The brash American was more than willing to talk, focusing on how desk-bound and vindictive superiors had left him no choice but to resign, rather than face a court martial. *'I was just doin' what my trainin' told me to do'*, was his recurring theme.

Frank played along, agreeing sympathetically that Allman had probably been treated unjustly by the Army. When the time was right, he didn't think he would have any trouble recruiting him. Especially given the amount of money Allman would be offered for his cooperation.

Carlos had also instructed Frank how future communications between them were to be handled. Yesterday he had set up a new Hotmail account, and bought a cell phone to be used exclusively if he thought it necessary to contact Carlos. He was only to access the Internet from locations away from his condo to send or receive messages regarding the plot.

The rain was an annoyance in another way: it meant no sex with the horny Elizabeth today. On Wednesdays, he and Liz usually spent an hour or so at the motel after they'd finished with tennis. Liz had laid down strict rules for their affair, including no exchange of phone numbers. He didn't have hers and she didn't want his. She'd been most definite on that point. That way, she told him, there was no chance of her husband getting wind of their affair by a misdirected call. Although slightly bemused at her security precautions, Frank had readily gone along with them. He knew she wouldn't show up at the club for lunch on a rainy day, either. That was another of her rules.

He wondered if Tom Allman might, but quickly rejected the idea of looking for him at the club's restaurant.

Keep to your routine at all times, Carlos had emphasized. He'd probably see him tomorrow, anyway.

16

TUESDAY, JULY 13

Don was chairing the monthly staff meeting to discuss the active cases his investigators were working on. The sessions were always low key, just a chance for the boss to be brought up-to-date on investigations he wasn't involved in on a day-to-day basis.

Forty-five minutes after the meeting began, Don was satisfied with their progress. He'd checked over the individual reports, suggested a few minor changes, and declared four of them ready to hand over to clients. Three were law firms handling contested divorce cases and the fourth was a farmer who'd had a number of market-ready cattle disappear. Don's personal investigation wasn't mentioned, although he took some good-natured ribbing about dashing off to Europe at short notice.

After the others had left, Don caught up on the paperwork. He signed a few checks Joanne had prepared, and okayed a lunch date for the following week with a prospective client. When they were finished, she reminded him to call Tom Allman.

THERE HAD BEEN A MESSAGE from Tom this morning requesting a meeting. He suggested tomorrow at 12:30, and asked that Don call back if he couldn't make it. The message had piqued Don's curiosity because it was a departure from Tom's normal routine, a weekly phone call on Wednesday nights to Don's unlisted home number.

There had been no mention of where to meet because the venue had been agreed beforehand. Their simple code meant that Don would meet him a day earlier and an hour later than specified. He left his office at ten past one to keep the rendezvous.

DON WAS THE FIRST TO arrive at Randy's Café on the lower concourse of a mid-town office tower. Most of the usual lunch crowd had dispersed, and Don had no trouble finding an empty booth. He was studying the menu when Allman joined him a few minutes later. .

"Hey Tom!" smiled Don, half-standing to shake his hand. "I'd say you've dropped a few pounds."

"Huh! It's all this damned exercise! Next time get me into a 'seniors only' club. This bunch takes their tennis too damned seriously," complained Allman, wincing as he settled into the bench opposite Don. "Pulled a calf muscle yesterday," he explained.

Don chuckled. "Ahh, you'll be thanking me for it down the line!"

"I doubt that, pard," muttered Tom. "Anyway, I could sure make fast work of a beer. How about you?" he asked, looking around for a waiter.

"So what's happened?" Don asked after their frosty pints arrived, along with a bowl of nuts.

Tom drained half his glass and grabbed a handful of peanuts before replying. He'd had lunch with Frank Archer after playing tennis yesterday, he began. "Looks like this guy is into something sinister after all, pard."

"Aha. So this was his idea? He invited you, not the other way around?"

"Yes, sir. Caught me by surprise. Other than the occasional drink together after playing, I haven't had much to do with him. There's always been other guys around. But he just came up to me in the locker room and suggested we go to lunch. We went to one of those bistros down on the waterfront not far from his condo."

"Well, I'm all ears, Tom. Fill me in."

ARCHER HAD MADE A STARTLING proposal. *How would the American like to make some money and get back at the US government at the same time?*

"Suggesting I come on as a pissed off ex-army type with a grudge was a good call on your part, Don," said Allman. Don had mentioned the ploy when he had first briefed him about Archer.

"How did you pull it off?"

"Ahh, it wasn't that difficult. Just played the redneck from Colorado to a broad audience. Never voiced my opinions directly to Archer."

"Sounds like you played yourself, Tom!"

Allman let out a hearty laugh. "Walked right into that one, didn't I?"

"Just kidding, of course, but glad it worked. So what did he offer you?"

Archer had contacts who would pay big dollars for a man with expertise in explosives, and who wouldn't have any qualms about taking part in a plot to embarrass the present administration in Washington. The group was planning an attack to rattle the American public, and turn them against the president. Allman would receive $100,000 up front, and a further $100,000 when he was no longer needed. At a later time, All-man would be given details of what his role entailed.

"He wouldn't tell me who these people were, either. If they were al-Qaeda types, I didn't want any part of it, and I made that perfectly clear," Allman said. "I may be seriously pissed at the government, I told him, but if they're planning a 9/11-type operation against individuals, then I wasn't interested. In fact, I even suggested I'd rat on them."

"What did he say to that?"

"Not what they were planning," he told me. "The object is to cause panic on a massive scale, something to bring the whole country to a standstill and bring about a crippling economic crisis."

Don shrugged. "Well, that scenario has been threatened by radicals before, hasn't it? Poisoning the water supplies, spreading deadly viruses, that sort of thing."

"Yeah, you're right. And if you believe the feds, it's only a matter of time before it happens. But whatever they're up to, it involves explosives."

"Blowing up bridges, or dams, maybe? But I don't see how that could be accomplished without causing casualties."

"My thoughts exactly."

"That's a lot of money, too. What did you tell him?"

"Said I was definitely interested, but wanted to think on it."

"...And?"

"He said he could wait a few days. We're gonna meet again on Friday."

"Good show, Tom. Does Archer chum around with any of the other regulars at the club?"

"No, not that I've noticed. Not that he's standoffish, just a bit reserved. I don't think he gets a lot of the ribbing and sexual innuendos the other guys start throwing around after a few drinks, if you know what I mean. His English is pretty good, though, at least when he speaks."

"Does he drink alcohol at all?" Don asked.

"Well, he had a glass of wine at lunch, but he usually sticks with soda."

"What about the girlfriend?"

"The married babe at the club? Yeah, she's still in the picture," Allman replied. "But he seems to have split with the McNeil woman. He hasn't been seen with her since he got back from England."

"Hmm...wonder what brought that on?"

Don scratched his chin, and sat back with his arms folded. They were at a turning point in the Archer case, and had to decide what to do next. Should he talk to the police? They tossed the pros and cons around for a while. So far Archer hadn't done anything illegal. Talking about subversive activity and actually carrying it out were two different things.

Allman's conversation with Archer wouldn't arouse much interest from the local police, Don knew. Although the offer was made rather casually, Archer had warned him to keep it to himself. If he decided not to take up their offer, that would be the end of it. But those behind him, he'd stressed, were not to be taken lightly. If Allman didn't want in, he'd better keep it to himself, implied Archer.

For now, Don decided they had nothing to gain by talking to the police. Don suggested he use the meeting with Archer on Friday to push for more details; who he'd be working for, the time frame for the job, that sort of thing. He should also stall, telling Archer he needed more time before making a commitment. If and when they had more convincing proof of a suspected plot, Don planned to pass the information to RCMP Inspector Brian Roberts.

17

WEDNESDAY, JULY 14

Don had debated taking the day off to lend Yvonne a hand with her garden make over. She had been working on plans for the changes ever since moving in with him. With the help of a professional landscape architect, the task got underway a few weeks ago. Don had volunteered to do the heavy digging, and had made a start last Saturday. Yvonne had scoffed when he quit after an hour and settled in his lounge chair with a cold beer.

"Sorry, hon, but my back's bothering me," he'd pleaded this morning at breakfast. Tell you what, though, I'll knock off early this afternoon. Should be able to handle the business end of a shovel again by then."

"Sore back my foot!" Yvonne retorted. "Maybe I'll just have to hire a young man with muscles to help me."

"You have my blessing, sweetheart," Don laughed, as he headed out the door.

AFTER HE GOT TO HIS office, he left a message for Brian Roberts at RCMP headquarters. The inspector was in a meeting and it would probably be close to noon before he would be free, according to his secretary.

Her estimate was right on: Roberts called at 11:55. Don began with a rundown of his trip to London.

"Sure, I remember Derek," said Roberts, when Don mentioned Superintendent Houghton. "Cant say I envy him his new job, though. Have you had any follow up from him about this Archer fellow or his contacts in London?"

"No, not yet. But I'm sure he'll let me know if they uncover anything I can use."

"Well, I wouldn't hold my breath, Don."

"Oh, and why is that?"

Roberts had checked out the Amaras' using data from various intelligence agencies with which the RCMP shared information, including Interpol and the Central Intelligence Agency. Although no activity by the clan had been uncovered in North America, their history in France and North Africa was well-documented. Information that may have prompted the Department of Homeland Security [DHS] to put members of the Amara family on their 'no fly' list, Roberts suggested. Although Francois Amara wasn't named, his uncles and a cousin, Carlos, were on the list. None of them had attempted to enter the US since the list was compiled. But just having the same surname and a French passport was no doubt why Francois had been stopped and questioned a few times. He had been 'fast tracked' for citizenship, Roberts had discovered, and agreed with Don that his wife's position and connections probably played a part.

Obviously then, the man Todd had observed meeting with Archer in Toronto last fall wasn't on the 'No Fly' list or had used a false passport.

TRUE TO HIS WORD, DON was on his way home by 2:30, even though his thoughts weren't on performing 'grunt work' in the garden. He was still thinking about the carefully-worded caution Inspector Roberts had delivered during their conversation this morning.

Is there anyone left who hasn't warned me to be careful yet? he wondered, as he pulled away from the last of the traffic lights along Airport Road on his route home. The advice came from professionals he respected, though, so it was worth keeping in mind. It would only be a matter of minutes before the warnings were dramatically—and fatally—brought to bear...

Don saw the flashing lights of emergency vehicles as soon as he turned east on County Road 12, five kilometers from his rural home. The vehicles were blocking the two-lane road where an old iron and stone bridge crossed a narrow creek. He eased off the pavement and stopped behind the line of cars parked along the south shoulder. A blast of hot, muggy air hit him as he opened his door, a sharp contrast with the air-conditioned interior. He shrugged off his sports jacket, tossed it onto the passenger seat, and walked towards the quiet group of people standing behind an Ontario Provincial Police cruiser parked diagonally on the bridge. An ambulance with its rear doors open, another police vehicle and two fire trucks were clustered at the far end of the bridge.

"What happened?" he asked the young man who turned at his approach.

"Looks like someone ran off the road and rolled down the embankment," he answered.

"Probably drivin' too damned fast and missed the curve," piped up another of the bystanders, a white-haired senior wearing coveralls and a faded John Deere cap.

As Don watched, an emergency worker hurried up to the ambulance, pulled a white sheet off a stretcher and headed back towards the accident scene. The curve in the road and the steepness of the embankment obscured the wreck from the bystanders' view. All Don could see was two wheels of the vehicle, suggesting it had come to rest upside down. He slid carefully down the embankment towards another silent knot of people gathered beside the creek across from the wreck.

"NO!" Don screamed when he got his first glimpse of the vehicle. It was bright yellow, just like Yvonne's Volkswagen Jetta. Don burst through the startled spectators and into the creek. The water was only a foot or so deep, but he stumbled midway across and pitched forward on his knees.

"No! No!" he groaned as he scrambled to his feet and covered the short distance to the far bank. His pants were soaked and he'd lost a shoe.

Two police officers were hurrying towards him as he regained dry land. "Sir! Stay back!" shouted one of them.

"That's my wife's car!" he agonized as an officer, his arms spread wide, attempted to block his path. Don barreled into him, and they both tumbled awkwardly onto the grassy slope. The second cop picked up his partner's cap and helped him to his feet.

Don groaned an apology as he caught his breath and stood up. "I'm sorry fella, but I think that's my wife's car. I want to... is she...?" He was less than ten yards now from the upturned car and the white sheet covering a body.

The older of the two, a burly sergeant, now had him in a firm grip. "Just take it easy, sir, take it easy," he said calmly. "Let's make sure you're not mistaken. Could be someone elses car.

But Don knew it wasn't. If Yvonne had needed to go into town for something she would have driven along this road. It was the only route she ever used to get from his nearby home to the main highway. He was sure it was her car...

Don identified himself and explained all this to the officers, anxiously glancing over their shoulders at the wreck. The car had suffered extensive damage. It was resting on its roof, which had been crushed to within a foot or so of the engine's hood. The bottom had been sprayed with foam, although the vehicle did not appear to have caught fire.

The sergeant asked him if he knew her licence plate number. The front plate was buried in the ground and the rear plate wasn't visible from where they were standing.

"No, sorry," he gasped, "uhh, I can't think... the last number is seven, I think."

"You're doin' fine, buddy. Just breathe slowly now," cautioned the policeman.

"... Yeah, I'm tryin'. Oh, she had a bumper sticker on the back." Don didn't realize he'd used the past tense. "Something about farmers..."

The sergeant nodded towards his partner, who went to check. He was limping. Don's heart continued to pound as he anxiously watched the officer bend down, peer at the bumper, and slowly make his way back.

Maybe the cop's right and it's not her car... Yvonne wasn't planning to go out as far as he knew. He'd called her only an hour ago to say he would be home early. *Please God, let it be someone else!*

The cop's somber expression told him his uncharacteristic prayer had not been answered.

"Green and white sticker, says '*THANK A FARMER TODAY*'?" he asked.

Don groaned aloud and nodded, sinking to his knees.

"I WANT TO SEE HER, please." Don asked quietly, after the officers helped him to his feet. They stood silently as the coroner lifted the corner of the sheet to examine the victim.

"I'll check that out with the doctor as soon as he's finished, Mister Carling."

The coroner's examination didn't take very long. When he was finished, he waved the sergeant over. After a short discussion, Don was beckoned forward. He couldnt feel his legs at all and had to look down at his feet to stop from falling. The doctor said his name, but it didn't register with Don. He stared numbly at the shrouded form, and nodded when the doctor asked him if he was sure he was up to viewing the body.

"She's not disfigured in any way. I believe cause of death was a broken neck. She was wearing her seat belt, according to the EMTs."

"I see, thank you," mumbled Don.

He took a step forward and an EMT lifted the sheet to uncover the woman's head. Don shuddered and felt his heart stop. Thinking he was about to collapse, both policemen grabbed an arm.

"It's not her! That's not Yvonne!"

TEN MINUTES LATER, SITTING IN a police cruiser, Don's heart was still racing and he was soaked with sweat. Part of the mystery had been solved. He'd phoned home and Yvonne answered. Yes, she told him, she knew her car wasn't in the driveway. Marlene, her gardening lady, had borrowed it to run into a nursery on Airport Road . She'd offered her the use of it because her vehicle, an older pickup truck, wouldn't start.

"Why?" Yvonne asked.

"Uhh, I just saw your car. I'll explain when I get home. Be there in a few minutes, hon." He rang off before she could speak again.

Don was giving the sergeant Yvonne's explanation when another officer approached the cruiser holding the victim's purse. It had lodged under the dashboard during the crash. The dead woman's name was Marlene Hastings, according to her driver's licence. Don had never met her, he told them. The sergeant said he would have to talk to Yvonne and Don suggested he follow him home. The emergency vehicles had been moved enough to allow traffic to get moving again.

"Are you sure you're up to driving now, sir?"

"Yeah, I'm okay now," he sighed. "It's only a couple of minutes from here."

"OH MY GOD! WHAT HAPPENED to you?" a startled Yvonne gasped when Don came through the door. "Are you hurt?"

He probably did look a sight, he realized. His pants were still wet, there was a tear in one knee, and he was carrying the shoe that had come off in the creek. One of the officers had fished it out and handed it to him as he was about to drive away from the accident scene.

Don wrapped his arms around her and held her tight. "I thought I'd lost you," he murmured, his head on her neck.

He sat her down at the kitchen table and told her, as gently as he could, what had happened. Not surprisingly, the news brought her to tears. Almost fifteen minutes passed before her sobs subsided and she indicated that she was ready to talk with the OPP officers. They had agreed beforehand to let Don break the news to her, waiting in the driveway until he signaled for them to come in.

"This is Sergeant Milton, hon, and Constable—?" Don had forgotten his name and apologized.

"No problem, sir. It's Lewicki, Stan Lewicki."

Don invited them to join Yvonne at the table, then excused himself. "Just be a minute. Gonna change into something drier," he said, heading for the bedroom.

BY 7:30 THE PIZZA THEY had decided would do for supper sat largely untouched. It was attracting flies as it cooled, so Don picked up the platter and their plates and took them into the kitchen. When he returned to the patio he had a fresh scotch and soda in his hand. Yvonne was sipping white wine.

The police had left two hours ago, after Yvonne had told them all she knew about Marlene Hastings. Marlene was a single woman in her thirties, and Yvonne had hired her, on the recommendation of a friend, to revamp her perennial garden. Marlene had been working on it one day a week since mid-May. They had both agreed that some new shrubbery would enhance the design. Marlene was going to pick them up, but her truck wouldn't start. Rather than waste the rest of the day, Yvonne had suggested she use her vehicle.

Neither the police nor Don could offer a viable explanation for the accident. Sergeant Milton told them a complete mechanical check of the vehicle would be part of their investigation. It didn't appear any of the tires had blown out. The 2001 VW had new brakes installed just last month.

Did Miss Hastings like to drive fast? the police had asked Yvonne. She couldn't answer that, she'd answered, but volunteered that Marlene had struck her a reliable and level-headed sort, not one who would take a borrowed vehicle and try to see how fast it would go.

Had she consumed any alcohol while she'd been at the house? was another question asked.

When Yvonne became visibly annoyed at his line of questioning, the officer apologized, saying it was just routine. Don thought he could have been a little less blunt, but held his tongue. Instead he'd stood behind her with his hands on her shoulders, massaging them gently.

Notifying Marlene's next-of-kin was already being taken care of by the police, he'd told Yvonne when she'd asked. As dusk fell and the mosquitoes began their nightly assault on the nearest red-blooded targets, the quiet couple moved inside. Thirty minutes later, Yvonne flicked off the television, unable to concentrate, and took a sleeping pill.

Don held her in a long embrace, thankful again that it hadn't been her under the white sheet beside the wreck.

THURSDAY, JULY 14

Don couldn't sleep. At 5:30, he eased his weary frame off the king-sized bed and padded softly out of the bedroom. He needn't have worried about disturbing Yvonne. She had barely stirred all night, thanks to the sleeping pill.

Too many disturbing questions were on his mind.

Was the gardener's death really an accident? Did she oversteer or misjudge the curve leading up to the bridge? Was speed a factor? Or did driving an unfamiliar car have something to do with it?

They were all possibilities, but there must be more to it, he kept thinking. After all, she must have familiar with the road. She'd made at least four or five trips to work on Yvonne's garden, and probably had other customers in the area as well.

He took his first coffee of the day out to the rear patio, wiped the dew off a lounge chair, and sagged into it. The sun rising into a cloudless sky heralded the promise of a beautiful summer day. But nature's wonder didn't register on him. An unnerving trio of questions that wouldn't go away ...

Was the accident somehow connected to his case? Was Yvonne the real target? Had the car been forced off the road to kill her as a lethal lesson to him?

DON HADN'T BEEN ON HIS bike for over a month and his thigh muscles made that known during the first few kilometers. He was riding towards the accident scene. He had little recollection of anything about it after learning that Yvonne hadn't been the victim. Perhaps this morning he could look at it as an investigator.

The first clue that jumped out at him was obvious by its absence: there weren't any skid marks. Tire tracks in the gravel shoulder indicated the Volkswagen had been driven straight off the road. Any braking the startled driver applied then would have been too late, resulting in the rollover. The wrecked vehicle had been removed from the scene, but he estimated it might have rolled at least three times before it came to a stop. He made his way down the steep slope to the exact spot where it came to rest, easily recognized by the trampled grass and clods of dirt around it. The visible gouges in the soft earth on the embankment were probably made when the wreck was being winched up to road, he thought.

There wasn't much here to go on. Some fragments of broken glass, a dented hub cap, a few crumpled strips of metal trim, and a splotch of oil. Yesterday, he remembered, the smell of fuel was noticeable, but not this morning. He scrambled back up to the road, none the wiser for his efforts.

Well, perhaps the poor woman did just have a moment of inattention and lost control, he thought as he mounted his bike and headed for home.

Seconds later that hypothesis was shattered. His peripheral vision caught a glint of yellow to his left. He braked quickly and made a U-turn. Sure enough, the slanted rays of the rising sun were reflecting off something near the road's white center line marking. Don knelt to examine them. They appeared to be paint chips.

Yellow, just like Yvonne's Volkswagen.

18

A week had passed since their last meeting. The pre-chosen location, a bar in a downtown hotel, was filling up with Happy Hour patrons. Tom had arrived first, and taken a seat at the end of the bar with a clear view of the entrance. He was on his second Cuba Libre when Don walked in and sat at an empty table. He ordered a beer from the cocktail waitress and turned his attention to the baseball game on the large, wall-mounted television set. Fifteen minutes later Tom sauntered over and joined him.

"Looks good, pard. Haven't spotted any tail on you," he said.

"Neither have I," Don replied, shaking Tom's outstretched hand. "Let's get you a refill and I'll explain. What're you drinking?"

"Rum and coke today. Have to call it a Cuba Libre, though, don't I? Seein' as how you Canucks are so 'palsy walsy' with Mister Castro." He was smiling as he said it and Don knew he was kidding.

"Yeah, well, our politicians don't have to woo all those Cuban exiles in Florida to get elected, you know!"

Don had contacted Allman the day after the accident involving Yvonne's Volkswagen. It had been a brief call to warn him to be extra cautious from now on. When asked why, Don suggested that maybe others involved in the plot with Frank Archer were active here in Toronto, persons that Archer himself might not even be aware of. Now he gave Tom the full story.

Don had wasted no time in calling Sergeant Milton after finding the paint chips. He'd gathered up six pieces, placing them in a plastic freezer bag. The largest fragment was about the size of his thumbnail. Milton had dispatched a constable to pick up the chips and take them to the OPP forensic team poring over the wrecked Volkswagen.

"So, after cleaning the mud off the left rear fender, the cops concluded that the chips were from that area," explained Don.

"And they said 'Eureka!' another vehicle must have clipped her and caused her to lose control, right?" said Tom.

"Exactly. Whether on purpose or accidently remains to be determined." Don had taken a few measurements at the scene. "I found the chips about twenty-five yards, give or take a few feet, from where the car left the road. I figure a vehicle on the curve driving at about sixty-five, seventy kilometers an hour would cover that distance easily before going over the side."

"How come the cops didn't find the paint chips, one wonders?" mused Allman.

"Probably hidden under one of the emergency vehicles on the scene. By the time the last of them left, it would've been dusk," said Don.

The bar was almost full by the time Don finished his account. Allman leaned forward to avoid the couple at the next table from overhearing him and asked. "Do ya think she'd been hit on purpose?"

Don shrugged. The subtle warnings to watch himself flashed through his head before he answered. "I don't think there's any doubt. But it was probably because the 'perp' thought Yvonne was driving. Won't be easy to prove. And maybe she wasn't meant to die, just banged up because she was easier to get at than me."

"Because of Archer, you mean?"

"Yeah."

Don was fairly certain that no one had it in for Yvonne. He'd played the detective with her to rule that out. No enemies among her co-workers, no former beaus who might want to harm her, absolutely no evidence of that sort. The police had asked her much the same questions and reached the same conclusion. Don had been cautious with the police when discussing his thoughts about the accident. It could have been an attempt to intimidate him, he'd told them. When asked if he'd received any threats recently, he answered 'no' truthfully. Still, *if* it had been a deliberate attempt to cause the crash, then someone he'd investigated in the past may have been behind it, he suggested.

Allman was still skeptical and said so. "Could'a just been a case of hit and run, you know, boss. Maybe the driver had other reasons for not sticking around after bumping her. There weren't any witnesses, I take it."

"Nope. At least no one has contacted the police so far." Don toyed with his beer coaster, waiting to see if Tom had anything else to add. When their silence stretched to a minute, he spoke again. "I did find something else, though.

After finding the paint chips, he'd figured that someone must have been watching his house. *How else would they know when the Volkswagen pulled out of the driveway?*

Later on the day after he'd found the chips, Don had stood in front of his house to consider how that might have been accomplished. The field directly opposite, on the north side of the road, had been used to grow hay in the past, but this year was lying fallow. No cover there. The only other permanent residence nearby belonged to the Marlow family. Their neatly kept lawns bordered Don's acreage on its east side. He got out his bike again and rode slowly past Marlow's, stopped when he came to the stretch of road with wood lots on both sides.

Don dismounted, laid his bike on the shoulder, and turned to look back towards his house. From here, his driveway was clearly visible. But a parked vehicle would also be visible from the house. He walked slowly along the road until he could no longer see the front of his house, just the driveway. He was now twenty-five to thirty yards from the edge of the woods. From this point, he reasoned, anyone watching the house would be able to spot a vehicle leaving the driveway, yet remain unseen.

After a short search, Don found evidence to back up his reasoning.

A pile of cigarette butts littered the gravel shoulder, no doubt having been dumped from a stationary vehicle.

"Yeah, I see your point," said Allman. "If the ashtray had been emptied from a movin' vehicle, they woulda' been strewn over a wider area."

"You got it. And I also found a couple of paper coffee cups and two soft drink cans in the ditch on the passenger's side," Don said. "The stuff was dry, which meant it hadn't been there long. We had a thunderstorm two nights before the accident," he explained.

"Good work, pard," lauded Tom. "So more than one guy, and they'd been sittin' there for a while, is that your take on it?"

Don shrugged. "Yeah, I think it all fits. But proving it won't be easy, will it?"

DON HAD TAKEN THE CIGARETTE butts and the pop cans to a forensic lab headed by a retired police officer, Douglas Dixon. To friends and colleagues he was simply 'DD'. Determining the brand of cigarettes wouldn't be a problem, he'd told Don. It was a possible clue to the driver's identification, but not a strong one. The soda pop cans, on the other hand, held more promise. The lab tech, who first checked them over, thought he detected at least partial fingerprints, but it would take a few days to lift them.

"That was last Friday," said Don, "so I should hear from DD this week. If they come up with some prints, I'll get the OPP investigators to run them." It was now close to six o'clock and Don suggested they have something to eat rather than head off into the rush hour traffic. Allman quickly agreed.

They chatted about sports until their orders arrived along with fresh drinks. While they were eating, Tom told Don about his follow-up meeting with Frank Archer last Friday.

"I tried to put him off for a few more days, told him I wanted to know more about what they expected me to do," he explained, but Archer wouldn't budge. Rather than risk makin' him suspicious about my intentions, I told him, 'Okay, count me in'."

"Good. So he was still being tight-lipped about your role in whatever it is they're planning."

"Yeah, he sorta' hinted that it would probably be September before he had that information. So I played up the 'show me the money' angle, and told him I'd need to see the hundred grand before then or I wasn't interested."

"How did he take that?"

"Said that could be arranged, but the money would have to be transferred to a bank in the US. He was more concerned with whether or not I was free to get back into the States, but I assured him that I wasn't wanted by the feds or any police agencies."

"I wondered about that," said Don. "Realistically, whoever he's involved would want to know as much as possible about you, make sure you're who you say you are, that sort of info, before they put out a hundred thousand bucks, if you get my drift."

For the first time, Allman seemed a bit concerned. "Well, even if they can access my service record—which I very much doubt—they'll only learn that I was honorably discharged. That was part of the agreement when I resigned."

ALLMAN HAD TOLD ARCHER THAT he'd have to return to Alberta for a few weeks to wrap up his ties there. After that he would be free to return to the States. He intended to settle in Mexico or some other Central American country after the operation ended, he'd let on to Archer.

"I really do need to go back to Edmonton, but only for a few days," said Allman. "In the mean time, I think we should put someone on him 24/7. I'll be available to help with that as soon as I get back to Toronto."

"Okay, Tom, I'll set that up while you're gone."

19

Don hadn't given much thought to Danielle Clyde lately, what with the car accident and monitoring Tom Allman's attempts to gain Frank Archer's confidence. He'd left a message for her after he'd returned from London two weeks ago, but she hadn't called back until today. The delay had puzzled him, but he didn't bring it up before he gave her a brief report about what Frank did and didn't do in London. "He did spend most of his time at Wimbledon. I didn't see any indication that he'd spent any time visiting art galleries or dealers. So, I'm still not sure exactly what he's up to," he told her, "but I think we'll know before too much longer."

Danielle didn't challenge this rather vague remark, and he saw no reason to tell her about Tom Allman's undercover role vis-a-vis Frank or the British counterterrorism squad's interest in him. Her uncharacteristic lack of interest in his investigation rankled him. When it seemed she was about to end their call without any questions or comment, he asked rather abruptly, "Do you want me to continue with the investigation?".

Danielle hesitated, but when she answered it was with a definite 'yes'.

"Okay then, we'll continue our investigation. I presume he usually goes to New York for the US Open matches?"

"Yes," she replied. "He has ready mentioned it to my PA."

Don looked up the dates for this year's tournament. Labor Day fell on Monday, September 6th, and the matches got underway the week before.

"As soon as his reservations are made, let me know," Don instructed her. "And call me yourself with the details. I can't be sure if someone in your office hasn't tipped him off about you hiring me. Understood?"

He hung up before she had a chance to ask for an explanation.

DANIELLE HAD GIVEN SERIOUS THOUGHT to ending her contract with Carling, which was why she had taken so long to return his call. Her husband's demand that he wanted a divorce now had surprised her. According to their agreement, they were to remain married for a few more years. And his disclosure that he knew of her affair with Charles—and threatened to expose it—meant she might have to give in to his demand. Not only did he want the divorce moved up, he wanted a doubling of the promised financial settlement amount for his silence.

How did he find out? They had been so careful, she'd thought. Both she and Charles would suffer immeasurably if word of their liaison was made public, not only from embarrassment, but in Charles's case, financially. It had something to do with his pre-nuptial agreement, apparently, and the vast sum he would be on the hook for if he filed for divorce before his teen-aged children reached legal age. And that was still a few years away. They did plan to marry once they were both free, but until then they were hoping to keep their relationship secret.

She hadn't said anything to Charles yet about this disturbing development, but she would have to tell him about it sooner or later. Or would she? Had Frank turned the tables on her and hired a private investigator? she wondered. On reflection, she didn't think that likely. Most of their local trysts took place in her penthouse apartment, only reachable via stairs from her office or the private elevator from the firm's main reception area two floors below. More likely a staff member was behind the leak, someone with an axe to grind, perhaps. But who? And what was the connection to Frank? The women Frank was involved with were not Empire North employees, according to Carling.

FRANK WASN'T GOING TO WAIT much longer for his wife's answer. It had given him great pleasure to startle her with his demands. Gerald Tupman, the Empire North accountant who'd run afoul of Danielle Clyde, had called him a few days after his return from England. The man she was having an affair with was Charles Rothwell, President and CEO of one of the largest investment firms in Canada, Tupman informed him. He didn't say what proof he had, but Frank wouldn't need any. From her stunned reaction he knew his information was true and she wasn't going to call his bluff.

No, Tupman's revelation was fortuitous timing in more ways than one. Once the mission was over, it would be prudent for him to leave North America for good. To that end, it would be best if he was divorced, and free of all ties in Canada. His long-held dream to have his own art gallery in France would then be possible. Money shouldn't be a problem, even if he had to settle for something less than two million from his wife's fortunes. A large bank balance—plus the art work he had already acquired and stored away in France—would make for a successful start.

Although his cousin Carlos had assured him his role would be over before the actual operation took place, he was still worried that something might go wrong. Frank wasn't convinced that Carlos and his co-conspirators weren't underestimating the capabilities of various police agencies in Canada and the US. He'd have to assess his personal risk factor again, no later than after his upcoming trip to New York City.

Frank had been having these thoughts as he drove home from the club. After parking his leased BMW in the building's underground lot, he took the stairs up to the lobby and emptied his mailbox. He dropped the assortment of flyers into the recycling box, and sniffed at the only remaining item. He knew who the mauve envelope was from without opening it—his ex-girlfriend, Jill McNeil. He slit the perfumed missive open as he waited for the elevator. This was the second such note she'd sent him, hoping to rekindle their relationship. She missed him terribly, she wrote, and he could still call her anytime. He shredded the card and dropped it in the waste bin.

Once he was inside his apartment he turned on his computer, intending to browse the websites of New York City galleries. He'd be expected to look for another painting or two during his trip to the US Open. But it was beginning to bore him, he realized. On his last trips abroad, he hadn't had much enthusiasm for his job. In Paris, and again in London, it had been an effort to make the rounds. In fact, he hadn't bought anything from the English dealers this time, and that was a 'first'. He pushed himself away from the computer and sighed.

Maybe I should apply myself more determinedly to Carloss operation. That, plus the chance to break away from Danielle sooner rather than later, will set me free to call my own shots from here on...

The personal pep talk worked. Ten minutes later Frank drove out of the building's parking garage, heading for Bayview Village and one of the three Internet locations he now used. Following directions from Carlos, he had set up two Hotmail accounts after returning from London. Carlos had warned him not to use his personal computer for correspondence any longer. It was a bit of an inconvenience, but he hadn't objected. Midday traffic was light, and twenty minutes later he lucked into a just-vacated parking space less than a block from the café.

He was hoping there would be a message from Carlos. At their meeting in London, Carlos had informed him that he would get to meet the cell's top man in the US in New York. That's when he would be given specific instructions as to his role as the date of the American presidential election drew nearer. Carlos had told him to be prepared to spend most of his time after mid-September in the US. That wouldn't be a problem for him. Now that he could hold knowledge of his wife's affair over her, he could pretty well come and go as he pleased. He had a satisfied smile on his face as he signed in to check his mail.

ROLLIE PARSONS, ONE OF KAYROY'S part-time agents, had followed Archer to the Internet cafe. He'd almost messed up, because he hadn't expected Archer to leave his building again so soon after returning. He'd just bought a hot dog from a street vendor and was walking back towards to his car when the distinctive light blue BMW pulled onto the road in front of him. Fortunately for Rollie, Archer was held up at a road construction site three blocks east, giving him time to catch up to the BMW before it disappeared.He parked a block away from the narrow-fronted cafe he'd seen Frank enter. When Archer emerged twenty minutes later, Parsons was standing on the opposite side of the busy street. He raised the newspaper he was carrying as Archer's BMW pulled away from the curb.

His cell phone rang, and he knew Hank Neely had seen his signal. "Okay, Rollie, I'm on him! I'll take it from here."

Neely was another KayRoy investigator, and Parsons had called him for back up while he was following Archer towards Bayview Village. Parsons, Neely and Micki Held were the team Don had assigned to watch Archer around the clock. Held, 42, was a retired Toronto cop. Don had hired her on the spot when she'd answered his ad three months ago. Archer had driven straight home, and Parsons was still watching the parking garage when Held arrived to relieve him at 8 p.m. She would stay in position until 1 a.m., the routine they'd followed since the 24/7 surveillance began last week.

20

MONDAY, JULY 26

Archer hadn't made any unexpected moves or met with anyone of interest over the weekend, according to the surveillance team's log. It had rained for most of the day on both Saturday and Sunday, and Don and Yvonne had dropped their plans to go sailing with her avid boating friends on Georgian Bay. Don was secretly relieved, not a big fan of spending hours keeled over at a thirty degree angle, wiping spray off his sunglasses.

His ill-disguised expression of regret had brought forth a loud hoot of derision from Yvonne. "Hah! And you're probably all ready working on an excuse for the next time they invite us!

Sunday afternoon Yvonne and a girlfriend went to a movie. Don flicked channels between the Blue Jays game and the weekly PGA tournament. By four o'clock, the baseball game was over and the outcome of the golf tournament was no longer in doubt: Tiger Woods had a four stroke lead with three holes to play. He turned the TV off and wandered into the kitchen.

He thought of opening a beer, but decided to wait until Yvonne got home. She expected to be back by five. A better idea struck him, one that had occurred to him earlier this morning.

The *QUIK STOP ON 12* variety store was housed in an older, wooden building at the corner of Airport Road and the Twelfth Line. Until they retired a year ago, the store had been owned by a couple named Mason. Don had stopped in occasionally, usually when he needed something he'd forgotten to buy in the city. He hadn't been inside since the Mason's sold out and moved away. The faded *'Under New Management'* sign was still on the entrance door. Inside, it was apparent that the new owners still hadn't gotten around to making any visible improvements. He made his way past the crowded racks of snack foods intended to lure impulse buyers and approached the checkout counter.

"Hello," he said to the slight Asian man bent over what appeared to be an inventory form.

"Yes?" he replied, frowning.

"Trouble?" Don asked.

"Shoplifters...many things gone."

Don couldn't quite place his accent. He introduced himself, mentioning that he lived just up the road, and had known the previous owners. Luis was from the Philippines, he said, in answer to Don's friendly probing.

"Well Luis, if you don't mind a suggestion, why don't you move this checkout counter closer to the front door, just inside it, maybe. That way you'd have a better view of customers as they're leaving."

Luis sighed and nodded. "Yeh, we want to make changes to whole store," he said, spreading his arms. "We can do it then, maybe."

"And you should consider putting up a couple of the big mirrors, too. Makes people think they're being watched, even if they aren't."

"You a policeman, Mister Don?"

"No, not really, but that's very perceptive of you, Luis!" he chuckled. "I'm a private investigator."

Don had stopped in on spec, hoping to see if anyone in the store remembered selling cigarettes or drinks to a stranger on the day of the fatal accident. Someone who didn't fit the profile of the store's average customer. It was a long shot, he realized, and even though Luis was aware of the accident, he couldn't recall anything odd about customers that day. Don thanked him for his time and turned to go. The aroma of fresh-brewed coffee caught his attention as he neared the door. A woman was straightening up a table holding two large coffee urns. The Masons had never sold coffee 'to go', and he hadn't noticed the set-up when he'd come in.

"You like a hot coffee, sir?" asked the lady, whom Don immediately took to be Luis's wife.

"Uhh...sure," he shrugged. "I'm already over my daily limit but it smells too good to pass up!"

If she hadn't asked, he would have missed the clue now staring him in the face. The cup she handed him—no logo, no name, just a red and white checkerboard design—was the same as the used cups he'd found in the ditch near his house the morning after the accident.

WELL, THAT WAS A LUCKY *break*, Don thought as he drove away. Unlike her husband, Maria did remember something out of the ordinary. The customer had complained that the coffee wasn't hot enough, also that the store didn't offer real cream, just the powdered variety. The rude customer was a woman. She'd bought the coffee anyway, plus two cans of Coke and a pack of cigarettes, and slammed the door on the way out.

Maria had trouble explaining her appearance, the English words she wanted to use apparently not part of her vocabulary yet. She used 'sicky' and 'no meat', which Don took to mean the woman was thin and ill-looking. Her brown hair was 'very bad', and she agreed with Don's suggestion that maybe she meant stringy. When she mentioned that the woman also had noticeably red eyes, Don knew she was describing a drug addict. And she remembered that the vehicle she'd arrived in was not a new truck and the driver had a beard.

Still, it was promising evidence to build on, he reflected. If Doug Dixon has been able to lift prints off the soft drink cans they might be able to identify her. Especially if she had a criminal record.

"YES, WE LIFTED A FEW partials off the Coke cans," said Doug Dixon. They were standing at a table in DD's forensics lab, just off the 401 freeway and five kilometers from Don's office.

"That's encouraging, DD. Wouldn't happen to be those of a female, would they?"

"Aren't you the smart one, mister private detective. No wonder you're so expensive!"

"Ha! Wish that were true!" laughed Don.

"Got a name for her yet?" asked Dixon.

"Nope, but I'll bet she has a record, though."

"Right again, my friend. Are you making educated guesses or just lucky?"

"Modesty forbids me to answer that!"

Don told DD how the his casual visit to the variety store yesterday had provided him with the promising clues.

"So you think that these two were probably the 'perps' involved in the accident, and had just stopped at the store for supplies while they were watching your place," DD said.

"Yeah, exactly," replied Don. "And letting themselves be noticed at the store so close to the crime scene—then leaving their garbage behind tells me they weren't pros, either."

Dixon nodded. "I'd go along with that. We found evidence of a second set of prints, but they were too smudged to be usable, other than to indicate they were made by a male with large hands. The identifiable prints are those of one Shirley Jane Cuddy, age 39. She has a long rap sheet for prostitution, forgery, fraud, plus and a couple of things."

"Prostitution?" said Don, arching his eyebrows. "Must'a been a while ago."

Dixon handed Don a sheet of paper. "Fifteen years to be exact. Got busted a few times in her early twenties. Got off with the usual fines. Yeah, she would've been a bit of a looker back then," said DD.

Don studied Cuddy's mug shots, one taken in 1990, and another dated March, 2003.

Shirley Jane Cuddy's hair was neatly styled and she wore makeup in the earlier photo. Last year's edition was a stark contrast. Her hair was lank and stringy. She had prominent bags under her eyes, the left one displaying the vestiges of a shiner, and her shrunken cheeks attested to her noticeable weight loss over the years.

Don scanned the information. Cuddy was arrested last year in Toronto for trafficking in cocaine and released on bail pending a hearing. So far, one hadn't been scheduled. The delay didn't surprise Carling. The backlog for such crimes in the Ontario court system was long and getting longer.

Don and DD tossed around their thoughts about Cuddy. The woman had been picked up by undercover drug squad officers drug at a rundown bar in the city's east end. She was using herself and probably selling for her supplier to pay for her habit. No one else had been arrested with her.

Don hadn't heard of the bar where she'd been apprehended, but a thought popped into his mind. "Do you know anything about this bar? he asked DD. "Is it a biker hangout?"

The former cop shrugged. "You know, I do believe it was at one time. Maybe it still is. Why?"

"Just thinking out loud, DD. Listen, thanks for your help. You know where to send the bill. And I'll drop off a little something for your buddy at headquarters who ran the prints."

Don wondered how best to use the information from DD. He had two options, he decided. The first was to contact the OPP with the woman's ID straight away. The accident file was in the hands of their detective division and Don had already spoken to the officer in charge. His other choice was to take it a little further himself. That would mean a visit to Sonny's Bar and Grill. Maybe Cuddy still hung out there. And just maybe the guy she was with when Marlene Hastings was killed also hung out there. If they were really lucky, they might spot a dark-colored pickup truck with front end damage in the parking lot.

But he couldn't show his face there himself. As the perpetrators knew where he and Yvonne lived, it was possible that they knew him by sight as well. He wouldn't use Tom, either. Best call on one of his other operatives, a fellow that rode a Harley and wasn't from the Toronto area. He made a mental note to find out if Sonny's *was* a biker bar first, though.

As quickly as he'd formulated the plan, he rejected it. One, it couldn't be carried out in a day or two. And secondly, he wasn't even sure yet that the rollover accident near his home had anything to do with his investigation of Frank Archer. Suspicions, yes, gut feelings, yes, but no hard evidence. No, the better option would be to let the Provincial Police run with it.

Detective Sergeant Leon Belcher answered on the second ring. "Sure, I'll be glad to see you. I was just looking over the file this morning, as a matter of fact."

The OPP's division headquarters was a squat, two-storey brick structure erected in the early 1960s. It was an oddity amid the more modern structures surrounding it. Don joined a short line of civilians at the screening area just inside the front entrance. After passing unchallenged through the X-ray scanner, he signed in, received a visitor's pass, and was directed to Belcher's office.

It was their first face-to-face meeting. Belcher stood six foot, four, weighed two hundred and fifty pounds, and had a mass of curly black hair. He was wearing dark glasses, and Don thought he looked more like an Italian opera singer than a cop. His greeting was accompanied by a wide smile and Don knew right away that this was a man he could work with.

"Don, we're still not entirely convinced that this was a deliberate attempt to run the victim off the road. Yes, it would appear that her car was hit from behind, which probably lead to it ending up in the ditch.

We're not disputing that. But it could've happened by accident. A careless attempt to pass her, inadvertent contact, et cetera. And that leaves us with a 'hit and run' scenario," Belcher explained, after Don asked him how the police investigation was coming along.

"I have no quarrel with that thinking, Leon, however this might change your mind." Don passed him the photos he'd taken of the cigarette butts and other litter on the roadside near his home. "Prints from the Coke cans belong to this woman," he said

Don gave Belcher copies of Shirley Jane Cuddy's mug shots and rap sheet and explained how he'd made the connection to her purchases at the *QUIK STOP ON 12* corner store.

"Very resourceful of you, Don, to put it mildly. I won't ask how you came about these," he smiled, tapping the copies. "I guess a successful private investigator has to have contacts inside the system, right?"

Don returned his smile. "Well, at least we're all on the same side, aren't we?"

Their meeting had ended on an amiable note. Belcher assured him the police would immediately start looking for the Cuddy woman. Don didn't think it would take that long to find her, but if it did he could go with his second option and put his investigators on her trail.

Little did he know that the search for Shirley Jane Cuddy would come to a shocking end only days after it started...

21

SUNDAY, AUGUST 1, 6:30 A.M.

Yvonne's screams jolted Don awake from a deep sleep. He sat up just as she rushed into their bedroom, a look of stark horror on her face. She screamed again as she collapsed on the bed beside him.

"Wha—'? What's the matter, hon?" he asked, struggling to kick start his brain.

"A body! There's a body on the front lawn!" she sobbed.

Don wrapped his arms around her and held her tightly against his chest until her breathing slowed to a more normal level. "It's a woman, I think... by the bird bath. You can see it from the front window."

"Stay here."

He quickly pulled on his jeans and a T-shirt and padded barefoot down the hall and into the living room. Yvonne had opened the drapes and Don saw what had shocked her. Yvonne's eyes hadn't deceived her: there was definitely a body propped against the pedestal of the stone bird bath, thirty feet from the window. Don closed the drapes, found his sandals, unlocked the front door and stepped cautiously outside. He scanned the yard slowly, looking for signs of intruders. Satisfied he was alone, he approached the body.

He muttered a curse under his breath as he knelt in front of it. The victim's forehead was a blotch of matted hair, stained dark red with dried blood. He was looking at the exit wound, he knew.

Shirley Jane Cuddy had been executed by a shot to the back of her head.

Don mustered his thoughts before returning to the house. *Somebody is sure trying to scare me off, but it isn't going to work. I'll get the son'ova bitches no matter how long it takes, he vowed.*

THE REST OF THE MORNING was a blur to Don. After draping a sheet over the body, he made two calls. The first was to the OPP branch office in Caledon East, the closest to his home. The second was to Sergeant Leon Belcher, a call that was routed to his voice mail. Two police cruisers responded to Don's first call and arrived within minutes of each other. Sirens could be heard in the distance and by 8:30 three more cruisers, an ambulance, and the coroner's SUV were parked in the driveway or along the road. By ten o'clock, reporters and film crews from three Toronto television stations had arrived, adding to the congestion.

Plastic privacy screens were soon erected around the murder scene and Don ushered Yvonne out to the back patio. She was still shivering despite the temperature rising rapidly towards the day's forecasted high of 29C. Don made coffee and brought her a cup, and stood behind her with his arms around on her shoulders until she calmed down.

"I can't stay here any longer," she told him softly. "Not until you know what's going on."

Don had no honest answer to allay her fear, and didn't even try to dissuade her. Although he'd told her that the gardener's death might have been a 'hit and run' accident, he'd stopped short of telling her that his investigation said otherwise. And now definitely wasn't the time to tell her that he knew the identity of the murder victim lying on his front lawn.

By the time the coroner had examined the body, confirming what Don had already surmised, Detective Sergeant Leon Belcher had arrived to take charge of the investigation.

"Doc says she died from a single shot to the head. Type and caliber of the bullet not yet ascertained.

"And I agree with you, Don, it has all the earmarks of an execution-style killing," Belcher said. They were alone at the kitchen table, Yvonne having retreated to the bedroom.

"Did they find any identification on her? I had a quick look around for a purse or wallet before the cops arrived but didn't find anything," Don said.

"Nope, nothing. I've got men searching the road and ditches in both directions, but I'd be surprised if they find anything. She was probably 'offed' at another location or in the vehicle used to bring her here."

Don nodded. "And they must've dragged her body across the lawn. There was a trail of sorts through the dew earlier, but that had disappeared before most of the officers got here."

"Well, it wouldn't have taken much effort, eh? Looks like she was all skin and bones."

"Yeah, well, I guess the poor woman was a junkie of some sort. I'm pretty sure it's the Cuddy woman," said Don.

"I think so, too. But positive ID will have to wait until we run her prints. The coroner estimated she'd been dead for five or six hours," he added.

Don glanced at the wall clock. "So she was killed between three and four in the morning, then, but not necessarily dumped here until later. We went to bed just before midnight and I never heard a thing until Yvonne woke me."

It was well into the afternoon before the police finished their on-scene investigation. Yvonne had agreed to spend the night as long as Don was with her. Over dinner, she agreed to Don's suggestion for the week ahead.

Yvonne had lent the two-bedroom apartment she owned to a girlfriend when she moved in with him. The agreement she'd made with her friend meant she still had the use of one of the bedrooms if and when she needed it. Don suggested she stay there on week nights for the time being, returning to spend the weekend with him.

"Nothing is going to happen to you, I promise," he said, hugging her. "Whoever killed this woman is trying to shake me up, not you." He was speaking quietly, but firmly. I don't know yet if it's someone connected to the case I'm working on now or something from the past. But between me and the cops we'll get to the bottom of it."

As they sat silently, holding hands, Don fought to hold back the anger welling up inside of him. Anger at the audacity of the murdering bastards who, for the second time in two weeks, had brought their vicious ways to the quiet rural community he called home.

TUESDAY, AUGUST 3

For the second day, the story about a body having been dumped on a private investigator's front lawn was front page news in the morning papers and on most television newscasts, so Tom Allman wasn't surprised when Don called.

"Oh yeah, I've seen the reports," he said. "What the hell's goin' on, pardner?"

"Wish I knew, Tom," replied Don. "But I'd bet my last nickel it has to do with our investigation."

Allman had been working with the team of KayRoy investigators watching Archer 24/7 since he'd returned from Edmonton. There had been no change in Archer's routine. He went to the tennis club on most mornings, dropped into an Internet cafe two or three times a week, and hadn't been seen with any unknown contacts.

"Which supports my theory that he probably doesn't have a clue about these murders, or who's behind them," said Don when Allman finished.

They had a lengthy discussion on the Don's theories regarding Shirley Jane Cuddy, specifically why he thought she had been in the vehicle used to run Yvonne's gardener off the road, and how her apparent increased drug use recently—and maybe her loose tongue—led to her demise.

OPP Sergeant Leon Belcher had informed Don that undercover drug squad officers had traced the woman a few days after he'd identified her. They found out that she been buying cocaine in larger quantities to feed her habit. The autopsy on her body showed that her system was almost at overdose level when she died, and the coroner suggested she may have been unconscious when she was shot.

"Hmmm," offered Allman. "So, maybe, just maybe, whoever had hired her and her partner got wind of her ahh... *big spending*, got nervous that she could be linked to them, and decided to take her out."

"Yeh, that's it in a nutshell, Tom," agreed Don. "And that's how the police see it as well."

"What about the driver? Guess he hasn't been found yet, huh?"

"No, but who knows? Maybe he's the one who put the bullet in her head."

Allman gave an audible snort. "Yeah, or maybe he's a goner, too. Maybe they should check the car trunks in the long-term parking lot at the airport!"

His facetious remark brought a chuckle from Don. "Well, it wouldn't be a 'first', would it?"

"Very strange, very strange indeed, offered Allman. "I 'm goin' to the club tomorrow, though, and I'll check in with you afterwards."

Tom Allman wasn't the only one surprised to see the stories about Don Carling in his morning paper, along with his photograph. The photo showed Carling standing with a group of policemen on his front lawn. Frank Archer didn't recognize the man, but the name rang a bell. Carling, he recalled, was the private detective hired by his wife to follow him to Paris. No motive for the murder was mentioned in the article, and the police response was 'no comment'. The victim had not been officially identified yet, but her name was being reported on the all-news radio station he was listening to while he read the paper. He had never heard of Shirley Jane Cuddy.

Should he let Carlos know about this? After mulling it over for some time, he decided he should. After all, it was Carlos—or someone in his cell—that had discovered that Carling was a private detective. His mind made up, he dressed and headed off to send an email to Carlos.

BY FRIDAY, THE MEDIA'S INTEREST in the murder had waned, including calls to the KayRoy office by reporters wanting to speak with Don. He had politely refused all requests, saying only that the police were handling the case, not his firm. Sergeant Belcher had aired a message asking anyone with information about the killing to contact the police, but so far there had been no response from the public. A search for relatives of the dead woman had taken days, but finally turned up an aunt and uncle living in a small Cape Breton Island outpost. According to them, Shirley Jane had left Nova Scotia while still in her teens, and had not been heard from since. She probably never knew that her widowed mother had passed away ten years ago.

EVEN HIS FRIEND, RCMP INSPECTOR Brian Roberts, was aware of the case. It was the first thing they had discussed when he'd called Don Thursday morning, yesterday. Don brought him up to date, explaining why he was certain Cuddy's death was connected to his investigation of Archer. "So there you have it, Brian," he'd said. "I know it may seem a bit far-fetched, but I can see no other motive for both these deaths. I think they were just clumsy attempts to scare me off. Why? I don't know, but my instincts tell me it's all to do with Archer."

"Well he's certainly a person of interest since you brought him to our attention," Roberts said. As promised, Roberts had his staff check their files for any info on Archer/Amara. Although the man had no criminal record either in Canada or his native France, he would now be flagged by the CSIS, the Canadian Security and Intelligence Service. "You were right to give us his identity, Don. Given the current situation vis-a-vis terrorism, any link, however tenuous it might seem, can't be ignored."

When Don asked exactly what being 'flagged' meant, Roberts explained that from now on every time Archer's passport was scanned, his movement would be stored in the system's computer. The data would be noted not just at airports, but at vehicular border crossing checkpoints to and from the United States as well.

The same information would be registered if he used his still-valid French passport, Roberts said, when Don asked. "If he tries to enter the

US using his French papers, he'd probably be subjected to a lengthy grilling. The Amara name is definitely on Homeland Security's A-list."

"Yes, I gather that's why he wanted Canadian citizenship in the first place," said Don. "Well, thanks for this, Brian. One of my agents has worked his way into his Archer's confidence, and I'll let you know what happens next."

AT THE VERY TIME CARLING and the RCMP officer were discussing him, Frank Archer was poring over Danielle's response to his ultimatum. It had arrived much quicker than he'd expected. Obviously his threat to make public her affair with Charles Rothwell had hit a nerve. But he wasn't going to look a gift horse in the mouth, and, as he read through the revised divorce agreement he'd just received from her lawyers, he felt a sense of triumph.

The document was short and surprisingly straightforward. They would jointly file for divorce due to irreconcilable differences. She'd even agreed to the two million dollars he'd demanded on one stipulation: their divorce was not to be made public until after it was granted. Frank had no problem with this. The money would be shown as a severance payment from Empire North. He was to resign from the firm and vacate the condominium no later than thirty days after the decree was issued.

He briefly thought about challenging the clause concerning their daughter, but on reflection decided it wouldn't be worth the effort. In effect, the clause prohibited him having any contact with Gabrielle. Actually, he had no strong feelings for her one way or the other. Their last so-called 'family' lunch had been over two months ago. No, it would be no great loss to him if he never saw her again. But, 'never say never' his mother had always admonished him. Perhaps when she was grown up, Gabrielle might want to know more about him, and by then she could take the initiative, he reasoned.

He had insisted on one change to the document: the time and disposition of his payoff. He wanted half the money before the divorce was final, but her lawyers were adamantly opposed to this. The result was a counter offer that would pay him $250,000 now, and the balance within 30 days of the divorce becoming final. Frank agreed to the revised terms, and signed the papers. The initial funds were to be deposited in his Swiss bank account within twenty-four hours. He'd had the foresight to set up the account in Zurich when he'd been in Switzerland in May, using his French name and his sister's Paris address as his domicile on the application. The account had been opened to handle the funds Carlos had promised for his cooperation, but the first major deposit to it would now come from the divorce severance.

He opened a bottle of ten-year-old Cote-de-Beaune wine, poured a glass, and silently toasted his good fortune. It still bemused him that he'd ended up married to this rich Canadian woman. If she wasn't such a devout Catholic, it probably wouldn't have happened. He'd almost walked away from her demand that they marry only weeks after what, to him, had been nothing more than a sexual romp on the Riviera. Once she had spelled out the easy and lucrative possibilities that a marriage to her would bring, however, he had quickly changed his mind. And it had been a good move, he thought, as he sipped the excellent vintage from his native country. With his travel experience, the knowledge of the art world he'd gained, plus the financial nest egg from Carlos, he should be free to pursue any number of business opportunities once he said farewell to Canada.

As he looked around the condo's spacious living room, he realized there were very few items that he would want to take with him. Most of the furnishings came with the place. The few items he'd acquired himself —the wine cooler with rack attached, the stereo system, and a number of books and CDs—would all be left behind. Most of the CD's could be replaced, anyway. Whatever clothing he could fit into two large suitcases, some art books, and his laptop computer were all he'd take with him. When he left for New York, he couldn't foresee any reason to return to Toronto. The rest of his mission would be on American soil, and he'd be free to return to France afterwards.

22

MONDAY, AUGUST 9

Joanne buzzed Don. "Sergeant Belcher on line one, boss."

"Morning, Leon. Just touching base to see how your investigation is coming along," said Don.

Belcher told him the police were still in the dark concerning the Cuddy murder, but there had been a promising development in the accident investigation involving Yvonne's car.

"We still haven't been able to trace or even identify the driver, but we did get a hit on the probable vehicle he used," he said. "After you found the paint chips from the yellow Volkswagen, I had our men search that part of the road thoroughly.

"What did they find?"

"Just a few scrapings, but they matched bits we found on the left rear panel of the Volkswagen. Spectrometer analysis determined they were from a GM product, either a Sierra or a Chevy Silverado, '97 or '98 model."

"Wonder how I missed them myself? Guess I was too excited when I saw the yellow chips."

"Well, don't beat yourself up over it, Don. They were almost invisible, apparently. The truck we're looking for is grey in color, almost the same color as the road surface. If you hadn't pointed the area out to us, we probably wouldn't have thought to look there," Belcher explained.

Because of manpower restraints, the police hadn't been able to launch an intensive search for the truck yet, Belcher admitted.

An idea struck Don. "Maybe we can help you out there, Leon. I've got a few guys available and it won't hurt to spend some time on it."

The officer agreed, and as soon as they ended their call, Don speed-dialed Rollie Parsons' cell phone. Rollie answered just after he had three-putted the fifth green...

"It wasn't just the damned putts that pissed me off, Don," exclaimed an exasperated Parsons, "but it took me five friggin' shots to get on the green!"

Don chuckled. "Well, Arnie, when you've brought the course to its knees again, stop by the office. I've got a job for you."

ROLLIE WAS ALL SMILES WHEN he entered Don's office. "Birdied the last hole!" he enthused.

"Always something to bring you back, eh?" They chatted about golf until Joanne brought them coffee. "Here's a challenge for you, he began, once they were alone again. "Might require a bit of luck, but if it's still in the area you may be able to track it down."

Don briefed Rollie on the models of GMC trucks to look for, and the name and location of the bikers' bar where the Cuddy woman had uses and sold drugs. There was a good chance the guy seen in the pickup with her probably hung out there, too. The police had never made public the possibility that the gardener's death hadn't been an accident, or that another vehicle might have been involved.

"Hey, it's worth a try. Especially if he thinks no one's looking for the pickup" said Rollie.

"Good point, and the cops don't think the vehicle would have suffered much damage, either, probably just some paint missing, and some gouges near the front right wheel."

"Yeah, that makes sense," agreed Rollie. "And he probably wouldn't have bothered to get it repaired."

"Right. So I wouldn't waste too much time checking out body shops, but here's something we could try..."

"Hey, I like that!" said Rollie, after Don laid it out for him. "In the mean time, I'll snoop around the biker scene, maybe get a lead on him."

"I've been wondering what's been happening with you and Archer, Tom," said Don. His American investigator had called him with an update on his undercover assignment.

Tom Allman hadn't spoken to Frank Archer since he flew to Edmonton almost three weeks ago. Last week, when Tom showed up at the tennis club, there was no sign of Archer. Finally, on Friday morning, he asked one of the regulars if he'd seen Frank lately.

"No, but then he's never around when pros are in town. He'll be over at York University watching the ladies play, you see," he told Tom, referring to the annual Canadian stop on the Women's pro tennis circuit.

Archer confirmed as much when he greeted Tom yesterday morning in the locker room. He'd casually inquired about Tom's trip to Edmonton, and, after the other members were out of earshot, asked him if he was free for lunch.

Allman had quickly agreed, hoping Archer would tell him more about the plot, specifically what they needed him to do. He came away from the restaurant none the wiser, though. Instead of providing information, Archer had a question for Tom. Could he be ready to move down to the States no later than mid-September?

"So Archer never mentioned explosives, or what they were going to be used for?"ask Don.

Allman shook his head. "I don't think he knows himself."

"All a bit weird, isn't it?" offered Don. "But then again, I don't see him as one of the leading players in whatever it is they're planning. Seems to me that recruiting you was all they needed him for, and maybe he's to be the buffer between you and the real brains behind the operation from now on."

"Could be, Don, could be. And you're probably right about him just bein' a ' gofer' of sorts. There's gotta be some assholes in the plot who've been trained in terrorist ops".

"But if that's true, and we're talking about a cell whose members are," Don paused, searching for the right words, "... well, at least I would expect them to be Islamic radicals who've been trained in terrorist tactics. And carrying that hypothesis a bit further, one wonders why they would resort to using an outsider."

"Like me, you mean," said Tom.

"Exactly! You'd think they would have their own guys who knew their way around explosives."

"Yeah, that thought had crossed my mind," Tom agreed, "but I'm thinkin' that it could be because I'm less likely to draw attention than some brown-skinned foreigners with 'look at me, I'm an Arab' written on their foreheads. Know what I mean?" said Allman. "Especially if they're runnin' around in areas where there aren't a hell'uva lot of people about."

" It could be that simple, all right," agreed Don, and, changing the subject, asked, "Did he talk money? What about the advance you'd insisted on?"

"Should be in my account in Denver by tomorrow. I'll need some of that for expenses, of course."

"Okay ... well, if we can screw up their plans that's all the bucks we'll see, I guess."

"What's this 'we' bit, white man?" Allman chuckled.

Don laughed at the age-old Lone Ranger joke. "You'll get your share, Tonto, don't worry!" It was the only lighthearted moment in their conversation.

"Tom, there's been an unexpected development that will impact our investigation of Archer. Danielle Clyde, phoned me this morning and canceled my contract with her," Don said

"What? You're jokin' aren't you? Why in hell would she do that?"

"Haven't a damned clue!" answered Don. "Just called and told me to drop it. Didn't want a written report or anything. Basically said her husband's actions were of no concern to her any longer." Don had never let on to her that he suspected her husband was somehow involved in a terrorist plot. "But that doesn't mean we've given up the chase, Tom. We're going to stay on him. At some point we'll have to turn it over to the federal authorities. But I don't think we're ready to do that just yet."

"I'm with you there, pardner," replied Allman. "I gather the Feds and the CIA are workin' together better'n they were before 9/11, what with this Homeland Security deal, but they probably wouldn't be too interested in what we have on this guy right now."

THURSDAY, AUGUST 12

"Miss McNeil? Could you spare me a few minutes? Maybe over a coffee? Don handed the slightly startled woman his business card.

"Private investigator?" she read. "What's it about?"

Don had approached Frank Archer's former lover as she left the travel agency that handled travel arrangements for Empire North employees. He gently steered her out of the busy lunchtime pedestrian stream towards the curb, quickly explaining that his interest was in Frank Archer, not her.

"He and I are no longer friends, Mr.—" she looked at the card again. "... Carling."

"Please, call me Don," he smiled. "Honest, I just need to ask you a few questions about him. Nothing personal, I assure you."

The attractive blonde still wore a wary look on her face. "Why? I don't see—"

"Just give me ten minutes, Miss McNeil, that's all. How about at the Starbucks across the street?"

THEIR MEETING TOOK UP MOST of her lunch hour. Don insisted that she order something to eat, and, once Jill realized Don wasn't a threat to her, she talked openly about her past relationship with Archer. Her frankness was no doubt fostered by the hostility she still harbored towards him, Don felt.

With that in mind, Don didn't think there was any harm in telling her that he was checking into Archer's activities on behalf of Empire North. Not exactly true, now he was no longer working for Danielle Clyde, and he made it clear that Frank's affair with her was not the issue.

"Well, I'm sure I wasn't the first and probably not the last to fall for him," Jill admitted. "So what *are* you after?"

Frank and Jill's affair started in 2002. He'd never seemed to take anything seriously and their conversations usually centered around tennis or her work. He always took her to upscale restaurants, and occasionally to a movie afterwards. Every two or three months they would leave the city and stay overnight in the Muskoka region north of Toronto. Frank drank only French wine, and never more than two or three glasses. She had never seen him inebriated.

"Our overnight trips stopped early this year, though, and he started to shove me aside about that time, too," she added, almost wistfully. From her tone, it was obvious that she was still hurting from their breakup.

"Did he ever talk politics, Jill?"

She thought for a moment before replying. "No, not really. I know he didn't like the Americans very much. The government, you know, especially the president. He would get really mad when he heard him talking about the war in Iraq. He'd grab the remote and switch the TV off."

"Really?" said Don, feigning surprise. "Is he a Muslim, is that why?"

"Oh, no. He wasn't religious like that or anything. He just didn't think the US had any business in those countries."

Don switched subjects. "What about men friends? Did he ever talk about the fellows he played tennis with?"

"I don't think so. If he did, I don't remember any names. I remember some relative, or maybe he was just a old friend from France, coming to visit him. He was quite looking forward to that. But I never met him."

"Do you remember when that was?"

She shrugged and shook her head. "Last fall, maybe? Sometime before Christmas, I think. But I'm not really sure. Sorry."

"That's all right, Jill. I'm just fishing," he smiled. "I know he made lots of trips for the company. Did he talk about those when he got back?

"Oh, just in general. I don't know much about art, but I know that was his job."

She glanced at her watch, and Don took the hint. "I'm sorry I took up so much of your time," he said, rising and offering his hand. "Thanks very much for your cooperation. Believe me, what we talked about will remain confidential as far as I'm concerned."

Jill shook his hand and preceded him to the door. Just before she was about to step off the curb she turned and said, "Now I remember you! You took the same flight to Paris as Frank a few months ago. I booked those tickets, but Frank said he'd never heard of you."

Aha! So that's what happened! Jill was behind the leak, inadvertent perhaps, that led to Frank's spy-like actions in Paris! Probably orchestrated by others, but designed to throw me off his trail.

FRIDAY, AUGUST 13

"Bonjour, Paul, good to hear from you! Anything new on the hotel murder? asked Don.

Don was at home and munching on his breakfast cereal when the early call surprised him.

"That's why I'm calling, mon ami," said Paul. "The police investigation has suddenly become enshrouded in secrecy, at least as far as my access to it."

"Oh? Any idea why?"

"Not exactly. But Inspector Monet called me in a few days ago, not as I had hoped to give me an update, but to go over again the timing of your last evening in Paris."

"What? I thought he was happy with both our accounts of that night."

"Yes, so did I. And I reiterated my testimony exactly as before. However, he did ask more questions about how much we'd had to drink."

"Meaning was I pissed enough to order a whore and then kill her in a drunken rage?" asked Don incredulously.

"No, no, I can't see how he could get that impression. No, it struck me that as no viable suspect has been identified, the police are just going back over everything. You know how it works."

"Yeah, but it's still bugs the hell out of me," Don replied. "What about my DNA? That should have cleared me." There was a long pause from across the ocean, and it was left to Don to speak again. "... What aren't you telling me, Paul?"

"Well... that's when my source dried up," sighed Boutin.

"What do you mean?"

"I had called him a few weeks ago to chat, and specifically asked if they had the results of the test yet," he explained. "As diplomatically as he could, he informed me that I was now persona non grata as far as discussing the police investigation." There was another lengthy silence. The lingering uncertainty that had been bothering him ever since Boutin first called about the murder, surfaced again. "And it was a few days after that when Monet called."

"Well, that's most disconcerting, Paul. In fact 'highly pissed off' is how I feel at the moment," said the exasperated Canadian.

"I can understand that, Don. But don't let it get you down. Here's what I'm going to do now that I've been cut out of investigation..."

All his instincts and experience told him the key to solving the murder still lay in finding the connection to the prostitute: be it a hotel employee, a taxi driver, or the pimp that sent her to the hotel that night. Even though the police had supposedly exhausted all avenues to find the person, Paul thought they must have overlooked something.

With that in mind, he told Don, he had launched his own search for the missing link. And he didn't expect or want to be paid for his efforts, he said, when Don brought the subject up. It was more a matter of honor, was how he phrased it, and he wouldn't be satisfied until he'd been able to lift the cloud of suspicion still hanging over his friend's head, thanks to the inability of the Paris police to find the killer.

"It may take some time, but I'm putting my best people to work on this," he told Don emphatically, "and we'll stay with it until we find who's behind it."

Nothing good ever happens on Friday the thirteenth, his superstitious grandmother used to tell him when he was a young boy. Her words struck him suddenly as he was shaving. *Well, Grandma, you're right again...*

23

"Your brainwave paid off, Don," said Rollie. "I got a call yesterday about the ad."

Don had placed an advertisement in a weekly publication that was distributed free through variety stores, service stations, coffee shops and restaurants. Under *VEHICLES WANTED*, he'd advertised for a *'seven or eight year old large pickup truck in good running condition. Appearance not important, needed for a back woods mining operation. Must be cheap.'*

"Yeah, this guy rang me and said he had a '97 GMC Sierra with some dents and scratches on it, but a good engine and 'tranny'. Told him I was interested, so we arranged to meet."

"But the guy didn't fit the description of our suspect, right?" said Don.

"No such luck. No, it was a young guy, mid-twenties, clean cut, works for a small used car lot way out in the east end," answered Rollie. "Anyhow, I drove out there and had a look at it."

The truck had a lot more damage than it would have sustained from bumping a car from behind. There were dents in the sides and tailgate, and lots of scrapes. But there was a recent tear in the body work just ahead of the right front wheel well. "Must of been used in construction, or for carrying bikes or ATVs. But I think it's the one were lookin' for, Don. And it is grey. I took it for a test drive, said I was interested, would run it by my partner and get back to him. He couldn't—or wouldn't—tell me how they'd acquired it."

"Doesn't matter, Rollie. We'll leave that to the OPP. Give me those details again, please, and I'll call Belcher right now."

Ten minutes later, Sergeant Belcher had the information. "Thanks, Don, I'll have a team out to there within the hour," he said.

FRIDAY, AUGUST 20

It hadn't taken the police long to realize the tip from the private investigator was valid. A court order to seize the GMC pickup on suspicion of possible involvement in a fatal 'hit and run' accident had been issued less than twenty-four hours after Don's call to Sergeant Belcher. The young salesman Rollie Parsons had dealt with watched in open-mouthed amazement as a no-nonsense team of officers loaded it on a flatbed trailer and towed it away. His boss, the owner of the business, wasn't around when the police acted.

He was in his office yesterday, though, when the police returned, but not in a cooperative mood. They asked to see the paperwork regarding his acquisition of said vehicle. The conversation turned testy when he couldn't come up with any. It was only after he was threatened with charges that might lead to his business licence being canceled that he came clean. He'd bought it for cash, he confessed. And no, he hadn't received any documentation with it, or licence plates. He was planning to register it in his company name, but hadn't got around to it yet.

Belcher knew such a move was illegal, but greasing the right palms could make it happen. And he knew that George, the owner, wasn't too worried about being caught out. He'd been fined before for similar offences.

"When did this happen?" Belcher asked him.

George, whose real name was Gregor Malkev, a landed immigrant from the Ukraine, scratched his unshaven chin and ran a finger under his smudged collar. A guy brought it in ten, maybe twelve days ago," he shrugged. "Said he was movin' out west and didn't need it anymore."

"So, being a shrewd operator, you low-balled an offer and he took it, right?"

The wary dealer shrugged again, as if to say 'business is business'.

"What did this person without a name look like? And don't tell me you can't remember or we'll continue this conversation at the station," ordered the sergeant.

Another shrug. "...Maybe forty, big stomach...how you say it? 'Beer gut'?" he said. "And with a beard. Yeah, could be a Santa Claus," Malkev laughed, hoping to get a smile out of the cops. He failed.

"Height? Weight? Any other features?" pressed Belcher.

"Two meters or so. Many kilos, I can't guess how many."

"Who was with him? I don't suppose he left on foot after you took it off his hands, did he?"

Malkev thought for a moment before replying. "Some guy drove him. I didn't see him. Another truck...not big like this one."

"Don't suppose you got the licence number. Make? Color?"

He shook his head. "No, too far away. Other side of street. Black, I think."

Belcher was taking it all down on a note pad. After a few more questions that Malkev couldn't answer, he gave up. Before leaving, he also jotted down details of Malkev's passport, immigrant visa, and business licence. He threw a curt 'Thank You' towards him as he headed for his cruiser.

"Will I get it back?" Malkev called.

"We'll be in touch," replied Belcher, closing the door.

MONDAY, AUGUST 23

Don wasted no time getting to OPP headquarters after Detective Sergeant Belcher called, anxious to hear the latest information regarding the GMC pickup.

"We've confirmed that it is the vehicle used to run the Volkswagen off the road," Belcher said. "There was just enough yellow paint from it on the truck's front end to make the match."

"Probably why he wanted to get rid of it," said Don.

"Perhaps. But they also found DNA of the Cuddy woman in it."

"From bloodstains?" asked Don hopefully.

"No, nothing to suggest it had anything to do with her murder, or moving the body. Her prints were on the dashboard on the passenger side, and a few strands of her hair on the seat," explained Belcher.

As far as other prints, the police were still checking them out. Only smudged prints were found on the steering wheel, suggesting the driver wore gloves or there had been a cover on it at one time. The dealer, Malkev, confirmed this during a follow-up visit. There had been a fleece cover on the wheel when he bought it, but he'd taken it off and discarded it. The only identifiable prints were found on the tailgate, and were those of an ex-con named Daniel Belanger. His whereabouts were still unknown.

"But Belanger doesn't match the description of our suspected driver, or the guy who sold the vehicle to Malkev," said Belcher. According to his sheet, he's 1.65 meters tall, and weighs 70 kilos. He would be 35 now, and he's also prematurely bald."

Don did the math in his head, still not willing to deal strictly in metrics. "So he's about five foot, seven inches or so, and thin," he said. "What's his history?"

"He's from Quebec, and has been in and out of jail since he was a teenager. Your typical small-time hood, basically. Extortion, aggravated assault, and armed robbery, to name a few of his transgressions."

"But he's on the street now?"

"Yeah, says here he was released a year ago after serving three years for his part in a credit union hold-up near Montreal. Still on probation."

Locating the truck moved two police investigations forward. The fatal accident near Don's country home and the murder of Shirley Jane Cuddy. In the first case, they could now prove it was the vehicle used to run the yellow Volkswagen off the road. Cuddy's DNA put her in the truck, and the statement by the Philippino woman at the corner store put her in it the day of the accident. Her brief description of the driver matched the more detailed one given by the car lot owner. At this point, though, there was no proof to connect the missing driver and the truck to the Cuddy murder. An intensive police search for this man was still underway.

"Well, you may not be able to prove it yet, but I'd bet my last dollar that this bearded guy had a hand in both of the deaths," Don said, and added, "and the odds are that he's an ex-con, too."

The policeman nodded. "Yeah, I go along with that. But we probably won't have confirmation until we apprehend one of these suspects. There are a number of scenarios we're working on."

"Does one of them have Belanger as the killer? Maybe he was brought in to take Cuddy out," said Don. Belcher offered a non-committal shrug, and Don continued. "Even without obvious evidence that her body had been in the truck, they could have wrapped her up in a tarp or something. Remember the marks on the lawn?" Again Belcher nodded. "I mean they used something to drag her from the road."

"Or perhaps these two had nothing at all to do with her murder," cautioned Belcher. "But no, there's nothing wrong with your thinking, Don. We're looking for both suspects. Belanger's photo and a composite drawing of the other suspect will be circulated to the news media tomorrow."

24

Frank Archer had no trouble entering the US, thanks to the email from FARMER telling him to drive to New York instead of flying. If he'd put off his trip for a day or two, it might not have gone so smoothly. Today, however, the customs and immigration officer at the border crossing from Ontario to Niagara Falls, New York, had found no reason to pull Archer aside for detailed questioning. He ran Frank's Canadian passport through the scanner and asked the usual questions. What was the purpose of his trip, and how long was he planning to be in the States?

Heading for New York City for a week to watch the US Open tennis tournament, he'd answered. There were no more questions and he was waved through.

If he'd gone with his original plan to fly, he would have likely faced a different reception. At the very least, he would have faced a barrage of questions from the American officials at the pre-clearance check point. At worst, he could have been refused entry without explanation. His name on the watch list issued by the Canadian Security Service would have triggered the action. However, the latest update to the watch list wouldn't show up in the computer system at the Rainbow Bridge entry point for another forty-eight hours, on Tuesday, the day after the Labor Day holiday.

He had picked up the email from FARMER on Friday morning. Before he left London, Carlos told him he would be meeting both FARMER and FOX, the operational leader of the mission, during his trip to New York.

The past two days had left Frank with little time to ponder why he'd been told not to fly. He'd never had any problems traveling by air on his Canadian passport, including flights to the US.

What had changed? he wondered, as he sped eastwards on interstate I-90. *Were they just being overly cautious as the date for the operation drew closer?* He hoped so. As the afternoon wore on, other thoughts ran through his mind. *Will they want me to go back to Toronto? Or will I be staying in the US to work with Tom Allman?*

As far as he was concerned, it didn't really matter. All his personal effects and clothing were stuffed into two large cases in the trunk. That might have raised a few eyebrows if they'd searched the car at the border, now that he thought about it. He would've had trouble convincing even the most gullible official that he needed it all for his short stay in New York. He hadn't thought about that possibility, and Carlos would have come down on him like a ton of bricks if he'd known about it.

And what about this car? It was on lease to his wife's company. Presumably the dealership Empire North dealt with would want it back when the lease expired in December. Until then, he supposed, no one would be looking for it.

Frank had never driven for more than four or five hours at any one stretch in his life before today. Driving distances between major cities—even countries—in Europe were small compared to North America. At four oclock , he'd been on the road for almost seven hours. After he turned south near Albany, he started looking for a place to stop for the night. Forty minutes later he pulled into a motel just off the freeway at Kingston, New York. He could easily cover the remaining distance to New York City in the morning. After checking in, he called the contact number he had been given.

THE MESSAGE LIGHT WAS BLINKING when Don entered his den at 1:45 p.m.

"He never showed, Don, and I couldn't have missed him. I had a clear view of every passenger coming down the jetway off that flight. And he didn't appear at the baggage carousel, either. Maybe he changed flights? Call me ASAP."

"Son'ova bitch!" Don uttered softly, after replaying the message. Richie Flanagan, a New York PI, had called twenty minutes ago, when Don and Yvonne were still a few kilometers from home on their bikes.

Flanagan, a fifth generation Irish-American and an ex-cop, was working on information Don had received from Jill McNeil. As promised, she had called Don with Archer's itinerary after she had booked it. Air Canada flight 742 departing at 10:15 this morning and a return flight on the 13th. Her agency had also made a booking for him at a Marriott hotel near Central Park.

"Bad news, hon?" asked Yvonne. "It must be by the scowl on your face."

"Sorry, babe. Just have to make a call. You go ahead and shower first. I'll be there in time to scrub your back," he said.

"Don't be too long, then. And you'd better be smiling," she answered lightly.

"RICHIE? IT'S DON." THERE WAS a lot of background noise on the line and he couldn't make out the voice. He was about to ring off and try later when the noise disappeared.

"Yeah, I'm here. Just cleared the tunnel. Got me now?"

"Yep, you're loud and clear. Any sign of the bugger yet?"

"Naw, I'm sure he didn't arrive on that flight. I'm headin' for the Marriott to see if he shows up there."

"Check that. I'll see what I can find out from this end," Don told him. "Maybe he switched flights, or even the day. But I might not be able to confirm that until Tuesday."

He left a message for Jill McNeil on her answering machine asking her to call him after the holiday weekend. *Maybe Archer had changed his reservation to a later flight,* Don thought.

"I'll do some checking with the airline today, Richie, and let you know what I find out," said Don. "This isn't the first time Archer has pulled a disappearing act on me."

Yvonne was still in the shower when Don got off the phone. He stripped off his biking clothes and entered the ensuite bathroom off the master bedroom. Yvonne peeked out from the steamy shower stall. "That's not much of a smile, lover boy," she said. "Get your sweaty body in here and I'll see if I can do something about it."

Ten minutes of mutual and sensual body rubbing later, Don was definitely smiling. The caressing continued after they stepped out of the shower and put on their towel robes. Don nibbled on her neck as he pulled her into the bedroom. "Hmm...you're going to have me all wet again if you keep that up, darling," she whispered, as they bumped into the bed. He pulled her robe open, let it drop to the floor, and kissed both her firm nipples slowly and then moved up to her lips.

"I love you, you know. Why don't you move back in so we can do this more often?"

LATER, AS THEY LAY WITH their warm bodies entwined, Yvonne traced her fingers along his jaw line. "That was, on a scale of one to ten, hmmm...at least a—"

"A twelve," interrupted Don.

"Yvonne blew in his ear. "I was going to say fifteen."

AFTER DINNER DON EXCUSED HIMSELF and phoned New York again. Richie Flanagan answered immediately. Frank Archer had not checked into the mid-town hotel. Nor had he canceled, according to the desk clerk. Don had checked with the airline and found that there was a late flight scheduled into LaGuardia at 9:30, but his instincts told him Archer wouldn't be on it. Asking Flanagan to go back to the airport would be a waste of time, and he suggested a better way to find out if and when Archer arrived.

"Yeah, that might work, Don. I'll leave the message for him, and get back to you if he replies."

MONDAY, SEPTEMBER 6, 11:25 AM

Frank was relieved to find traffic on Labor Day was lighter than he'd been expecting. He had never driven in the big city, and wasn't looking forward to navigating his way around central Manhattan. But the new instructions he'd received last night spared him the challenge. The sign for the Holiday Inn was easily visible from the middle of the George Washington Bridge. Two right turns after exiting the bridge brought him to the motel on the east bank of the Hudson River.

The attractive African-American clerk on duty greeted him with a wide smile. Yes, he was expected, she assured him, and all she needed was a credit card imprint and his signature on the registration form.

"Your reservation is for three nights, but you can extend if you wish, sir," she said, handing him his room key. "I hope this nice weather lasts for your visit!"

Frank made no comment about the length of his stay or the weather. His original reservation had been for a week. "Uhh...yes, thanks," he managed. "Are there any messages for me?"

"Oh, almost forgot!" She pulled an envelope out from under the counter and handed it to him.

"This was dropped off earlier this morning for you, Mr. Archer."

Frank's room was on the second floor and looked out over the river. The room was stuffy, so he turned the air conditioner to 'high' before opening the envelope. Inside was an embossed invitation card and a slip of paper with a phone number. The invitation was to a reception at the Cote Verde Consulate tomorrow afternoon at 3 p.m. The reception was in honor of dignitaries from that country in New York for the opening session of the United Nations next week. Frank stared at the card for a moment, dredging his memory for what, if anything, he knew about the country. Puzzled, he set the invitation aside, reached for the phone, and dialed the number.

Cote Verde...a new country somewhere on the west coast of Africa? He vaguely recalled reading about it some time ago, but couldn't remember details.

THE MAN WHO ANSWERED THE phone was friendly enough, and identified himself as Karim. He apologized for having made the change to Frank's original hotel plans, and asked if he was comfortable at the inn.

Archer muttered a non-committal 'yes'. The motel itself was adequate in that it had a decent restaurant plus all the usual in-room amenities. But, from studying the city guide and maps, he learned he was miles away from the tennis stadium. Karim agreed, and for that reason a car and driver would be available to him throughout his stay. The change was a security precaution, he added, without further explanation.

"Did you notice any sign that someone might have been following your car?" Karim asked.

During his trip to France in June, Carlos had given him a short lesson on how to spot a tail; vary his route when driving to and from the club; use different locations to check his email, note the other patrons in restaurants, that sort of thing. Francois took it all with a grain of salt, and half-heartedly followed his cousin's advice for a week or so before giving it up as a waste of his time. *I can't play the spy game*, he'd mused. *I'll leave that to Carlos and his band of conspirators.*

"Not that I noticed", answered Archer brusquely. "So what should I do now that I'm here? Stay in my room until you come for me?"

Karim picked up on Archer's evident frustration from his curt replies. "No, no, Francois, that's not necessary. Please be patient. A car will pick you up tomorrow afternoon and bring you to the reception. I will make myself known to you soon after you arrive," he said. "All your questions will be answered and then you can enjoy the tennis matches.

25

TUESDAY, SEPTEMBER 7

The diplomatic plates on the black sedan were the first thing Frank noticed when it pulled up in front of the Holiday Inn. The vehicle belonged to the Cote Verde Consulate, according to Raoul, the driver. He asked Raoul about the unfamiliar country. Archer was right as to Cote Verde's location, but not its age. The small country had gained its independence more than fifteen years ago.

The trivia about Cote Verde was all Raoul was prepared to talk about, so Frank abandoned his efforts to engage him in conversation for the rest of the one hour trip.

"Welcome, Francois." The man extending his hand had been standing just inside the entrance to the salon where the reception was underway. "I'm Karim."

"Thank you," said Frank, as they shook hands. Karim, like himself, was light-skinned and approximately the same age. Forty at the most, was Frank's guess. His slick-backed dark hair and pencil-thin mustache reminded him of the actor David Niven.

"Can I get you something to drink? Tea or coffee? Or something cold, perhaps?" he asked, steering Frank towards a nearby corner. Frank opted for iced tea, and his host headed for the long serving table laden with beverages and canapes. It gave the visitor a chance to look around the noisy room.

The salon was a lot smaller than it had first appeared to Frank, which probably contributed to the high noise level. He didn't think there could be more than fifty to sixty people in attendance, most of them men. A nearby group in African tribal dress were having an animated discussion in French, although Frank couldn't make out the topic because they were all speaking at once.

When Karim returned, Frank asked about the guests of honor. "Ahh," he shrugged. "They have been delayed, apparently. We may not see them at all. But that's not why I arranged for us to meet this way."

Frank quickly lost interest in Karim's small talk, but nodded politely from time to time. He was dismayed when he sneaked a peek at his wristwatch to see that only thirty minutes had passed. It felt more like two hours. His host appeared to waiting for someone. The only thing he'd learned was that Karim was not FOX. Even though Frank had almost whispered the question, Karim blanched noticeably and cautiously peered around before replying with a shake of his head.

Frank was about to apologize for his 'loose lips' when Karim interrupted him. "Just a minute, Francois," he said, and answered his cell phone. "Yes, we will leave now," he heard Karim say. "Come Francois, time to go. Follow me, please."

They left the consulate via stairs to the basement level. Karim ushered him into a beige Toyota that was parked in the small compound behind the building. Archer noticed its New York plates and absence of a CD designation. A few minutes after leaving the consulate, Karim turned onto First Avenue, heading north, and they were immediately caught up in rush hour traffic. A clock on a bank building read 4:22, as they inched their way past the United Nations building. Traffic began to move slightly faster once they reached the Queensboro Bridge. After they had crossed the bridge, Karim turned left. An overhead sign told Archer they were headed for La Guardia Airport. Just after they passed a sign indicating the airport was one mile ahead, Karim veered into the right hand lane and exited the freeway.

"Not that far now," he said, when they stopped at a red light. They were in the borough of Queens, according to a sign post, and traffic had once again become a stop-and-go cacaphony. Three lights later, Karim turned down a narrow side street lined bumper-to-bumper with parked vehicles. From movies and TV shows he'd watched, Frank realized that they had entered a working class neighborhood; post-war clapboard houses on narrow lots; a small, dusty park full of black and white kids playing football; and a tavern on the corner. Most of the houses were in good condition, with neatly-kept lawns, as opposed to the few with broken windows and badly in need of a new coat of paint.

Frank was still baffled as to where they were heading when Karim turned up a back alley and pulled into a wooden, one-car garage. Without a word, Karim led him through a small backyard and into a shed attached to the two-story house. "Go through the kitchen. Someone is waiting for you in the front room," he said, opening the back door.

The blind on the kitchen's only window was pulled down, and Frank paused in the dim light to get his bearings. Sunlight was still visible through an alcove to the front room, and he stepped hesitantly through it.

"Welcome my brother," said the room's lone occupant, rising from a sofa to greet him.

Frank went into shock—there was no other word for it—and his legs gave out. Only the back of a chair he grabbed prevented his complete collapse. He tried to speak but words wouldn't come. The ghost stepping forward to hug him was his 'dead' brother, Rene.

THEIR REUNION LASTED WELL INTO the early morning hours. Hours that saw Frank's emotions range from disbelief, anger, and fear, but ending with a slight sense of relief. Rene began with a long and apologetic explanation about his disappearance, the subterfuge that led his siblings to believe he had been killed in the mountains of Algeria in 1993.

Unlike his brother, Rene had heeded their uncles' wishes and converted to Islam. Restless and out of work, he had jumped at the chance to join the Islamic uprising in Algeria. He'd taken part in savage battles against the heavily armed and well-trained government troops for almost two years. During one of the last battles between the opposing forces, he had been seriously wounded. His cunning and bravery in combat had caught the attention of his leaders, however. Instead of being left behind to face certain death at the hands of the army, he had been whisked away to a rebel safe haven. Eventually he was moved to Libya, where he endured a long recovery from his injuries. After the insurgency ended in defeat and he was well enough to travel, he ended up in Afghanistan.

Two years of intensive training and indoctrination at a training camp funded by Osama bin Laden followed. In 1997, he returned to France with a new identity, living in and around Bordeaux, and strictly forbidden to have any contact with his family. He was a sleeper agent for the soon-to-be infamous al-Qaeda. He was never given an assignment during this time in France. Three months after the 9/11 attacks in New York and Washington, he received new orders. He was to move to New York and live undercover until called on. He arrived in the US after a circuitous route in the summer of 2002. Once again, he had a new identity and papers, and access to funds for his daily needs.

He turned aside Frank's questions about how he'd made his way to the US, and wouldn't reveal the identity he was using now. He had a job with a cargo handling company at nearby JFK International Airport, one that let him maintain a low profile and provided a decent income, he told his brother.

When Frank came right out and asked him if he had played a role in the 9/11 attacks, Rene quickly denied any involvement. "I never set foot in America until two years ago, and this is my first assignment for the cause, Francois."

"Then you... are you—" Frank stammered, a stunned look on his face. "Yes, I am FOX."

Before his bewildered brother could speak, Rene launched into a fervent explanation of how and why he came to be a soldier for al-Qaeda.

"Our goal is to put fear once again into the minds of the American public, and we'll do it without causing civilian casualties. Think about the aftermath of our 9/11 triumph. People were afraid to leave their houses. The airline industry collapsed almost overnight. Not just here in America, but around the world! Some airlines will never recover. And look at the money being spent on security! Old people in wheelchairs being searched just to get on a flight from a small city in the middle of nowhere. Amazing!" The words were spilling out of Rene's mouth so quickly he had to stop to catch his breath. "So you see, brother, we can accomplish the same results with our plan as the 9/11 martyrs," he continued, calmer now. "No, we will leave the blood-letting to others, and believe me when I tell you that there are plenty of our brethren working on such plans. For my part, I am humbled our great leaders have chosen me for this task, and I pray that I can fulfill their trust."

Frank was reminded of similar exhortations he'd heard from Carlos, as Rene rambled on, peppering his speech with references to 'the cause', and infidels, and the hated enemies of the Muslim world, the American and British governments in particular. Israel and Zionists were also mentioned disparagingly.

"Well, as I told Carlos more than once, I am only in this for the money," Frank stated, when Rene finished. "If that upsets you, then maybe you don't want me involved."

Rene held up his hand and offered a rueful smile. "...I know that, brother, and we're happy with your commitment as it stands. We won't ask any more of you. Agreed?"

Frank nodded, and asked, "Who suggested approaching me in the first place?"

Rene smiled. "It was my idea, Francois. I had been informed about your marriage to the Canadian woman. And when you let on to Carlos that it was, ah-h... perhaps just for appearances sake, and you weren't really happy, that I thought you might consider joining us. And I hope you can understand that I couldn't reveal myself until you had agreed."

Frank shrugged, and for the first time since he arrived, showed obvious anger. "You mean that if I had turned Carlos down, I was never to know you were still alive? And what about our sister... was she ever to know your secret?"

Rene paused for a long time, and Frank thought he saw a tear trickle down his cheek. "...I don't know if I can answer those questions truthfully, brother."

Frank let the subject drop, and emboldened by Rene's obvious desire to make amends, said, "Then I think it's time someone told me just exactly what it is you're planning, don't you?"

"Of course. That's why I had you brought here tonight. Now what did Carlos tell you during his briefings?"

"Not very much," answered Frank. "Mostly he asked me to be patient, saying that I'd be given details of the plot after an American with a knowledge of explosives was recruited."

"Yes, and you are to be commended for finding him for us, Francois. We had been checking out possible candidates here in the US. By 'we' I'm referring to myself and Karim. There are plenty of right-wing extremists we discovered, most of them greedy. The greedy ones are also reckless, by and large, and we were looking for someone we could trust. Ruthless, perhaps, but not irresponsible."

"Well, I think we'll be okay with Allman, he seems quite level-headed to me."

"Good, he was checked out by resources available to people above me after you gave Carlos his name, and apparently nothing was found to indicate that he's other than an opportunist who has a beef against the army."

"Are there other members of the cell here or in Canada?" Frank asked. When Rene didn't answer, he continued, "I can't help thinking that there must be a connection to a few ah-h...*accidents*, shall I say, that centered around the private detective Carlos warned me about."

"We are a very small group, and that is by design," Rene eventually explained. "Karim, or should I say FARMER, has developed certain contacts—outsiders—that have been paid to carry out a few tasks on our behalf. I leave these dealings to him, and the less you and I know about these things, the better."

As the head of the cell's American arm, Rene's task was to put into action the plot that would see explosive-laden rail cars scattered about the country. Mobile bombs, in effect, that would be detonated at an opportune time. He'd studied maps, rail networks, and satellite images of prime target areas while deciding how this could best be achieved. His initial thought was to target the heavily-populated eastern seaboard region, but quickly rejected that scenario.

"Too crowded, and too hard to find a remote site," he said, when Frank asked why. "And that's the first task I want this American to undertake. Find a suitable location where trains can be accessed without fear of discovery."

Rene let on that there was a plan to smuggle the devices into the

States, and Allman's help would be needed both before and after the shipment arrived. "They'll be coming in via Mexico," Rene said, "and Karim will provide you with details once the time frame for the delivery is known."

When Rene was finished, Frank had one last question for him. "Am I missing something? You keep referring to 'explosive devices'. I thought that's why you needed a guy like Allman—to the make bombs."

Rene shook his head. "That was the original plan, but we need him for these other tasks now."

"I see. Should I tell him about the change?" Frank had told Rene that Allman was waiting in Denver for further instructions. "I'm supposed to contact him by the middle of September."

"No, leave it until later. If there is a problem getting the shipment across the border, we'll need him to assemble bombs for us," said Rene.

It was past midnight when Frank declared that he was exhausted and wanted to return to his hotel. Discussion of the plot had ended an hour ago, and they'd been reminiscing about their younger, innocent days. At the door, his brother hugged him again, kissed him on both cheeks. Rene's gesture was an unspoken apology, Frank realized, for the years he'd been just a sad memory to him

26

WEDNESDAY, SEPTEMBER 8

Don chuckled. Flanagan's Irish accent was most pronounced when he resorted to profanity. "Archer did cancel his hotel reservation. Did it on Monday morning, Don. The feckin' mental midget at the hotel who told me otherwise hadn't checked the proper file, apparently. Incompetent piece of shite!",

The message that Don had suggested be left for Archer hadn't been answered. The message asked him to call concerning an important change to his flight reservations. If he had responded, his call would have reached an answering machine and not been returned. But Flanagan would know that their suspect had checked in.

Two days after his supposed arrival, there was still no sign of Archer. Don had spoken to Jill McNeil yesterday and been told that the travel agency hadn't had any request to revise Archer's itinerary. She confirmed that her office had ordered a tennis pass for him, and it had been sent to his condo by courier two weeks ago.

Would it be worthwhile having Flanagan spend more time to try and locate him? Don wasn't sure. Once again Archer's actions were no doubt meant to foil any surveillance attempts. Identifying any contacts he met with in New York might advance his investigation, but probably more important was having Tom Allman on the inside. If, as expected, Allman heard from Archer in the next week or so, he should be able to keep tabs on him from then on.

THURSDAY, SEPTEMBER 9

It was an unexpected call from Chuck Todd, Empire North's security chief, that filled in some of the blanks for Don. "Hey, great to hear from you, Chuck. What's up?"

"Got time for a beer today? Might be a good time to pick each others brains."

An hour later they were seated in a bar near the Empire North building. Don had to park three blocks away and when he entered the bar he was sweating from the unseasonably high temperature. He paused just inside the door and took off his sunglasses. The dimly-lit room was nearly empty, and it was only a few seconds before he heard his name called.

"Over here, Don!" said the burly Todd, rising to greet him. Although they had never met, Don recognized his distinctive deep voice. "A bit on the warm side, eh? Looks like you could use a beer," said Todd as they shook hands.

"What was your first clue?" chuckled Don, sliding out of his suit jacket and loosening his tie.

He pointed at the frosted pitcher of lager the waiter was just depositing on the table. "That should be enough for me, what're you going to drink?"

By the time they had emptied the first jug, the two ex-cops had traded backgrounds and shared a few laughs. Chuck Todd had put in twenty years on the Toronto police force before taking early retirement to work for Danielle Clyde. Don got the impression that Todd hadn't been a big fan of the changes demanded by politicians in recent years. The so-called 'political correctness' rules, his perceived leniency afforded to criminals by the courts, and the public's increasing lack of respect for the men in blue had soured him on the job.

"So I've been told your work for my boss has ended. When did that happen?" asked Todd, after the waiter had delivered a fresh jug.

"Came as a bit of a surprise, actually. I got the impression that whatever had spurred her to hire me in the first place didn't matter anymore.

"Did you ever find out what her husband was up to?"

Don hesitated, but only for a few seconds. Here was a man he could trust, and one who might be able to help him. It took him fifteen minutes to recount what he discovered so far about Archer and the suspicious organization he was associated with. "There's no doubt in my mind that the attempt to kill Yvonne and the body on my front lawn are somehow connected to him," he summed up. "But I don't know how they got wind of my investigation."

Todd listened without comment, and hadn't touched his beer for the last ten minutes.

"Boy, that's all rather disturbing," he offered quietly. But why would this uhh... *conspiracy*, need someone like him? Or taking it a step further, why would he want to get involved? I mean the son'ova bitch has it made, doesn't he? Cushy job, no hassles from Ms. Clyde."

"Well, yeah, those are good questions, Chuck. I don't know what his motives are, other than his apparently strong feelings against the US government," said Don.

"Money?"

"Probably an incentive, yes. These terrorist organizations always seem to have unlimited financial backing. I'm sure he's gonna get a good pay off for his help." Don pause and drained the last of his beer. "But I can see why he would be an advantage to them. He's been living here for some years, and knows his way around, that sort of thing. Apparently he speaks almost flawless English, and he doesn't have the swarthy features one would expect from a man whose father was native of North Africa."

"He can pass for a white man, you mean. Not an Arab."

"You got it. After 9/11 that's an advantage, especially moving about the US."

"And since that's where the plot is supposedly to take place, you're sticking with him, right?"

"Uh huh, and with Allman in his confidence, I'm hoping we'll get enough warning to thwart it. Or turn it over to the authorities."

"Yeah, well, don't play the hero, my friend. Take my advice and get them in the picture as soon as you know for sure what they're up to."

Don nodded. "Yeah, we will," and on a lighter note, added, "I know my limits, Chuck. I'm a lover, not a fighter!"

"Hey, nothing wrong with that," he said, reaching for his glass. "So at the moment he's supposed to be in New York, but hasn't been spotted."

Don nodded. "Allman should be hearing from him soon, and we'll pick up his trail from there."

"I see. Well, I don't know how—or if—what Ms. Clyde let on the other day will impact on your investigation, but here's what I learned..."

Danielle and Frank were to be divorced, sooner rather than later.

"Well I'll be damned!" exclaimed Don. "She had sort of explained their relationship when she hired me. But I thought they were to stay married for a few years yet."

"And you were right. She didn't offer any reason for the change, just told me that once Frank moved out of the company condo I was to check it over, and inventory it."

"Any time frame mentioned?"

"Not really. Said she'd let me know when he moved out."

THEY EXCHANGED CARDS, SETTLED THE bill and were on their way out when Don glanced up at the large TV screen over the bar. It took a second look to register what he was seeing...

"There's the SOB right now!" he said, grabbing Todd's arm and pointing at the TV. A banner under the picture proclaimed 'Live from the US Open'. A sportscaster was interviewing a towel-draped player at courtside. The sound was muted. "The guy in the blue shirt, second row, just to the left of the announcer with the mike. That's Archer!" Don told the puzzled Todd.

"RICHIE! WHERE ARE YOU?"

"Uhh...at Shea stadium watchin' the Mets. Why?"

"I just spotted Archer. He's watching tennis right now." Don described Archer's distinctive blue polo shirt with a yellow logo over the breast pocket. "He's sitting just to the right of the tunnel the players use to get to and from the court, said Don, checking his watch. It was 2:35. "He'll probably be there for another two hours or so. Think it might be worth trying to pick him up when he leaves?"

"Definitely! I'll head down there right now. The Mets are gettin' their asses kicked by the Dodgers anyway. Will call when I get there."

"Good show, Richie. I'm sure he won't have his own wheels, so I'd watch for him near the taxi stand."

AS SOON AS HE GOT home, Don tuned into the tennis telecast. The cameras panned by Archer's seat location three times in the next hour, and each time he called Richie on his cell to let him know that Archer was still inside. Just after 5:30, the match between two top-ranked female players ended. Cameras were on them as they shook hands, and made their way towards the tunnel. Archer was gone. He speed-dialed Richie's number.

"He's on the move, Richie! Sometime since my last call."

"I hear ya'. No sign of him yet," came the reply. "I've got a good...oh shit! There he is! Call ya' back!" The line went dead.

TEN MINUTES LATER DON'S PHONE rang. "There was a guy with him, and they were picked up by a Mercedes with diplomatic plates," Flanagan reported, sounding out of breath. "There's no way I could follow them. Couldn't get a cab in time."

"Well, nice try, anyway, Richie. At least we know he's there," said Don.

The vehicle was sporting a country flag alongside the CD decal, but Flanagan didn't recognize it. Its description didn't ring a bell with Don, either. "Hang on while I get to my computer. I'll Google it," he said. He typed 'National flags' and the search engine came up with a number of sites. The second link he clicked on gave him the answer. "Here it is, yellow and green diagonal stripes with one red star, right?"

"Yeah, that's the one," replied Flanagan. "So where's it from?"

"A place called Cote Verde. It's on the Atlantic coast south of Morocco," Don replied.

27

MONDAY, SEPTEMBER 13

Frank's thoughts were still riding an emotional roller coaster four days after the reunion with his brother. The shock and disbelief brought on by his brother's reappearance was slowly waning, but one thought wouldn't go away. The fear that both of them might spend the rest of their lives in prison if authorities got wind of their plot.

On the other hand, he was glad that his brother, Rene, and not the more radical Carlos was in charge, now that the plot was entering the operational phase. He'd been trying to clear his mind and concentrate on driving, but isn't wasn't working. He still wasn't sure of their real motives, for instance. Were Carlos and his brother committed jihadists? He didn't think so. He couldn't recall either of them using the term 'holy war', which radicals usually meant when they spoke of a jihad. And he did think they were being honest about not wanting to kill people.

Karim—FARMER—on the other hand, struck him as a completely different case. Frank came away from their meetings thinking that he would relish a little blood on his hands. He'd read and heard enough about terrorist training camps to know that recruits had hate and loathing for infidels drilled into their heads before they graduated. And Karim, had been schooled at one of the most notorious camp, Rene had let on.

At their last meeting they had discussed what Frank should do with his car. *Should he just abandon it at the Buffalo airport? Wouldn't it eventually arouse suspicion?*

Probably, but it could be weeks before it was noticed, Karim had suggested. "The longer it sits there, the greater the odds that thieves targeting expensive cars in the long-term parking lot will notice it and make it disappear. "Voila! Problem solved."

FRANK WAS ABLE TO PUT the flashbacks of his New York visit on hold for a brief time when he stopped at a travel center for gas and coffee.

When he pulled back onto the freeway, a sign told him he was fifty miles from Buffalo. He was thinking again about Rene, Karim, and what was expected from him in the weeks ahead when he encountered a line of thunderstorms just east of Buffalo. It was still raining as he took the off-ramp to the airport.

Seconds later, his lack of concentration and the road conditions almost cost him his life...

The driver of the semi-trailer he was close behind had taken the tight turn on the still rain-slicked pavement too fast. When he hit the brakes the large rig jack-knifed right in front of Frank's BMW, leaving him only a split second to react. Rather than smash head-on into the mass of wheels rapidly filling his windshield, Frank jerked the steering wheel hard to the right. The BMW cleared the rear of the semi by inches as Frank instinctively ducked across the passenger seat. The car spun twice down the slippery grass slope before the rear bumper crashed against the corner of a cement culvert.

In shock, Frank slowly opened his eyes and struggled to sit up straight, a move made difficult because of the incline. Eventually he heard a woman's voice, but couldn't see her.

Then it hit him. The jarring stop had activated the onboard emergency communications system. The woman asked if he was injured. Did he need an ambulance?

Dazed, Frank realized a response was necessary. He didn't seem to be hurting anywhere, and managed to assure the concerned operator that he was okay. When she asked again if he needed assistance, he was able to convince her he didn't need help. The first person to reach him was the driver of another semi-trailer who had witnessed his wild ride off the road. He asked the same questions. Frank managed a weak smile and told him he wasn't hurt. The seatbelt had saved him from serious harm, although he'd twisted his back. The driver helped him from the car as a siren announced the approach of the first police cruiser to reach the scene.

AN HOUR LATER THE BMW had been winched back up to the pavement. Remarkably it had sustained very little damage. Hitting the culvert had left a large 'V' in the rear bumper, and the resulting jolt had set off the alarm system. The trunk lid was also creased. Other than that, the vehicle appeared to be unmarked. It was still driveable, he told the state trooper.

"Then you were very lucky, sir," the trooper answered, as he handed back Frank's driving licence. "And you're free to go. My report will be on file at this office," he said, handing Frank a card with the contact information. "Just give it to your insurance company when you get home."

Frank thanked the policeman. *No way that's going to happen,* he told himself.

The jack-knifed semi had been straightened out and moved to the shoulder. Another trooper was directing traffic past it. He stopped the slow moving stream to allow Frank to pull out and get past the wreck. Twenty minutes later he pulled into the long-term parking lot at the Buffalo airport, shut off the engine, leaned back, closed his eyes. He sat motionless for the better part of five minutes, giving his still-racing heartbeat time to slow to a more normal pace.

Frank checked his watch while he waited for the shuttle bus to the terminal. Had it not been for the accident, he would have had three hours to kill before his flight departure. Now, though, his wait was down to an hour. During the short ride to the terminal, he rechecked his pockets to ensure he had his valuables: wallet, passport and e-ticket and sunglasses. He was traveling light, with only a carry-on bag. The cases he'd left behind in New York City would be shipped to Arizona after he was settled.

By the time he checked in, made his way through the security process, and bought a coffee and sandwich, his flight was boarding. He had asked for a window seat at the rear of the plane and was one of the first passengers to board. After a cursory check of his new passport and boarding pass, the gate agent said, "Enjoy the flight, Mr. Gagne."

The nearly-full aircraft pushed back from the gate on time. As the Southwest Airlines flight to Phoenix taxied towards the runway, a bubbly flight attendant gave the usual emergency briefing to a mostly disinterested audience. She did get a few chuckles when she invited the passengers to relax and enjoy any turbulence they might encounter. Her light-hearted remark went right over the head of the petite, white-haired lady seated beside him. Her death grip on the armrest between them tightened noticeably at the mention of turbulence.

EVEN THOUGH HE WAS DEAD tired, having been up since 6 a.m., sleep eluded him as the Boeing 737 cruised over the Midwestern states. The mental comedown from his near miss on the freeway probably accounted for some of his restlessness. Adding to it was how best to handle what needed to be done after he got to Phoenix.

Supplies critical to the operation were to be brought into the country from Mexico, smuggled across the border somewhere in southern Arizona. The time frame was early November. Frank would receive details two or three days in advance. He should reconnoiter the area to familiarize himself with the roads and check points, and accomplish it no later than mid-October.

"Do it during the day to lessen your chances of drawing attention from the Border Patrol or local police officers," Rene had advised.

Frank wasn't too sure he could handle it on his own, and suggested that he should get Allman to help him. Rene balked at first, because he was against Allman knowing more than necessary about the overall operation, but eventually relented and gave his okay to involve the American. Arranging a safe location to hide the shipment was also to be Frank's responsibility.

I'll need Tom's help with that, too, Frank thought, but kept it to himself.

RATHER THAN BE DRAWN INTO conversation with the still-jumpy lady seated beside him, Frank feigned sleep when a flight attendant stopped the food and drink cart at their row. He was thinking again about his last few days in New York. He'd met Karim twice at restaurants near Arthur Ashe Stadium. Karim had accompanied him to the matches on Thursday afternoon and their box seats were only yards from center court.

"Connections," he'd smiled, when Frank had asked how he'd managed the choice location.

Reflecting back on it now, Frank realized that no matter how innocuous Karim's probing seemed to be, he was being vetted again as to his commitment and able to handle his role.

He was also grilled about his future once his part in the mission ended, specifically, whether he would need to return to Toronto to finalize his divorce. Frank didn't think that would be necessary, and he planned to fly directly from the US to Europe. The initial money he'd demanded from his wife had been deposited in his Swiss bank account, he'd told Karim, and any documents requiring his signature could be handled by courier. Rather than phone his wife and tell her that he wouldn't be back—as he'd been planning—Karim suggested an alternative.

Frank agreed, and last night he'd left a message on Danielle's private office line, knowing she wouldn't pick it up until this morning. He told her that he would be leaving for France directly from New York. A trip of indeterminate length to deal with possible business ventures, he'd lied. That way, Karim reasoned, no one should be looking for him in the US. He could put off contacting her until he did actually return to France. Saturday morning they'd met for the last time. Karim had greeted him with a big smile, and their meeting lasted only as long as it took them to drink a cup of coffee. There had been no further talk about the plot. Frank would be given further instructions after he got to Arizona.

Karim had wished him luck and gave him weekend tickets for the same box at the stadium. The seat and the tennis action on Saturday and Sunday were the best Frank had experienced in his years of attending Grand Slam tournaments.

A faint smile crossed his face as he finally drifted off to sleep. In his head he was running down the list of code names that Karim had insisted he memorize as they were be used in all future correspondence between cell members. His brother, Rene, was FOX, while Karim was FARMER. Carlos was BREEDER and his own code name was GROWER. Omar, the spooky man who'd been with Carlos in London, was VET. Frank was to his 'minder' after he arrived in Phoenix. Details of his travel plans would be forwarded to Frank at the appropriate time.

Secrets, secrets, thought Frank, as his mind clicked off...

28

Don had just returned from a workout at his health club when Chuck Todd called.

"So what happened after you spotted Archer on television? Did your man catch up with him?" asked Todd.

"Yeah," Don told him, "Flanagan got to the stadium in time to see Archer leaving. But it was a one-time sighting." The New York PI had watched for Archer again on Saturday and Sunday without success. "Too many people and too many gates to watch, although I'm sure he was there."

Don had Rollie Parsons stationed at the airport to see if he returned to Toronto on his booked flight, but that had been no sign of him. "So I'm still in the dark as to where he is now or how he's moving around."

"Well, I can tell you how he got to New York—he drove there," said Chuck..

"Hmm, I wondered about that. There hasn't been any sign of his 'Beemer' all week. We've been checking his parking spot."

"That's because it's sitting in a parking lot at the Buffalo airport."

"Buffalo? So he drove that far, and then—"

"Got on an airplane, most likely. All I know is that Archer was in the Buffalo area on Monday," Todd replied. "And I'll tell you why,"

The leasing dealership had been contacted by the company that monitored the onboard alert system. It was a follow up inquiry to advise they had received an onboard alert from one of the dealership's vehicles. The leasing manager hadn't no knowledge of the accident, and, when he was unable to contact the registered driver, Mr. Frank Archer, he called Empire North.

"When this query reached Ms. Clyde, she called me in and asked me to check it out," explained Todd. "She also told me that as far as she knew, her soon-to-be ex-husband was in France. Maybe he is, but his car is sitting in the airport parking lot. The BMW's onboard GPS confirm it."

Todd had contacted the State Police and eventually tracked down a clerk with access to the report written up after Archer's accident.

Don was having a hard time putting this latest information into perspective. If Archer had been driving back to Toronto before the accident, why did he change his mind and head for the airport? Or was that his destination all along? Presumably, he was headed there to take a flight. After all, the plot he and Allman were part of was to go down somewhere in the US. Perhaps he planned to fly back to Buffalo to pick up the car sometime later... but when?

"Jeezus, Chuck, I don't know what to make of this. But the bugger's trying hard to keep his whereabouts a big secret. He heads off, supposedly to watch a tennis tournament, and then disappears. Probably met with another cell member."

"Well, we might get a chance to throw him off stride. How'd you like to take a drive to Buffalo with me? I'm heading down there on Saturday to retrieve his car."

SATURDAY, SEPTEMBER 18

Don had quickly accepted Chuck's invitation, and by 10 a.m. on a misty morning they were inching forward in the lineup on the Peace Bridge connecting Fort Erie, Ontario to Buffalo. Fifteen minutes after starting down the US side of the bridge, Don pulled up to the customs and immigration booth in lane seven. He handed their passports to the unsmiling and youngish-looking agent.

As the agent flipped through them, he asked, "What's the purpose of your visit, and how long do you intend to be in the US?".

"Headin' for the stadium hopin' to get some tickets to next week's Bills game," smiled Don. The home opener for the city's NFL team was on the following Sunday. This broke the ice with the young agent and, after a short discussion about the team's prospects for the upcoming season, he returned their passports and waved them through.

Twenty minutes on the freeway brought them to the airport exit. The signs to the long-term parking lot were easy to follow, and Chuck spotted the blue BMW after a short search. There was an empty spot beside it, and Don wheeled in and shut off the engine. Both men got out and examined Archer's car.

"Boy, if this damage had been to the front end, he wouldn't have been able to drive away," said Todd as he ran his hand over the bashed-in trunk.

Don was on one knee, looking under the rear end. "Nope, he was lucky that way. Even the muffler and tailpipe have only been scraped."

The dealership had supplied Todd with a duplicate set of keys, and he used them to open all the BMW's doors. Archer had not left any personal effects inside, but he had overlooked two items that provided the investigators with clues.

"Yeah, this make sense," said Chuck, studying the parking ticket he'd found on the floor. "It's time-stamped at 4:17 p.m. on Monday. The accident happened about two-thirty. He must have been on the road real early if he started from New York City."

Don had been studying an area map of the city left on the passenger seat. A circle had been drawn around exit 38. It was not the exit one would take to reach central Manhattan, he surmised. But it might be why Archer never showed at the hotel he'd been booked at originally. He checked the glove box and under the seats hoping to find a receipt, a brochure, or any evidence of where he might have stayed.

"Nothing?" Chuck asked, when Don straightened up.

"No, this is it," he said, handing him the map.

While Don was searching the interior, Todd had been trying to open the trunk. "Guess we'll have to wait until we get it back to Toronto to find out if he left anything in here."

After a short discussion, the two investigators decided there was nothing to be gained by hanging around any longer. Todd started the BMW and checked underneath for leaks. "It's clean, so I'm off. They had agreed to return via the Rainbow Bridge at Niagara Falls, approximately twenty miles north of the airport.

"I'll be about twenty minutes behind you if you have any problems with the Beemer," he told Chuck before he pulled away. "I'm gonna' make a quick stop at the terminal."

AN HOUR LATER DON PULLED into a Tim Hortons coffee shop in Niagara Falls, Ontario, where Todd was waiting for him.

"Any hassle at the border?" Don asked.

"No problem. The officer looked at the damage but didn't say anything. Think he was nearing the end of his shift. What were you after in the terminal?"

Don had gone into the terminal building to study the flight departures board. He was only interested in those scheduled to leave from five o'clock onwards. There weren't that many, and he eliminated those to east coast cities and Florida. There were none shown to Toronto or overseas. Four caught his attention. He jotted down their flight numbers, departure times and destinations: Dallas, Seattle, Los Angeles and Phoenix, Arizona.

"He could've gone anywhere, I guess. But I don't think he flew to France. Tom Allman is expecting to hook up with him out west somewhere," said Don. "Odds are he's still in the US."

After finishing their coffee, they continued their homeward trip. Westbound traffic was heavy on the Queen Elizabeth Way [QEW], and Don rather enjoyed tailing another car, something he'd hadn't had occasion to do for some time. He was still maintaining a seven or eight vehicle gap behind the BMW as they approached the turnoff for highway 410 North.

Don broke off his brush-up exercise and took the exit for Brampton and Yvonne's apartment. He had arranged to pick her up to spend the rest of the weekend with him. He vowed to forget about Archer until Monday and devote his full attention to the woman whom he still hoped to marry. And once this case was over he wasn't going to take 'no' for an answer...

TUESDAY, SEPTEMBER 21

Morning Chuck, what've you got for me?"

Not a hell'uva lot, Don," answered Todd. "Had a call from the car dealer's body shop yesterday afternoon. The trunk was empty when they finally got it open. Guess your guy had his luggage inside the car with him."

"I see. Don't suppose he's contacted Danielle Clyde, either."

"Nope, nothing, Don. But listen, are you free this afternoon?"

"... Well, I can be," he replied, guardedly. "What've you got in mind?"

"How'd you like to have a look around Archer's apartment?"

"Now you're talking!"

"Meet me in the lobby at one. And as you're no longer working for Ms. Clyde, this visit is just between us, okay?"

THURSDAY, SEPTEMBER 23

Don Carling was going over expense account reports from his team of investigators when Joanne buzzed him. "Tom Allman on the line, boss,"

Don swung his chair around and grabbed the phone. "Hey there! I was starting to worry about you, Tom. Everything okay?"

Allman's only contact with Don since he'd left for the States last month had been via two short email messages. The first had informed Don that he was established in Denver. The second, a week after Labor Day, advised that he still hadn't heard from Archer.

"Yeah, I'm good. Didn't have anything to report until now. Archer called last night with a job for me."

"Aha! Bet it has to do with explosives, right?"

"Well, not exactly, but it's leadin' up to that," replied Allman. "They want to me scout some locations, places that can be used to attach explosives to freight trains. I'm expectin' a package today with photos of suggested sites to get me started."

"Railways, eh? So that's what they're planning," mused Don.

"Yeah, that's what Archer let on. He didn't say—or maybe he doesn't know—what happens after I suggest a suitable location. He's still only the messenger for someone higher up in the cell, is my guess."

"Yeah, that makes sense," Don agreed. "When are you supposed to do this?"

"I'll get goin' as soon as I get this package. Probably head out tomorrow or the next day. It'll mean a lot of drivin', and they want it done by the middle of October."

"How did he contact you?" asked Don.

"Oh, via cell phone. I have two now, and I'm calling you on the one I brought with me."

"Good, let's restrict our calls to that number. Did he tell you where he was calling from?"

"No, but I've gone 'high tech' with the new phone. Got caller ID. He called from the 602, the area code for Phoenix, Arizona."

"That doesn't surprise me, he spends some time there most winters, apparently,"said Don. "Anyway, update me as often as possible. Oh, and did you give some thought to what we talked about before you left?"

"Yeah, I did, and I took your advice, pardner," replied Tom. "Couple of old army buddies, guys I can count on to cover my ass if needed."

The last time they met, Don had voiced his concern about Tom acting alone, especially once he learned when the plot was to occur. They didn't see Archer himself as a threat to Allman's well-being, but then again they figured other cell members would show up soon. If that happened before they were ready to turn their findings over to US authorities, Don worried that it could put his American investigator's life in danger. Tom had shrugged it off, but conceded he would think about it.

"That makes me feel better, Tom. Who are they?"

Hank 'Razor' Gillette and Charlie Minh were both ex-Green Berets whom he thought might welcome the challenge. Like Tom, they had found the grind of routine training boring after the adrenalin 'highs' experienced during their covert missions during Operation Desert Storm in 1991. They had stuck it out a few years longer than Allman, but were now on 'civvy street'. Both were eager to help after hearing Tom's story.

Gillette, a helicopter pilot, flew pipeline patrol for a natural gas company from his base near Amarillo, Texas. Gillette had been home when Tom called and assured him he could be available on short notice.

Charlie Minh now lived in Los Angeles and had been harder to find. The message Tom left for him two weeks ago wasn't returned until yesterday. Charlie, then aged 7, and his parents were among the last South Vietnamese to be airlifted out of Saigon during the American withdrawal in April,1975. His father had been a translator for US army intelligence and would have been high on the Viet Cong's hit list if he hadn't been extricated.

Minh had quickly been nicknamed 'Charlie Chan' by the members of Allman's team when he joined it in 1989. Despite his protestations that he wasn't Chinese, the moniker stayed with him. He didn't even look like the fictional detective's number one son', he claimed, but the team wouldn't budge.

Minh was at loose ends, he told Tom, having just returned from a fruitless trip to Vietnam. Although he couldn't prove it, his dead father's past probably figured in his failure to obtain the necessary permits to set up an export business. Like Hank Gillette, Charlie would welcome some action and could be ready on short noticed when required.

Don didn't mention the visit he and Chuck Todd had made to Archer's vacant apartment two days ago. The apartment had been vacated for good, was their joint opinion. A maid service cleaned his apartment once a week, and their last visit had been on Friday, September, 10. That explained the bed made up, and the towels and linens all clean and stowed in closets. The kitchen was spotless as well. The only personal items Archer had left behind were a pair of casual trousers, two shirts, and a pair of well-worn tennis shoes.

The only item of interest Don turned up didn't mean anything to him at first glance. The slip of paper, two inches square, was folded up in the breast pocket of one of the shirts. Two words were written on it, *'farmer'* and *'breeder'*.

"Any idea?" asked Todd when Don showed it to him.

"Nope, not a clue. Looks like a piece of paper from a memo pad, doesn't it? Something he just grabbed because it was handy to write on." The paper had an auto glass company's logo on it. They rechecked the kitchen drawers and the desk in the den but couldn't find a matching pad.

Don knew that his operatives had tailed Archer to Internet cafes around the city. *Maybe he was online when he wrote down the words?*

TWO DAYS LATER HE HAD his answer. His investigator, Rollie Parsons, found an Internet café using memo pads from the auto glass company. The manager had placed the pads at each of the outlet's twelve cubicles for the convenience of customers. When shown Archer's photo, he scratched his shaved head and shrugged.

"Yeah, he comes in here once in a while," he told Parsons, "but I haven't seen him lately. Why are you asking?"

Rollie ignored the question. "Can you remember anything about him? Was anyone with him, for instance?"

"Dunno. Never said much, always paid cash. That's about it."

"Do you keep records of your customers? Something to indicate when he was here last?"

"No, just log the number of the computer they use for time charges, that's all. Just a daily log. You sound like a cop, you know."

Rollie shook his head and smiled. "Thanks for your time, sport. I'll be on my way."

Later, over coffee in Don's office, Rollie recounted his visit to the café. "It would be like looking for a needle in the haystack to try and find email messages he might have received or sent," Don replied when Rollie suggested it. "Too many hard drives to check, even if he agreed to let us access them."

The two words, *farmer* and *breeder*, had been running around in Don's head ever since he'd found the note in Archer's shirt. Just like the refrain from a song that kept replaying on one's mind, and just as frustrating. About the only conclusion he'd come to was that they were probably code words. *But for what? Or who? Was there really an agricultural connection?* It was fruitless, he realized, to make anything of it without more to go on. After Rollie left, he decided it was time to pass the information on. He had Joanne place a call to Inspector Brian Roberts.

"Hi'ya, Don. What's up?"

"Well, it may be nothing, but here's something I've come across in my investigation ..."

29

SCOTTSDALE, THURSDAY, SEPTEMBER 23

Frank Archer had been holed up in an Inn Suites hotel since he'd arrived in Arizona. His original plan had been to stay at the Empire North condo. It was vacant, he knew, because he'd called the office at the complex before he left New York. The first Empire North clients weren't expected until late October. But Frank had second thoughts after his flight landed in Phoenix and changed his mind. Better to pick an unknown location, one that he hadn't used in the past.

The package containing the satellite photos had arrived in his luggage from New York. They didn't mean anything to him, but he was sure the American would know how to use them. He could see now why having a 'local' on the team was an advantage. Scouting remote locations would have been beyond his capabilities, and he was glad they'd left it to Tom.

Now that he was going to be staying in Phoenix for the foreseeable future, he needed a place to play tennis. He searched the yellow pages for likely venues, narrowing the list down to tennis clubs that advertised 'visitors welcome'. He'd already rejected the club that guests of the company condo had access to, in spite of his past success there with certain lady members. He was sure there were other clubs in Scottsdale where he could score, it was just a matter of finding the right one.

He mentally flipped a coin between the two clubs that looked the most promising from their ads. His decision made, he dialed the winner. The perky receptionist was most accommodating. Mister Gagne from Montreal would be more than welcome. Weekly or monthly memberships were available to visitors, and she was sure she could fit him into this afternoon's mixed doubles schedule.

DENVER, FRIDAY, SEPTEMBER 24

Tom rose early, eager to make an early start after sitting around for so long. His sunglasses cut the glare of the rising sun as he drove northeast on Interstate 76, heading for Nebraska. By 10 a.m. he had reached the town of Julesberg, Colorado, and pulled into a truck stop for breakfast. He was driving his four-year-old Jeep Commander, which he had placed in storage before moving to Alberta.

While he ate his breakfast of ham and eggs, he studied the aerial photos again of the sprawling Bailey Yard, the largest railroad facility of its kind in the world. He knew a bit about the yard because he'd watched a television documentary on it a few years ago. The grainy photos appeared to have been downloaded from the Google Earth website. The same applied to the other suggested locations, one in Texas and the other in New Mexico.

After reviewing the contents of the package Archer had forwarded to him, he'd gone online to update his knowledge of the Bailey Yard. He learned that an average of 120 trains passed through the yard each day. They wouldn't be able to target rolling stock, but in any twenty-four hour period there were hundreds of coal and freight cars waiting to be assembled into trains via a computer system specially-designed for the purpose. Two key questions, however, couldn't be answered from photos.

Did a reasonable number of trains stop at a given site for a short period? And could one approach them without being observed? A physical reconnaissance of the locations was needed...

As Tom approached the Nebraska border an hour later, it dawned on him that the rather loose terms of the search he was undertaking could work in his favor. He could pick a location that left him the best chance of sabotaging the operation.

Tom arrived in North Platte, home to the multi-use operation known as the Bailey Yard, by mid-afternoon. His first glimpse of the yard was from the bridge on Highway 83 where it crossed over the multiple track layout. The lines of idle cars, designed to carry various commodities, stretched for miles in either direction.

He checked into a motel, and watched television until he got hungry. After dinner at a nearby chain restaurant, he took a power nap. At eleven o'clock, he set out to begin his mission.

There were still plenty of vehicles on the road bordering the yard, and he blended in with the traffic until he found a spot where he could pull over unnoticed. He was now near the western boundary of the yard's eight by three mile area, all of which appeared to be well-fenced. He watched for half an hour before driving around to the south side and stopping again. By 1 a.m., he had rejected the Bailey Yard as a viable location. It was too well lit up, and a scene of constant activity. There was also a visible and random security presence inside the fence, jeeps he observed driving slowly along the perimeter, probably manned by armed guards. He returned to the motel and hit the sack. By ten the next morning he was heading south for Texas, en route to the second suggested location...

SATURDAY, SEPTEMBER 25

At noon he crossed into Kansas. With no reason to hurry, Allman kept his speed close to the posted 65 MPH speed limit for most of the afternoon. There was little traffic, and even the occasional stench from the vast feedlots near the highway didn't spoil his enjoyment of the rolling countryside. Daylight was beginning to fade when he pulled into a Best Western motel in Liberal, only a few miles north of the Oklahoma border. He was hungry and thirsty, and after a quick shower he headed over to the Beef Baron Steakhouse across from the motel. Happy Hour was in full swing and the sound system—too loud for his liking—was belting out Country and Western music to a noisy crowd.

Actually the music isn't that bad, he told himself as he drained his second Rolling Rock beer.

But I'll never admit that to Don! After a third beer, he moved on to the dining room and was quickly seated.

The sixteen ounce porterhouse steak, a fully-loaded baked potato, and a generous portion of beans took care of his hunger. He waved away the dessert menu, settling instead for coffee and Kahlua. In his younger days he would have returned to the bar to keep his buzz going, but 9 p.m. found him back in his room. Before turning in, he pored over a map of the western states and marked the route he would follow tomorrow to Amarillo.

Hank Gillette, his Green Beret buddy whom he hadn't seen for five or six years, lived near Amarillo. Tom called his number, hoping to catch him at home, but an answering machine picked up. He left his number and a brief message saying he would call again after he got to Amarillo.

When he woke up Sunday morning morning and drew back the drapes, he saw that a heavy fog had settled over the area during the night. So thick in fact that he couldn't make out the restaurant across the four-lane road where he had dinner last night. He spent the next couple of hours chatting with stranded truckers in the coffee shop next to the motel. From them he learned that the route he'd chosen paralleled railroad tracks for the most part. When the fog began to dissipate rapidly around 9:30, he set off to continue his quest. By the time he'd crossed the narrow Oklahoma Panhandle and entered Texas he knew he'd have to keep looking. The tracks were accessible enough, and there were any number of suitable spots to approach them under cover of darkness. However, he'd only seen three trains in the two hours it took him to reach Stratford, Texas.

After a coffee break, he turned onto Highway 287 and followed it to Amarillo, arriving early in the afternoon.

The city stretched out on both sides of Interstate 40, and he pulled into a no-name motel on the south frontage road. He checked in and paid cash for one night. His room was on the ground floor and faced south, which muted the constant hum from the busy Interstate traffic. The desk clerk had explained where the Amtrak station was located and, after checking to ensure the room's plumbing, lighting, and television were all in working order, he headed off to find it.

"How many freight trains pass through Amarillo every day?" he asked, once he got the attention of the bored-looking clerk in the booking office.

The pasty-faced young man scratched his right ear and wrinkled his forehead before replying. *Maybe answering questions about freight traffic didn't fall within his job description*, Tom thought.

After a second shrug, he guessed there could be as many as thirty or more, but most of them didn't stop.

"What about the ones that do? Where is the freight yard ?" Tom didn't think he was asking difficult questions, but once again the clerk hesitated, and Tom was glad he wasn't trying to book a trip to New York with overnight stops along the way.

"Must be somewhere out east," was the best he could manage.

Tom decided he could find it on his own. "Thanks, Einstein," he muttered, as he turned away.

He'd found the freight yard without difficulty, but almost immediately rejected it for his use. The only activity in the yard centered around the cattle industry. Beef on the hoof, no doubt destined for slaughter houses on the west coast or east of the Mississippi. Not much was happening on a Sunday afternoon, and, after watching a crew loading cows for thirty minutes, he drove away.

I'm wasting my time here, no doubt about it, he told himself. The ideal location wouldn't be found on these dusty, sun-baked prairie lands. The answer had to be further west.

Back at the motel, he got his laptop up and running and logged onto Google Earth. He was looking for passes where major highways crossed the Rocky Mountains. With so few options, he reasoned, the railroad builders probably used the same routes. After an hour's search, he'd make notes on a few 'possibles'.

The nearest site was in New Mexico, a few hundred miles to the west. As he had already paid for the room, he was left with the rest of the day to kill. He walked to a 7-11 convenience store near the motel and bought a six-pack of Lone Star beer. Back in his room, he debated calling Archer to see if there had been any new developments, but decided to wait until he had finished his search.

Halfway through his second beer, Razor Gillette called. His friend was flying pipeline patrol and wouldn't be back to Amarillo for another two days. "Stick around until I get back!" he urged.

"Sorry, pal, but I've got to move on before then. Maybe next time, huh?"

MONDAY, SEPTEMBER 27

The beer had worked as well as any sleeping pill, and Tom woke early and refreshed. The first light of day was filtering into his room after he'd showered and shaved, and packed his overnight bag. A cool breeze greeted him when he stepped outside, and a pink and mauve pastel was spreading across the horizon as he wiped dew off the Jeep's windshield. Fueled by a sixteen ounce cup of surprisingly drinkable coffee from the same 7-11, Tom was well clear of the city before most of its residents had stirred.

He was headed west for Albuquerque, Interstate 40 all the way. Shortly after 7 a.m. he stopped for breakfast at the first small town he came on after crossing the New Mexico state line. 'Land of Enchantment' read the large sign at the welcome center, but the first few miles didn't look any different than the last eighty or so of flat west Texas plains to Tom.

The topography started to live up to the state's slogan, though, as he approached Tucumcari. Traffic was still light, allowing him to take in the scenery while still watching the road. Small mountains, some dotted with oak trees, began popping up along the way. The subtle increase in the engine's RPMs was evidence that he was now gaining elevation with every passing mile.

His immediate plan was to check out the rail layout around the state's largest city. And at one location he'd spotted using satellite imagery, there was only one track across the highest point. If that were so, and two trains were approaching the pass from opposite directions, one would have to stop until the other cleared the pass. *How else could the system work?* Tom had thought as he scrolled the map.

THE FIRST HE HEARD OF the accident on the Interstate came via a traffic bulletin on the Classic Rock FM station he was listening to. When he stopped to gas up at a truck stop on the outskirts of Santa Rosa, he heard more details about the accident from the gaggle of big rig drivers clustered around the coffee machines. Two semi-trailers were on their side, completely blocking the westbound lanes thirty miles west of town. One driver had picked up a police bulletin on his CB radio advising that it would be two to three hours before the lanes were re-opened. Tom asked him if there was an alternate route.

"Nuthin' for rigs like ours, we just hafta' sit it out," the hefty, bearded fellow told him. "Real fuckin' piss off," he added for emphasis. "What'er ya drivin', Bud?"

When Tom told him, the driver steered him over to a large wall map. "You can cut down here on 60, and wind yer way over to I-25 this way." He traced the route with a crooked finger. "Narrow road, only two lanes, but it'll save ya sittin' on yer ass here all day."

"Thanks, pard, that's a good idea. Good luck to ya'," said Tom, extending his hand.

Sometimes when fate intervenes, good things happen, Tom mused two hours later. The unexpected detour had taken him to the ideal location...

30

PARIS, TUESDAY, SEPTEMBER 28

As Tom Allman racked up the miles in the southwestern United States, two seemingly unrelated murders occurred thousands of miles away, in Paris and London. Both were linked to Don Carling's investigation, although that wouldn't be known until much later. Finding the connection would involve anti-terrorism forces in four countries and private investigator Paul Boutin.

"DID YOU SEE THIS, PAUL? Wasn't this guy on the list?" Jacques Brunelle, Boutin's young agent, was pointing to a photograph in today's copy of Le Figaro. The body of twenty-two-year-old Salif Farka, a landed immigrant from Mali, had been discovered last night behind an apartment building in an eastern Paris suburb. Mali, a land-locked African country, had once been part of the French colonial empire.

Boutin pulled a file from his desk drawer and scanned the list of the Nouvelle Monde employees. "Yes, he's on it," he said, "a room service waiter, apparently." Boutin had obtained the list from his police source early on in the investigation.

"Did we check him out at the time?" Jacques asked.

"No, I don't see any reference to...ah, here it is. The police cleared him. He wasn't working that night."

Boutin returned his attention to the newspaper article. The victim had died from a gun shot to the head. The police were conducting their search for possible witnesses, hoping to establish a motive for the killing. The experienced investigator put his hands behind his head and tilted his chair back. Jacques remained silent, waiting for his boss's next words.

"Well, young man, there must be more to this than meets the eye!" Boutin was on his feet now, thinking out loud. "For one thing, most slayings in this area are gang-related, are they not?" Jacques nodded. "And," continued Boutin, "the victims are usually done in with knives, or switchblades, or maybe beaten to death. A bullet to the head—that has the mark of a different criminal element. I think it is time for another visit to the hotel."

BOUTIN'S CONTACT AT THE HOTEL Nouveau Monde agreed to see him this afternoon, after her lunch hour. When Paul surprised her by inviting her to lunch, she quickly agreed. And yes, he could come by her office first, in that case. He arrived at 12:30 and was immediately shown into her office. Fifteen minutes later he had all the pertinent information available on Farka.

The young African had worked at the hotel for six months before he was murdered. As part of the kitchen staff, his job was to retrieve trays, dishes, and other items delivered by room service waiters.

"Ah, so he wasn't actually a waiter in May," said Boutin.

"No, he was still apprenticing, then," answered Denise, the hotel's personnel manager, "although he probably did deliver the occasional order. He was promoted to room service waiter just a month ago."

And soon after that he suddenly quit. He hadn't given a reason, just called the kitchen and never appeared again. He would have been entitled to some pay, but hadn't arranged to pick it up.

"Hmmm...most unusual," offered Boutin. "Tell me, would he have had access to the rooms when he first started? A skeleton key, perhaps?"

"Well, we don't use keys anymore, but he would have had a card that opened all doors, yes."

"What about the security of these cards? Do employees take them home with them, for instance?"

"Oh no, that's not allowed. They must put them in a cabinet when they go off duty."

This information raised more questions for Boutin, but not ones Denise could answer. He'd have to see someone in the kitchen. "Thank you for your help, dear lady," smiled Boutin as he closed his notepad. "Now it's time for lunch and a glass of wine!"

The discovery of a young woman's body behind a vacant storage building was front page news in most daily newspapers. Faiza Kayani, 22, daughter of landed immigrants from Pakistan, had been stabbed to death. Her body was found less than a mile from the family home. The tabloids were playing up the 'honor killing' motive, even though there was no proof yet to warrant such speculation. The police were tight-lipped, saying only that it was too early to suggest a motive.

Detective Superintendent Derek Houghton and three members of his counterterrorism squad were huddled in his office, debating how her murder might affect their work. Her death had cast a pall of gloom over them: Faiza had been a confidential informant for Derek's squad.

The woman and her Muslim family—father, mother, brother and two younger sisters—lived in the large house at 786 Kilburn High Road. The house that Francois Amara/ Frank Archer, had been followed to by the Canadian private investigator, Don Carling, during Wimbledon week earlier this summer. At the time, the dwelling had been on a watch list because of her brother, Saahir. He'd become a 'person of interest' after being photographed at rallies led by a radical sheik. The counterterrorist force had marked the house for increased surveillance after Carling had given the information to DS Houghton.

Nothing came of the squad's renewed interest in the house, however, until Faiza called the anti-terrorism hotline. Houghton had authorized a covert meeting between Faiza and one of his officers, and subsequently interviewed her himself. Faiza was concerned about what she called her brother's suspicious meetings'. On three occasions that she was aware of, unknown men had come to the house late at night. The meetings were none of her business, Saahir, had told her in no uncertain terms. As a strong believer in her faith, Faiza didn't believe in the violence encouraged and abetted by an increasing number of young Muslim men in Britain, including her brother. She also believed that he was using his computer to communicate with the late night visitors.

Derek had serious doubts about using her, but she was most insistent that she wanted to help. Her apparent intellect—she was an 'A' student at the University of London—and her sincerity finally convinced him to enlist her. She readily agreed with the stringent terms he'd laid down. Faiza was to maintain a passive role only, not 'play the spy' by asking questions or trying to listen in on her brother's meetings. Houghton assigned a female officer, Sergeant Barbara Norman, to be her contact.

She'd met twice with Norman, but only to report that strangers had been to the house again. Surveillance teams had also noted the night visitors, but no worthwhile intelligence came from their monitoring efforts.

Sergeant Norman suggested a more risky move. In her meetings with Faiza, usually in coffee bars near the university, Norman learned that the Kayani family kept budgies, three cages of the chatty little birds.

Why not bug one of the cages? she thought, and suggested it to Faiza. When she was shown the small disk—only slightly larger than a fifty pence coin—the young woman was immediately keen on the idea. She assured Barbara she could easily hide one without risk. It was her task, with the help of her younger sisters, to keep the cages clean and replenish the bird feed. The cage in the large kitchen room, where the family took their meals, was the best place for the bug, she decided. Her father and brother entertained male relatives and visitors there, drinking coffee and talking, sometimes into the early morning hours. DS Houghton took a few days to think about it before he okayed the plan.

When the police revealed that the victim's brother had flown to Karachi, Pakistan, the day before her body was found, it provided the media with even more fodder to push the honor killing theory. But the continuing investigation by Scotland Yard threw doubt on that theory. Raiza did not have a boy friend of any religion, and her parents were genuinely distraught over her death. Her father could not explain his son's sudden departure for Pakistan, telling the police that he'd only learned of it the night before Saahir left. Nor had he said when he would be back.

"Do you think they found the bug, and realized she must have been planted it?" suggested one officer.

Houghton replied. "We don't think so, apparently it's still 'live', right Barbara?"

"Yes sir, it was still picking up voices as of last night. Her parents were mourning her, according to the translator." The older couple always spoke Urdu, their native tongue, when they were alone.

"Well, let's hope whomever takes over cleaning that cage doesn't find it," said Houghton.

"If it wasn't the bug, then perhaps something else she did may have raised warning flags," offered Sergeant Norman.

"That's certainly a possibility," agreed Houghton, "and sending Saahir off to Pakistan was just a ploy to mislead the police. I'd bet my last fiver it was a contract killing, ordered because of a misstep by the young lady."

"We'll go with that theory for now, and maybe the Yard's murder squad will find answers to back it up. No need to tell them of her connection to us just yet," Houghton told them. "So get out there and lean on our informants, all of them, let them know you'll pay well for good gen."

ALTHOUGH HE HADN'T INFORMED HIS team, there was one man the superintendent was going to share the information with. After the meeting broke up, Derek called Detective Inspector Rex Hart. Hart had first come to Derek's attention when he was assigned to Paddington Green Station in the late 1990's, as a newly promoted detective sergeant. He'd impressed Houghton with his work ethic and shrewdness in sorting through dozens of clues in complex investigations. His rapid rise through the ranks was due in part to the well-deserved high marks Houghton had given him in his periodic assessments. Their partnership ended shortly after 9/11 when Derek was tabbed for his new job. Hart was now second-in-command of the Yard's homicide division, and quickly agreed to meet Derek's for a drink later that afternoon.

Their meeting was productive, and when it ended Derek was satisfied that they were on the same wave length regarding the young Muslim woman's death. Hart was not directly involved with the investigation, but the officer in charge reported to him. The police were still working trying to determine a motive, including the possibility that a male relative had killed her.

Her mother told them that Faiza left for the university as usual around noon on Monday, and wasn't expected home until late. She'd said she was going to stay for an evening lecture at 7:30 p.m. From interviews with fellow students, detectives were able to confirm that Faiza had indeed attended the lecture. But no one recalled seeing her after the talk, and best estimates had her leaving the building at approximately 9:15. Her parents had not heard from her before they went to bed at 10:30.

Faiza usually traveled by Underground to and from the university, and often got off at the Maida Vale Station rather than the much closer stop, Kilburn Park on her way home. The longer walk was for the exercise it gave her, apparently. The building where she was found was approximately half way between the stations. A pedestrian had spotted the body just after dawn, and the coroner's report suggests she'd had been dead for approximately six hours.

"With that in mind, we started with two possible scenarios," Hart told him. "One, she'd been the victim of a robbery attempt that she resisted, or two, her killer had followed her from the university. But she hadn't been robbed. There was twenty or so pounds in a change purse in her book bag. And that area hasn't logged a violent mugging for two years."

"I see. And no leads from students at school that night, I take it," said Derek.

Hart shook his head. "Nor has an intensive canvass of the neighborhood found anyone who might have heard or seen what happened. The few tips received from the public have been discarded as well."

"But she was stabbed to death, right? I haven't seen the report, of course."

"Definitely. The autopsy confirmed that she'd been stabbed twice in the heart, killing her instantly."

"Just twice?"

Hart was quick to see what Derek was thinking. "Yes, I thought that unusual as well. I checked the files on so-called honor killings. Most of the victims had been stabbed a number of times, the relative venting his anger in a frenzy, if you will. This is different, though."

"Couldn't agree more, Rex. Doesn't fit the profile. And I'll tell you why."

Houghton revealed Faiza's role as one his confidential informants, and explained why he thought her brother's flight was a decoy to foster the honor killing motive. Hart nodded knowingly as he digested this information.

"Obviously I can see why you don't want this to become public knowledge, and I'll keep it under my hat for as long as you deem necessary," pledged Hart. "But I'll suggest to the investigating team that they steer their thinking towards the 'murder for hire' motive."

"Yes, I don't think you'll find that it was a relative," said Derek. "But locating her brother should remain a priority. It might lead the real perpetrators to believe they're in the clear."

"Right, it won't be easy, and it could take weeks. Have to jump through hoops with the authorities both here and in Pakistan, as you well know."

The two officers agreed to exchange any tips gleaned from informants, and Derek assured his colleague that if it would help solve the crime, he wouldn't hesitate to reveal her role as a confidential informant.

But he fervently hoped it wouldn't come to that. A number of threats had been made against Britain by those claiming ties to the 9/11 bombers, threats to punish the country for its support of the American-led war on Iraq. Scotland Yard's counterterrorism squad, in cooperation with MI5, had already thwarted two plots meant to rattle the British public. In both cases timely intelligence provided by CIs had been the key.

The alert status remained high, especially in the major cities, and the watch list of known radicals and possible recruits to their cause continued to grow. Developing reliable informants took time and patience. If word got out that Faiza Kayani had been an informant, DS Houghton knew others would be scared off immediately. Without inside information, uncovering future plots would be that much harder.

Derek had no doubts that homegrown terrorists were already planning future attacks. And, he feared, the possibility was high that eventually they would succeed. The fact that al-Qaeda, the Taliban, and other radical factions, could recruit suicide bombers with such apparent ease in the Middle East conflicts was never far from his thoughts. He'd racked up many sleepless hours wondering if the same tactics would be tried in Britain. Intelligence sources had already reported attempts to brainwash young English-born Muslims, hoping to turn them into martyrs. A recent secret report from MI6, the British equivalent of the CIA, noted that seven young males from the Birmingham area had attended training camps, known as Madrasas, in Pakistan last year. The religious schools were well-known breeding grounds for future suicide bombers, and MI6 figured the seven they knew about were but a tip of the iceberg.

31

NEW MEXICO, WEDNESDAY, SEPTEMBER 29

Archer answered the call in his usual brusque one-word manner. "... Yes?" A trait that the American found both ignorant and annoying.

"It's Tom. I've found a suitable location. Do you want the details now?" There was a hesitation on Archer's part and Allman thought he might have lost the connection.

"How far from Phoenix?" Archer asked.

"About a day's drive. It's in New Mexico."

"I see. Do you have any other places to check out? It might be better if it were closer."

It was Allman's turn to pause. He had marked an area in southeastern Arizona as a possibility, but didn't think it would have the same advantages. "Well, yeah, there's another one I can check. I'll head down that way tomorrow."

"Good. You're still ahead of schedule. Call me when you've seen it. Then I'll need you to come to Phoenix." Archer ended the call before Tom could reply.

"Friggin' jerk," he muttered, as he snapped his phone shut.

ALLMAN SPENT THE NIGHT IN Socorro, sixty miles south of Albuquerque on Interstate 25. As he nursed a frosted bottle of Corona in the Mexican restaurant next to his motel, he realized the small city would make a good jumping off spot for the planned operation. It had plenty of motels and restaurants, and lots of people about. But it was a good hour's drive from the location he'd surveyed. Albuquerque might be a better bet.

The next morning he headed south again, before turning west on I-10 at Las Cruces. It wasn't long before he spotted the rail line paralleling the freeway. A few miles on, he slowly overtook a long freight train. He was approximately two hours from the New Mexico-Arizona border, and the rail line was visible for most of the way. Although he passed a few stopped trains, there was no cover to work from. The same applied to the tracks in southeastern Arizona. By the time he reached Tucson, he was convinced that the mountain pass area in New Mexico was the best location to approach idling trains.

He reached Tucson by mid-afternoon and checked into a recently-renovated motel just off I-10. He'd opted for a room on the third floor, one that faced north towards the desert city's downtown skyline. He still had two beers left in his small ice chest, and opened one as he stepped through the sliding door to the room's small balcony. The outside temperature was pushing ninety, and Tom savored the still-cold brew as he studied a row of boarded-up motels on the north side of the highway, relegated to a slow death when construction of the Interstate cut off easy access to them.

32

LONDON, MONDAY, OCTOBER 4

"Barbara, I want you to listen to these," DS Houghton said, handing her a stack of tapes. The recordings had come from the bug Faiza Kayani had hidden in her family's kitchen. "The translator noted a few words that didn't make any sense to him, English words spoken in the midst of the native language the speakers were using. I want you to listen for them."

"Okay, sir. I not sure what you're referring to, but I'll have a go," Norman replied.

"Shouldn't be too hard to pick out, the rest of the talk will be gibberish to you. Get right on it, please, could be important," her boss instructed.

Houghton had enlisted a professor from Cambridge, a native of Pakistan and fluent in most languages spoken in the region, to translate the tapes. He had underlined the words in his printed transcripts, and commented that he wasn't sure if he'd heard them correctly.

"What were the words?" his sergeant asked.

Houghton shook his head. "I'd rather not say, Barbara. I don't want you to have a pre-conceived notion of what to listen for. They are probably code words, and I want to verify that."

Nor did he tell her why the confirmation was necessary. He was acting on a query from his colleague in Canada, Brian Roberts of the RCMP. Roberts had passed on the information that Don Carling had given him. The Canadian security forces couldn't shed any light on the words, but knowing that Carling's investigation had a UK tie-in, Roberts had contacted London.

The request from Roberts had actually arrived in DS Houghton's office last week, two days after the death of the squad's confidential informant, but Derek had been too busy to deal with it until now.

Derek's phone rang just after Sergeant Norman left his office. DI Rex Hart was on the line.

"We have a copy of everything on the hard drive," said Hart. "It wasn't easy, but the lads managed it."

"Excellent! Did they follow my suggestion?" he asked.

When Houghton had told Hart about Faiza Kayani being a CI for his task force, he'd made a request. Would it be possible for his officers to access the computer in the Kayani residence? The one Houghton thought her missing brother probably used?

"Yes, and it worked a charm."

At Houghton's suggestion, the officers investigating the murder called on the parents again, and told them it might help find the killer if they could check the computer for possible leads. As expected, the elderly immigrants were not computer-literate, and terms like 'email, viruses, and 'address book' went right over their heads. They had no objection, and showed them to the spare room where the computer rested. Neither parent had been in the room while the squad's computer expert downloaded everything on the hard drive.

"Good show, Rex. Anything on it to help your investigation?"

"Not really, but there are some emails that make no sense to us, but may to your chaps," said Hart. "I had them make a copy of the download for you. Just have one of your lads drop by for it."

TUESDAY, OCTOBER 5

"How did you make out, Norman? Thought it would have taken you longer," said Houghton, when his sergeant dropped a folder on his desk. "You look tired, though," he added, almost as an after thought.

Barbara bit her tongue. She had spent fifteen hours listening to the tapes yesterday, pausing only to use the toilet and refill her coffee cup. Dinner had consisted of a stale sandwich from the cafeteria at nine last night. Wired on caffeine, she'd taken a taxi back to her flat just before midnight. It was 3 a.m. before she fell into a deep sleep, only to be jarred awake a few hours later by her alarm clock. And now she had a splitting headache.

"Those were the only English words I heard them speak. There are the occasional exchanges in English on the tapes, usually between Faiza and her sisters. But these words were mentioned by men in another context." Barbara pointed to the first sheet of paper in the folder.

Houghton studied them for a moment. *Grower* was used four times according to Norman, *Farmer* at least a dozen times, and *Breeder* seven or eight times. And she'd heard one usage of the word *Fox*. To complete her report, she had referenced them to the dates they were recorded. All occurred during a three week period from late July to mid-August.

"Interesting," remarked Houghton eventually. *Grower, Farmer,* and *Breeder* coincide with what the translator heard, so that's the confirmation I was looking for. You're sure about hearing *Fox,* are you?"

"Yes, sir. I replayed it four times," she said, stifling a yawn. "That reference was on the last tape, by the way."

"Right. And we won't getting any more from the bug. It's been silent for three days and the techs figure its micro battery has died."

Houghton dismissed Norman with a "well done" and suggested she try to get more sleep. Once again Barbara held her tongue, putting down her superior's uncharacteristic manner to the tension she'd noticed in him since their informant had been murdered.

After Sergeant Norman left his office, Houghton composed a message concerning the code words, sent it to RCMP Inspector Brian Roberts in Ottawa, and the Department of Homeland Security in Washington.

At RCMP headquarters, the message was added to the file containing the first reference to the words received from Don Carling. The file was designated as 'active'. As such, information received from any source regarding the suspected code words would require immediate attention.

In Washington, however, it was a different story. When a search of the Homeland Security database returned a 'not known' tag to the words, the information was assigned a Class 3 rating, which basically assigned it to a 'back burner', so to speak. It would only be reclassified higher if newer or more detailed references were received. The vast majority of tips—hundreds a day—came from the public and were given a Class 4 or 5 rating.

33

TORONTO, TUESDAY, OCTOBER 5

"Morning, Sergeant. I hope it's good news. I was beginning to think you must have hit a dead end."

"Yes, well, we had stalled for a while. But we caught a break last week and we now know who was behind the wheel when Marlene Hastings was run off the road. And we're pretty sure this guy killed the Cuddy woman, too."

"Well done, Leon," praised Don. "How did you find him?"

"Well, this 'perp' isn't in custody yet. He's probably back in the States. We've asked the police there for their help in finding him."

"Sounds as if you're on the right track, though."

"Yeah, but it gets better...and more complicated. The break came when we caught up with Daniel Belanger, the ex-con from Quebec, and he started talking."

"The fingerprints on the pickup, right?

"That's him. He told quite a story..."

BELANGER WAS ARRESTED IN MONTREAL on September, 28th. The Quebec police were acting on a warrant issued by the Ontario Crown Attorney's office. Belanger's fingerprints had been lifted from the tail gate of the GMC pickup the police had confiscated. He'd been returned to Toronto and interrogated by Sergeant Belchers team.

"You're headed back to the penitentiary for violating your parole, for one thing," Belcher told him when Belanger demanded to know why he'd been arrested. "You weren't supposed to leave Quebec without your parole officer's permission, yet you've been here in our fair city consorting with some rather bad apples, haven't you?"

"No way, man! Never been here till now. You're makin' it up!" Belanger protested.

"Daniel, Daniel," sighed the detective. "You never learn, do you?" Belcher waved a folder containing a copy Belanger's rap sheet in front of him. "How many times has your sorry ass been hauled before the courts? Six? Seven? We don't have to make things up where you're concerned. We're smarter than you! You're just a dumb ass 'gofer', and you get caught every time!" Belcher slammed the folder on the table, startling Belanger. "And now you've been mixed up in a couple of murders. Guess you should've stuck to holding up corner stores in La Belle Province, eh?"

Belanger laughed off all allegations about his probable involvement in the murders until Belcher played his trump card. "Well, smart guy, your fingerprints are all over the pickup truck. How are you going to explain that to the judge. It's enough evidence to charge you with more than one serious offence, including murder." Taken aback by this revelation, his cockiness quickly wilted and he asked for a lawyer.

AFTER BELANGER'S COURT-APPOINTED LAWYER HAD reviewed the police file, he advised him that there was probably enough evidence to see him charged, not with Shirley Jane Cuddy's murder, but certainly with aiding and abetting. Without making any promises, the police suggested that if he cooperated, he might only face a charge of violating his parole conditions. The lawyer recommended he take the offer.

Belanger came clean. He had driven his ten-year-old van to Toronto to pick up a shipment of cocaine and transport it back to Montreal. A week after his arrival, he still hadn't been able to make contact with the drug dealer. He'd been directed to show up at the biker bar, and wait until he was approached. That's all. He had no name or phone number for the contact. When he let Montreal know, he was told there had been a problem and the deal had been delayed.

'*Sit tight*' he was instructed. He was basically broke, having run through the money he'd been given for expenses. The big money would only be paid to him after he delivered the drugs safely to Montreal.

On Saturday night, July 31, he was approached by a big guy he'd noticed drinking in the bar. This man introduced himself as 'Smoke'. Belanger already knew his name because he'd heard others use it.

"Anyway, to make a long story short, Belcher went on, "this Smoke character offered Belanger a few hundred bucks to help him 'drop off a parcel', as he put it."

"And that parcel was the body that ended up on my front lawn, I'm guessing," said Don.

Belcher agreed with him. Belanger had been using drugs while he was hanging out at the bar, he'd confessed, and that's why he was broke. He couldn't describe where he'd gone with Smoke, other than to recall it was about an hour's drive from the bar and in a rural area. And he had the date right. He knew it was the long weekend because he was going to head back to Montreal on Monday now that he had gas money. As it turned out, though, he hung around for a few more days and drove Smoke to the car lot when he sold the pickup. He denied having anything to do with Cuddy's murder, admitting only that she'd been in the bar most nights and was usually stoned. He couldn't be positive, but he thought he'd overheard her and Smoke arguing more than once.

"What the story on this guy? I presume he's an American."

"Well, we not sure yet, but yes, he's probably a Yank. We didn't get much info from the bar's manager, but one of the bartenders called us the next day. Calling, he said, because he had tried to help Shirley Jane Cuddy, and was pissed off when he heard she'd been murdered."

"Help her? How?"

"He'd tried to talk her into seeking help for her coke habit, but she wasn't having it. And apparently it was easy to score somewhere in the area, although he couldn't say who supplied her."

"So it wasn't Smoke, then?" Don asked.

"Don't think so. The bartender thought Smoke had first shown up around the beginning of July. Description fits with what you gave us initially and matches what we pried out of the Russian car dealer."

"So, early July. The fatal accident happened on July 14th, Don recounted. "That would've given him time to scout out the area around my place. But he must of had some local help. The Cuddy woman, maybe?"

"He did take up with her, apparently, although one of the bartenders didn't think it was a 'love at first sight romance, as he put it. And he didn't do drugs, if this guy was telling the truth. So it's not unrealistic to suggest that she just came in handy for his purposes."

"I see. But the unanswered question then is who was Smoke working for?" asked Don.

"Don't know, and that's where it gets complicated," replied Belcher.

THE OPP HAD CONTACTED AMERICAN authorities, hoping they could put a name to him. Their starting point was the New York State Police, whom they provided with his description and nickname. It would not have been the first time that a hit man from New York had been hired to carry out a contract north of the border. Most of them came from one of the crime families operating in Buffalo or New York City. But there were no references to this Smoke character in any of their data bases, including those devoted to the Mafia. The State Police then turned the information over to the FBI.

Two days later, a surprised Belcher received a call from the FBI. An agent from the Bureau's New York office wanted to know why the OPP was interested in the man. Belcher explained that the he was a suspect in two murders, and he would appreciate the Bureau's help in finding him. He did not mention the probable connection to Don Carling's investigation of Frank Archer. The agent thanked Belcher for his cooperation, but politely refused to reveal what, if anything, they knew about the man.

"So, the plot thickens, as the saying goes," said Don.

"For sure. I told him that a warrant would probably be issued soon for his arrest, and he assured me they would give it 'due consideration', whatever that means, said Belcher. "But I definitely got the impression that this guy is known to them.

BELCHER WAS RIGHT. THE FBI did have a file on him. 'Smoke' fit the description of one Lionel Jesse Barr, 41, six foot, two inches tall. The only discrepancy was the nickname. According to the FBI file, Barr's nickname was 'Crash'.

Barr had come to the Bureau's attention when he'd been observed with a man they had under surveillance. The man's name was Karim Ahmad Bakir, a trade attache to the Cote Verde UN mission. His position afforded him diplomatic status. But intelligence suggested that trade issues might not be his only interest. Bakir bore a striking resemblance to a man with a different identity who had been active in Hamburg, Germany, in 1999-2000. A man that German intelligence suspected of being the paymaster for Arab students in that city. Two such students, Egyptian nationals, were subsequently identified as members of the suicide teams that brought down the World Trade towers on September 11, 2001.

This information regarding Bakir only came to light during post 9/11 investigations undertaken by global intelligence agencies. He'd disappeared off the German radar screen in the fall of 2000, and nothing had been seen of him until the summer of 2003. An astute FBI analyst spotted his likeness while checking the list of newly-accredited diplomats arriving in the United States to take up posts with UN member countries. Bakir was subsequently listed for occasional surveillance by the FBI's New York personnel.

34

DON HAD ONLY BEEN HOME long enough to change into shorts and a T-shirt, when his cell phone beeped. He'd been going to take advantage of the still mild temperature and mow the front yard, hopefully for the last time this year.

"Don Carling," he answered, as he stepped out onto the patio deck.

"Don, it's Paul Boutin."

He immediately recognized the Frenchman's voice, but it came with a somber inflection that told him he was not about to hear good news. Not when a glance at his watch told him it was almost midnight in Paris.

"Hi, Paul. What's happened?"

"Well, a rather disturbing development, unfortunately."

"Okay, Better tell me about it."

"Don, I just got a call from someone I trust at the Surete. I can't believe it, but apparently they are close to charging you in connection with the prostitutes death. It's—"

The Canadian ran off a string of expletives, then quickly apologized for his outburst. "Sorry, Paul. Didn't mean to subject you to that. But Jeezus, what can they possibly base that on?"

"My friend, that's all I can tell you at the moment. This information came to me in confidence, and I don't know anymore about it yet. But I know you're innocent, and I'm still working to prove it. And on that score, there had been a promising development."

Don exhaled a frustrated sigh. "Well, I sure hope so, Paul. What happened?"

Boutin gave him a quick account of the murder of the former hotel employee, and why he thought his death was somehow connected to the murder at the Hotel Nouveau Monde. It had taken Boutin four days to track down a relative of the dead man. The young African immigrant had been living with an aunt, a woman with a different surname. From her, Boutin learned that Salif Farka's parents were both dead and she had sponsored his entry into France.

The aunt was surprised when the private detective showed up at her door. He'd finally found her modest apartment in a rent-controlled apartment block, two kilometers from the spot where Salif's body was found. The police had interviewed her twice, she told Boutin. The first visit was from a female officer who broke the news of his death, and the second, later the same day, when detectives questioned her about the victim.

Their questions centered on her nephew's known friends and whether or not he belonged to a gang. Salif had spoken of a few friends he'd made, buts she didn't remember any names. And he'd never brought them to the apartment. She was certain, she'd told the police, that her nephew would not have been involved with a gang, a point she emphasized again when Boutin brought it up. What she told him about his work, though, was more informative. Salif had been well-schooled in his native country, and got his job at the hotel through a local government placement agency less than a month after arriving in Paris.

As far as she could tell, he'd been quite happy at the hotel. She was taken by surprise when he suddenly quit. She became even more upset when Salif wouldn't tell her why. Instead, he took to staying in bed until late morning, then disappearing for the rest of the day. She had no knowledge of where he went or with whom he might have been hanging out.

Boutin mentioned money. How did he handle his pay? Was he careful with it? Did he give his aunt some of it, perhaps?

The proud woman dabbed at her tears and gazed out the window. Salif's death had been the second tragedy for her in less than a year. Her husband, who'd never been sick in his life, had died of a brain aneurysm on his forty-ninth birthday. She dabbed at her tears and Boutin sat quietly, giving her time to answer. Yes, she told him, Salif had been frugal with his pay. He gave her more than she'd asked for to help with household expenses, and was saving for his first car. It was her next remark that tweaked his interest.

"But he did buy real nice clothes. He was a smart dresser."

Boutin knew that the young man was still being paid a minimum wage when he quit. "Mind if I have a look at his room?" he'd asked. She had no objection and showed him the small bedroom next to hers.

Salif's tiny closet was stuffed with shirts and trousers, mostly brand name items. They were not cheap designer knock-offs like those sold at flea markets, Boutin realized.

Boutin had then gone back to the hotel. Farka hadn't been working the night of the prostitute was killed, but that didn't necessarily mean he had nothing to do with it, the private investigator reasoned.

"After talking with the room service manager, I have reason to believe that Farka must have been a party to the murder. Indirectly, of course, but help he probably received cash for."

"Go on, I'm listening."

Boutin explained the system whereby room service staff had a card to access guest rooms, and were supposed to place in a cabinet when their shift ended.

A few days before the body was discovered, a card went missing. Not Farka's, but one assigned to a female maid. The young woman, apparently quite reliable, denied any knowledge of its disappearance. She hadn't misplaced it, she swore, or taken it home. And it never turned up. The boss posted a notice about the missing card in the staff locker room, but nothing came of it. It wasn't a high priority, he'd told Boutin, and she was issued a new one.

"Do these cards have the employee's photo on them?" Don asked.

Boutin chuckled. "They do now, but not at the time of the murder. And shift supervisors now check them in and out."

"In theory, then, this guy could've taken the card, sold it to someone, and it somehow figures in the prostitute's murder. A crime intended to point to me as her killer, eh? And it appears they may have succeeded," Don sighed.

"Yes, it could have happened that way. Farka had been spending a lot more than what his wages would have allowed."

With this new information to go on, Boutin was redoubling his efforts to solve the puzzle of Farka's unexplained decision to quit his job, his extra cash, his murder, and that of the prostitute's. "And I'll stay with it until I can clear you, my friend," he vowed, before he rang off.

HALF AN HOUR LATER DON was still sitting on his deck, hunched over the patio table with his hands tightly gripped around his second scotch on the rocks. He'd lost all interest in mowing the lawn. He was almost too pissed off at the situation confronting him to think straight.

How did it get to this? What started as a seemingly routine 'follow and report' surveillance case is turning into a nightmare.

Am I going to be charged with murder? Boutin didn't come right and say so, but that's sure what it sounded like. He finished his drink and shook his head, trying to make sense of it all.

Three women have been killed since I took on the Archer case. And for what? Just to intimidate me from pursuing Archer? Well, it won't work, you sick bastards. I'm not going to quit now, and even though you may not know it, this French playboy is your weak link, and eventually he'll be your downfall.

Don splashed another liberal shot over the remaining ice cubes and drank half of it. If Yvonne were here, he'd be talking it through with her instead of Johnny Walker Red. *And that's another reason I won't let go: I want her back in this house permanently, but she's still too spooked to return.*

He quickly drained his drink and put the top back on the bottle. *No more tonight,* he vowed. He headed for his den and looked up Clay Simmons's home number...

Clay's wife answered. For some unexplained reason they had never got along, and tonight was no exception. Her suggestion that he call her husband tomorrow to discuss his problem hit a raw nerve.

"No it damn well can't!" he exploded. Thirty seconds passed before his lawyer came on the line. Time enough for Don to rue his outburst.

"Listen, I'm sorry to bother you at home, Clay, but I need your advice tonight. And please, *please,* tell your wife I'm really sorry for snapping at her, will you?"

Unlike his wife, Clay was a good 'people person' and his small law firm had handled all of KayRoy's legal business since Don first hung out his shingle. He listened without interruption to Dons tale and questions regarding the possibility of the French issuing an arrest warrant for him.

"Unfortunately, Don, I've never had anything to do with an extradition request. However, I agree that's probably what will ensue, if your colleague's information is correct. How do you handle it? I really can't say. But let me make a call first thing tomorrow morning. I've an old friend at a firm downtown who'll know about these things."

Don thanked him, apologized once more for interrupting his dinner hour, and told Clay he'd be in his office all day tomorrow.

WEDNESDAY, OCTOBER 6

Don was stuffing paperwork into his briefcase when Clay Simmons called. An extradition request from France—particularly one dealing with a manslaughter or murder charge—would be treated seriously by Canadian authorities, Clay stated. "But that doesn't mean you'd be arrested immediately and bundled on to a flight for Paris. You could launch an appeal, which would certainly delay proceedings. One thing for certain, though. You would have to surrender your passport while an appeal was working its way through the system. And that process could be quite lengthy."

"That would be a problem for me. Any idea what my chances of clearing my name without going over there might be?" Don asked.

"Not very good, Don," Clay answered. "To be honest, I don't think the police would lay a serious charge if they couldn't back it up."

Don waited to see if Simmons had anything else to add. When he didn't, Don spoke again.

"Yeah, well, if it comes to an extradition request, I'll appeal, that's for sure."

"Sure, and my colleague will be glad to handle it for you. He's a partner at Price, Price and Wilson. Did your contact know when this request might be issued?

"No, but it'll probably be sooner rather than later. At least that's my guess," sighed Don.

35

PARIS, MONDAY, OCTOBER 11

Boutin had returned to the Hotel Nouveau Monde last week with more questions for the room service manager. He learned that Salif Farka had been pals with a waiter named Farouk, also a recent immigrant from North Africa. Rather than talk to him at work, Boutin decided to approach him at home on his days off.

This morning Boutin and his assistant, Jacques, tracked him down. They found him sitting on a bench across the street from the apartment building where he lived. He was reading a newspaper and watching a pick up soccer game. Farouk was wary of Boutin at first. He'd already been questioned by the police, he told him, twice in fact. He had been working on the night the woman was murdered, and the police had fingerprinted him and taken a DNA sample. He hadn't had any contact with the police since then.

When Boutin explained for the second time that he wasn't looking to tie him to Salif's murder, Farouk relaxed a bit. He and Salif had become close friends, and spent their days off together getting to know the city. They'd talked for hours over coffee planning for the future. They had hopes of one day being able to move into an apartment together. Eventually Boutin brought the conversation around to Salif's last weeks.

How had his friend acquired the money for expensive clothes and why had he quit his job? The detective quietly explained why he thought Salif had somehow got mixed up in the murder at the hotel. Unintentionally perhaps, but an involvement that may have led to his death. Farouk glanced around, as if to ensure no one was watching or listening to them. Boutin, sensed that Farouk had something he wanted to get off his chest, and waited patiently for his reply. When he started to explain, it all came out in a rush.

There had been a very attractive woman—Salif had described her as a 'knock out'—staying at the hotel that week, and she always chatted to him when he picked up trays from her room. The woman had used room service as often as three times a day. She tipped well, and his friend found her interest in him quite flattering. It was not a sexual relationship, Farouk emphasized, when Boutin touched on it. A week or so after she checked out, Salif started buying fancy clothes. Farouk didn't know her name, and he had never been to her room.

When he kidded his friend about his seemingly good fortune, Salif had clammed up. Farouk didn't know why he'd quit his job, and Salif had uncharacteristically brushed him off when he'd asked. They had gone for coffee a few days after he quit, and that was the last time he saw his friend alive. Salif had talked about leaving Paris, but he didn't know where to go. Neither of them had anything to do with gangs, he said, and he was at a loss when Boutin asked if he could think of a possible motive for his death.

After Salif's body was found, the police had questioned him and the rest of the room service staff. He'd given the police the same story: he hadn't seen Salif for ten days, and wasn't aware of anyone who might have had it in for him. Boutin asked him if he'd mentioned to the police about the female guest Salif had apparently been enamored with. No, he'd replied, he had just answered their questions, and nothing more.

As Jacques manoeuvred their car through the narrow side streets and back onto the Autoroute, his boss was thinking about the female guest that had supposedly taken an interest in Salif.

Hmm, an attractive woman, eh? One that stayed in her room and used room service frequently. Perhaps it was time to have a chat with a certain Mademoiselle Amara...

Boutin had delved into her background in the days after Don Carling's stay in Paris. His search didn't turn up anything to suggest she'd ever been involved in the criminal activities attributed to her late father's male relatives. Her presence in the hotel, though, was puzzling, to say the least.

Had her lengthy stay been a ploy designed to make the Canadian PI think her brother was still in the city? That was the most plausible explanation, both he and Carling agreed.

As they approached the exit from the Autoroute towards their office, Jacques cut into the right hand lane and slowed. "No, no!" urged Boutin, tapping his shoulder. "Go straight ahead until we reach St Cloud. We'll have lunch and a glass of wine there. Then I'll introduce you to an attractive, dark-haired woman."

They lunched in a quiet bistro on a tree-lined square in the exclusive Paris suburb bordering the Seine. The food was excellent, as was the bottle of Beaujolais Nouveau, the first of this year's harvest. By the time they'd finished their coffee, Boutin had briefed Jacques on the Amara clan, Don Carling's investigation, and why he wanted to interview Archer's sister.

"Let's walk," he said, as they left the restaurant. "I believe she lives in that monstrosity just there." He was pointing at a high rise building overlooking the Seine, a few short blocks from the square. "Thank God they don't allow this sort of tower in the city proper," Boutin offered, with a disgusted shake of his head. He was still scowling as they slipped into the shadow of the building, which, from below, appeared to be nothing more that twenty-plus floors of glass walls and concrete balconies.

At the front entrance, Boutin signaled to a man standing beside a small Peugeot van double-parked across the street. He was wearing coveralls sporting a local telephone company's logo and carrying a tool box. Boutin scanned the tenant list: 'F. Amara' occupied suite 1406. He was just about to buzz her apartment when an elderly man pushed the door open from the inside. Boutin grabbed it, offered the pensioner a smiling 'Bonjour m'sieu', and stepped in, followed by the other two. The tenant gave them a questioning glare before he turned and walked away. While Boutin and Brunelle waited for the elevator, the technician opened the door to the basement stairs. "Apartment 1406, Claude," Boutin told him.

"WHO IS IT?" ASKED A woman's voice asked in response to Boutin's knock.

"The police, Miss. May we come in?"

The lock clicked, and the door opened six inches, the length of the security chain. Boutin held an identity card from the Paris Police Department up to the opening. "I'm Detective Boutin, and with me is Officer Bluet." Jacques remained out of the woman's line of sight and didn't show a card. "You are Francoise Amara?"

"Yes, but how did you get in?" She was noticeably rattled, which Boutin took as a plus.

He shrugged off her question with a smile. "We were already in the building, Miss. Another case, you see," he lied. "Not the one I'd like to ask you a few questions about. Purely routine, I assure you."

"You want to talk to me about a case? What case?"

"Perhaps we could talk inside?" asked Boutin, still smiling. "We'll be brief."

The puzzled woman reluctantly unchained the door and showed them into a large living room. A quick glance around the tastefully-appointed room spoke to the private detective of one thing: money. If not Ms Amara, then someone else had spared no expense when it came to the decorations. Boutin commented on her choices as he settled into a padded chair across from hers. The paintings, statues, figurines and wall hangings all spoke of a Mediterranean influence, he remarked.

He was right, she said, adding that her late father had been born and raised in Algeria.

Now that he was face-to-face with her, he saw how remarkably identical her facial features were to those of her brother, Francois, whom he only knew from photographs.

"So what is this about?" she asked curtly, cutting off any further attempt by Boutin to put a friendly spin on their intrusion.

"Miss Amara, our investigation shows you were staying in the Hotel Nouveau Monde in early June. Would you confirm that?"

Her frown told him he'd caught her off guard. She nodded slowly, "... Yes."

"And did you know—perhaps from television or newspaper reports—that a woman had been murdered in the hotel around the time of your stay?"

Again Francoise paused, trying to figure out where his questions were leading. "Yes, I heard that."

"Were you questioned by the police at the time?"

"No, no I wasn't. In fact I remember thinking when I read about it that it happened after I had left the hotel."

"Quite so, Miss Amara," nodded the veteran investigator, leaning towards her. "And, as you so aptly put it, you *left* the hotel. You didn't actually check out because you never checked in. Isn't that right?" Boutin asked, arching his eyebrows. Francoise quickly turned away, her discomfort visible. "Why *were* you staying in the hotel, by the way?"

"I'm not sure that's of any concern to the police, but there's a simple explanation, really," she replied.

On the surface, Francoise's version was believable. When she finished, Boutin realized her explanation must have been contrived beforehand. The room had been rented and paid for by her brother, she admitted. He'd come to France on business, but, only a few days after arriving in Paris, he unexpectedly had to travel elsewhere to complete it. As Francoise was having her apartment redecorated—and was allergic to paint fumes—he suggested she move into the hotel until the work was finished.

"So you see, it was just a convenience for me. Nothing more," she summed up. Her trace of a smile suggesting check mate.

"Ahh, I see. Well, they did a nice job," said Boutin, scanning the walls again. "But it's not the murder that happened that week that concerns me at the moment. It's just possible you might be able to help us with another homicide."

TWENTY MINUTES LATER BOUTIN AND Brunelle were walking back to their car. "That was brilliant, chief! You found out that she did know about Farka, even though she denied it," lauded Jacques. "I could tell she was lying."

"Yes, the blushing alone gave her away, didn't it?" Boutin said. "And earlier I got strong vibes telling me she may know something about the prostitute's death as well."

Boutin had spun her a tale about thefts from hotel guests' belongings during her stay at the hotel. Not all those who had been victimized had reported their loss, it seemed. To make a long story short, he'd lied, a room service waiter was eventually suspected of the thefts. And now the man named Salif Farka was dead. Murdered, in fact. Boutin described the young African emigrant, then asked her two direct questions. One, had she had anything taken from her personal effects, perhaps something she didn't miss until after she'd returned home? And secondly, could she recall having any contact with this particular waiter?

No, Francoise hadn't had anything stolen. She acknowledged that she had used room service a few times, but couldn't recall a waiter matching Farka's description. Her lying was most evident when Boutin showed her a photo of Farka. She'd quickly shook her head and handed it back to the detective.

After they left, Francoise poured herself a large vodka and sipped at it as she replayed the unnerving visit from the police. *Obviously they suspect something about the waiter and me. But what?*

The detective hadn't asked if she'd had any contact with him since returning to her apartment. She would have lied again if he had. She wondered if Farka's surprise call—and her telling Carlos about it may have led to his death.

"So, now we wait and see what she does next," said Boutin as they reached the car.

"You're not worried that she might call the Surete to check on you, chief? Your false identity card, I mean?"

"No, no, that's not going to happen, Jacques, believe me. Her next call will be a revelation for us, if I'm not mistaken. Let's hope the phone line she uses is the one our man Claude tapped into."

Claude was a bonafide technician for one of French capital's largest telephone company. But he was also a part-time agent for Boutin's agency. Boutin had paged him while they were en route to St Cloud, and he'd agreed to meet them in front of Francoise Amara's apartment building.

Claude had tapped her phone line by the time they had returned to the lobby. "All set, chief. The tape will record both incoming and outgoing calls. But as a precaution, I'd rather not leave it there for more than two days, three at the most. We get a lot of service calls to this building and another technician might spot it."

"I'll bear that in mind, Claude. Not to worry, though. I think we'll get a hit on it before the day is out," Boutin replied.

PAUL BOUTIN HAD CALLED IT: Francoise made a call twenty minutes after they left her apartment. An answering machine picked up, and she left a message.

The answering machine prompt was generic, and Francoise hadn't used a name. The return call came at 11:30 that night. Without any preamble, a male voice asked, "What is the problem?"

"The police were here today. Two detectives. They were on about when I was using my brother's room at the hotel. They knew he had checked in.

"Go on."

"Well, they were on about the waiter, you know, the young black that—"

The caller cut her off harshly. "Don't say anymore! He's no longer a concern to us."

"They told me he'd been murdered," Francoise persisted. "Don't tell me you had—"

"That's enough!" he said, interrupting her again. "And don't call from home again. Use an outside phone."

Carlos cursed out loud. No one heard him, though. He was alone in one of three Paris apartments he had access to. Hiding places he moved between at random when he was in the city. Not that he had ever suspected anyone was watching him. At least not until Francoise called. He'd had second thoughts about his decision to use her before, and now it appeared his doubts were justified. It had seemed like a relatively safe move at the time. If Farka, the hotel waiter, had kept his mouth shut he'd still be alive.

But after his call to Francoise, he had to go. Carlos didn't want to take the chance of him losing his nerve and going to the police.

36

FRIDAY, OCTOBER 15

As far as Don was concerned, this week had been a big zero. He hadn't heard from any of the sources he was relying on to move his investigation along. He thumbed through his daily log. Ten days had passed since he'd spoken to the OPP, and it was even longer since he been in touch with Inspector Roberts of the RCMP. He hadn't heard from Tom Allman for some time, either.

He'd tried to reach Paul Boutin in Paris yesterday, only to learn that he was out of town and not expected back until early next week. The threat that he could be facing charges in France was never far from his thoughts. His lawyer's advice was to 'sit tight'. Nothing could be done until the French police made a move. He realized that, but the consequences of what would happen to his business if he were charged continued to worry him. His licence would be suspended at the very least, he felt.

Oh, well, at least I have the weekend with Yvonne to look forward to.

The expectation of being with all weekend gave his morale a boost and he started to straighten up his desk. *It's only 2:30 but I'm not accomplishing a hell'ova lot here.*

He was about to tell Joanne she could leave early, too, when she buzzed him. Richie Flanagan was on the line from New York.

"Hey Richie, good to hear from you! What's the latest?"

"That Smoke guy you asked me to check out? Are you still interested in him?"

"Oh yeah, anything you've got."

"Well, I think I've got a good lead on him."

"Hey, you've just made my day, Richie. Actually my whole week."

"Well, don't get too excited just yet. It's just a name so far. And it'll probably cost a grand to find out more."

Don swiveled his chair around and put his feet on the credenza. "I'm listening, Richie."

WHEN OPP SGT LEON BELCHER told Don about the suspect known as Smoke, Don had called the New York PI and given him the nickname and description of the bearded biker. *Did Richie have any sources that might help identify him?*

During his 22 years with the NYPD, Flanagan, had been a respected and honest cop, leaving many good friends behind when he retired. And he hadn't overused such relationships since becoming a private investigator. For the most part, he called on just two contacts, former partners who were now both detectives. The lead came from one of them, Sergeant Pat Regan, now working narcotics out of the Queens precinct. Previously he had been assigned to the arson squad.

Flanagan had asked him to run the man's description and nickname through the NYPD data base. It wasn't much to go on, and the search came up empty regarding any known felon using the nickname 'Smoke'. But Regan had a great memory, and recalled an arson investigation he'd been part of five years ago. A club house had been torched, and even though the police were certain a rival gang was behind it, no help was forthcoming from the victimized bikers. Their 'playing dumb' didn't surprise the cops. They knew the bikers would rather settle the score themselves down the road.

During that investigation, Regan and his partner had questioned members of the rival motorcycle club suspected of the torching. As they were leaving the club's parking lot, their squad car was bumped from behind by a large Harley. The damage was slight, a broken tail light and scratched fender. The burly, bearded biker feigned an apology for his 'accidently on purpose' mistake. This brought loud guffaws from the other five or six gang members watching. Cries of *'Hey Crash, watch where you're going!'* and *'Sorry officers, but Crash is just an accident waitin' to happen!'* followed.

The cops heard more derisive hooting as they pulled away, but Regan had noted the nickname. And it was the biker world's penchant to label each other with descriptive monikers that led to the suspect's identity. When the 'Crash' nickname, physical description, and biker gang connection were entered in the data base, two names came up. One was that of a man serving a life sentence for murder in an Ohio prison.

Regan gave Flanagan the second name. "The man you're looking for is probably a 'head banger' named Lionel Jesse Barr. Known to police here in New York State. He's been charged with assault and battery three times but never convicted. Also beat an extortion rap six years ago upstate. In Rochester, to be exact," said Flanagan. "Never been charged here in the greater New York area, but suspected of being an enforcer for hire. He'd be 41 now. Six foot three, and probably weighs at least 240 or 50."

"Well, that a reasonable fit, description-wise, with what we have. No manslaughter or murder charges, though?" said Don.

"No, but a lot of the wet contracts in the northeast go unsolved, you know. Maybe he's just smarter than most of these perps," offered Richie. 'Wet contract' was underworld jargon meaning the target was to be killed.

"Okay, I'll pass that info on to the local cops. Anything else? Can you get me a photo?"

"Yeah, I'll have his mug shot for you by Monday. One other thing, and this would be a dead giveaway. He's got a ten inch scar on the inside of his left arm, above and below the elbow."

"Great, I'll pass that on, too. So, what's the thousand bucks going to get us?"

"Don, you know I wouldn't hold you up for it, but if this guy is on somebody's watch list, we can probably find out where he's hanging his helmet these days." Flanagan let his words sink in for a few seconds before adding, "Understand what I'm sayin'?"

Oh I do, my Irish friend, you're loud and clear! mused Don. With multiple law enforcement agencies—city, state, and federal—all operating in the metropolis, information concerning the more than eight million inhabitants was a commodity, just like those traded on Wall Street. Particularly data on the criminal element. Even though he personally might have reached a dead end, Flanagan's contact might be able to move the query up the information chain a bit further. He told Richie he'd arrange to wire the money before leaving the office today.

The welcome call from Flanagan had brightened his day, and a second unexpected call, only minutes later, buoyed his spirits even more. Inspector Brian Roberts at RCMP Headquarters was calling. He asked Don if he had time to talk with two members of his team.

"Definitely, Brian. Still too early for Happy Hour!"

"Same here," chuckled Roberts. "We have you on speaker phone now and I'd like you to repeat for their benefit how you came across the code words you gave me on September 23."

Don told them about searching Archer's apartment, finding the crumpled note with the mysterious words, *farmer* and *breeder*, and how the note had been traced to an Internet café frequented by the suspect. He reiterated what had happened since then, including the fact that Archer had left Toronto, supposedly to return to France after the end of his marital arrangement

"Do you know where Archer is now?"

"Somewhere in the US, probably Arizona," Don replied. He paused to see if he'd be asked how he knew that, but the question never came. Instead, after a mumbled conversation at the Ottawa end, Roberts spoke again.

"Thanks for that, Don. The speaker is off now and my guys have left my office," he said.

"So what was all that about?" asked Don.

"Well, these officers are liaising with the UK on certain security matters. Seems the Brits have come across something similar and wanted further info on how we got wind of them. And that's where you came in. Just to clarify what you'd told me, I guess."

"I see. I'll bet the inquiry came from our mutual friend in London, Derek Houghton."

"I'm not sure, Don. As I mentioned before, we're in constant contact with British security these days, sharing anything that could be terrorism-related. Whether Derek was directly involved, I couldn't say."

"Maybe I'll ask him!" Don said, only half in jest. "What about the Americans? Are they part of this joint cooperation you're talking about?"

There was a lengthy pause before Roberts replied. "Let's just say they're getting better at it. Don't quote me on this, but there seems to be a lot of jockeying for position in Washington at the moment. Ever since the Department of Homeland Security was set up. Now the FBI and CIA have it looking over their shoulders."

Don was aware of the second-guessing and finger-pointing between the two federal agencies after 9/11. Most of the criticism originated with those now working for the new department.

Could the wait the OPP was experiencing for information on Smoke have anything to do with politics south of the border? He kept that thought to himself, though, and also the warning from Paul Boutin that charges against him were apparently in the offing.

"Well, I'd hope your guys will keep me in the loop if they come up with anything that might have a bearing on my investigation. I'm talking about the code words," said Don.

Once again Roberts took his time before answering. "Don, I'll see that you get any info that's within my power to share. It's not that I don't trust you, I'm sure you know that."

"I'm reading you loud and clear, Brian," said Don, "and I'll be in touch again if I come up anything worth mentioning to you."

Before they finished, Roberts again urged Don to be extra careful. The danger wasn't Archer himself, but those he was connected with, was the gist of his caution.

Well, if I do end up with my ass in a sling, it won't be because I wasn't warned often enough, Don thought, feeling for the small revolver in the holster strapped to his right ankle. He'd taken to carrying it a few days after Shirley Jane Cuddy's body ended up on his front lawn.

MONDAY, OCTOBER 18

Don was in a cheery mood as he drove to his office. The weekend with Yvonne had buoyed his hopes of having her back on a full-time basis as soon as the Archer affair was behind him. He'd been worried that Yvonne, rather than being married, might just decide that she still preferred being on her own during the week.

"You are such an insecure teddy bear at times, my sweet," she laughed when he mentioned it. Their casual, yet impassioned intimacy, and Yvonnes unmistakable warmth towards him even when they weren't in bed, allayed his lingering fears.

He was still smiling inwardly when his computer came online and he opened the email from Richie Flanagan. It contained an attachment of a mug shot of Lionel Jesse Barr. He immediately forwarded it to the OPP and followed up with a call to Sergeant Belcher.

"Well thanks, Don. This will be a great help," the police officer said. "Your sources are certainly better than ours, it seems. We'll see if Belanger can make a positive ID from this photo."

DANIEL BELANGER, THE EX-CON WHO had informed the police about the bearded biker, had been released. The crown attorney elected not to charge him, even though the police suspected that he had something to do with the dumping of the Cuddy woman's body on Carling's front lawn. According to the prosecutor, the fingerprint evidence wasn't strong enough to hold him.

He'd been re-arrested immediately, however, on a warrant from the Quebec police and returned to Montreal to face parole violation charges.

Barr's mug shot allowed the OPP to move closer to solving two murders. The used car lot owner, the Ukranian immigrant Gregor Malkev, was 'fairly certain' that Barr was the man from whom he'd bought the GMC pickup. He commented that Barr's beard was much bushier now, but there was no mistaking his heavy eyebrows and broken nose.

Yesterday a detective from Sergeant Belcher's squad flew to Montreal to interview Daniel Belanger, still in custody awaiting a hearing on his parole violation charges. Belanger positively identified Barr as the man he knew as Smoke, mentioning the same facial features as Malkev. But the clincher came when Belanger was asked if Smoke had any visible scars. "Oh yeah," he replied quickly. "An ugly one on his arm. Somebody must've tried to carve him up once."

Now that the police had a positive ID of the murder suspect, finding him became the priority. Don called New York, hoping Flanagan's sources—plus the thousand dollars—had provided information on Barr's present whereabouts.

It was not to be, however. Richie's report was brief. Information on Barr was 'off limits' to anyone below the federal level. "Sorry, pal, I know you were expecting more," said Flanagan. "But that came from someone either at or close to the FBI."

"So you're telling me that even though the police here have ID'd him as a probable murderer, a formal request to apprehend him probably would be ignored by the Feds?"

"A real son'ova bitch, huh? But that would be my take on it."

"But why, Richie? Am I missing something here?"

"No, and there's only one reason I can think of for their silence."

"And that would be?" asked Don, still puzzled.

"...He could be an FBI informant."

AFTER TALKING TO FLANAGAN, HE told Joanne to hold all calls, and closed his office door. Thirty minutes later he was still sitting at his desk, trying to make sense of Richie's information about Barr.

Did the OPP homicide squad have it wrong? Was the case they'd been building against Barr, the biker known as Smoke while he was in Toronto, all a mistake? Had his own input and theorizing also contributed to erroneous conclusions? After going over every aspect—both known and surmised —of Barr's involvement in the women's deaths, Don was still convinced they had it right. Including his gut feeling that it was all tied into a terrorist plot involving Archer/Amara. But what could he do next to keep the investigation on track? Without help from the American authorities, how could they get their hands on Barr?

Informant or not, the man is probably a murderer, and just giving up the search for him is not an option, Don concluded. *And there's one person who might be able to help…*

He checked the time: 3:40 p.m. With luck Inspector Roberts would still be in his office. He was, and a minute later the familiar voice of the head of the RCMP's counterterrorism bureau greeted him. "Afternoon, Don, what can I do for you?

Don gave Roberts a quick update on the problem concerning the American murder suspect.

"Okay, let me see if we're on the same page here," said Roberts when Don finished. "The OPP want this Barr fellow on suspicion of murder, not for any terrorist-related activity. Correct?"

"That's right. I've shared my thoughts with Sergeant Belcher, though, about why I think the murders are connected to Archer, but that's as far as it goes."

After a short pause, Roberts said, "Well, I can't promise anything, Don, but leave it with me for a few days. The only approach I can make to my counterparts in Washington regarding Barr will have to be based on his supposed connection with a suspected terrorist. And I'm going with your judgment on that." Again the RCMP officer paused, and Don could hear him sigh. "There has been action on that front, but I'm not at liberty to talk about it yet.

THE DEVELOPMENT HAD TO DO with the suspected code words that first came to light when Don Carling found them and subsequently passed them on to the RCMP. Roberts had forwarded the information to the Department of Homeland Security in Washington. Nothing came of it until he received a signal from Scotland Yard on the fifth of October. British sources had come up with two additional code words, *grower* and *fox*.

Roberts received a call from the DHS in Washington that same afternoon. All of a sudden the newest US department dealing with national security had a heightened interest in the suspected code words. The agent identified himself as Bob March, and politely asked Roberts how and in what context the words *farmer* and *breeder* had come to the RCMP's attention.

Roberts explained that his source, a private detective named Don Carling, had been investigating a Canadian citizen named Frank Archer, also known as Francois Amara, a native of France. It was believed that he probably still held French citizenship—and a passport—in his birth name. He gave an account of Archer's suspicious actions, beginning in May and continuing until he disappeared after a trip to New York City in early September. These movements had been tracked by Carling and convinced the PI that Archer/Amara was involved in a possible plot aimed at the USA. He did not know to whom the words referred to, nor did the Canadian Security Services have any knowledge of them, prior to Carling's discovery. They had also drawn a blank when it came to the two additional code words contained in Superintendent Houghton's message. When Roberts pressed March as to what Homeland Security knew about them, the American hesitated.

"Rather than get into specifics at this point," he said, "I'm going to suggest to my boss that we set up a conference call with the Brits to discuss this, ahh, *situation*. Can I get back to you after I get the OK and arrange it with London, Inspector?"

"Sure. I'll be available anytime. Let's hope it's sooner rather than later, though," Brian replied.

To Robert's surprise, Agent March called again two days later. Would he be available for a conference call that afternoon? He was, as was Derek Houghton in London. He was even more surprised when one of the participants in Washington was March's superior, Assistant Director George Egan. The AD began by thanking the Canadian and British policemen for contacting them with the information and apologized for not responding sooner.

"As you might imagine, Homeland Security has been swamped with tips about possible terrorists and plots, and even though we give information such that supplied by your services a much higher priority than tips from the public, it still takes my understaffed team time to check them all out."

The American authorities were faced with a daunting task, trying to keep critics at bay and reassuring a frightened public. The constant reporting of the color-coded terror alert status by the media probably had a lot to do with the nationwide anxiety. The status had been 'orange', for 'high', for most of the time since the 9/11 attacks. Unfortunately it was the only way for the DHS to keep the population vigilant to the continuing threat posed by their country's avowed enemies.

"No apology necessary," offered Roberts, sentiments echoed by Houghton.

Egan thanked them for their understanding and told them that the code words in question were now a top priority for his department and the file devoted to them was being monitored on a daily basis by Agent March.

Communications to and from locations suspected of housing radical groups were being monitored 24/7, he told them, by both CIA and the National Security Agency [NSA]. "We've requested both agencies to check through their intercepts from June to the present for mention of the suspected codes," said Egan.

Roberts offered his opinion that one was probably Archer/Amara's code name, and Houghton agreed. The British policeman then mentioned Saahir Kayani's name, the brother of his murdered informant. "He flew to Pakistan at the time of the murder," he said. "I believe he might have been working as a clearing house for messages, and possibly one of the code words refers to him. We suspect he acts as the relay, forwarding emails originating in France to a cell member in Canada and perhaps to others in America. He hasn't returned to London yet. We do not suspect him of being directly involved in his sister's murder, though."

"Very interesting," said Egan, who had been leafing through a file while listening to the others. "This trip Archer made to New York recently. Is there any evidence that he was in contact with anyone there?" he asked Roberts.

"Yes, there is, actually," the Canadian replied.

Roberts pointed out that most of the information they had on Archer's suspicious activities came via a private investigator. While he was in New York, Archer was observed in the company of a man driving a vehicle registered to the Cote Verde consulate."

In Washington Egan and March exchanged startled looks. "You're positive of this?" March asked.

"Yes, according to Carling," answered Roberts. "And this is a man I have complete faith in."

Derek Houghton interjected to agree with Roberts. "I've worked with Don Carling, as well. He's an excellent investigator. His information has always been reliable."

There was another pause as March and Egan conferred, their voices too low to be heard by Roberts and Houghton. Then Egan addressed them again. "Gentlemen, I want to thank you for your input. We'll attempt to put names to these codes, and Agent March will update you as to our progress. I trust you will do the same. Is there anything else either of you wish to add?"

Roberts spoke up, mentioning Lionel Barr. "We have strong evidence that this man may be responsible for two murders, hits he was probably hired to carry out at the behest of this terrorist cell we're talking about." Roberts explained that the Ontario police had hit a brick wall when they inquired about Barr to US authorities. "Apparently he's known to the FBI, but they're reluctant to share their information on him. Given our suspicions that Barr and the Archer investigation are related, it would be nice to know why the FBI is stonewalling."

"Leave it with me, Inspector. Won't hurt to make a few calls."

37

ARIZONA, FRIDAY, OCTOBER 22

Don picked up his phone as soon as Joanne told him who was calling. "Hey, Tom. About time you called. What the hell are you doing up this early? Bladder problem? Or haven't you been to bed yet?"

"Wrong on both counts, pard! And there's nothin' wrong with my waterworks," chuckled Allman. "Plenty of your fine Canadian beer available down here to keep the pipes clear."

It *was* early, just after 6:30 a.m. in Arizona. The lack of traffic on the quiet street two blocks from his motel let Tom check for a possible tail before he used his cell phone, he told Don.

"Just routine, or do you suspect they're keeping tabs on you?"

"Nope, no sign of that," replied Allman. "Just followin' your advice to check my rear end once in a while."

"Right on. So what have you been up to?"

"Still in a holding pattern, basically. Or at least I was until this past week. Finally wormed more information out of Frank about what is supposed to happen and my role in it."

Allman had been working hard to show Archer he was taking his role in the plot seriously. A man with an axe to grind and wanting to get on with the mission. Pay back time for the raw deal that forced me to quit the army, and a chance to put my Special Forces training to use again, was how he put it to Frank.

And slowly his charade was paying dividends. He was confident that he now knew as much as Frank did about the cell's plans. The date and authority to actually launch the plot hinged on the Presidential election on November 2nd, he'd learned. If the Bush administration was re-elected, Allman figured the plot would take place soon afterwards. If, on the other hand, the Democrats won, things might be put on hold until the new president's policy regarding Iraq was clarified.

Frank also let on that another member of the cell would be arriving in soon, probably via Mexico, and would become Frank's responsibility. He was to expect him around the end of the month.

"I'd been pushin' him to find out exactly what they wanted me to do about the explosives, asking questions, you see."

What type and how much would be required? Enough to knock a few cars off the rails, blocking tracks for a while? Or a real shit load...Massive explosions designed to scatter debris over a wide area. Was I goin' to have to wait until this other fellow arrived to find out?

"I kept tellin' him I'd have to know soon, Don. Roundin' up the stuff can't be done overnight, I told him, and dependin' on how much is needed, I'd want to get it from more than one source to avoid suspicion, ya see. Well, Frank agreed, and told me he would contact someone about it.

"And what was the outcome?" asked Don.

"A big surprise that's what! Seems they no longer need me to acquire explosives for them."

"No shit! Why?"

"Well, that's where Frank's info gets a bit fuzzy. He was just to tell me not to do anything along that line for now. Apparently that part of whatever they're plannin' is bein' looked after by others. They still have plans for me, but Frank doesnt know yet what they are."

"Sounds like they're trying to keep you in the dark as much as possible, doesn't it?"

"You got it, pard. But I picked the location for targeting the trains, and they need me for that, if nothing else. The guy that's supposed to show up soon will have be the one with all the answers, and he'll have to level with me or we'll call a halt and let the feds have them, right?"

Don agreed, and urged Tom to call whenever he learned new information about the plot. Their call ended on a lighter note when Don asked if he saw much of Archer on a day-to-day basis.

'Not really," replied Tom. "I play tennis with him a few times a week, but for the most part we go our separate ways, which is fine by me. But I did drag him off to a western bar the other night. One of those places with all that honky-tonk music you're so takin' with," he said, raising a chuckle from Don. "He only agreed to go after I'd suggested there would be lots of available women hangin' about."

"Don't tell me—you both got lucky!"

Allman response was a loud guffaw. "No, not even close! Don't think the talent was sophisticated enough for his European tastes. But he hasn't applied to the priesthood, either. He's beddin' down with a gal he met at the tennis club he's been playin' at on a regular basis."

"So you're the celibate one, right?"

"No chance of that, pardner! Let's just say that I'm learnin' to appreciate country music myself."

"Then there's hope for you yet, Tom!" Don laughed.

38

MONDAY, OCTOBER 25

Although Paul Boutin had warned Don that the French police might charge him, the news that it was actually going to happen still stunned him. As incomprehensible as it seemed to him, French authorities had linked his DNA to the murder victim. An irrefutable match, according to Boutin. According to his source, the paperwork for his extradition was in the government's hands as of this morning. Paul couldn't say how long the process might take.

"Well, for what it's worth, I've talked to my lawyer about it and he'll take all legal steps to oppose my extradition, Paul," Don sighed. "I know I'll have to clear my name eventually, just not in the near term. The Archer affair should be coming to a head in the next few weeks. After that I'll be free to travel. By the way, the last time you called you suggested you'd had a breakthrough. Anything more on that?"

"Yes, as a matter of fact. As we both suspected all along, his sister's presence in the hotel after Amara slipped out of Paris was not as innocent as it seemed."

He told Don about visiting her apartment, bugging her phone, and the call she made only hours after he'd questioned her about the room service waiter. "I had obviously spooked her, and she tried to tell the man she called that she was worried. He shut her up quickly, but I have no doubt that they had involved the waiter."

Boutin had agents watching her after his visit, but other than having lunch with a female acquaintance Francoise hadn't met with anyone else. The original tap on her phone line had been removed and replaced with one less likely to be discovered. But no more calls to the unknown male were recorded.

"If she has been in contact with him, she's been using public call boxes or a mobile phone. She was observed twice using public phones. I was on the verge of giving all this information to the police and letting them run with it when she left for Hong Kong and Singapore," said Boutin. "Won't be back until some time in November, apparently."

Francoise Amara was a model, but not one seen on the runways of the Paris fashion designers. She was too old and full-figured for that work. Her elegant hands and neckline were the tools that earned her a yearly, six-figure income in US dollars. Her clients were famous jewelry designers in Europe and Asia, who used her in photographs displaying their latest creations in fashion magazines, explained Boutin.

"You gotta be kidding!" marveled Don. "Do you think they wanted her out of the way, or was the trip already planned?"

"Can't say for sure," replied Boutin. "But we'll keep digging in her absence. Like her brother, she doesn't come across as a trained agent. She's the key to clearing you, I'm positive of that. And I'll be on her again once she returns.

"I really appreciate your efforts, Paul. Stay in touch. Au revoir."

WHAT A WAY TO START the week, Don was thinking after hanging up. He had just refilled his coffee and returned to his desk when Joanne buzzed him.

"You'll never guess who called while you were on the on the other line, boss," she said.

"You're right, I can't. And I'm not even going to try."

"Miss Danielle Clyde. She wants you to call her at your earliest convenience."

"Really! Well, I suppose my *earliest convenience* has arrived, now that I've got a refill in my hand. Give her a ring, please. Thanks, Jo."

ALTHOUGH DANIELLE AND HER HUSBAND had both signed the divorce papers in early August, the actual petition wasn't ready for her perusal until the end of the month. When she met with her lawyers to go over it, they urged her not to file immediately. There were two reasons for this. Her personal lawyer was still convinced she'd made a hasty decision, particularly by agreeing to double the amount payable to Archer. Secondly, her lover, Charles Rothwell, had found out about it.

Danielle was upset when Charles brought it up, because she wanted to tell him herself, but only after the fact. When she told him she was moving on it now because Frank had learned of their affair and threatened to expose it, he'd been stunned.

"I'm only doing it to protect you, darling," she'd told him.

He admitted that their affair was known to a very few of his trusted associates, one of whom was with the law firm handling her divorce. *Ah, how would our world survive without the old boys' network?* Danielle mused.

Charles was adamant that the leak to Archer could not have originated with his colleagues. After a lengthy discussion, Charles also urged her to delay the proceedings.

"What good will that accomplish?" Danielle asked. "He's already been paid $500,000. And the money isn't really an issue for me anyway."

"I know that, darling, but consider these possible ramifications..."

Charles explained his reasons for asking her to wait. Once the divorce petition was filed, he told her, it would be hard to keep it from becoming public knowledge. There was more than one reporter who went to great lengths trolling for gossip on prominent persons. And Danielle Clyde, president and CEO of Empire North, would make a juicy item for their columns. For his part, Charles couldn't chance having his name surface now, either. Even an unsubstantiated rumor could cost him dearly. His wife had already made veiled accusations about him having a mistress, even though she had named the wrong woman, an attractive divorcee on his staff.

Charles had only met Archer once. Danielle had introduced them at an Empire North reception a few weeks before their affair began. He'd been in the group chatting with the American executive when Archer let loose with his shocking anti-US rant. Recalling that scene, Rothwell remembered coming away with the impression that her husband showed little interest in Danielle's business, and even less in her friends and associates. *Perhaps he has an ulterior motive for demanding a divorce now.*

"So, if you agree, I suggest that we have someone take a close look at your husband. See what he's been up to lately. Might just find something that you can use to void your agreement with him."

Danielle reluctantly agreed. "...I suppose it's worth a try. I'll think about it.

And she did, for three weeks. Although Charles had casually suggested that he would be glad to 'ask around', as he put it, Danielle rejected his help and decided to go with someone she already knew.

"Good morning, Don. Thank you for returning my call so quickly."

"You're welcome," he replied, amused at her use of his first name without being prompted.

"What can I do for you?"

"I want to engage your services again."

"Uhh, well, sure. Always happy to accommodate past clients, you know. What is it you need?"

"I'd rather not discuss it over the phone. Are you free for lunch today?"

Don asked her to hold briefly while he checked with his secretary. He already knew he was free, but took a few sips of coffee before he spoke again. "Okay, Danielle. I can free up the time. Where and when?"

Danielle was flying to Edmonton this afternoon, on a flight departing at 2:30. She would have her personal assistant make a reservation for 12:30 at the *CLEAR SKIES* restaurant in Terminal One. Would that suit him?

Don agreed to the arrangements. The last time he'd dined in that exclusive eatery, hosting a pair of possible clients, the tab had set him back almost two hundred and fifty bucks. Which wouldn't have mattered if the clients hadn't changed their minds and backed out of what would have been a lucrative contract for KayRoy. He was sure he'd have better luck with Ms.Clyde—she'd already insisted that lunch would be on her.

Danielle was already seated at a corner table when Don walked in. After making small talk while they ordered, Danielle came right to the point.

"Do you know where Frank is now?"

The question caught him off guard. *Does she know that I'm still pursuing him? Has she somehow got wind of what he's up to?*

Their drinks arrived before he could reply. White wine with a dash of soda for Danielle, a pint of Alexander Keith's Ale for him. He raised his glass and offered 'Cheers', before taking a swallow. He was trying to decide whether or not there was anything to be gained by playing dumb.

"No, not exactly," he said truthfully. "But we are fairly certain he hasn't returned to France yet."

"We? Who's 'we'?"

Don gave her everything he knew about Frank's activities since they had last spoke. He ended with an account of Tom Allman's last update from Arizona.

Danielle tried to interrupt twice, but he waved her off. When he finished, he picked up his beer and sat back in his chair. "So that's where we're at as of today."

"And you've been doing all this on your own?" she asked, her tone slightly incredulous.

"Yes," he admitted. "Let's just say that Frank's suspicious moves while we were on your tab left a number of unanswered questions. Throw in a few murders and I decided to keep after him until we have enough on him and whomever he's associating with to call in the police."

Danielle stopped her glass inches from her mouth. "Murders?" she gasped, returning her drink to the table. "What murders?"

Don told her how Marlene Hastings, probably mistaken for Yvonne, had been deliberately run off the road and killed, and about Shirley Jane Cuddy, a drug addict, whose body had been dumped on his front lawn. He didn't mention the murder of the prostitute in Paris.

"Am I sure they're connected? You're damned right. I don't believe in coincidences, for one thing. And that's why I've still pursuing him."

"I see," she nodded. "Well, now you can go after him with my backing, Don."

"Well, just hold your horses, Danielle. Let's not get ahead of ourselves."

"What? You're turning me down? If it's more money you want—"

"No, no, that's not the case. My rates haven't changed. And I'd be glad to have you covering our expenses again. But only if you level with me."

A puzzled look came over her face. "What do you mean?"

"Just this. Tell me what's behind your renewed interest in Frank. And by the way, I know you're planning to start divorce proceedings now instead of later."

"You do? How?"

Her reaction confirmed what Chuck Todd had hinted at. "It doesn't matter how I came by that information," he said. "But I believe that's why we're here. So why don't you lay it out for me."

Danielle put down her fork and pushed her half-finished quiche away. "You're right, it does have to do with the timing of our divorce. A change that was forced on me, actually."

While Don continued to eat, Danielle revealed that she was involved with another man. An affair that Frank had somehow got wind of, and used to demand an early divorce and a doubling of the financial settlement he was to received. Public knowledge of their relationship would be particularly damaging to her lover, Charles Rothwell. She mentioned his name, even though Don hadn't asked her to.

"So Charles and my lawyers have pressed me to delay the proceedings. They feel his demands are unjustified, especially asking for another million dollars. Basically they think there must be more to his motive than meets the eye, and wanted to check him out."

"Did they say how they would go about that?"

"No, not really. But it's a moot point anyway. I told them I'd take care of it myself."

Ahh, the independent female at work, thought Don. "And that's where I come in, is it?"

"Exactly. And after what you've told me about him and his terrorist connections, I—"

"Not confirmed yet," he cautioned. "Let's just categorize them as 'probable' for now."

"Whatever. But my God, if he's involved with terrorists I want to know! And see him prosecuted for it!" Her emotional outburst was a 'first' in Don's presence. "So, please go after him. Spend whatever it takes."

"Deal," he said, extending his hand, which she quickly and firmly shook. They agreed on an advance for KayRoy's expenses, and finished their lunch in silence. They both passed on dessert, but ordered coffee.

"Well, I guess a divorce will be the end of Frank's buying trips for your art gallery," Don said.

Danielle nodded empathically. "Yes, and perhaps for the best. We just got the invoice from the Paris gallery where he bought a painting in June. Forty thousand dollars for a rather mediocre work by a little-known artist did not impress me at all. At least he only bought one."

Only one? A picture of Frank bundling packages into a taxi in Paris suddenly surfaced in Don's memory. He'd been carrying three packages when he came out of the gallery...

He asked Danielle to explain how the financial aspects of the artworks Frank acquired overseas were handled. How were they paid for? Did he use a company credit card? Was there a limit on what he could spend, for instance?

Danielle was puzzled by his questions. "What does this have to do with terrorists?"

"Maybe nothing," he shrugged. "But it could be that Frank was charging you for paintings that didn't end up in your company's collection."

"Really? How would you go about proving that?"

"I'd need invoices from galleries he's dealt with for starters, then I'll have a colleague in Europe check it out."

Danielle readily agreed. If he's been stealing from me, and it can be proved, then I'll have him charged. At the least, it should provide the leverage to counter his financial demands regarding the divorce, she thought. "Copies of the invoices will be delivered to your office by tomorrow afternoon."

"By the way," Don said as they left the restaurant, "if you should hear anything about me and a criminal investigation in France, don't worry about it. It will be taken care of. And I'll be in touch regarding Frank as soon as we know for sure what he's up to."

Danielle stared after him with a puzzled look on her face as he thanked her for lunch and left the restaurant.

39

WASHINGTON, TUESDAY, OCTOBER 27

"Good Morning, Inspector. It's Agent March at DHS calling."

The RCMP officer returned the American's greeting and added, "And you can skip the title, Bob, just Brian will do."

"Well, thanks, I sometimes wish we were a little less formal around here," said the Homeland Security agent. "Brian, I finally got an answer from the FBI regarding this Barr character you asked about."

"Great! As I mentioned, he's a suspect in a couple of murders up here."

"Yes, well, it may be some time yet before you get your hands on him, but this what I learned from their New York office..."

Lionel Jesse Barr was not an FBI informant. Quite the contrary. March explained how Barr had been seen with Karim Ahmad Bakir, the Cote Verde trade attache. It was the Bureau's thinking that Bakir might have ties to a terrorist cell in the New York area. The tenuous threads to cell, uncovered in the aftermath of 9/11, suggested that it had been in existence before the 9/11 attacks, but not involved in them. It was designated as a sleeper cell, possibly one planning a future attack in the United States. As this was an ongoing investigation—and it was still not clear exactly how Barr figured in it—the Bureau wanted to 'sit on him' for now. They would deal with the Canadian police concerns about him as soon as it was feasible.

40

Pakistani authorities had been alerted to Saahir Kayani's flight number when his passport was scanned at the airport in Karachi. It was the first indication the police had that he was still in the country. Neither his parents nor the uncle in Karachi, whose address he'd listed as his local contact when he'd entered a month ago, had heard from him. Pakistani Intelligence had telexed the information to London, and Scotland Yard was waiting for Kayani at Heathrow Airport when his flight landed.

After he reached the immigration desk, he was pulled aside and escorted to the interview room where Detective Inspector Rex Hart and two members of his squad greeted him.

Hart studied the puzzled traveler while his sergeant looked through the man's passport. "Mister Kayani," the sergeant began, handing him back his passport, "we have some bad news for you, I'm afraid. As no one has been able to contact you since you left London, this seemed the best way to tell you."

"I...I, don't understand...what..." Kayani stammered.

"Your sister Faiza was murdered the day after you flew to Karachi."

The news stunned him, and he sat heavily into the chair that Hart quickly shoved behind him.

THREE HOURS LATER, HART WAS briefing Detective Superintendent Derek Houghton about Kayani's return. They were alone in Derek's office. "The revelation that his sister was dead definitely came as a shock to him. His visible grief was certainly not put on. And when we drove him home to meet his parents, we got the same impression."

"Well then, that means the honor killing theory can be discarded for good, I should think," Houghton said.

"Yes, it does. In fact after he'd pulled himself together, he asked if we had found her killer yet. Not killers, plural, or did we have a motive, just killer. Almost as if he had someone in mind."

"Really? That could be the break you need, then."

"Exactly. As you know, we've been at a dead end. Nothing from the street, or from any of our usual informants. Which tells us that it was a singular act, probably not a killing for hire."

"That makes sense. So what's your next move?"

"He's agreed to speak with us tomorrow morning, and we'll go from there. I didn't see any harm in leaving it until then. Do you want us to press him about what he was doing in Pakistan?"

Houghton rubbed his chin thoughtfully before replying. "He'll probably be expecting it. But I suggest you tread softly, let him believe that you're only interested in solving his sister's murder," he shrugged. "That way, he might think his other activities have gone unnoticed."

"Right. And now that I think of it, his first reaction when we took him aside spoke to that. I'm sure he thought we wanted to know what he'd be up in Pakistan. He almost seemed relieved when we told him of the murder."

SUNDAY, OCTOBER 31

"Well done, Rex! Bet you didn't think it would be quite so simple, did you?" said Houghton, extending his hand.

DI Hart smiled his thanks. "No, it came together rather nicely after the brother steered us to the suspect."

The Sunday papers carried accounts of yesterday's arrest of a landed immigrant from Pakistan and his subsequent confession to the murder last month of Faiza Kayani.

Hart gave Houghton details that were not in the newspaper reports. Faiza's brother and the man worshiped at the same mosque in north London. His first name was Ali, and eventually their casual acquaintance led to Ali formally asking Saahir to introduce him to his sister. Saahir saw no harm in this—Ali struck him as a reasonable sort with a steady job in a bakery—and although hesitant, his sister went along with it.

Faiza agreed to meet Ali more to appease her parents and their traditional ways than out of a desire to get married anytime soon. That would not happen, even if she were attracted to her brother's friend. She'd had more than one heated discussion with the family over her independent and western views in recent months. The following week the three met for tea. Another three weeks passed before Faiza agreed to a second meeting, and once again joined Ali and her brother after Friday evening prayers.

"Apparently she never really took to this chap, but sticking with tradition, she bowed to her elder brother's request and accepted an invitation from Ali to have dinner with him. Just the two of them," explained Hart. "But that ended the relationship. She told her brother in no uncertain terms that she had no further interest in the man. Saahir informed Ali of his sister's decision and thought nothing more of it."

"I see, and what was the time frame on this?" Houghton asked.

"Approximately two weeks before he killed her. It was just happenstance that Saahir left for Pakistan the day before her slaying."

The young immigrant rented a room in an Earl's Court hostel and that's where the police arrested him Friday night. It was as if he had been expecting them. He broke down almost immediately, and made a tearful and apologetic confession. He had waited for Faiza outside the university on the night before her death, hoping to change her mind, but she'd brusquely told him to leave her alone. Her cold rejection set him off, and, the next night he stalked her after she came up from the Underground at the Maida Vale station.

"So her unfortunate demise had nothing to do with family honor, or her being a police informant," Hart summed up. "The defense will probably plead temporary insanity, but at least the case is closed as far as we're concerned."

AFTER DI HART LEFT, HOUGHTON held a meeting with his officers to tell them of the successful conclusion to the murder investigation. "In the end, it was just a senseless act perpetrated by a spurned suitor. Nothing to do with her being an informant. Any questions?"

Sergeant Barbara Norton spoke up first. "Did Saahir give any details about his trip to Pakistan?"

"Not much, but then I'd asked them to down play it. He gave them a half-baked story about just wanting to see a bit of the country, and moving around with no particular agenda, et cetera, et cetera," said Houghton. "Complete rot, of course, but for now we'll leave it at that."

"So we'll still keep an eye on him?" asked another officer.

"Oh yes, beginning today we'll be watching him around the clock. Every time he moves, every time he speaks to someone outside the family home, I want it logged. Understand?" There was a communal nod of agreement from his officers. "It will mean longer hours for everyone, at least for the next few weeks. I've put in a request for more bodies, but that won't happen overnight."

"But you're thinking he was probably on a training course, right boss?"

"Until we know differently, yes," said Houghton. "And if he was, we can assume he's been sent back with specific instructions to put that training to work. Probably in conjunction with others. That's why keeping track of him in the near term is a priority."

41

SINGAPORE, SUNDAY, OCTOBER 31

Paul hadn't been to Singapore for years and the changes blew him away. The modern airport was the first of indication that the small nation had arrived on the world's stage with a bang. Even if he'd been jet-lagged after the overnight flight from Paris, the efficient and airy terminal would have caught his attention. But he wasn't tired. When he'd outlined his plan to pressure Francoise Amara, Don Carling had been all for it, and told him the expense would not be a problem. With that in mind, Paul had booked a business-class ticket, and slept for six hours in the almost flat surface his seat converted to.

Rather than wait for Francoise's uncertain return to Paris—and the probability that his colleague would face arrest in the interim—Boutin decided a surprise confrontation with her was called for. He was certain he could break her, he'd told Carling, and now was the time to do it.

The taxi ride from the airport into the city proper revealed further amazing evidence of the country's modernization. The harbor on his left was dotted with supertankers and cargo ships stacked high with containers. The highway they were driving on, according to signs posted along it, could quickly be converted to a runway for the Singapore Air Force's state-of-the-art fighter aircraft in an emergency. The only thing that hadn't changed was the weather. The temperature in the city's business district was 33C and the humidity nearing ninety per cent. It gave him a blast furnace-like jolt as he stepped out of the taxi in front of the modern hotel. The momentary discomfort disappeared as soon he entered the impressive, three-story lobby and its air-conditioned atmosphere. An abundance of fresh flowers and potted plants provided a tropical garden-like ambiance.

"Just two nights, sir?" asked the attractive young Asian clerk as she studied his reservation information on her computer.

"Yes, that's correct. I may want to extend, though. Would that be a problem?"

"No sir, we have plenty of rooms available until late next week. Just let us know," she smiled, handing him a registration form. "All I need is your signature and a credit card for an imprint."

Five minutes later Boutin was ushered into a tenth floor room by a young bellhop, who, after carefully setting Paul's large suitcase on a luggage stand, quickly explained the room's controls for lighting, air conditioning and the large screen television. The hotel featured Internet access from each room and Boutin laid his laptop computer case on the table near the connection. He noted one of the languages on the easy-to-read instruction card for using the system was French. He thanked the bellhop, tipped him, and closed the door behind him.

If she hadn't changed her itinerary since leaving Paris, Mademoiselle Francoise Amara should also be staying in the hotel. Boutin knew that she had flown out of Paris on Thursday, the 14th, on a Cathay Pacific flight to Hong Kong. Paul's team had obtained a copy of her travel arrangements from her travel agency. Singapore was her next stop after Hong Kong and she was booked into the hotel as of two days ago.

Paul fished a bottle of Perrier water out of the minibar, and settled into one of the room's two plush armchairs. The local time was coming up on noon. He decided that his best chance to catch her in person would probably be later this afternoon, after four perhaps. But first he'd better ascertain that she was in fact staying in the hotel. An idea struck him, and after quenching his thirst, he exchanged his dress shirt and tie for a sports shirt, and made his way back down to the lobby...

BOUTIN KNOCKED ON HER DOOR at 4:30, and his unexpected appearance had the desired effect. Francoise's slender hand flew to her mouth when she recognized her caller. "You... you, what are you doing here?" she gasped. "Did you—" she hesitated, pointing at the small bouquet of roses resting on the hallway table. "You sent these, didn't you?"

Paul admitted as much. He'd had the florist shop in the hotel arcade deliver them. By doing so he'd confirmed that she was staying in the hotel and her room number. All he'd written on the card was 'See you soon'.

"May I come in?" he asked. When she moved to close the door on him, he placed his hand on it and said, "What I have to tell you may keep you out of jail."

Francoise turned without a word and sat in one of the large room's two well-cushioned chairs. Boutin stepped in and closed the door behind him. He took the chair opposite her without waiting to be asked. He gave her time to regain her composure, a few silent minutes that saw her facial expression alternate between fear and puzzlement with the occasional hint of hatred.

Eventually she sat back with her arms folded. "I'm listening."

"Ms. Amara, I didn't come all this way just to send you flowers. Here's the deal. I am not with the Surete. I am a private detective, and—"

"I'm going to call hotel security," she interrupted him, reaching for the phone.

Boutin caught her wrist and squeezed it. "No you're not, unless you want it known to your agency and customers that you could be charged as an accessory to murder, perhaps two murders."

She stopped trying to break free from his grasp and sank back into her chair. "Just listen to what I have to say, and maybe, just maybe, you might avoid going to jail," he said, releasing her wrist.

Fifteen minutes later, Boutin knew his decision to come all the way to Singapore to confront her was the right one. He'd given her his take on how he thought the killer—or killers—had been able to get into the room next to Don Carling's. "I believe you were responsible for obtaining the pass key used to access that room. And I'm certain that you got it from a room service waiter named Salif in return for a handsome amount of money. You told me in Paris that you didn't remember him, but I now know that's not true. And he became the second murder victim."

"You can't possibly prove that," she said.

"Oh? Young Salif had a buddy, another waiter, and he bragged to him about his friendship with you, and how much money you paid him," Boutin told her, flashing a brief smile. "I've got his sworn testimony and he's agreed to tell the police the same thing if necessary." Actually he had no such document, but Francoise couldn't refute his assertion because it was true.

She lowered her head and studied her long and colorful nails, flicking imaginary bits of dust off them. When she looked up again she said, without much confidence, "My lawyer will see it differently, and I have nothing further to say to you. Please leave."

Boutin started to rise and then dropped back into his chair. "Yes, I'll leave, but just let me say this. I don't think you had any idea of what you were letting yourself in for when you took your twin brother's room at the hotel. And you probably don't know who supplied the money to pay for the pass key. If you knew it was going to be used to abet a murder, you probably wouldn't have agreed to help. Am I right? He detected a slight nod of her head. "But what you knew or didn't know is immaterial now. Once this information reaches the police, your life is in danger, make no mistake about that."

The warning startled Francoise. "What do you mean?" she asked, almost whispering.

"Just this," he said, leaning closer and lowering his voice. "Your brother and those he's associated with are not into petty crime. They're part of a terrorist network." Stunned, she tried to speak, but Boutin continued before words came out. "Yes, *terrorists*," he emphasized. "They've sanctioned two murders so far and are plotting something you don't even want to know the first thing about." He was being overly dramatic, but it was having the desired effect. "And don't think family ties will save you if they see you as a weak link. Once you're regarded as a liability, however slight, you'll be a marked woman. And your brother won't be able to do anything about it..."

He eyed her silently until she turned away. He started to stand, but she held up her hand.

"Wait, please. What can I..." her worried voice trailed off.

"What can you do to get out of this mess?" he asked.

When she nodded resignedly, Boutin gave her an out...

42

WASHINGTON, MONDAY, NOVEMBER 1

DHS Acting Director George Egan exploded. "Godammit, that's not good enough! We need whatever they have *now*. Not next week...not three days from now, but *NOW!* Call the CIA again, March. If they still stall, let me know immediately. If necessary, I'll get the White House to light a fire under their asses!"

Egan's official title was Deputy Director, but he had been appointed to the temporary position last week after the director had suffered a near-fatal heart attack, which was expected to sideline him for at least two months.

Agent Bob March nodded and hurried back to his office two doors down from the AD's. He had contacted the CIA three weeks ago requesting any information they might have on the code words the Canadian and British counterterrorism task forces had discovered. Since 9/11, the CIA and the National Security Agency [NSA] had been monitoring suspected terrorist networks around the clock. Thousands of technicians, interpreters and analysts were involved. Electronic eavesdropping of satellite and land line phone communications in addition to email exchanges allowed them to keep tab on hundreds of terrorist suspects and their activities.

The information—billions of data bits—was stored on massive hard drives in a CIA building in Virginia and the NSA's enormous headquarters at Fort Meade, Maryland. Armies of clerks used unique software programs to correlate seemingly unrelated threads—names, cell phone numbers, ship movements— routed to or from known or suspected terrorist organizations, training camps and safe houses around the globe.

The CIA had taken a week to respond to March's initial request. His query had been 'prioritized', he was told, and would be dealt with as soon as possible. Apparently four or five suspected code words with no other details wasn't enough to warrant immediate attention from the agency.

March called the CIA staffer he'd spoken with previously, and had barely begun to relay his boss's threat to pull strings when the agent stopped him.

"Hold your horses! I was about to call you, Bob!" he chuckled. "There's been a development regarding your query. Our people had a 'hit' on a couple of the names you gave us."

Two of the code words, FARMER and FOX, were used on intercepted satellite phone calls originating in Yemen and answered in the US. The agency was now searching their data bases for any previous occurrences of their use. Did Homeland Security have any other information about them that might help their search?"

March had been reviewing his file on the words and noticed something he'd missed. "Here's a suggestion that might speed things up," he said. "Narrow your search to French-only communications. Our sources think the suspects are probably French nationals, or at least working out of France."

THE SCENE AT DHS HEADQUARTERS in Washington was being repeated at the FBI's New York office: an underling was catching the wrath of his boss to start the week.

Special Agent Dwight Ewing was on the carpet. "What the hell do you mean *'he's history'*?" The man dressing him down was his new boss, Special Agent in Charge [SAC] Jonathan Cannon. "The Canadian authorities have been in contact again about this Barr character. Why haven't we at least begun the process of handing him over to face the charges up there? From what I read, this asshole is probably a murderer." Cannon stared at Ewing, waiting for an explanation.

Ewing let out a deep sigh before he spoke. "It's complicated, sir," he began. "Barr was a person of interest to us for some time. He'd had contact with a suspected agent for what we believe is a possible terrorist cell based here in the New York. If our take on him was right, anything he was guilty of up in Canada was uhh... at their behest."

"Don't beat around the bush, Ewing! I know you've got a degree in English from Yale. Say what you mean, for God's sake! He was hired to carry out hits up there. Yes or no?"

And you went to Georgia Tech on a football scholarship, Ewing said to himself. "...Yes," he replied, biting his tongue. "Your predecessor thought we could sit on Barr a bit longer."

"I see. So your former boss, now happily retired and living on a golf course in Hawaii, I understand, sanctioned his termination."

"Yes, that's what happened," admitted Ewing. "It wasn't a decision taken lightly, but..."

"Stop right there, Ewing!" ordered Cannon, holding up a hand. "I don't want to know any more about it. If it comes back to bite the Bureau, your former boss can do the explaining."

"Fine by me, sir," said Ewing, rising to go.

"Hold on, Ewing. I presume we have his prints on file. What about his DNA?"

"We have both."

Okay, I want you to send whatever we've got up to these good folks in Toronto. Maybe it will help them close the files on the murders they want him for. Make up your own story as to why we can't produce the SOB himself. You're dismissed," he said, shaking his head. Ewing stood and made for the door. He resisted the impulse to slam it as he left.

Back in his office, Ewing took a few minutes to cool down. *If my first meeting with the new SAC was any indication, his reputation as a 'hard ass' definitely held true*, he thought. *Maybe it's a good thing I didn't have to explain how Barr was dealt with...*

Not that the FBI had a direct hand in his demise. They had been behind the rumor, though, naming Barr as a Bureau informant. The rumor was leaked to a notorious, Jersey-based motorcycle gang known to be part of an often violent dispute over drug territories with the outfit Barr rode with.

The rumor had accomplished its purpose, apparently. Word filtered back from underworld sources that Lionel Barr was no longer in the land of the living. Ewing shuddered to think how the hit on him may have occurred. The odds of his body turning up were slim to none, in his experience. It was either deeply buried at a construction site or resting on the bottom of Chesapeake Bay, weighted down by cement shoes.

WEDNESDAY, NOVEMBER 3

Although the US presidential election was held yesterday, Tuesday, the result was not made official until earlier this morning: President Bush had defeated the Democratic challenger, Senator John Kerry, by the narrowest of margins.

Don knew that the terrorist plot hinged on the outcome, and wasn't surprised when Tom Allman called just hours after the official announcement hit the airwaves.

"Okay, pard, things are pickin' up down here," said Tom. "Archer just got the word sayin' the plot is a 'go' now that the president has been re-elected. There's somethin' they need me to do regarding the explosives in a few days. Supposed to get me details tonight or tomorrow."

"Any idea what they want?"

Tom hesitated. "Nothin' definite, pard. How 'bout I get back to you as soon as I know more."

THURSDAY MORNING THE PACKAGE FROM the FBI containing Lionel Jesse Barr's DNA data arrived by courier at OPP Sergeant Leon Belcher's office and was immediately sent to the lab. Belcher was hoping the samples would match those collected by his homicide investigators. Although Barr's fingerprints had been found on the pickup truck he'd sold, that alone wasn't enough to support a murder conviction. They needed evidence to tie him directly to one of the victims.

Barr had never made any physical contact with the first victim, Marlene Hastings. However, evidence collected by PI Don Carling near the scene of the car crash that killed her tied him to the second victim, Mary Jane Cuddy. Carling had picked up and bagged cigarette butts and coffee cups he'd found strewn by the roadside near his country home. The spot, he'd surmised, where Barr had parked while he waited for Yvonne's yellow VW to leave his driveway. DNA from these articles and hairs found on the clothing Cuddy was wearing when she was killed were an exact match to the FBI samples.

"It may not matter now," Belcher told the chief prosecutor when he called him after hearing from the forensics lab, "because this character is now presumed dead, according to the FBI. Legally I don't suppose we can consider it a closed case, though, or can we?"

"No, not from our perspective, unfortunately," replied the lawyer. "I suggest you complete your report as if he were alive. I'll file it, but it will have to be entered as an open case. If you should get word that he is officially dead, then we'll close it."

"The odds of that happening are about the same as the Maple Leafs winning the Stanley Cup this year," remarked Belcher.

The lawyer was still laughing loudly as he hung up.

Toronto's National Hockey League club hadn't won the prized trophy for almost forty years, and were off to another poor start this season.

WASHINGTON, FRIDAY, NOVEMBER 5

Agent March was pleasantly surprised when he received a classified report from the CIA only four days after he phoned the agency with his boss's ultimatum.

The joint report from the CIA and the National Security Agency [NSA] was not extensive and didn't provide any information as to the locations of suspects linked to the codes. The report listed only eight intercepted transmissions in which the code words were used. The information had been culled from intercepts logged during the period between early May and mid-September.

NSA was prohibited by federal law from eavesdropping on calls made within the United States proper, although critics suggested this restriction was not always adhered to. The intercepts transcribed by analysts in the report had originated in three locations: France, Great Britain, and Yemen.

The FBI, on the other hand, and usually acting on a federal warrant, was permitted to monitor traffic between callers within the continental US.

MARCH TOOK THE REPORT TO acting Director George Egan immediately. When the AD had read it, March made a suggestion. "Give me a few days to contact our friends abroad to see if they can match these intercepts with names or locations in their countries. Meanwhile, I'll ask the FBI to work on them here," he said.

"Okay, get on it, March, and ask if they have any info as to a time frame for whatever this cell is supposedly planning," said Egan. "Wasn't there something from the Brits about the Christmas period?"

"That's right, sir, although they didn't provide any details. I'll try and find out what they based that assumption on."

"Good," replied Egan, leafing through the report again. "What about the French? A number of the calls originated from a French phone number according to this," he said. "Might be worth checking with them."

March had also noticed the references to France, and had planned to take the initiative and contact the French authorities. But he couldn't miss an opportunity to stroke his superior's ego. "Great idea, sir. I'll get in touch with their intelligence people right away."

TIME WAS NOT THE SIDE of the allied intelligence agencies, however. From discussions with his counterparts at the CIA and NSA, March knew that trying to identify parties at both ends of a given call or Internet message was like looking for the proverbial needle in a haystack. Trained terrorists changed their phones, user names, and Internet providers at random to thwart electronic efforts to pinpoint them. Unless an individual called the same number on a regular basis, chances of tracking him down in the short term were very low. And with the last reference to the code words having occurred almost two months ago, March was afraid the cell's plot might be at the stage where no further communications were necessary.

43

IN ARIZONA LATER THE SAME day, Agent Diane Jimenez, duty dispatcher for the Border Patrol's southeast sector, told the excited caller to speak more slowly and repeat his message. The call came on the toll-free line displayed on billboards for reporting suspicious activity.

"...There's twenny, mebbe' twenny-five,' of 'em. They're just millin' about and sittin' in some bushes in the desert by the road. Must be illegals!" said the caller. She couldn't place his accent.

"What is your location, sir?" she asked calmly.

The caller told her he'd passed through Bisbee about five minutes ago, heading east. When she asked him for his name, the connection began to break up, and she couldn't make out his reply. Ten seconds later it died completely. She logged the call at 9:15 p.m.

The caller probably wasn't from the area, she concluded, or he would've been able to pinpoint his position more accurately. Agent Jimenez studied the area map. She figured he must have been near the intersection of Tumble Mountain Road and Highway 80, only a few miles from the Mexican border. It was territory often used by guides, known to the Border Patrol as 'coyotes', to lead aliens across. It was a larger than average group, if the caller's estimate was correct, and they were probably waiting to be picked up and driven to safe houses in Tucson or Phoenix.

Jimenez made a quick decision. There were two patrol vehicles in the Douglas area to the east, and two more north of Bisbee. All were within 20 to 25 minutes of the reported sighting. She swiveled her chair around to face the communications panel and reached for the microphone. After a radio check with the patrol vehicles, she instructed them to head for the area.

Next, she called the Sierra Vista station and advised them of the situation. The Border Patrol kept a small fleet of aircraft at the airport just north of the city. When she asked if there was a chopper available, the duty officer replied, "Hold one, Diane..."

A minute later he was back on. "Yep... there's one on standby tonight. Let's give the fly boys something to do. I'll authorize their flight. They'll check in with the ground ops once they reach the area."

"Roger that, SV, and thanks," she answered, and signed off.

T HE CREW OF THE AS350 helicopter, commonly referred to as the "A Star', was ready to lift off at 9:32, twelve minutes after they were alerted.

"Sagebrush 12, you're cleared for take-off. Maintain a listening watch on frequency 119.3," the tower controller advised.

The low altitude the chopper would be flying at meant it would be below Air Traffic Control radar most of the time. They could use the radio, however, to advise ATC in the event of an emergency.

Weather conditions were favorable for night visual flight operations: cirrus cloud above twenty-five thousand feet, visibility approximately ten miles, and a south wind of seven to ten knots at 2,000 feet above ground. Both pilots decided their night vision goggles [NVGs] wouldn't be needed until they reached the rendezvous area.

With her part in the search mission over for the time being, Agent Jimenez got to thinking about the report from the anonymous caller. A couple of things about it bothered her. The call came via the 800 number and Diane could count the number of calls she'd received on the line on one hand. And she'd been on the job for five years. Most reports in the area regarding border crossers came from locals, ranchers whose land straddled the border. She thought about calling one of the area ranchers. She was about to dial his number when she checked the large wall clock. It was almost 10 p.m., and rather than disturb him, she put the receiver down. Most of the ranchers she knew turned in early and rose before dawn.

Diane replayed the call again. There was something about the voice that wasn't quite right. Eventually she decided the caller had been trying to imitate a southern drawl. She was also wondering why the caller hadn't tried again. *Maybe his phone battery died*, she surmised. *Oh well, the boys should be calling in soon. Nothing more I can do until they get to the area.*

IT WAS 10:45 WHEN SHE got the call. "No contacts, Diane. We've swept the area as far east as Douglas. Haven't seen anyone. The chopper has made three low sweeps of the area. Their heat-seeking gizmos picked up nothing but cattle and a few coyotes, the four-legged type."

"Check that, Donny. I'll log it off and you can resume normal patrol. See you at twelve. Be safe."

Mexican-American Donny Martinez was Diane's husband. Both their shifts ended at midnight, and Donny would pick her up for the short drive to their farmhouse home a few miles east of Douglas. Diane refilled her coffee cup and returned to her desk, still puzzling over the situation. It was unlikely that the border crossers had been picked up before the patrol vehicles converged on the area, Diane reasoned, but not impossible. Just to be on the safe side, she issued an alert to all units further north, advising them to be extra vigilant overnight for suspect vehicles. Any vehicle capable of carrying four or more passengers would be stopped and searched: SUVs, pickups, minivans, and trucks of any size would qualify.

THERE WAS A VERY GOOD reason for the fruitless search. The call had been placed by Tom Allman. A ruse that he hoped would draw patrols away from the area where he was to rendezvous with the smugglers at 11 p.m. Thirty minutes after his call, he saw evidence that his false report had worked. The Border Patrol helicopter passed directly over the shabby trailer he was renting in the Crooked Horn RV Park The chopper was tracking southeasterly, a course that would keep it just north of the border and along the highway towards the Bisbee area.

The park sat on ten acres of scrub land seven miles southeast of Sierra Vista. Allman had spotted the *'TRAILER FOR RENT'* sign on a coffee shop bulletin board yesterday morning after arriving in SV. One phone call, a short meeting in the same shop an hour later, and $120 in cash secured him a week's rental of the run-down unit with no questions asked.

The park had seen better days, and most of the thirty or so trailers scattered about would never be considered roadworthy again. He'd only exchanged a quick 'hello' with two of the permanent residents, both seniors who showed no interest in him, which suited Tom perfectly. If the rendezvous and pick up came off as planned, he'd be long gone before his rental period ended.

When Archer told him what needed to be done, he'd asked Tom if he needed his help collecting the shipment, but Tom had quickly assured him that he could manage alone. The last thing he wanted was an untrained accomplice trailing around after him in the desert. The message Frank received told him the shipment would consist of four small crates. If that was all that showed up, Tom didn't think he'd have a problem hiding them from a cursory inspection if he ran into a random Border Patrol check point.

At 10:30 p.m. he placed another call, this time to a cell phone with the southern Arizona area code, 520. The man who answered wasn't in Arizona, but he wasn't that far away, either. He was holed up in a secluded arroyo a few miles south of the border, less than ten miles as the crow flies from the park. Allman's message was short and simple: it was a 'go' for the rendezvous. The answer was a quiet 'Bueno'.

A few minutes later Tom pulled on a dark long-sleeved sweater, turned off the lights and left the trailer, closing the door quietly behind him. He got into his navy blue Jeep and drove slowly out of the RV park, turning south on Highway 92.

Tom had chosen the rendezvous location after an all-night reconnaissance of the area 24 hours ago, sitting unseen for hours watching for border patrol activity. He had only noticed one patrol vehicle driving slowly south on the winding road that lead to the Coronado National Monument, the mountain park overlooking the Mexican border region. Most of the traffic on the road consisted of visitors traveling to and from the park during daylight hours. The Border Patrol vehicle passed him again forty-five minutes later heading northbound.

He was positive his arrival tonight had gone unnoticed. He was leaning against the one wall that was still standing of a derelict barn, the only outbuilding remaining on the once-active ranch. The barn was three hundred yards down a dirt path from the paved road. There was even less evidence left of the original farmhouse nearby. Part of a stone chimney stood in stark testimony to the fire that had destroyed the building more than twenty years ago.

He had given the GPS coordinates of the barn to Frank to forward to his contact. Now he waited, leaning against the front bumper of his Jeep while he scanned the darkness to the southeast, towards the border.

At least that's the direction they should be coming from unless they screw up, he thought.

He checked the luminous dial on his wristwatch. Still three minutes before he was to signal. It was deathly quiet, the only sound a sporadic and barely audible 'ping' from the Jeep's still-warm engine.

Tom's night vision had peaked, yet the only images he could discern were that of the mesquite bushes and palo verde trees dotting the emptiness of the scrubby range land. He estimated his visual range at a maximum of twenty yards. With no moon, and a thin layer of high cloud obscuring most of the stars, it was much blacker than he had expected.

He donned his night vision goggles and peered into the desert, but there was still no sign of activity, human or otherwise. At exactly 11 p.m.

he flicked on his coned flashlight, pointed it to the southeast, and swept it back and forth while counting to five. He waited a minute and repeated the action.

This time there was an instant response approximately twenty degrees to his right. Three short bursts of dim light. A minute later Tom heard low engine noise, and almost immediately caught the outline of approaching vehicles.

There were three of them. Four-wheeled, customized ATV's that must have arrived at the rendezvous point earlier, and sat with engines off waiting for Allman's signal. Now they wheeled to a stop in front of him, the drivers clad in stocking masks and wearing NVGs.

Without a word, the driver of the lead ATV dismounted, uncovered two containers secured on the back of his rig, carried them over behind the Jeep and set them on the ground. The second driver placed the two boxes he'd been hauling on top of the first two. The leader remounted his ATV, directed a quick 'Adios!' at Tom, and wheeled back into the darkness, followed by the other two. The exchange took less than two minutes, and Tom stared after them as they high-tailed it back towards Mexico.

The ex-Green Beret grudgingly admired their actions. They had been suitably outfitted for the covert rendezvous, were in place at the right time, and had used three vehicles. The third was a back up in case one of the others had broken down, he figured. The vehicles had been modified to reduce engine noise to the lowest possible level. All precautions Tom would have taken if he had been in their shoes.

Tom loaded the boxes, which weren't very heavy, into the rear deck of his Jeep Commander and covered them with a tarp. He waited a further ten minutes before moving slowly away from behind the barn wall and back along the dirt path. When he reached a point beside a copse of trees twenty yards from the road, he stopped and stepped outside. He listened for traffic noise, but it was still remarkably quiet. He removed the makeshift hoods he'd placed over the headlights to dim them, slipped back into the driver's seat and quickly covered the remaining distance to the black top.

Twelve minutes at the 55 mph speed limit brought him back to the RV park. Most of the occupied trailers were in darkness as he rolled past them. Once inside the trailer, he slipped his boots off, undressed in the dark and got into his own sleeping bag lain out on the lumpy bed.

Sleep eluded him, though. He knew from experience that the adrenaline buzz would take time to wear off. A number of thoughts were keeping him awake. One dwelt with what would have happened to him if he had been stopped by police or the border patrol. He didn't know what was in the containers, but it sure as hell wasn't fruit from Mexican orchards. He'd end up it jail for sure—and not just for a few days—until the authorities could unravel his covert role regarding the terrorist plot.

The second thought, also one that he couldn't answer, concerned how and why the shipment came via Mexico. Those behind it must of had help getting it into Mexico in the first place, and then with the border crossing operation. But money talks in those circles, he knew, and Mexico was known to have more than its share of corrupt officials.

Tom was still thinking of possible scenarios when he finally drifted off to sleep. And his 'best guess' was close to the mark. The shipment had originated in Egypt, and arrived in the port city of Tampico on Mexico's gulf coast. The ship's cargo of farm machinery was destined a large implement distributor, and the boxes were listed as machine parts on the manifest. A few hundred dollars to a customs inspector ensured their clearance without inspection.

An al-Qaeda World operative based in Mexico City made the arrangements to move the contraband up to the border area and into the hands of the men who smuggled it into the US.

44

FRIDAY, NOVEMBER 5

Don decided that he couldn't wait any longer. Paul Boutin's rushed call as he was getting ready to leave Paris for Singapore had been worrying him all week. Boutin had just learned from a reliable source that the French government would be filing a request with Canadian authorities for Carling's extradition 'within days'. If he were to be of any use to Tom Allman he had to leave for the US this weekend.

DICK EASTON, YVONNE'S BROTHER, GREETED Don Carling warmly. "Hey, Don, what's up? It's been a while. How're you keeping?"

"Pretty good, thanks, Dick. Something's come up that you might be able to help me with, though."

"Well, as long as the leak is in your house and not your personal waterworks I'm your man!"

Don burst out laughing. "No, nothing like that! And don't worry. If I ever have a problem with my plumbing you'd be the last guy I'd call! Even for a family discount!"

Easton and his wife lived in London, Ontario, and Dick had his own small but busy plumbing business. Don and Yvonne had occasionally visited with the Eastons' during the past two years, usually spending Friday and Saturday night with them. The men had become good friends, partly fostered by their mutual interest in sports. They chatted about sports for a few minutes, including the woes of three teams they both followed: baseball's Toronto Blue Jays, hockey's Maple Leafs, and the Detroit Lions of the National Football League.

"So, what do you need, Don?"

"Do you and your buddies still go over to the Lions games?"

Don had an open invitation to join Dick and his buddies whenever they were planning a trip to a Detroit Lions game. Dick was the groups' volunteer co-ordinator, responsible for ordering tickets and chartering a bus to transport them to and from Detroit, a two-hour drive from London. It was a 'men only outing and plenty of beer was consumed, mostly on the trip home.

"Oh yeah, we still go, but not as often. Ticket prices are up and the team stinks. But yeah, we've still got enough faithful fanatics who sign up. In fact we're headin' over this coming Sunday," said Dick. "They're up against the Redskins. Should have a chance against them."

Don had already checked the schedule. "Got room for one more?"

"Uhh, yeah, we do. Got room for three, actually."

"Well, it'll just be me," Don said. "Can you still get across the border by just showing your driver's licence?"

"Haven't had any hassles so far. You hear rumblings that you'll soon need a passport, you know. All because of 9/11, right?"

Don agreed. The Department of Homeland Security had drafted plans to make possession of a passport mandatory for travel to and from the continental US. Even American citizens would be required to present a passport to re-enter their country, if initial reports were correct. Don wanted to enter the US without having to show his passport, and the bus charter presented a good way to avoid having to do so. He thanked Dick, and told him he and Yvonne would arrive tomorrow afternoon.

He laughed at Dick's suggestion Yvonne might have to drive them back to Toronto if the beer flowed freely on the bus trip back to London after the game. "Hey, I'm getting too old for that sort of nonsense, Dick!"

He wasn't planning to be on the bus when headed back to Canada. But Dick wasn't to know that until later.

SATURDAY MORNING, NOVEMBER 6

"Tell me again why you're in such a hurry to get to the States. You were rather vague when you called yesterday."

Don and Yvonne had enjoyed a quiet evening together last night. They were both tired, went to bed early, slept soundly, and woke within minutes of each other just after seven o'clock. Don prepared a full breakfast that they'd eaten in relative silence over the morning paper. By 9:30, they were en route to her brother's place in Yvonne's car.

"Yeah, sorry about that, hon," he said, easing back into the right lane after overtaking a transport truck. Yvonne had asked him what was bothering him. "It's a long story, really, and has to do with the case I've been working on since June. It started with my trip to Paris..."

Don had told Yvonne about the murdered prostitute right after he learned about it, and the attempt by people connected with Archer to lay the blame on him. "Well, I don't know yet how they managed it, but the French police say they have enough evidence to charge me in connection with her murder. Ridiculous, I know, but they want me extradited."

"Oh my God, how did you get into such a mess!" said Yvonne, shaking her head. Don didn't have an answer. "So why don't you just get a good lawyer and fight it? What are you going to gain by leaving the country now?"

"Well, I'm not sure, to tell you the truth. The extradition order will probably get to Ottawa next week, but I can't take the chance that I'll have to surrender my passport while it gets sorted out."

"How do you know all this?" Yvonne asked, her bewilderment showing.

Don shrugged. "Paul Boutin told me some weeks ago that this might happen. And I *have* discussed it with my lawyers," explained Don. "They'll launch an appeal. But just to make sure I'll be available if Tom needs my help, I figured I'd better get across the border while I still can."

"Ah, so that's where this man you're investigating is hiding out," she said, "and Tom is still keeping track of him, right?"

"That's it in a nutshell, hon," replied Don. "This uhh... *plot* we suspect Archer is involved in should be coming to a head soon, so I want to be there when we turn it over to the US authorities."

They drove in silence for another fifteen minutes with Yvonne staring out her window. "Well, sweetheart, I just wish you would turn it all over to the police now and be done with it," she said, taking his free hand in hers. "Fraud and divorce cases are one thing, but your chasing terrorists really worries me."

"I know, and I'm sorry. But its just turned out that way," he replied, squeezing her hand. "And we're not trying to be heros, believe me." He was about to tell her that at least three law enforcement agencies were aware of his investigation but thought better of it. It would only cause her more anxiety if she knew how complex and potentially dangerous his pursuit of Archer was becoming.

They continued the drive in silence, stilling holding hands and both lost in their own thoughts.

SUNDAY MORNING, NOVEMBER 7

The two US Customs and Immigration officers who boarded the chartered bus on the US side of the Ambassador Bridge were in good spirits. The bridge spanned the Detroit River between Windsor, Ontario and the American city. The officers quickly checked everyone's ID, mostly a cursory glance at their driver's licence. The older of the two officers, a burly six-footer with a shaved head, joked to his partner that maybe they should send one of the passengers back to Canada because he was wearing a Washington Redskins jersey.

"I'm going to remember you, pal," he told the fan, tapping his driver's licence. "You'd better be wearing a Lions shirt the next time I see you." His feigned severity drew hoots of laughter from those seated around the offender and chants of *Throw him off!* and *Arrest the bugger!*

Don had no reason to suspect the American authorities would be looking for him, but he still let out a sigh of relief after the officers left the bus and waved the driver on. Once they reached the parking lot at Ford Field, he followed Dick and the rest of the group as they filed into the stadium 45 minutes before kick-off time. The first half saw some exciting football, but Don couldn't get caught up in the enthusiasm of the others. His mind was elsewhere, but no one seemed to notice. When the first half ended, the home team was only down by three points, and bets were flying back and forth as to the final outcome. Dick and Don lagged behind as most of the group headed for the concession booths for food and drink.

"Okay, Dick, I'm going to split now," he said. "I really appreciate you helping me out like this."

"Yeah, well, you be careful. And like I said, just call if you want me to relay a message to Yvonne."

Last night, while Yvonne and her sister-in-law were cleaning up after dinner, the men adjourned to the basement family room for a post-meal brandy. While they were alone, Don explained why he hoped to enter the US unnoticed. "I just need to make myself scare for a week or so to wind up an investigation," he told Dick, without mentioning details of his problem with French authorities.

After slipping out of the stadium, Don hailed a taxi and asked to be taken to the downtown Greyhound Bus terminal. On the short ride he wondered again whether or not he was doing the right thing.

Only time will tell, he realized after running the pros and cons through his mind for the fourth or fifth time. And once again he concluded he'd made his best choice. Yes, he was going to get a lot of flack when it was over. He might even lose his private investigator's licence until he cleared himself. But Tom Allman was going to need help. Help that Don wouldn't be capable of giving him if he were locked up in Canada or France.

Just get on with it! he urged himself as the taxi dropped him at the terminal. The next bus to the Metropolitan Airport was leaving in twenty minutes, just enough time for Don to join the short line at the ticket counter and buy a one-way fare.

It was a quarter past five when the fugitive—as he was now thinking of himself—rode the escalator up to the departures level. His destination was Denver, Colorado. Carling had pre-planned this next step from his office Friday morning. He'd searched the Internet for flights between the two cities on Sunday evenings. There were three possibilities: a Northwest Airlines flight via Minneapolis, a United flight via Chicago, or a direct flight on Frontier Airlines. He scanned the overhead sign listing flight departures. He was glad to see that his first choice, the direct flight, was still scheduled

"Are you checking any luggage , sir?"

"No," smiled Don. "Traveling light!"

Even 'traveling light' was an exaggeration. All Don had in his nylon carryall bag was a few toiletries, two pair of jockey shorts, socks, an extra polo shirt and a light sweater. Another case contained his laptop computer.

He bought a one-way ticket to Denver on the Frontier Airlines 7:30 p.m. flight, using a credit card bearing the name James R. Wright, a fictitious employee of Don's company. The charge would be billed to Kay-Roy, the same as charges made on cards issued to real employees. It was Don's first use of the bogus identity. He had a driver's licence in the same name, and had presented it when asked for photo ID at the ticket counter.

After receiving his boarding pass and making his way through the security area, Don realized he was starving. Not surprising, as his food intake since breakfast had consisted of one tasteless hot dog at the football game. With an hour to spare before his flight's departure time, he found a restaurant and ordered a chicken and ribs dinner. His cash stake amounted to 300 US dollars, but he also had an ATM card that would access an account in James R. Wright's name, and held $10,000 transferred to it from KayRoy's line of credit.

Just before he dozed off after the Boeing 737 reached its cruising altitude, Don had prioritized what his first actions would be tomorrow morning. He needed wheels, more clothing, and another cell phone. Then, and only then, would 'James Wright' be ready to call Tom Allman.

DON'S FLIGHT ARRIVED IN DENVER at 9:20 p.m. Although most of the car rental agencies in the arrivals area had CARS AVAILABLE signs displayed, Don decided to forego the convenience of an airport rental. In the off chance that anyone did come looking for him—and discovered that he had flown into Denver—car rental companies would be the first thing they'd check, he reasoned. At least that's what he would do if the situation were reversed. Instead, he called one of the airport area hotels and booked a room for the night. The shuttle bus dropped him off at the hotel twenty-five minutes later. 'Mister Wright' was sound asleep with the TV still on half an hour after checking in.

MONDAY MORNING DON AWOKE PLEASANTLY refreshed after eight hours of sound sleep—and hungry again. After making quick work of the Rocky Mountain Breakfast Special—eggs, bacon, pancakes, hash browns, and two slabs of toast—Don was ready and anxious to get moving.

The hotel offered hourly bus service to downtown Denver. Don checked out and caught the 10 a.m. bus. The weather on this late autumn morning was right out of the Colorado tourism book he'd leafed through at breakfast. Clear blue sky, temperature around 65F, and red and yellow leafage gracing the maple trees on the shady streets they were passing through.

The bus dropped him across from the State of Colorado capital building. The distance to the Budget Rent-a-Car's city center location was three blocks, and Don enjoyed the fresh air and walk. The lone agent on duty was handing a customer a set of keys and telling him to 'have a nice day' as he entered the office. Don was offered a choice of cars and opted for a mid-sized, four-door sedan, and handed his credit card and driver's licence to the agent.

"Could be two days, but not more than four," Don replied, when asked. "I'm here to check out some real estate opportunities for a client back home," he told the curious agent when he remarked on the Canadian driver's licence.

Once the paperwork was completed, Don asked for directions to a shopping center. The agent produced a city map and circled an area with a marker pen. "You'll find a big mall on either side of the freeway right about here. Can't miss them," he smiled, handing Don the map.

Don familiarized himself with the Ford Taurus's instrument panel and adjusted the mirrors before he slowly exited the parking lot. Rush hour traffic had long since thinned out, and twenty minutes later Don turned off Interstate 25 and pulled into the vast parking lot surrounding the Cedarview Plaza. He locked his lap top and carryall in the trunk before heading inside.

An hour later he had purchased all the items on his shopping list. *Cripes, that's the longest time I've spent buying things for years!* he thought, collapsing into a chair at Starbucks in the food court. *And I shudda' bought the suitcase first.* The coffee was way too hot for his liking and he used the time while it cooled to transfer his new acquisitions into the medium-sized case.

As he munched on a grilled chicken sandwich, he thought about his next move. Should he call his office yet? Before leaving Toronto, he and

Joanne had agreed on a plan for communicating if and when he became a fugitive.

One of the first items he'd acquired was a phone card and Don studied the instructions on the foil package as he drained his coffee. To use it, he first had to dial a toll-free number, and then enter a 10-digit access code. It wasn't as simple as dialing direct, but it wouldn't be traceable, either.

After punching the numbers, a recorded voice told him he was now free to place a call...

Joanne answered on the second ring. "Good afternoon, KayRoy Services."

"Yes, may I speak to the office manager?"

"Oh, Hi Don, you're clear. No one looking for you yet." Her alternate answer would have been 'he's not available, may I take a message?'.

"Good. I've gotta a number for you. Ready to copy?" Don reeled off the number of the cell phone he'd purchased at Walmart. The phone came with sixty minutes of air time, and it could be topped up as necessary. "Use this number if you need to contact me," he said, "but don't call from the office." Don was probably going overboard with his precautions, he knew, but he wasn't leaving anything to chance.

45

"James, what would you say to a bit of sleuthing again for us?"

"I would say your chances are excellent, old boy!" replied retired MI5 officer to Inspector Houghton's question. "What have you got in mind?"

After he returned from Pakistan eleven days ago, and helped Scotland Yard identify his sister's killer, Saahir Kayani had resumed his normal routine. Surveillance teams had logged him returning to work, shopping on the High Street, and attending Friday prayers at the Regents Park mosque. None of his movements were regarded as suspicious. Until yesterday...

Two officers followed him as he made his way to Liverpool Street Station, where he entered British Rail's Advance Purchase office, spoke with a clerk and left with a ticket folder in hand.

One officer stuck with him as he took the subway home on the Circle Line. His partner used his warrant card to question the clerk who had served him. Kayani had purchased a round-trip ticket to Birmingham, leaving on Thursday.

Houghton sent a car for James and greeted his old friend warmly when he arrived at Scotland Yard. Over tea, Derek explained the surveillance job he had in mind for him. Forty-five minutes later, James had been fully briefed on Kayani. He was shown a number of colored photographs of the suspect, the most recent taken yesterday.

"Won't need those, Derek," he said, indicating the photos. "I've got his likeness locked in my memory box already. He'll be easy to recognize."

The inspector smiled his agreement. He'd had ample proof before that the senior citizen's mind was as sharp now as it was when he retired some twenty years ago. *I'll count myself lucky if I have most of my grey cells at sixty, let alone seventy-plus!* he thought.

Houghton gave James two addresses in Birmingham that housed known Muslim radicals. "In case you lose him after the train arrives, I'd suggest checking these places for him, Derek said. "I wouldn't doubt he'll show up at one of them. I don't expect you to stick around up there for more than a day or two, James. If you can just find out where he heads for in the city, that would be of great value. Anything else you uncover would be a bonus." He gave James the phone number of an officer on the local force to contact if he needed back up.

"Don't worry, Derek, I'm too old to play James Bond. But I will be careful," he assured his friend.

PHOENIX, TUESDAY, NOVEMBER 9

Omar Hadad—his real name—had flown from France to Tahiti, the holiday isle in French Polynesia. His round-trip excursion ticket showed him returning to France in three weeks time. He checked into an ocean-side hotel and lounged in the sun for five days. On the sixth day, he checked out, telling the curious clerk he was moving to another hotel on the other side of the island.

That was not his intention, however. He was headed for the island's international airport in Papeete. After completing the check-in formalities, Jean Clairmont, a French citizen and civil engineer according to the forged passport he was now using, boarded an Air New Zealand to flight to Los Angeles. Eight hours and thirty minutes later, the terrorist, code named VET, arrived on American soil.

He was in the United States to attend a conference on climate change sponsored by the University of Southern California, he told the Customs and Immigration officer. After a few more routine questions, the officer stamped his passport and beckoned to the next person in line. His explanation would have stood up if queried. The university *was* hosting a three-day conference beginning tomorrow. Two hours after arriving at LAX, Clairmont paid cash for a one-way ticket on a Southwest Airlines flight to Phoenix. Before boarding, he used the cell phone he had just purchased to call Frank Archer with the flight number and ETA.

Tom Allman had followed Archer to the airport. Archer had phoned him earlier this morning to tell him his colleague would be arriving today.

At the multi-level parking garage, he continued to the level above the one Archer parked on. He took the stairs instead of the elevator to the ground level in time to spot Archer heading into the domestic terminal. His decision to wait in the baggage area was rewarded when Archer and the newcomer descended on the escalator from the arrivals level fifteen minutes later.

Tom made mental notes of the man: late thirties or early forties, height a few inches over six feet, slender build, and weighing about a hundred and seventy pounds. His skin was deep brown in color, and All-man figured him for a native of an Arab country, perhaps from one the Horn of Africa region. His ill-fitting brown suit reminded Tom of those popular with Iron Curtain country diplomats twenty years ago. *At least he isn't wearing robes, but we'll have to outfit him in 'Arizona casual' cloth-ing, or he'll be noticed everywhere he goes,* thought Tom.

After his bags arrived, Archer led him back to the parking garage, and Allman didn't bother to follow them. Archer was to call him later regard-ing their next move.

He was stretched out on his bed watching a sports channel recap of the day's NFL games when Archer called. Without naming him, Archer told Tom that the newcomer wanted to inspect the shipment that had been smuggled across the border. "Right, I'll pick you guys up at nine tomorrow mornin'," Allman said, and hung up before Archer could reply.

"No problem, pard, we can talk freely. Archer and another cell member who arrived today are holed up at their motel three miles from mine," said Allman. "Where are ya and what's up?"

Don was spending his second night at the motel on the northern outskirts of Denver. He gave Tom a short account of his hurried depar-ture from Canada. "Didn't think I would've been much help to you if I couldn't enter the US, Tom. If you can believe it, they're still looking at me for the hotel murder back in June.

"You sure you didn't do it, pardner?" Allman joked, hoping to lighten the tenseness he perceived in Carling's voice.

It worked. Don laughed out loud, and was still chuckling when he managed a reply. "Yeah, temporary amnesia induced by too much red wine. That'll be my defense!"

"Ahh, it won't come to that, Don. But I'm glad you're stateside."

"So you've seen this new guy? And have they given you anything to do yet?"

"Well, I was at the airport when he flew in this morning. I'll be meet-in' him tomorrow when I take 'em out to check over the shipment I picked up a few nights ago. He's an Arab by the looks of him."

Allman told Don about the rendezvous at the border, and moving the crated supplies to a storage unit in Mesa, east of Phoenix. "There are four boxes, all sealed with tamper-proof locks," he said. "I hopin' to find out exactly what's in them tomorrow."

WEDNESDAY, NOVEMBER 10

Don had spent an uneasy night and had just got back to sleep when his phone rang. Joanne was on the line, and apologized for disturbing him. Groggy, Don rolled to a sitting position, and squinted at the clock radio. It was 7:04. " Uhh... no, that's okay, Joanne. My alarm should've gone off a few minutes ago." He reached over and turned it off.

"There have been two calls for you since I got to the office twenty minutes ago," she told him. "The paperwork requesting your extradition has arrived, apparently."

Don muttered a curse. Not that he was surprised: there had been enough hints from Paul Boutin that it was in the works. Both calls came from Ottawa, the first from Inspector Brian Roberts.

"I told him you were taking some time off and I wasn't exactly sure when you'd be back, just like you said. But I don't think he believed me, Don. He asked for you to call as soon as possible."

"That's okay, I'll handle it. Who was the other call from?"

The caller had identified himself as George Johnston, with the Federal Justice Department. "He also wanted to speak directly to you, and when I told him you were on vacation and couldn't be contacted immediately, he asked for your lawyer's name and number. So I gave it to him."

"Good work, Joanne. Sorry to put you on the spot, but it can't be avoided right now," said Don. "You'll probably get a call from Simmons sometime soon, but you'll have to lie to him as well."

Joanne laughed. "No problem, boss! Good practice for an agent in training, right?" Joanne had been taking courses towards obtaining a private investigator licence.

Don couldn't suppress a chuckle. "Not really! I'll try to get in touch with Clay this morning, and that should take the heat off you. Thanks, Joanne."

He debated when and who to call concerning the news from Joanne. He decided to put off calling Brian Roberts. He was fairly sure the call from the RCMP officer had to do with the extradition request. He didn't want to put his friend on the spot by ignoring the advice Roberts would probably give him: turn yourself in. Nor did he want to lie about his location. But he would call his lawyer. Clay Simmons picked up on the second ring.

"Where are you, Don?"

"Clay, I can't tell you that just yet. Did you get a call from the Justice Department this morning?"

"Yes... less than thirty minutes ago. The French have requested your extradition on a murder charge." When Don didn't reply, he continued. "As your lawyer, I advise you to come in and surrender your passport. Then we can start the appeal proceedings."

"Sorry, no can do, Clay. You remember what we discussed about this. Just refer it to your colleague's firm. I gave him the details after you put me in touch with him, and they'll launch the appeal. That should buy me time. That's all I can say now."

"You realize that by your non-appearance you will be regarded as a fugitive from justice, don't you?"

"Yeah, I do, Clay, and I know you're only telling me what any ethical lawyer would advise, but I'll have to take my chances for now." He hung up before Clay could reply.

DON SPENT THE AFTERNOON WANDERING around a grasslands park near the motel, and the combination of fresh air and moderate exercise had left him pleasantly tired, but had done much to relieve his anxiety. He wasn't happy now that he was officially on the run, but he still didn't feel he had any other option until he and Tom Allman were ready to give up their investigation and hand their findings over to US authorities. By 7 p.m. he was sitting in his room's well-worn easy chair staring at the television set. He only eaten two slices of the medium meat lover's pizza that he'd had delivered before pushing the box away.

He grabbed for his cell phone as soon as it rang. "How'd it go today, Tom?"

ALLMAN HAD DRIVEN ARCHER AND the new arrival out to inspect the shipment earlier today. "Frank introduced me to this Arab, who's usin' a French name. 'Shaw-n-n' or somethin' like that. I told him I wasn't into foreign languages so when I heard Archer refer to him as Omar, probably a slip up on his part by the way the asshole reacted, I told him that's what I was goin' call him. He doesn't like it, but fuck 'im. He sure as hell doesn't like me and I feel the same way about him."

Don smiled for the first time today. "Guess he's never met a American 'redneck' before, Tom! What about the supplies? Did you get to see what's in the crates?"

"Well, not much more than a quick look," replied Allman. "There are three crates of explosive devices, eight to a box. He didn't open the fourth box, which is about the size of one of those uhh... portable keyboard gizmos."

"You mean a synthesizer?" asked Don.

"Yeah, one of those. Anyhow, I'm thinkin' it's probably a control panel. From the glimpse a got inside one, it appears to be a fairly intricate set up. Probably got an electronic brain, for want of a better description."

"And that's all they need? You don't have to put anything together for them?"

"Nope, these things are in 'ready to use' condition, accordin' to Omar."

"Other than your mutual dislike for each other, what's your take on him? Is he going to be running the show from now on?"

"Looks like it. Or somebody who hasn't shown up yet. But this prick has been trained in terrorist ways, unlike my tennis buddy, Frank. He's a cagey bastard, but he couldn't keep from braggin' about how he had designed and constructed the devices himself."

"Shit, maybe we should just hand it over to the Feds now. Probably be much safer for you if we did," said Don.

"Don't worry about me, pard," replied Allman. "I'd rather take it a little further and nail more of the bastards. There's gotta be more than these two involved."

They had a long discussion about their options. In the end Don went along with the American.

"Okay, we'll hang in there a bit longer. If we take down Archer and this other guy now the rest will just go underground and try again later. What do you think?"

Allman agreed. He also knew that they might try to take him out once his part was finished, and said as much. "That's why I'll need back up."

Now that Don was in the US, they agreed that he should move closer to Arizona. Allman had a suggestion. "Let me make a call. If I can reach the guy right now, I'll run it by him and call you back. Keep your phone on, pard."

46

LONDON, THURSDAY, NOVEMBER 11

James Coates reached Liverpool Street Station early and easily spotted Saahir Kayani when he arrived fifteen minutes before departure time for the train to Birmingham.

To Coates's trained eye, the suspect looked no different than thousands of other Asian-born males living in the Greater London region. Kayani was neither tall nor short, weighed about ten stone, and his dark black hair was in need of a trim. He was wearing grey cotton trousers, and a plain blue shirt under a bulky fleece vest, no doubt to ward off the colder than normal temperature of plus 2C this morning. He was wearing cheap black shoes. His luggage consisted of a small suitcase with wheels and a sports bag bearing the Nike logo.

While Kayani stood in line waiting for the boarding announcement, he made frequent—and probably what he thought were nonchalant—glances behind him. Coates knew he was checking for a tail.

The former spy was also carrying a small case, containing a few items he could use to alter his appearance in a hurry. Once boarding was announced and the gate opened, he joined the line up and made his way along the line of coaches, well behind Kayani. He'd been furnished with an open second-class ticket like the one Kayani had purchased, and boarded the same car as the suspect.

He slipped into an aisle seat five rows behind Kayani. Both men remained seated during the two and a half hour trip. James put on a cap and wrapped a woolly scarf around his neck before leaving the train and stayed well behind Kayani as they walked towards the station's main entrance. Once outside, Kayani stopped and made a call on his mobile phone. Three minutes after his call, an older model Ford Vauxhall with faded red paint slowly approached the designated pick up zone, and stopped at the curb when Kayani waved. He quickly shoved his suitcase in the rear seat and got in beside the driver.

James thought about trying to follow in a taxi, but quickly discarded the notion. Instead, he strode towards the curb in time to get a glimpse of the car's registration number. He succeeded, and after the vehicle pulled away, he took out a small note book and jotted down the number. The red Ford moved into the lane leading to the City Center.

Time to get on with 'Plan B, he told himself, and headed for the taxi rank. When his turn came, a smiling driver clad in a colorful knitted toque got out of his vehicle and held the door open for him. James thanked him and gave him the first address to head for ...

BY FOUR O'CLOCK, JAMES HAD abandoned his attempts to find where the car that had picked Kayani up had taken him to. Henry, the Jamaican-born taxi driver, had driven him by the two addresses Houghton had supplied him with. There hadn't been any sign of the Ford on either street. James decided it would be prudent to put off any further attempt to locate him until tomorrow.

He had Henry drop him off at a medium-sized hotel a few blocks from the city center. James took a single room on the second floor and ran a hot bath. The seventy-five-year-old suddenly felt more tired than usual in the late afternoon and was looking forward to a good soak. He called Derek's private number while waiting for the bathtub to fill. His call was routed to the policeman's voice mail. James gave a description of the vehicle and its registration, a brief outline of what he planned to do tomorrow, and left his hotel contact information.

SEVEN TIMES ZONES AWAY IN Colorado, 'James Wright' had returned his rental car, taken a taxi to the airport, and bought a ticket to Amarillo, Texas. His flight on the regional airline made a stop over in Albuquerque, New Mexico, and it was late afternoon before he arrived in Amarillo. He'd called Hank Gillette with his ETA and the Texan was waiting for him in the arrivals area. The tall man in the black Stetson with the braided hat band greeted him with a firm handshake and big smile. "Everybody calls me Razor," he said, "Really original, huh?"

"What was the option? 'Blades'?" laughed Don. His host insisted on carrying Don's small suitcase and led him to a deep purple-colored Ford 150 pickup parked in front of the terminal. The truck body had more dents in it than most demolition derby entrants, it seemed to Don.

"Don't worry, nuthin' wrong with the engine. This is my workin' rig," explained Razor, who hadn't missed Don's once over.

"Let me guess, you run cattle for a living, right?" smiled Don.

Gillette nodded. "So you really are a private eye! But I gotta ask, how could you be so hard up that you had to hire a loose cannon like Trigger?"

"Trigger? That's Tom's nickname?"

"You mean he never told you that? Jeez, maybe that Canadian gal did drum some respectability into him before she saw the light!" he chuckled.

"Nope, never mentioned it," said Carling, smiling. "But now I can't wait to hear how he came by it!"

"Well-l-l, let's leave it for another time. It goes a lot better when he's there to defend himself!"

GILLETTE TURNED WEST ON INTERSTATE 40 after leaving the airport. Don had never been to Texas, and his first impression of Amarillo was that it was smaller that he'd expected. The freeway ran through the city, and was lined with motels and restaurants on both sides. When he remarked on the city's size, Razor replied, "Yeah, most of the state's population lives in the Dallas to Houston corridor. I think there's only about two hundred thou' in and round Amarillo."

Gillette exited I-40, heading south. "My ranch is twenty miles from here, near Hereford."

After a short stretch on I-27, Gillette turned west onto Highway 60 and it wasn't long before Don's nostrils were filled with the overwhelming stench of manure, a mixture of cow dung, urine and ammonia that was almost visible. The source was soon obvious. Thousands of beef cattle were milling about in feed lots straddling the road.

"That's the smell of money, Don! Steaks and roasts for a hungry nation! Take a deep breath, it's good for what ails you!" he urged, laughing.

"Well, it would definitely clear one's sinuses," agreed his passenger. He tried to imagine what the clothing—let alone the workers themselves—must smell like after a day in the yards. They drove past three or four men operating front end loaders amidst the mounds of manure. *Must be the entry-level jobs*, he thought.

Gillette explained that his ranch was minuscule compared to the average in the area, and he only had between 35 and 40 head of Black Angus cattle on his acreage most of the time. More of a hobby than a business, was the way he put it. His main source of income was evident when they reached his driveway and stopped while Razor checked his mail box. A helicopter rested on a pad behind the ranch house at the end of the driveway. Razor had learned to fly in the Army, and now flew pipeline patrol for a major natural gas company serving the panhandle area of northwest Texas.

"Can't introduce you to my wife 'cause she's not here anymore," said Gillette as he lead Don inside. "Seems she didn't appreciate the smell of cow shit on a daily basis. His wistful explanation told the visitor that there was more to the separation than that, but Razor didn't elaborate.

Instead, he pulled two beers out of the fridge and popped their caps. "Welcome to my humble abode, friend," he smiled, handing Don a long neck bottle of Lone Star. "Grab a couch and give me the lowdown on just what you and Tom are mixed up in."

They had finished two beers each by the time Don had answered Razor's questions.

"So now that the president has been re-elected, you expect these bastards to carry out their plan," said Gillette. And they need Trigger's help to get the explosives on trains."

"Yeah, that's it in a nut shell," nodded Don. "He should be calling me tonight or tomorrow with an update."

47

LONDON, SATURDAY, NOVEMBER 13

James made the trip from his flat on the south bank of the Thames River to Scotland Yard by bus, having spurned DS Houghton's offer to send a car for him. He had returned from Birmingham late yesterday, called Derek and assured him had no objection to meeting on the weekend. Derek gave him a warm welcome and introduced him to the three members of his squad already seated in his office.

"James, first let me thank you again for your help," Derek began. "You saved us manpower that was needed here in London."

"I'm glad to be of service, Derek, you know that," James replied modestly.

Yesterday morning James had resumed his search for clues as to where Kayani might be staying. As he neared the second address the police had given him, he spotted the red Ford that had picked up Kayani after their train arrived. The vehicle was parked half a block from the house itself. He strolled past the house, and found a busy café on the next corner. He bought a coffee and found a table by a window with a clear view of both the house and car.

Most of the café's customers were Caucasian, and seniors like himself. The passersby, on the other hand, were a mix of younger Asians and Blacks. James had only taken one sip of his coffee—served in a cheap plastic cup—when Kayani and another man came out of the house and headed towards the Ford. James breathed a sigh of relief when they walked right past it.

Neither of them glanced at the café as they passed it and rounded the corner. James counted to fifteen before he stood and casually left the café. He crossed to the other side of the street, dumped the still-hot coffee into the gutter and dropped the cup into a rubbish bin. He had no problem keeping the twosome in sight, and two blocks on they reached the busy Newbury Road and turned left. James closed the gap he'd been maintaining as the pedestrian traffic increased. A minute later he spotted the dome of a small mosque. Kayani and his companion entered it via a side door rather than through the main entrance. The mosque looked more like the office building it had once been than a place of worship.

"They were inside for the better part of an hour," James told the group. "When they emerged, another man, fully-robed and probably an imam, was with them. They got into a van parked behind the mosque and sped away. That was the last I saw of Kayani, unfortunately."

"Not a problem, James," lauded houghton. "The information you gathered has already put another piece to the puzzle."

The mosque was known to be frequented by a group of disaffected, Asian-born British youths attracted by the resident imam's anti-government rantings. All of them had been photographed at rallies to protest the British involvement in the US-led conflicts in Iraq and Afghanistan. Their role, at the mostly peaceful rallies, was to try and incite the crowds to violence, according to police reports.

"This particular Islamic cleric has already been put on notice by the government for his vitriolic and slanderous accusations voiced in his weekly addresses," said Houghton. "But your information connecting Kayani to him is a new development."

The ownership of the red Ford was traced to another Pakistani immigrant, thirty-two-year-old Zamir Lodhi, a hospital orderly. He had been living in Birmingham since 2002. Although the counterterrorism force wasn't aware of it yet, Lodhi had been in Pakistan at the same time as Kayani. In fact he had returned to London on the same date, October 28th, but on a different flight.

AFTER JAMES COATES LEFT, HOUGHTON'S team turned their attention to the recent request from the Americans asking for any information they might have concerning the code words. What little his team knew of them had been retrieved from Saahir Kayani's hard drive. The data had been surreptitiously downloaded by Scotland Yard detectives investigating his sister's murder. The messages were in French, yet the code words were in English. Three of the same code words had been heard on the voice tapes from the bug planted by his now dead sister: FARMER, GROWER and FOX. Most of the messages had originated from BREEDER, a new name to the enigma.

Several aspects of the messages had them puzzled. Although references were made to 'the plan' and 'our operation', no date or location was mentioned. *Was that information already known to the conspirators, or had it not been decided yet?*.

"I still think he's just being used as a 'go between', " said Sergeant Barbara Norman. "As they've all been in French, it's logical to assume they originated in France."

"Yes, I'd go along with that," added another officer. "Didn't the tip off we had from your Canadian friend involve a Frenchman?"

"That's correct," answered Houghton. "Don Carling, the PI, had been on the man's trail both here and in Paris. He's convinced this chap is a member of a cell planning an attack in the United States. One of these codes probably refers to him."

Norman held up her copy of the report. "Then I think he's GROWER, sir. Two of the e-mails addressed to him were routed to Canada, according to the note on the last page. Other recipients may have been 'blind copied'."

"Meaning what, Sergeant?" asked Houghton.

"I think it means they couldn't say where others getting the messages are located," suggested one of the male officers. "Right Barbara?"

"That's my understanding, yes," she replied, "but I'd guess they are somewhere in America."

"Summing up, then," said Houghton, "we've got e-mail traffic originating in France, sent to this computer belonging to Kayani, and forwarded to unknown persons in North America. The recipients are identified by code, as is the sender. These people are no doubt members of a terrorist cell. Probably backed by al-Qaeda or a similar, but as yet unknown organization, with the same goals."

He paused to see if anyone had anything to add, and noticed the skeptical look on his sergeant's face.

"Yes, Barbara?"

"Well," she shrugged, "any such far-flung plot would require a fair bit of financial support, wouldn't it?" No one disagreed with her. "Who's ever behind it would need deep pockets as well as willing recruits to pull it off," she added.

You're right, Barbara, but let's not fall prey to tunnel vision," he cautioned.

"Did Kayani's trip to Birmingham having anything to do with this supposed plot?" another officer wondered aloud.

"No, we don't believe there's a connection," Houghton said. "And I don't believe we'll find one." Any overt actions being planned by this Birmingham imam and his band of followers will probably be directed at British interests, according to the latest assessment I received." The report had reached Houghton's office this morning. This view was also held by the national security service, MI5.

After the meeting ended, Houghton summarized the team's thinking in regard to the code words and sent it off to Washington. In it he stated that GROWER was believed to be Archer/Amara, the Toronto resident, and two other codes referred to agents in the US. He added his team's thoughts about a possible time frame for the plot. Sergeant Norman and one the other squad members were positive they had heard the words 'turkey time' used on the tapes. There had been no usage of the words in the e-mail traffic downloaded from Kayani's computer, though. *Was it a reference to Christmas, perhaps, and could it mean that the plot was planned for the Christmas holiday period in the US?*

WASHINGTON, MONDAY, NOVEMBER 15

Agent Bob March wasn't much further ahead after poring over the message from London. If they were unable to put names to the codes, let alone locate the suspects, the information was tenuous at best.

However, Houghton's report did provide March with one alarming clue that had to be checked immediately. It was late afternoon in England, and his call caught DS Houghton just as he was about to leave his office.

His explanation as to why the British thought the plot was to be activated around the Christmas holiday period made the hairs on the back of March's neck tingle. If the words 'turkey time' did in fact refer to a date for the supposed plot, then the Brits had made an understandable but erroneous assumption, March realized. Houghton explanation centered on the British tradition of serving roast turkey as the main course on Christmas Day.

But ham, not turkey, was the centerpiece of Christmas dinner for most Americans. Turkey was a Thanksgiving tradition in the US. And Thanksgiving Day was only two weeks away ...

MARCH WONDERED IF THE CANADIANS had any new information regarding GROWER, whom the British suspected was the code name for the Frenchman now known as Frank Archer

He called RCMP Inspector Brian Roberts, and what he learned only added to his woes. The man that was investigating Amara/Archer—private investigator Don Carling— had disappeared. Roberts explained Carling's predicament with respect to the murder in Paris. "There's no way he killed anybody, Bob, but someone set him up and he's been charged because of DNA evidence that connects him to the victim. It's all probably tied to this terrorist cell. I tried to contact him via his secretary, but he hasn't returned my call."

March sighed. "Any idea where he would be now?"

"My guess is somewhere in the US. Probably working with his agent who has infiltrated the suspected cell."

IN PARIS, PAUL BOUTIN WAS waiting in the arrivals hall at Charles De Gaulle airport when Francoise Amara's long flight from Singapore landed. She had called him two days ago with her flight details. The attractive and smartly-dressed woman drew admiring glances from many of the males around Boutin as she descended the escalator to the baggage claim area. Once she had claimed her luggage—three heavy suitcases plus handbags—Boutin loaded them onto a baggage cart and led her to the parking building. Jacques Brunelle was waiting there with the agency's Peugeot station wagon.

Paul used the forty-minute drive to brief Francoise on how her next few weeks, perhaps months, would be spent. It was a scenario he had laid out for her in Singapore. An approach to the police that Paul thought offered her the best chance to avoid a jail term and preserve her professional career. She had agreed with him at the time, and now he asked her if she was still willing to follow his guidance. She had been staring out the window as he spoke, her eyes hidden behind large sunglasses.

Thirty seconds of silence passed before she turned slightly towards him and said softly, "Oui." Paul thought he saw a lone teardrop trickle from her right eye.

It was the only viable avenue open to her, and she knew it. Boutin had stressed that if she didn't cooperate, he would have no choice but to inform the police about her connection to the murdered room service waiter.

They drove directly to Saint Cloud and Francoise's apartment building. They helped with her luggage and waited in the lobby for her to repack. She was going to be staying at a safe house for the next few days, Boutin told her, and gave her one hour to get ready. He and Jacques waited in the lobby during the interval. There had been no indication, either at the airport or en route to the city, that anyone else had been expecting her, but the woman's safety was paramount if Paul was to clear his Canadian friend, Don Carling.

By 10 p.m. they had moved Francoise to the safe house. It was an apartment, actually, near the Porte de Champerret, approximately a mile north of the Arc de Triomphe. Boutin had purchased it while he was still in the army, and now his agency owned it. The one bedroom, third floor apartment was in older building, and smaller than Francoise's own flat. It had been remodeled last year, though, and had all the necessary conveniences for an extended stay. The neighborhood featured plenty of shops and restaurants, all within easy walking distance.

"I'm sure you are jet-lagged, Miss Amara, and we're going to leave the next step until tomorrow," said Boutin. "I'll be here in the morning along with an Inspector Monet of the Surete. One of my men will be nearby all night, just as a precaution. You may use this phone to make calls to friends, if you wish," he said, indicating a phone on the living room table, "but use this to contact me." He handed her a mobile phone that he'd had in his jacket pocket.

He didn't tell her that any calls she made on the apartment phone would be recorded in his office.

48

The arrival of Inspector Jean-Luc Monet caused Boutin to shake his head in amazement. He was standing at the coffee bar a few doors from the safe house sipping on a café crème as the patrol car screeched to a halt across from him. The unexpected police presence in their quiet neighborhood drew questioning looks from shopkeepers tending to their outdoor displays.

So much for discretion on their part, Paul mused.

Monet and a female officer climbed out and the driver drove away, presumably in search of a parking space. The inspector saw Paul wave, nodded in reply, and crossed the street to meet him. They shook hands and Monet introduced him to his aide. Boutin signaled the waiter for three coffees. Monet lit up a Gauloise cigarette, ignoring the No Smoking sign behind the bar.

Boutin had paid a visit to Monet's office the day after he returned from the Far East. He'd told the inspector that he now had evidence that would explain how those behind the young prostitute's murder had been able to gain access to the room next to Carling's. Evidence, he was positive, that also had a bearing on the death of Salif Farka, a former employee of the hotel. Monet had heard him out, but was skeptical.

"What about the Canadian's DNA we found in the bed and on the body?" he asked. "How will this new ahh... *evidence* deal with that?" Boutin admitted he didn't know, but suggested an explanation might emerge once the police interviewed his informant.

Boutin shook his head when Monet asked for her name. "She's away on a business trip and I'd prefer she return to Paris on her own accord," said Boutin. "I have her word that she will answer your questions at that time."

Monet didn't particularly want to go along with Boutin's plan, but finally concurred. As the police investigation of the prostitute's death had stalled anyway, he agreed that nothing would be lost by waiting a few more days. Now that she was back, Monet was anxious to question her. The two men chatted about football while waiting for the driver to reappear. He did so five minutes later and politely declined Boutin's offer of a coffee.

When the others had finished their coffee, Boutin led them to the apartment building. He buzzed the apartment and identified himself to Francoise. There was an audible 'click' as the door unlocked and he ushered them inside and up to the third floor.

Francoise opened the door to his quiet knock and showed the visitors in. Boutin introduced the officers to her and left. He had hoped to sit in on Monet's interrogation but the inspector wouldn't hear of it. Instead, he went back to the coffee bar to wait.

Monet started by asking Francoise to give her full name, permanent address, and present occupation. He continued with a few questions about her recent trip and showed genuine interest in her modeling career, questions that she was comfortable answering. His manner wasn't the least bit confrontational, and her initial nervousness had eased noticeably by the time he took her back to her stay in the Hotel Nouveau Monde in June.

She told the same story she'd given Boutin: her apartment was being painted, her twin brother's business had taken him out of Paris unexpectedly, leaving his hotel room available and paid for. Boutin had checked out her alibi about the redecorating job, and found that she'd told the truth.

Who had put her up to obtaining a master key from the room service waiter? Was it her brother? Where did the money come from and how much was he paid for it?

The questions came in rapid in succession, signaling the end of informal chat Monet had opened with. Boutin had told her to expect them, but she still stumbled through her answers.

"No, my brother wasn't behind it. Actually the only contact I had with him was when he phoned a day or so after he arrived. He had the key card to the room delivered to my apartment. I never did see him while he was here."

"Then who put you up to it?"

"A cousin...Carlos Amara." She knew the consequences of this admission. Boutin had made it quite clear that she would have to go into hiding or risk being killed. But giving him up was her only chance of avoiding a jail term, he'd finally convinced her.

The money—500 hundred euros in 50 euro notes—was delivered to the hotel room by a man she didn't know. They'd only exchanged a few words, and she couldn't remember much about him. Her vague description literally fit thousands of men in Paris. Age 30 to 35, average height and build, short brown hair.

Monet checked his notes. "When did you actually pay the young man for the pass key?"

Francoise thought for a moment before answering. "It was on the Tuesday morning when he delivered my breakfast order."

"I see...Tuesday, the eighth, then," he said, looking at his notes again. "And how and to whom did you turn over this key?"

"I returned to my apartment later that morning and someone came by for it the same afternoon."

"Really? Why did you go home?"

"That's what Carlos told me to do. I returned to the hotel that evening because my clothes were still there and left the following morning. That's when my brother's reservation expired."

"Hmm...And this man who picked up the key. Was he the same one who'd delivered the money to you?"

Her reply was a slight nod of her head and a soft 'yes'.

"How do you communicate with Carlos?" Monet asked.

She only had one phone number for him, and her calls went directly to an answering machine. He usually called back within a day or so.

"When did you last speak to him?"

"Before I left on my trip."

"You're sure? You haven't called him since Monsieur Boutin talked to you in Singapore?"

She had briefly thought of calling him last night, but just as quickly decided not to. "No, I haven't talked to him since the week before I left for Hong Kong, and he hasn't called me, either," she added, anticipating his next question.

"I see. But tell me, was Carlos behind your rather sudden decision to travel? I would have thought an extended trip like the one you made would have been booked well in advance."

She hadn't expected the question, and her surprise showed. *How did they know that she had called the travel agency only hours after Carlos had practically ordered her to disappear for a while?*

"Uhh, no. My agency called just a few days before I left," she lied. "The model who'd been scheduled for the assignment had to cancel for medical reasons."

Monet knew she was lying, but didn't press her on it. Instead, he asked her if she knew why Carlos wanted the key.

She didn't, and never broached the subject with him. She also vehemently denied any knowledge of the girl's murder. She defended her brother when Monet suggested he might have been involved in the crime. Even though she'd had very little contact with her brother since he'd married and moved to Canada, she was positive he would never get mixed up in any criminal activity, she stated.

"What about Carlos? Is he also an innocent?"

Francoise hesitated again, toying with the large jade ring on her right hand for long seconds before replying. "...I really don't know what he does," she admitted. "Perhaps his father or uncle have been a bad influence on him. I wish I hadn't agreed to help him," she shrugged.

Monet paused and lit a cigarette, ignoring her brief look of disgust.

"Okay, let's talk about this waiter. You say you knew nothing of his death until Monsieur Boutin told you about it. Is that correct?"

She brushed at the smoke drifting her way before answering. "Yes, that's right."

"But you had spoken to him after you moved back to your apartment, I believe."

Monet knew she had because Boutin had wormed the information out of her in Singapore. Francoise had been surprised by the call from a worried Farka to her unlisted number. Then she remembered giving him her business card while she'd been 'making friendly' while setting him up to steal the key.

Farka had called her because there was a rumor going around the room service staff that the police were going to have them all take a lie detector test. He was worried that he would fail the test if the police asked him about the pass key that had gone missing.

What should I do, Miss? he'd asked. Francoise had no advice for him, but told him to sit tight for a few days until she could talk to someone about his concern. She had spoken to Carlos later that night. He forbade her from calling Farka back, and she never heard from the young man again.

"Doesn't take a genius to surmise that Farka's call to her sealed his fate," offered Boutin.

"No, not after she told this Carlos character about it. She maintains that was the only time she spoke to Carlos about Farka."

Boutin and Monet were chatting in the coffee bar after the inspector had finished his interview with Miss Amara. They discussed their individual assessments of her while the other officers went to retrieve their vehicle. Neither of the experienced investigators felt she was as gullible as she made out regarding the need for the pass key. Her culpability might emerge more clearly down the road, they agreed.

"Tracking down this cousin of hers now becomes our priority," said Monet. "And I have no doubt that you are already looking for him.

Paul smiled. "Of course! But we've found very little to go on so far. I think you'll agree that the odds are that he had a hand in these murders. And the sooner he's found, the sooner you'll be able to drop the preposterous murder charge against my Canadian colleague, won't you?"

"We'll see," Monet shrugged. "Just make sure you let me know if you get a solid lead on Amara."

"Certainly, Inspector. You can count on it."

MONET TOLD BOUTIN THAT THE police would be returning later with equipment to trace the call they wanted Francoise to make, hoping to get a lead on Carlos. "Not necessary, Inspector, the line is already bugged, you see."

Monet laughed softly. "Of course, of course...silly of me not to realize that! Let's you and I go back up there, then, and have her make that call now."

Francoise was surprised to see them. "Miss Amara, we would like you to try and contact Carlos today, just in the off chance that he is in Paris. The sooner we can locate him, you see, the sooner it will be safe for you to return to your apartment. Is that all right with you?"

Francoise agreed, and rang the number she was to call if there was a problem. An answering machine picked up as expected, and Francoise left her message. "Carlos, I'm back from Singapore and need to talk to you. I'm staying at a friend's house in case the police are watching my apartment. Please call me as soon as you get this message at this number."

"Well done, Miss Amara. If he calls, please try and keep him on the line as long as possible. Just ask him for his advice on how to deal with the police if they contact you again," the inspector told her.

Neither man doubted Carlos would stay on the line long enough to allow a trace, even if he did return her call.

"Where did you get this?" demanded Saahir, staring at the small round object his fourteen-year-old sister Reza had just handed him.

"It fell out of the bird cage when I was cleaning it," she answered. "What is it?"

Saahir muttered a curse under his breath. He knew exactly what he was holding. During his training at the remote camp in Pakistan, he'd been shown examples of electronic bugs used by British spy agencies.

"Never mind, little sister. It's probably something the store put in the cage, perhaps a miniature tape player to teach the birds to speak. But it's broken now so I'll throw it away," he told her, speaking now in a friendlier tone and mussing her hair. "It's nothing you need to be concerned with."

But it was definitely a concern for him: a warning sign that he—and perhaps the whole cell—had been compromised.

He left the house in a rush ten minutes later, crossed Kilburn High Road, and entered the nearly deserted park known as Bracket Gardens. He followed the main pathway with no particular route in mind, trying to make sense of the bug and its possible ramifications.

How long had it been there? Who put it there? Could it have been in place when Carlos came to London to meet with his cousin?

If, as he feared, one of the British security services was responsible, he'd have to alert Carlos immediately.

Helton, the undercover officer assigned to watch Kayani tonight, slipped out of his unmarked vehicle at the suspect's unexpected appearance and fell in behind him. A hundred yards into the park the Pakistani slumped onto a bench lit by an overhead lamp.

Helton turned off onto a narrow side path and stopped behind a large chestnut tree. From this vantage point, he had an unobstructed view of Kayani. To Helton, the suspect seemed to be studying a small object in his hand. Two minutes later Kayani pulled a mobile phone from his pocket and made a call...

"DERBY ONE TO BASE."

"The muted but audible reply was immediate. "Go ahead, One."

"Suspect exited his home ten minutes ago and entered Bracket Park. He is now on his mobile as we speak."

"Is he alone, One?"

"Affirmative, and he seems quite upset about something."

"Can you pick him up on the directional?" Helton was equipped with a portable microphone gun and recorder.

"Negative, Base. He's too far away and I can't get closer without being spotted."

"Understood...okay, standby, One. Will have further for you shortly, over."

Helton was just about to initiate another call to base when the green light on his phone flashed.

"Base to Derby One. Advise situation now please."

"The call he made was a short one, and he's still just sitting there. Maybe he's waiting for a call back, but I'm...okay disregard, he's on the move again.

"Roger that, One. A *YELLOW CARD* 'op' has been authorized. Say suspect's position now.

"He's heading for the north gate to Bracket Street."

"Roger, stay with him. Derby Two on the move now for that location. Will advise when they have a visual on him."

Seven minutes later Helton received word that Derby Two, a two-man team in a ten-year-old Toyota sedan with no visible licence plates and a cracked windscreen, had spotted Kayani. After exiting the park, Kayani turned left on Bracket Street and walked slowly along the park's dark perimeter.Unknowingly, his route away from the busy High Street made him easy prey for what befell him moments later...

HELTON HAD A PERFECT VIEW of the suspect being handed his 'yellow card', a rapid response tactic undercover officers routinely practiced, but the first time the Derby Two team was conducting it in the field. Its use had to be sanctioned by a senior officer, in this case DS Derek Houghton. The football terms, yellow card and red card, had been picked by the officers themselves to designate their tactics.

The battered Toyota stopped alongside Kayani and both officers, wearing worn jeans and dark shirts, jumped out and surrounded the startled pedestrian.

"Money, arsehole!" demanded the first attacker, shoving a handgun at the terrified victim's chin.

Before Saahir could move or respond, the second officer put him in a tight headlock from behind. His partner fished Kayani's mobile phone out of his pocket, along with a handful of coins and a few bills.

"Cheap bastard!" he spit out. "Let's go!"

The second officer released his strangle hold and shoved Kayani roughly to the ground. The attackers were back in their vehicle and speeding away as the victim struggled to a sitting position.

Helton gave his mates an admiring 'thumbs up' as they sped past the hedge he'd watched the takedown from. It had only taken them twenty-eight seconds by his watch, well under the optimum one-minute limit for the operation. If it had been a *RED CARD* op, the target would have been bundled away to a safe house for interrogation.

Shaken and dazed, Kayani remained on the ground for a full minute after the car disappeared around the corner to his left. His heart was still racing as he struggled to his feet, peering into the darkness in both directions, looking for possible witnesses to the attack. Most of the houses opposite were in darkness, and set well back from the street.

Should he head for home and call the police? Would they even take a serious interest in his mugging? What could he tell them about his assailants?

He tried to recreate the attack in his mind, but it had happened so quickly only a few details came back to him. Both men were masked, and the one who spoke was English, and probably white. Not much to go on. As to their vehicle, he could only describe it as being 'not well looked after'.

Other than having a sore neck, he was uninjured. He hadn't been carrying a wallet, and they'd only taken the ten pound note, leaving the coins for him to pick up. He was almost home when he suddenly stopped and felt his wrist. His gold watch was still on it...

The phone! They were after my phone! And it has the emergency number for Carlos in it!

As soon as they were well clear of the area, the team leader radioed Base again.

"*YELLOW CARD* successful. Have the last number the suspect called. Ready to copy?"

"Roger, Two. Go ahead." The comm operator wrote down the number and read it back.

"Good copy, Base. We're twenty minutes out."

DS Derek Houghton arrived at the squad's operations room a few minutes after the phone number had been called in. He had been at home when the duty officer called requesting his authorization for the interdiction on Kayani. He grabbed a coffee from the large pot that had been brewing since the evening shift came on duty four hours ago.

"The area code tells us it's a Paris number, sir, the officer advised him. "Should we ring it and see who answers?"

"No, I don't think that's a good idea. Best we let the French handle it." He checked his watch: it was 8:04, an hour later in Paris. Had they called the number, they would have heard a busy signal. Saahir Kayani was on the line from a pay phone on the High Street, leaving a message for Carlos. He told of being jumped by thugs who stole his phone, the one he'd just used to call Carlos.

Although it was late, Houghton decided to act on the information now instead of waiting until tomorrow. "Please ring the National Police HQ in Paris for me, Susan," he instructed the comm clerk. "Buzz me when you've got him on the line, please."

The duty officer who answered assured Houghton that Commandant Rheaume, his superior, wouldn't be upset by a call from London, and patched him through to the inspector's home phone.

"No apology necessary, Derek," said Rheaume. " I'm always available to Scotland Yard, you know that. Especially when it concerns terrorist activity."

Houghton quickly explained about the suspect they'd been watching, and how his team had got hold of his phone. "He called a Paris number less than two hours ago," Houghton said.

The Frenchman needed no further explanation and copied down the number. "I'll have my men start checking on it immediately, but it may be morning before we have a result. I'll get back to you by midday tomorrow, Derek."

Houghton thanked him and rang off. Now he had to decide whether or not to move on Kayani. *Did they have legal grounds to haul him in for questioning? If he was still rattled, it could be to their advantage...*

After some thought, he decided to leave him alone for the time being. If the French authorities could put a name to the number Kayani had called, theoretically they would have more 'ammo' to use against him.

Before Houghton left for home, he had the duty officer check with the local police stations to see if Kayani had reported the attack. The responses were all negative.

It was just on one o'clock in the morning when Derek turned off Edgware Road, heading for his home alongside the canal in the Little Venice area. As he turned into his narrow driveway on the darkened street, an idea struck him. A plan to make use of the Pakistani's mobile phone. A ruse that might provide them with more valuable clues if it succeeded...

First thing tomorrow morning, he told himself as he unlocked the door, slipped into the quiet house, removed his shoes, crept upstairs and got into the king-sized bed without disturbing his soundly sleeping wife, Sonya.

CARLOS SLIPPED INTO THE DRAB and mostly darkened building and entered the apartment where he kept the answering machine. It was just after midnight and his arrival had gone unnoticed. There were three messages on the emergency phone line.

The first was from Francoise. He rewound the tape and listened to it a second time. He'd been expecting a call from her because she was due back in Paris two days ago. He'd thought she might have called him right away.

Why did she wait? Have the police already contacted her? He listened to her call again. She didn't sound especially worried, but his instincts told him she wasn't completely at ease. *Was she being coached?*

He played the second message. It was from a rattled Saahir in London, upset about the electronic bug he'd found in the bird cage.

Now what? This is an even more disturbing development...

He made himself a coffee and sipped it, mulling over possible ramifications of the bug.

If it had been in place during his visit in June to meet Francois, it meant only one thing: Kayani had drawn the attention of the British police.

Then why hadn't he been arrested, or at least taken in for questioning? For that matter, if they'd been overheard during that meeting, one would think the authorities would have come down on me as well. Or Francois, who apparently hadn't attracted attention as he traveled back to Canada and eventually to the US...

Relax, Carlos told himself, as he tried to make sense of it all. *No, the bug probably wasn't installed until sometime after that. Since June, the limited contact he'd had with Saahir had been by email. Perhaps it has to do with Kayani's trip to Pakistan.*

WHEN HE LISTENED TO THE second message from Kayani—made less than an hour after his first call—he knew that wasn't the case. He had to act, and quickly. At the end of his message, Kayani weakly suggested that he might just have just been the victim of a random mugging, but Carlos didn't buy it. Kayani's missing phone, the discovery of the listening device, plus the rather stilted call from Francoise all spelled trouble. It was time to burn a few bridges...

HE WOULDN'T BE RETURNING ANY of the calls, that was his first decision. He was remembering the warning delivered by instructors at the training camp in Pakistan two years ago: sever ties immediately with anyone that may have been compromised during a mission, even if that link is a blood relative or trusted friend.

As far as he was concerned, Saahir and Francoise would now have to fend for themselves. The plot had progressed to the point where he no longer needed the Pakistani to relay email messages to North America. And Francoise's only role had been to help obtain the hotel pass key months ago.

In hindsight, his decision to try and scare off the Canadian detective had been a bad move. With regard to Salif Farka, he'd had no choice but to order the 'hit.' The spooked hotel waiter's call to Francoise expressing his concern about a possible lie detector test meant he had to go.

He disconnected the answering machine, ripped the phone from the wall, and shoved both instruments into a plastic sack. He spent another forty minutes sanitizing the apartment by wiping all surfaces he might have touched. He rarely slept here, and never left any clothing or toiletry items behind.

A few minutes after ten, he locked up an left the apartment for good. He took a random route along the quiet streets and fifteen minutes later reached the banks of the Seine. After checking to make sure no one was watching, he threw the bag containing the phone and answering machine into the dark waters. It disappeared immediately. He fingered his cell phone, wondering if he should ditch it as well. He was fairly sure that he'd never given its number to anyone.

But why take a chance? He tossed it into the river and headed off in search of a taxi. He'd head for one of his other hideaways on the city's southern perimeter, and tomorrow he'd obtain a new phone and call FOX.

49

PHOENIX, SATURDAY, NOVEMBER 13

Tom Allman hadn't heard from Archer since the trip to the storage unit on Wednesday, and decided it was time he called the shots. Last night he'd called Frank and given him an ultimatum: tell Omar he wanted to know more about the explosives or he was calling it quits. Archer had been at a loss for words—exactly the reaction Allman had expected. Archer called him back 30 minutes later.

"Okay, Tom, Omar isn't happy about it, but he will do as you wish."

"Good, I'll pick you guys up at ten o'clock tomorrow morning," said Allman, and hung up.

IT IS UNFORTUNATE THAT WE need the likes of him, but it won't be for much longer,." Omar told Frank after he'd called Allman. Omar's dislike for the American was obvious to Archer from the moment he first introduced them. Archer had remarked on it when they were alone that night. "I still see him as our enemy, a greedy opportunist with blood on his hands from fighting against us in Iraq," Omar had explained.

Nothing that Archer offered as proof of Allman's hostility to the US government could sway Omar, and more than once he'd suggested that they were taking a chance by using him. In the end, though, he had reluctantly admitted that recruiting an American helper versus bringing in others from abroad was the best option and he would work with the man.

It's ironic, Archer thought, *I'm only in it for the same basic reason: money.* The Arab didn't seem to be aware of this, however, and hadn't questioned Archer's commitment.

They were sitting in Omar's motel unit, next door to Archer's. Other than eating together at night, usually at one of the nearby chain restaurants, Omar had kept to himself, which was fine with Archer. On the plus side, Omar had altered his appearance for the better. His long black hair had been thinned and shortened and no longer reached below his collar, and the straggly beard that had been so noticeable in London was gone, replaced by a neat goatee. This morning they had gone to a department store and purchased casual clothes for him—jeans and khaki pants, polo shirts, a pair of running shoes and a sun hat. With his sunglasses on, he looked just like most foreign tourists visiting Arizona for the first time.

Allman was also impressed with Omar's appearance when he picked them up for the short drive to Mesa. Omar no longer looked out of place dress-wise. Allman's friendly 'Howdy' greeting was returned by Archer, but met with a sullen look from the Arab, who made no attempt to dispel his dislike for American. He made no effort to join the conversation between Tom and Frank.

At the storage compound, Omar opened one of the devices, explained its inner workings, and answered most of Tom's questions. "Okay, Omar, that looks safe enough to handle. So why don't we head on up to New Mexico early next week and get these things planted? That will give us plenty of time to do the job right."

Omar shook his head. "The devices are not to be armed until the seventeenth or eighteenth. So we must work to that time."

Aha, just as I figured, the power source is limited, Tom told himself.

"Okay, then, let's plan on arriving up there about a week from now? I figure we'll need two or three nights."

The Arab shook his head again. He wanted to see the location Tom had chosen before then.

"It not like there are thousands of people in that area, Omar," he argued. "Why spend anymore time there then necessary?" He went out to his Jeep and came back with maps and photos of the region. "I've already made a thorough recon of this area," he explained, pointing out the rail yard and the surrounding empty fields. Omar still wasn't convinced, and their discussion became rather heated. They finally agreed to leave next Thursday, the 18th. "I'll take you around the whole area on Friday, and we'll start getting the explosives set on Saturday night."

"Where will we stay?" asked Frank.

"Leave that to me," replied Tom. The drive back to Phoenix was even quieter that the drive out.

TOM CALLED DON IN TEXAS that night, and they had a long talk.

"Problems?" Razor asked, after Tom hung up.

209

"Maybe. Tom thought he might get a chance to sabotage the devices before they were used, but that may not be possible. He and the Arab aren't getting along and Tom doesn't think he'll ever be left alone with the devices. This guy is going to be looking over his shoulder all the time."

"So what's supposed to happen next? Are they still going with the Thanksgiving date?"

"Yeah, they confirmed that today. Tom told him they had allow two, maybe three nights to get all the devices loaded, and that's now planned for next week. Apparently the Arab doesn't want to arm them until six or seven days before they're to be used. Something to do with the power supply, according to Tom."

"Must be usin' a battery, then. Probably one that will only last about a week without recharging," Gillette suggested.

Don told him how Allman had described the devices. On the outside, the case resembled a thin laptop computer, matte black in color.

"He had a good look inside one of them, and figures the charge itself consists of an upgraded plastic explosive surrounded by another type of charge. Something I didn't quite understand, but it will ensure an instantaneous and powerful blast when triggered," explained Don.

"Probably 'det' cord," said Gillette.

"Yes, that's the term he used. What is it?" asked Don.

"It's short for detonator cord. You remember those old western movies where the bad guys used a long fuse to blow up a train or a cave where they'd left the hero tied up?"

Don chuckled and nodded. "Yeah! Complete with the melodramatic music as it burned down!"

"That's it. Well, det cord is the modern version. It can be triggered electronically and explodes in a millisecond. Combined with the PE', it will make one helluva blast, especially if it's attached to a tank car full of flammable liquid."

"Well, that seems to be their plan."

"How are they gonna fix them to the cars?" asked Gillette.

"Apparently they're coated with some sort of adhesive on the bottom. A 'peel and stick' set up designed to adhere to a metal surface. It will have to be a strong substance that'll counteract the constant and bumpy motion of a moving train," said Don.

"Sounds like they've thought it all through," Razor observed. "I wonder how they're gonna, uhh… 'communicate' , you know, with the things once they're on the move. Maybe they're just timed to go off automatically."

Don shook his head. "That's a possibility, I guess, but Tom figures they must be fitted with a satellite phone receiver, and a call made will be made to either set it off, or at least start an arming sequence."

"Yeah, that would work. And they'll no doubt be equipped with a transponder or a GPS unit for tracking purposes," said Gillette.

Don admitted his knowledge of satellite phones and their capabilities was sketchy, and wondered how the terrorists could be sure it would work .

Gillette scratched his chin thoughtfully before answering. "Well, in theory a call would be placed from anywhere in the world to a given number, for instance. Simply put, the signal would be relayed via a comm satellite to what are known as earth stations. As long as the receiver in the device is within range of one of these stations, the call would go through. And I think technology exists that'll allow them to call multiple numbers at the same time. Maybe five or more at the flick of a switch."

"I see," said Don. "And presumably there are enough of these relay stations sited across the US to ensure calls to most regions would make the connection, right?"

"Yep, that would be my take on it. These guys would've considered all these factors. I mean why risk the chance of having their plot fail because they can't trigger the bombs remotely?"

Don agreed with him. "I have to keep reminding myself that we're dealing with a terrorist organization, not just a couple of amateurs with a hate on for the government, Razor," he sighed.

50

PARIS, WEDNESDAY, NOVEMBER 17

Carlos Amara's decision to abandon his hideaway last night had been a prudent move.

At 5:45 a.m., while most of the building's occupants were still asleep, a four-man National Police squad kicked in the door to third floor apartment that Carlos had cut and run from only hours ago. The address had been retrieved from the phone company's data base shortly after the call to Inspector Rheaume from London. Rheaume had authorized the predawn raid and anyone found inside was to be taken into custody.

The apartment was unoccupied, however, and the team had just finished a thorough search when Rheaume arrived at the scene. The squad leader in charge of the raid gave him a thumbs down.

"No one here, sir, and very little to indicate permanent occupancy, he reported. "Looks as if as if a phone was ripped out of the wall in a hurry. We haven't found any usable fingerprints yet, either."

"Well, it was apparently in use as late as last night, according to the British. Two calls in a relatively short time," said Rheaume. "Okay then, seal the place up for now. And talk to these people," he added, indicating the curious neighbors who kept peeking out of doors along the hall corridor. "Find out what, if anything, they know about the occupant. I'm going to have a chat with the concierge."

The elderly concierge was not very helpful. He knew nothing about a 'Francoise Amara', the name of the person listed as the tenant of apartment 312. The building was a privately-owned 'adults only' complex with 200 units on five floors. A majority of the tenants were pensioners. The leasing of the units was handled by a management firm and all financial arrangements were handled by them.

A new tenant would have received their keys from him, though, he acknowledged. If he'd been out his wife, who had passed away three months ago, would have handled it. Personally, he had never spoken to the supposed tenant of apartment 312, and couldn't say whether the woman named was the actual occupant. He suggested Rheaume get in touch with the management firm for any other information. The senior officer thanked him and left.

HE WAS ONLY SLIGHTLY FURTHER ahead after speaking to the firm's office manager. The rent for a one-year lease had been paid for by an electronic transfer from a Marseille bank. As of today the firm didn't know if the occupant planned to extend the lease beyond the December 31 expiry date. Rheaume left with a copy of the lease signed by 'F. Amara' on December 15, 2003

THE DAWN RAID BY THE National Police wasn't the only turn of events today that saw the noose drawing tighter around Carlos Amara's neck.

"Sometimes when we least expect it, my young friend, Lady Luck comes through," smiled Boutin, handing Jacques a note with a licence plate number on it. "Remember our chat with the superintendent, Monsieur Caron, at Miss Amara's condominium?" Boutin and his aide had spoken to him after their surprise visit to Francoise

"Uhh...vaguely. You offer a reward for information, didn't you?"

"That's right! Fifty euros. It was a long shot, but it has paid off. Better late than never, I suppose."

Boutin had told Caron that he would pay for any useful information regarding unknown callers to the building in June, or since then. The type of person not normally seen around the building, suspicious vehicles, that sort of thing. With only forty units to look after, Boutin reasoned that any 'super' worth his salt would notice these things.

It wasn't Caron who came up with the information, though. The tip came from the elderly gentleman in the first floor apartment that overlooked the entrance to the building. After Caron called him yesterday, Boutin hurried around and spoke with the resident, Georges Surette.

Surette spent most afternoons sitting by his window. One afternoon he'd noticed a dirty panel truck pull up and stop in the handicapped parking space right below his window. A passenger got out and entered the lobby. While he was inside, the driver rolled down his window and emptied an ashtray onto the pavement. This upset the senior citizen so much that he used his binoculars to take a closer look at the vehicle. When it left a few minutes later, he jotted down its licence number. He'd completely forgotten about the incident until Caron mentioned Boutin's request in passing yesterday.

"He couldn't remember much about the men, other than to say they were rough looking characters," said Boutin. "And the building isn't equipped with CCTV, not that the tapes would still be available."

"What about the timing? Any help there?"

"Yes, and this is most interesting. He's almost certain it was on Tuesday, June the 8th."

"Really? Didn't you say he's in his eighties? How could he be so sure?"

"Now you're stereotyping! Many seniors are just as sharp as you, young man," Boutin smiled. "But it's a good question, and one I asked him myself."

Monsieur Surette left Paris on Wednesday, June 9th to visit his son in Bordeaux. He was gone for three weeks. He'd insisted on showing Boutin the note he'd made on a calendar with his train's departure time.

"From this information, we can assume, can we not, that they were there to pick up the stolen room key from Mademoiselle Amara," offered Brunelle. "And the key was then used to gain access to the room next to Monsieur Carling's where the police believe the prostitute was killed."

"That's how I see it, yes," agreed his boss. "If the police can trace this vehicle, we should be a step closer to finding the real killer. Shouldn't take them too long. It's a local registration." The last two digits were '92', indicating that the van had been registered in the French capital.

TRUE TO HIS WORD, COMMANDANT Rheaume called Houghton with details of this morning's raid on the suspect's apartment. He had barely started when the Houghton interrupted him. "Excuse me Claude, how is that name spelled?"

"Amara... *a-m-a-r-a*," replied Rheaume. "The lease for the apartment was signed by a 'T. Amara', and the same name was used to order the phone installation. But the phone was no longer there this morning. Why do you ask?"

Houghton quickly flipped through the Kayani file and pulled out a sheet of paper. "Well, there's a connection here between that name and the man who made the calls to Paris last night."

Houghton broke it down for him. Don Carling, the Canadian PI had been investigating a male originally named Francois Amara, but now known as Frank Archer. He had also discovered that Archer/Amara had a sister with the same first name, and she probably lived in Paris. Her brother, now a Canadian citizen, was believed to be a member of a terrorist cell directed from France. A cell planning an attack in the United States sometime soon.

"Well this really complicates things, doesn't it?" Rheaume offered. "If my memory serves me right, I do recall a crime family by that name that was active here some years ago. They eventually ended up in jail for quite some time, and would be quite old now. However, it's a lead we'll follow up. And I'll have my people start looking for this twin sister."

"Yes, probably wouldn't hurt. And here's something else to throw into the mix, especially as it adds to possible terrorist activity..."

Houghton told him about the code words use in correspondence between suspected cell members. "The US and Canadian authorities are working on them as well as us. I'll pass on any developments regarding if and when I receive them," said Houghton before ending the call.

WHILE RHEAUME HAD BEEN TALKING to London, his officers were trying to track down the' F. Amara' shown on the lease. There were four with that name in the Paris region and they had already eliminated two when Rheaume buzzed their office.

"The Amara you're looking for is likely to be a female," he advised them.

A half hour later he received a message from the officers. They were at the residence of a Miss Francoise Amara, but the woman has been away since sometime in October, according to the concierge.

WHEN THE SHADOWY MEN BEHIND al-Qaeda World initially sanctioned the plot conceived by Carlos Amara, they had agreed to provide him with two of their key assets: Rene Amara, their sleeper agent in America, and the Egyptian bomb maker.

The revelation that his cousin, Rene, was alive and living undercover in New York had stunned Carlos. The group's spokesman, an unsmiling man with coal-black eyes and a beard to match, revealed that he had fought alongside Rene in Algeria and subsequently attended training camps in Afghanistan with him. It was suggested to Carlos that Rene was the ideal man to guide the plot in its final stages on US soil, and he quickly agreed.

A face-to-face meeting would have to wait until the operation ended, but Carlos had often fantasized about what a wonderful reunion and celebration that would be. It was on his mind again as waited for morning to dawn in New York. He checked his wristwatch for the umpteenth time in the last hour. The moment it showed 11:00 a.m., five hours earlier in New York, he made the overseas call using his new mobile phone...

"I NEED TO SPEAK TO Mister Green, but I'll call back later," Carlos said, after the 'beep' from the answering machine.

In his modest bungalow in New York, Rene put down his coffee cup, reached for the phone and hit the machine's STOP button. The coded phrase let him know it was Carlos calling. If, for some reason, he didn't want to speak to Carlos, he would have picked up and told him he had the wrong number.

"There have been a few disturbing occurrences here in the last twenty-four hours," Carlos said, when Rene answered. "Is everything okay at your end?"

"...Yes," replied Rene guardedly. "What's the problem?"

Carlos recounted the attack in London on Saahir Kayani, his suspicion that police may be trying to get at him through Francoise, and why he had severed his ties with them.

"You have followed the proper procedure, then, "said Rene, stifling a yawn. "And as long as you cannot be traced, no one should be able to thwart our plans. The final preparations for our feast are underway. There has been no indication of trouble from GROWER and VET. However, I will advise them again to be watchful."

Rene pushed away his breakfast plate of yoghurt and fruit after the call from BREEDER. He was no longer hungry, and debated not showing up for work today.

Should he call in sick? He couldn't remember the last time he'd taken a day off, so he didn't think it would be viewed with suspicion. And he *was* extremely tired. He hadn't had a good night's sleep for weeks, he realized. Yes, he would stay home today. His decision made, the al-Qaeda World sleeper agent called the cargo company he worked for to say he was ill.

Now, with the day free, he had time to carefully consider the necessary moves that he must make. He brewed another cup of tea while he pondered Carlos's disclosure of possible trouble across the Atlantic. It was the first indication that, despite their careful security measures, their plot might have been compromised. He'd been telling the truth when he'd told Carlos that there had been no sign of trouble at his end. However, with only a week to go before VET was to begin the final stage of the plot, the ominous inklings of trouble voiced by Carlos couldn't be ignored.

He toyed with his teacup, thinking about the American. Using Allman, the seemingly disgruntled army veteran, had not caused any problems so far. Recruiting him had been viewed as a stroke of luck, actually, and negated the need to bring in operatives from abroad. Men much more likely to draw attention in the less populated regions of the American west. Allman's role would be over in a few more days and he might, as he'd suggested to GROWER, just disappear from the United States forever.

But after much deliberation, FOX concluded that he couldn't count on that happening. He had to go with Omar's distrust and suspicions of Allman, opinions that he'd voiced more than once since he'd first met him. Therefore, he concluded, he had to give more weight to Omar's judgement than that of his brother, Francois.

Yes, the American had to be terminated. He'd call FARMER today and have him arrange it.

NEW MEXICO, WEDNESDAY, NOVEMBER 17

Tom Allman glanced over at Frank Archer, slumped in the passenger seat sound asleep. Omar was sitting behind him, staring out the window. They were an hour out of Albuquerque, heading east on I-40 in his Jeep. The four crates of explosives and their small bags were secured behind the back seat. He had booked two rooms at a medium-priced motel a few miles from the city's airport. The busy area would afford them a sense of anonymity, he'd explained to Frank, and there were plenty of restaurants to chose from for what he expected would be a 3 to 4 day stay.

They arrived just after dark, and checked in. "Be ready to go at 8:30 tomorrow morning," Tom told Omar. "The area you want to see is about an hour from here." He left them on their own to eat, not wanting to spend any more time with the sullen Arab.

51

PARIS, THURSDAY, NOVEMBER 18

The police wasted little time acting on the plate number provided by the private investigator, Paul Boutin. A few minutes after 8 a.m., Monet and six members of a rapid response squad arrived at an auto body shop owned by Emile Brest, age 62. The panel truck was registered in his name. The 'hole-in-the-wall' repair shop was located on a back lane in a northern suburb. Brest didn't fit the descriptions of the suspects they were looking for, but two of his employees did. One of them was his son, Marc. The duo stood in open-mouthed awe as armed officers in combat fatigues fanned out around the dingy garage. The shock effect was exactly what Monet had counted on. After demanding to see their identity cards, Monet had them handcuffed and waved away their angry protests, telling them only that they were suspects in a murder investigation. Marc yelled to his puzzled father to call a lawyer as they was led away and hustled into separate police cars.

FOUR HOURS LATER, INSPECTOR MONET had broken Marc Brest...

"I was not there when he strangled her!" protested Brest. "There's no way you can pin her murder on me!"

"Monet smiled, nodding slowly. "Strangled? Who said anything about her being strangled?" He leaned across the table, bringing his face within inches of the suspect's sweating brow.

Brest pulled away and brushed perspiration from his nose. "It was in the papers," he pleaded weakly. "That's where I read about it."

How she had died had never been made public. Now that Brest had given himself away, Monet was quick to capitalize on his gaffe. His full cooperation might just see him avoid a murder charge, the inspector explained, settling back in to his chair. It wasn't long before the frightened man caved completely. The 35-year-old mechanic gave the police a full account of his involvement in what he thought was just to be an extortion attempt, but ended in the prostitute's killing.

LONDON, THURSDAY, NOVEMBER 18

DS Houghton had spent most of yesterday putting together his plan to 'return' Saahir Kayani's cell phone to him...

"Norman, do you recall the name of that young Asian constable we used last year? Mingling with the protesters at the Israeli embassy?" Superintendent Houghton asked.

Sergeant Barbara Norman looked up from the file she'd been studying.

"Hmm...Khan, wasn't it?" she replied, after a moment's thought. "He was assigned to one of the east end precincts, I believe."

"That's the chap! I need him here as soon as possible, even if he's off duty," said Houghton. Tell his superior we'll need him for a few days," he added, as Norman reached for her Rolodex file.

Constable David Khan arrived at Houghton's office at two o'clock. By four, he had been briefed on the ruse the counterterrorism squad hoped he could pull off. After a last run through of questions he might be asked, Houghton was satisfied that Khan was ready.

"Be here tomorrow morning dressed in casual clothes," Derek told him, "and we'll put it in motion."

The modestly handsome officer, 23, was born in London in 1981, a year after his parents had been granted landed immigrant status. Khan was exactly the type of recruit the Metropolitan Police Force had been targeting since 9/11: well-educated, no run-ins with the law as a youth, and fluent in at least one of the languages spoken by the growing Asian population in the United Kingdom. He grew up speaking Urdu at home while quickly becoming fluent in English at school.

AFTER ANOTHER QUICK REHEARSAL, KHAN call the Kayani residence on the Kilburn High Road. They had waited until receiving word from the surveillance team that their suspect had left for work, knowing then that one of his parents—probably the father—would answer. They had figured correctly, and Khan had left his message. At 11:30 a.m., he slipped out of the unmarked patrol car a half mile north of the Kayani residence.

Khan was window shopping along the busy shopping district at 11:45 when he felt his phone vibrate. It was the watchers calling to advise him that Kayani had just arrived home. "Roger, I'll make the call in ten minutes."

"SOMEONE FOUND MY PHONE? WHO? Where did he find it?"

The elder Kayani held up his hand. "Patience, my son! Let me explain."

He told Saahir as much as he remembered from the call, and stressed that the caller spoke excellent Urdu. He had told the caller to ring back between 12 and 12:30. "That's probably him now," he said, when phone rang.

"Is that Saahir Kayani?"

"Yes," he replied, cautiously. "And you are?"

"My name is Mohir Khan, sir," the policeman replied, switching to Urdu. He'd used a false first name, but stuck with Khan, one of the most common Pakistani surnames. "I think I have found a phone belonging to you. I took a chance that the first number on your list was your home number, so I tried it. Your father thought it was probably yours, you see."

Kayani's felt a flood of relief. Perhaps he shouldn't have reacted so hastily the other night by calling Carlos. But he'd better be sure this man was not a police plant...

"Yes it's probably mine, and thank you for being so honest," said Saahir. "Where did you find it, by the way?"

Khan launched into his prepared explanation. He'd found it earlier this morning, just after getting off the all-night bus on the High Road. The bus stop was four blocks from the rooming house where he lived. He worked for a catering company at Heathrow Airport, and his shift didn't end until 2 a.m. The phone was lying in the gutter at the corner of Bracket Street and the High Road, partially covered by leaves. Because of the late hour, he'd waited until after he got up this morning to try and find its owner.

His explanation sounded plausible enough to Kayani, and they arranged to meet in front of the Tesco Market in fifteen minutes. "Don't be late because I have to get the bus before one o'clock. It takes me almost two hours to get to work," Khan urged.

The handover took less than a minute, ending when Khan saw the number 249 bus approaching and told Kayani that it was his bus. Kayani thanked Khan warmly and they embraced, both praising Allah for Khan's supposed 'good Samaritan' deed and Kayani's good fortune in having it returned.

Other than a few new scratches on its casing, the phone looked the same to Saahir. There had been mud on it, but Khan had cleaned it up, he'd explained. He wasn't exactly sure how one took it apart, but it didn't appear to have been tampered with. He hit the 'quick dial' button for one of his co-workers, who answered promptly and assured Saahir the signal was loud and clear. Kayani told him he'd be 30 minutes late returning to work. He'd thought of a way to check to see if Khan was on the up and up...

WHEN KHAN MENTIONED THAT HE lived in the area, Saahir had almost asked him for the address. But that might have been perceived as impertinence on his part by a fellow Muslim, he realized, and he'd rejected the notion. But Khan had mentioned the name of the company he worked for, and as soon as he returned home Saahir looked up the company's number in the business directory.

"Good afternoon, ma'am," said Kayani. "Does Mohir Khan still work for you? I wish to pass on a message from friends in Karachi."

"Let me check, sir," the receptionist replied, "I'll have to put you hold for a few moments." Thirty seconds later she was back on the line. "Ah, yes, he does work here. However his shift doesn't start until 3 p.m. Can I have him call you, perhaps?"

"Unfortunately not. I'm only in London for the day. But I have another contact with whom I can leave the message. Thank you for your help. Goodbye."

Kayani felt even better after ringing off. *Perhaps those men who'd jumped me were just a couple of thugs after all, and not the police.*

THE MOOD IN DS HOUGHTON'S office was upbeat after Constable Khan returned. He had ridden the 249 bus as far as Oxford Street, where an unmarked car picked him up. By the time he reached the police station, Kayani had already made his call to check on him.

The catering company Kayani had called inquiring after a 'Mohir Khan' was a front, a fictitious company set up for use by various British Intelligence services. The small office was located in a corner of the vast Royal Mail complex at Heathrow Airport. An agent/operator was on site eight hours a day, but the few calls to it were normally routed to answering machines. Kayani's call, though, was answered by the duty agent. She responded using the prepared script that had been faxed to her from DS Houghton's office just before Khan left to contact Kayani.

"Good work, everyone, and particularly you, Constable Khan," lauded Houghton. "I'm sure we'll be calling on you again, and perhaps there will be a spot for you on our squad in the not too distant future."

After he left, Houghton and his officers reviewed the Kayani situation. During the hours his phone had been in their possession, it had been modified. A microchip had been inserted that gave the squad an instant record of any number he called from it. His call to his friend at work and the second one to the bogus catering company confirmed the chip was working as planned. Unfortunately the techs had not had time to devise another chip that would tape calls.

"Well, let's hope he uses his mobile to call another cell member," said Sergeant Norman. "That would give us a leg up, wouldn't it?"

"True enough, Barbara," agreed Houghton. "If it were me, though, I'd throw it away and get a new one. But Kayani is showing his inexperience, it would appear."

A knock on the door interrupted their session. A young constable entered and handed Houghton a slip of paper with a number written on it. "Righto, team! Kayani is running true to form. He's just tried to call the Paris number again, the one he called before we brought him down the other night.

STANDING OUTSIDE THE REAR ENTRANCE to the dry cleaning plant where he worked as a presser, Kayani stared at his phone, mystified. Had he misdialed Carlos's number? Again, but more slowly, he punched in the numbers and got the same result: no ring tone, just an indistinct static-type sound on the line.

52

NEW MEXICO, THURSDAY, NOVEMBER 18

Omar was alone when he came out of the room he and Archer were sharing and slid into the front passenger seat. "What's the matter, Omar? Couldn't get Frank out of bed?" asked Tom with a smile, hoping to set at least a civil tone for the morning.

"Not feeling well," he says. "His presence is not necessary in any event," replied Omar.

Probably as tired of your company as I am, thought Tom.

Fifteen miles east of the city, Tom turned off the Interstate and onto the two-lane secondary highway heading south. It was a typical November morning at the 5 to 6,000' level: cloudless skies, a light southwesterly breeze, with the temperature slowly climbing towards the predicted daytime high of 50F. The highway paralleled the Manzano Mountains and Tom remarked on the stark but stunning view as they rounded a sharp bend to face the range head on. Omar also appeared to be impressed by the scene, Tom thought, but his only response was a slight nod.

There were no other vehicles in sight when they reached the dusty, gravel road Tom was heading for. He made a left turn onto it and a few minutes later the twin tracks of the Great West Railway were visible to the right. At a slight rise in the road, he pulled off onto the narrow shoulder and stopped.

They were now looking down on the tracks. "This stretch of track," Tom explained, sweeping his hand from left to right, "is where the eastbound trains stop and wait, sometimes for up to an hour."

"Why is that?" Frank asked.

"Because there is only one track through the mountain pass up ahead. It's about three miles from here. They stop here to give way to a train, sometimes more than one, coming down through the pass on the single track section."

"How do you know this?"

"Because that's what I was doin' on my earlier trip. I spent the better part of two days around here checkin' it out."

Omar glanced around. "And no one noticed you stopping here?" he asked skeptically.

"No, but it's not exactly a freeway, is it? Besides, I had a cover story ready." He pulled a pair of binoculars from under his seat. "Birdwatching. Eagles nest in the mountains behind us."

Omar was still dubious and said so. "Well, you wouldn't be bird watching at night."

Allman chuckled. "Of course not! And this isn't the spot we'll approach the trains from, either. See all that empty land on the far side of the tracks?"

Omar nodded. The grasslands that stretched to the another mountain range on the southern horizon were mostly devoid of any sign of activity. A few head of cattle were scattered about, grazing in lonely splendor. The only buildings visible were five or six widely separated and derelict farm structures.

"Let's head over that way," said Allman. He started the jeep again, now sporting a film of fine dust, and pulled back onto the road. Five minutes later they reached the intersection with Highway 60. He turned onto the pavement, heading southwest. A mile further on they reached a bridge crossing over the single track. He stopped, and pointed to his left. "The pass itself is a mile or so up there around the bend. You can see there's just the one track now. Once a train gets over the pass, it reaches the dual tracks again near the town of Mountainair. Westbound trains stop up there if necessary, but the location is too close to town for our use."

Traffic was light on the highway, and Allman kept his speed near the posted limit. They were now driving along the vacant ranch lands he'd pointed out when they had stopped earlier. He explained his plan to get the explosives to the railcars, using one of the abandoned sheds between the road and the tracks as a base.

"We'll come back tonight after dark and get started. It'll probably take us two, maybe three nights, to complete the job."

THEY HAD RETURNED TO THE city and dropped Omar off at the motel. Tom went out to buy the supplies needed to sustain them during the next few days and nights. They left Albuquerque again at 7 p.m., this time taking the I-25 south and Highway 60 to the area.

After checking to make sure there were no other vehicles in sight, Tom had turned off onto the dirt path that had once been the main roadway to the abandoned ranch. He parked the Jeep behind a derelict building a hundred yards from the highway. It had taken them two trips to move the crates and supplies to what Tom was now thinking of as their forward operating base, a second crumbling shed not visible from the road.

"TIME TO GET MOVIN', OMAR. There's two trains waitin' now," Allman said.

The Arab grunted a reply, and rolled to a sitting position. He had been dozing in his sleeping bag while Allman was out reconnoitering the tracks.

Omar took the thermos of tea Tom handed him, poured a cup, and drank it quickly. Both men donned black coveralls and pulled dark wool caps over their heads to ward off the cold desert air. There was no visible frost, but Tom knew the temperature was at or near the freezing point. Not that he was concerned with the cold: once they were busy, body heat alone would keep them warm enough. There was just enough star light filtering through the high, thin overcast to let them pick their way around the sparse vegetation and rocks without stumbling. They were both carrying four of the devices, which weighed about three pounds each.

They were able to attach all eight of the laptop-like units to tank cars by 2 a.m., on three different freight trains stopped to allow westbound trains to clear the pass. With at least another four hours of darkness left, they returned to the shed for more devices. There was a longer wait for the next train to stop, and they were on the verge of quitting for the night when an appropriate target slowed in front of their hiding position. It was a mix of boxcars and tankers and they were able to fit four more devices before it moved on.

"That's it until tonight, Omar," whispered Allman, as they trudged back towards the shed. "Time for sleepin'."

LATE SATURDAY NIGHT AND EARLY Sunday morning they repeated the operation. By 4 a.m. they had successfully fixed the last of the devices to targets. The operation had gone without a hitch: there had been no sign of either human or electronic surveillance while they'd been going about the task. They had targeted 24 cars, securing the devices under or behind metal frames or supports. Most of them had been tank cars designed to transport flammable liquids.

They gathered up their sleeping bags and remaining supplies and made their way back to the Jeep. Without using the headlights, Tom drove slowly back to the highway and turned west towards the Interstate. It was still dark when he pulled into the motel parking lot a few minutes before six.

AFTER ENTERING HIS ROOM, TOM realized he wasn't especially tired. Just as he had after the rendezvous on the border when he'd picked up the devices, he'd gotten a rush from the covert action conducted over the last two nights. It brought back giddy memories of crawling around the Iraqi desert in the dead of night attaching explosives to tanks, heavy artillery guns, and ammo dumps.

He pulled off his boots and dropped into the easy chair. *It mighta' been a blast, but for all the wrong reasons...I just helped a fuckin' terrorist plot get closer to happening...and it might be too late to stop it.*

He was thinking again of the strange request made by Omar Friday morning, the day after they had arrived in Albuquerque. They had stopped for breakfast at a restaurant a few miles from the motel before heading off to look at the site Omar wanted to see. Tom was reading a newspaper while they waited for their orders to be served when Omar interrupted him.

"What are all those vehicles doing there?" he asked, indicating the RV park next to the restaurant. Tom folded his paper. "Those are what we call recreation vehicles, and that's a park where they can stay overnight or even longer." He pointed out the different types—fifth wheels, trailers, and motorhomes.

"For some people, the RV is their home on wheels," Tom explained. "They're known as 'full-timers'."

Omar asked about prices, and Tom pointed to a 40-ft. long deluxe model Holiday Rambler coach pulling out of the park. "That big brown one there? That baby probably set those folks back around 500,000 dollars.

"But you don't have to buy one," he continued, indicating a class C model with a *CRUISE AMERICA* logo on its side. "You can rent one like that for anywhere from a week to a few months. An alternative to stayin' in motels or hotels. Not exactly luxury, but comfortable enough to get around in."

Omar had asked Tom a number of questions about the vehicles and then made his surprising request. He wanted Tom to rent one of the smaller ones for them after they got back to Phoenix.

While they had been laying low yesterday waiting for nightfall, Tom had given a lot of thought about how to turn this to his advantage. Theoretically, his role was to have ended after the explosives were planted. But now that they needed his help to rent an RV, he just might have one last chance to find out exactly how and where Omar planned to detonate them. If he could manage that, then it would be time to hand it over to the federal authorities.

He didn't want to think about how their 'lone wolf' tactics would be viewed if the plot succeeded. After all, it had been his call to carry on a bit longer before stepping aside, and Don had gone along with him. *Let's hope I can pull it off*, was his last thought as he fell asleep.

He awoke with a start two hours later and made for the shower. As he toweled off, he decided what his next move would be. He slipped out of his room, started the Jeep, and drove to the service station two blocks away. While the gas tank was filling, he called Charlie Minh in Los Angeles and explained what his plan was and how he needed Minh's help to make it work. His former Ranger buddy was ready to go, and said he'd leave for Phoenix within the hour.

53

PARIS, SATURDAY, NOVEMBER 20

Paul Boutin was mildly intrigued by the call from Inspector Monet last night and had quickly agreed to meet him this morning. He didn't offer any details, only telling Paul that it would be worth interrupting his weekend for. Little did the PI know when he rang off that the call would see him caught in a whirlwind of activity lasting all weekend.

Monet greeted Paul with a big smile as he approached the café across from Police Headquarters. He'd been sitting at an outdoor table and rose to shake hands. "Sit, sit, I have good news for you!" he urged. "The tip you gave us about the licence plate paid off big time!" A pot of coffee and two glasses of brandy were already on the table. He pushed one over to Boutin.

"Sante!" said the happy policeman, raising his shot glass.

"And to you, Inspector," replied Boutin, bemused by his host's jovial mood, a noticeable change from Monet's usual dour demeanor.

They were seated under an electric heating element and the warmth radiating down from it was welcome, warding off the chilly breeze whipped up by a late autumn storm tracking across the capital region.

"Your lead led to the of two suspects, and the quick confession by one of them, Marc Brest. His partner in crime, on the other hand, wasn't so eager to talk," Monet explained.

Unlike Brest, the second suspect had a criminal record. Michel Drouin, 48, was a native of Marseille. He had served time for assault, extortion, and burglary. He'd been released from his last jail term three years ago, and started his new job at the garage a month later. He had refused to answer any questions after they took him in, other than to deny any knowledge of the murder at the Hotel Nouveau Monde. His co-worker's confession, however, had left him out on a limb, and Monet struck quickly to lop it off.

By Friday afternoon Drouin gave in and agreed to plead guilty to manslaughter rather than face a murder charge. It wasn't just the plea bargain arranged by his public attorney that swayed him, rather it was his knowing how precarious his life would be if he were released on bail. The cartel that hired him was to be feared more than prison life, in his mind.

Monet's face carried just the hint of a smile throughout his account of the arrests and confessions, and he signaled for another brandy when he finished.

Boutin complimented Monet on solving the prostitute's murder and asked, "What was their motive? Did you find out who had put them up to it?"

"Oh yes, and that's where it gets interesting..."

Drouin had been tight-lipped about who had hired him until Monet suggested it was a terrorist organization. Even murderers could muster up a sense of patriotism at times, it seemed, and Drouin opened up and told how he had been recruited. The former convict had worked for the Amara gang as a young man in Marseille. His first arrest and conviction came about when he'd been caught during a bungled kidnaping and extortion attempt the Amaras' were behind. In spite of offers of a reduced sentence if he would identify his bosses, he'd kept his tongue.

After he was released from prison three years ago, keeping his mouth shut back then paid off. He was certain the elder Amara brothers had a hand in his being hired at the Paris body shop. He was content with his new life and had every intention of staying out of trouble.

Until Carlos Amara came calling...

He was given almost no time to think about the younger Amara's offer, and the amount dangled in front of him was too much to turn down. The ex-con's good intentions were quickly forgotten. He was provided with the hotel pass key and the number for the prostitute's pimp. After she showed up at the hotel, Drouin and Brest took her up to the vacant room adjoining Don Carling's.

"How did you know it wasn't in use?" Monet had asked.

A contact—he never knew the man's name—was also at the hotel and told them which room to use. This contact also assured him that Carling was out and probably wouldn't be back for a few hours. The pass key let them enter both rooms and open the connecting doors between them. All was going according to plan until the young prostitute refused to go along with the plan to entrap the Canadian, a set up that it was hoped would see Carling charged with rape.

"And how was that supposed to happen?" Monet had asked.

"The bitch was to enter his room naked when he got back, because we figured he'd be at least half-pissed when he returned. She was to try and get him to fuck her and then cry 'rape'," Drouin explained in a monotone voice.

"So you killed her just because she wouldn't co-operate, is that what you telling me?"

"Yeah," Drouin shrugged. "Something like that."

Monet had to reign in the impulse to smash his fist into the murderer's unemotional face. "*Something like that?*" he exploded. "What the hell does that mean? Spell it out for us!"

Drouin had slapped her around and forced himself on her before strangling her to death. He'd used a condom.

"And the hairs of the man we found on her body? You planted them there, didn't you?"

"Yeah," he admitted. "Got them from the guy's hairbrush."

"Why did they move her body to the other room down the corridor?" asked Boutin.

Monet snorted. "Another silly move by these cretins. They thought someone might check into the room and find her before Carling got back, giving him an alibi."

"Well, that wasn't the only dumb thing they did, was it?" opined Boutin. "Tell me about the phone call you were so interested in. The one that also pointed the finger at my friend."

The hotel's phone system had logged a local call from Don's room at 10:33 p.m. According to testimony from both Carling and his French host, they had left the restaurant 'after 10:30 but before 11p.m.' Neither one could narrow it down any further.

"But that call was made by one of the perpetrators of the crime, n'est ce pas?" offered Boutin.

"Indeed it was. Drouin admitted he'd had his accomplice make it. It turned out to be the pimp's number. The first call to summon the girl was made earlier using his mobile phone."

Boutin declined Monet's offer of another brandy. Instead he filled his coffee cup and stirred in a sugar cube.

"So you see, Paul, why we couldn't eliminate your Canadian colleague from our list of suspects. And when the his DNA matched the hairs found on her body, well..."

Boutin nodded slowly. " It's too bad you weren't able to break the pimp's story. It might have led you to these bastards sooner."

"Yes, we did eventually get his identity from an informant, but he turned out to be a dead end. That was just a few weeks ago. He admitted that the girl had approached him, but he'd turned her down because he thought she was lying about her age. He told us he had no idea how Drouin or someone else had found her or how they came by his phone number. That's probably complete bullshit, but we couldn't prove otherwise. She'd only been in Paris for three days at the most before she was killed. Might've been her first job," said Monet.

"In hindsight then, it was just a poorly conceived plan from the start,"offered Boutin. "A clumsy attempt to incriminate Carling, or at least embarrass him. But it only adds to the savagery this Carlos character and his co-conspirators will resort to, doesn't it?"

"It certainly does, Paul," replied Monet. "And for that very reason I'm meeting with the security service tomorrow morning. As I've probably already ruined any plans you had for the weekend, I'd like you to be there, too. Your findings and insight regarding Amara will be most helpful."

Boutin assured Monet that he would attend, and jotted down the time and location.

"You mentioned the Farka murder. Did Drouin have a hand in that?"

Monet shook his head. "Apparently not, even though I got the impression this Carlos character might have approached him for the job. His alibi for the time frame checked out. But I'm confident we'll be able to wrap up that case as well before too much longer. His killer probably has ties to the Marseille crowd as well. We're searching for a few possible suspects, and my instincts tell me they are losers just like Drouin."

"Then you'll be dropping all efforts to extradite Don Carling, I presume." said Boutin.

"That's correct," nodded Monet. "I've let the authorities know that he has been cleared and I expect they will get on with rescinding the order."

The long drive from New Mexico had been made longer by an accident south of Flagstaff that held them up for thirty-five minutes. It was almost midnight when Tom dropped Frank and Omar off at their motel. Charlie Minh had arrived two hours ago and checked into a motel across from Tom's. They had exchanged phone numbers when Allman called him from Albuquerque, and arranged that he would call him the next morning.

SUNDAY, NOVEMBER 21

Paul Boutin didn't think Don would complain about the timing of his call. His colleague had phoned from the Texas ranch last week and left his contact number. I know it's the middle of the night where you are, Don, but you might sleep better after you hear my good news."

Don yawned, and flipped on the bedside lamp, and fumbled for his watch. It 01:50. "Okay...no problem, Paul," he answered, stifling another yawn. "But it better be good..."

He sat up, swung his legs off the bed and reached for the non-existent pack of cigarettes, the habit he had given up fifteen years ago. He was wide awake by the time Boutin finished with his account of the arrest of the prostitute's killer and his subsequent confession. "What can I say, Paul, other than damned well done and thanks a million. That should make it easier for me to move about during the next few days."

Boutin's welcome news did make it easier for Don to get back to sleep. He was dead to the world when Tom Allman's call woke him at 7:30.

"Morning, pard. I expected Razor to answer."

"He's not here, Tom. He was called out yesterday to check for a pipeline for a leak. He's probably down Oklahoma way, and wasn't sure how long he'd be gone," Don said. "Left me in charge of feeding the cattle, if you can believe it."

"Cow shit and country music, what more could ya ask for, huh?" chuckled Tom. It was the only light moment in their talk.

"Jeezus, Tom! I think we should let the authorities take it from here, don't you?" Don protested, when told about the Arab wanting an RV. "They're going to hang us by our scrotums anyway! What the hell does he want that for?"

"Good question, pard, and one I insisted he answer before I go along with it."

He'd put the question to Omar while they were driving back to Phoenix yesterday. The terrorist had balked at first, but Tom stuck to his ultimatum.

"It turns out he wants a mobile base that can be used to track the devices, " said Tom. "Whether he just thought of it while we were in

New Mexico, or the need was there all along, I don't know. But it gives us another chance to stop them before it's too late."

Don let out a nervous sigh. "And presumably detonate them from. But how are you going to pull that off, Tom?"

Allman and Minh had a plan to rig an RV, thus allowing them to keep tabs on it. "Charlie and me are gonna set that up today," he explained. "Omar wants to be on the road by tomorrow, and that gives us enough time to get ready."

There was a long silence before Don spoke again. "Okay...I guess it's worth a try. Call me again as soon as you've arranged it. Once Razor returns, we'll get on our way to Arizona."

54

EARLIER THE SAME DAY IN Paris, Commandant Rheaume had made a key breakthrough in their quest to apprehend Carlos Amara.

Rheaume had been flabbergasted when told that Francoise Amara, the woman his officers had been searching for, was actually holed up in an apartment belonging to private investigator Paul Boutin's agency. Boutin had accompanied Inspector Monet to the morning meeting in Rheaume's office at the Directorate of Territorial Security [DST]. That revelation, plus evidence they presented regarding the known and suspected activities of the Amara family members, fueled his hunch that it had been a man using the apartment, not the woman shown on the lease. And that man was probably Carlos Amara.

"Excuse me, gentlemen," said Rheaume, pulling a file folder from a desk drawer. The folder contained the report he'd received from the Department of Homeland Security earlier this month. His department had been unable to correlate the phone numbers and code words with any information in their data bases. He had signed off on a reply to Washington to that effect just last week.

But now he saw a connection. Two of the phone intercepts noted in the DHS report were calls from Yemen to Paris. The number was the same one used by two other persons attempting to contact Carlos Amara recently—his cousin, Francoise, and the terrorist suspect in London..

His officers had discovered other signs to suggest that the apartment was only used for short stays, probably as a message drop. The telephone connection box and a cord for an answering machine were the main clues. A check with the electricity company showed that apartment 312's usage was considerably less that of the average unit in the building. When questioned, the postal carrier added to the mystery about the occupant. The letter box for 312 had never been activated, he told the police.

"Sorry about that," Rheaume apologized, closing the folder. "When I add the classified information in this report from the Americans with your findings, I have to agree with you. It seems highly likely that a terrorist plot is being concocted right under our very noses. And I find that most offensive, don't you?"

Both men nodded. "Yes, Commandant," said Monet, "You've hit the nail on the head. The terrorism may be directed at overseas interests, but the murders in our city are connected to the plotters, of that I have no doubt. And there is only one prime suspect."

"Right. Let us go and have a talk with your Miss Amara," said Rheaume.

RHEAUME SHOWED FRANCOISE A COPY of the lease for the apartment. "Miss Amara, is this your signature?" he asked.

The puzzled woman used her reading glasses to study the document. "No... it's a close resemblance, but I've never seen this before," she replied, handing it back. "And I'm not familiar with that address, either."

"Do you have an account with this bank in Marseille?" He showed her a copy of the transfer document for the monthly rent. Again, Francoise denied any knowledge of the banking arrangement.

"Would your cousin Carlos resort to using your name without telling you?" wondered Rheaume. "From what these gentlemen tell me, he has already involved you in his nefarious doings. Are you sure you haven't been a willing accomplice, Miss Amara? And let me be absolutely clear— these are not petty crimes we're talking about." It was the same stern warning that had convinced her to cooperate with the private detective in the first place.

Francoise shook her head emphatically. "No! No! I have no idea what he's up to! That's why I've agreed to stay here. Monsieur Boutin thinks my life would be in danger if Carlos knew where I was."

"And I would agree with him," said Rheaume. "The sooner we can apprehend Carlos, the sooner you'll be able to resume a normal life. Now, this is what we need you to tell us..."

Rheaume grilled her about her uncles, her brother, and any other family members still alive. He was after their addresses and phone numbers, and wanted to know when she had last been in touch with them. She answered all his questions truthfully, but nothing she told them shed any new light on what Monet and Boutin had already discovered. Except for one rather innocuous revelation...

DURING INSPECTOR RHEAUME'S INTERROGATION OF Francoise Amara, she'd let on that the family had once owned a chalet near Marseille. She'd mentioned it almost as an afterthought when asked about possible hideouts Carlos might be using if he'd fled Paris.

The chalet was used mainly during the summer when Francoise and her brothers were growing up. She thought it was jointly-owned by her father and his brothers. She wasn't sure of its exact location because she'd hadn't been to it since she was nine or ten years old, more than twenty-five years ago. Pressed for more details, she recalled that it didn't seem to be too long a drive from the family home on the northern outskirts of Marseille. When she told them she might have a photograph of the cha-let, Boutin's interest perked up. He drove her back to her condominium to look for it.

Not only did the shoe box of old photographs Francoise had tucked away in a closet contain a black and white snapshot of the chalet, it also had pictures of family members taken at her mother's funeral in 1993. In one photo, her brother Francois and their cousin Carlos were standing to-gether, unsmiling. She and her brother were twenty-five at the time, four years older than Carlos, she told Boutin. Both young men appeared to be clean shaven, had short hair, and were wearing dark suits, all in keeping with the somber occasion.

If Carlos had left Paris, might he head for the chalet? Boutin won-dered, as he studied the undated photo of the chalet. An idea struck him, a longshot at best, he realized, but worth a try. Francoise had no objection to Boutin borrowing the photos.

As soon as he'd returned Francoise to the safe house, Boutin called a friend. Denis was a keen rock climber, an activity that took him to south-eastern France two or three times a year. Fortunately Denis was home, and agreed to see him. Sunday was the only day that traffic was relatively light in central Paris, and Boutin double-parked in front of his apartment block ten minutes after he'd called.

Boutin declined his friend's offer of a drink. Time was critical, he explained, as he showed Denis the photo of the chalet. *Did he recognize the unique rock formation behind it? Could he pinpoint its location?* Boutin wondered.

"Sorry, mon ami," he replied, shaking his head. "It looks vaguely fa-miliar, but that's all."

He made a suggestion, though, and with a hurried 'thanks' Boutin was off again. His luck held traffic-wise, and at five minutes to five by his watch, the private investigator arrived at the Paris club house of the National Rock Climbers Association. The club house usually closed at five o'clock, Denis had warned him. He need not have hurried, though. A reception was in full swing for a group of the club's instructors who'd just wound up a weekend seminar.

He had the information he was seeking literally before he opened his mouth. The geological formation was known as the Cliffs of Clermont, he learned, from the first two men he showed the picture to. The cliffs were situated in the Bruelle Valley region north of Marseille. The almost vertical rock face rose three hundred feet above the surrounding forest and was a favorite climb for club members from all over France.

Meanwhile in Phoenix, Tom had been checking out RV dealers that advertised they had rental units available. He found it at 'SAMMY'S RV', an independent dealership with thirty units in its inventory. The lot was in an industrial area northwest of downtown. Tom approached the lone salesman and asked about rentals.

"Those two back there," said the disappointed salesman, pointing at a fifth wheel and a Class C camper parked by the back fence. He'd lost interest when Tom told him he wasn't looking to buy. The Jayco Class C had a few dents and scratches, but it was exactly what he was looking for. Tom glanced around, checking for security cameras, but not spotting any. An eight-foot high chain link fence surrounded the lot.

Sammy, the owner, handled the rentals according to the salesman, and he wouldn't be in until Monday morning, he told Tom.

"That's okay, pardner, tomorrow will be just fine. I'll call him then. Have a nice day!"

Tom and Minh returned to the deserted industrial area just before midnight and parked a block away from the rear fence. Minh used wire cutters to breach the sagging fence behind the chosen RV. Tom stood watch while Charlie fixed a tracking device to it. Ten minutes later he'd finished and climbed down from the RV's roof. Without a word, they retreated through the fence and hooked the cut wires together to make it look whole again, retreated to the Jeep, and left the area unnoticed.

55

. . . .

MONDAY, NOVEMBER 22

Tom called SAMMY'S RV as soon as it opened at 9:a.m., confirmed the Jayco RV was available, and called Frank. Tell your silent friend I've found a camper for him. I'll pick you up in half an hour."

By noon they had been to the dealership, completed the paperwork, given Frank a quick checkout on the RV, and were on their way back to the motel. Frank was driving it and Tom followed in his Jeep.

"Good drivin', Frank. Nuthin' to it, huh?" Tom said, approaching the five-year-old 23 foot RV.

Archer offered a weak smile. He wasn't looking forward to his new role as Omar's driver. He had hoped to be done with the plot days ago, leaving him free to return to France. Instead, his fear of ending up in an

American prison for God knows how long was front and center again in his mind.

Omar came out of his room and looked over the RV. "Here ya go, Omar," said Tom. "This'll do yuh just fine. No problem rentin' it. The guy was happy to have the dollars and didn't ask Frank any embarrassing questions."

He suspected Omar planned to abandon the RV once they were finished with it. Tom had coached Archer to list the Grand Canyon and southern Utah as his intended destinations on the paperwork. "You're all set fellas. This rig looks just like hundreds of others out there. I don't know what your plans are, but if ya don't smash it up, no one will be lookin' for ya for at least two weeks," said Tom. "By then I'll be sittin' on a beach somewhere nice and warm, and Uncle Sam can kiss my butt goodbye forever!"

ALLMAN HAD NO INTENTION OF going anywhere—at least not until Omar and his obviously reluctant helper were behind bars. He was thinking of the calls he would make as he drove back to his motel. After calling Don Carling to update him about the RV, his next call would be to the FBI.

A few miles from his motel, traffic came to a complete stop while cars involved in a minor accident were cleared from an intersection. Tom used the delay to call Charlie Minh. "We're set, pardner! I got 'em into the rig you wired. Are ya pickin' up a signal from it yet?" Tom asked.

Minh had hidden a transponder in the air conditioner mounted on the RV's roof. "Yes, I'm getting it now. I'm parked about two miles from their motel," replied Minh.

"Then you're good to go, pard. They'll be headin' north in an hour or so. Advise me as soon as ya can confirm that. I'll call the Feds then and give them your radio and phone info."

"Roger that, Trigger. I'll be in position in one zero minutes," Minh advised. "Will call as soon as they move out."

It was a call that Allman would never receive...

JAMES WHARTON II, 35, WHITE, blonde-haired, and athletic-looking, had been watching when Allman drove away from the motel earlier this morning. His room was three doors away from Allman's.

Wharton's All-American appearance belied his part-time occupation: he was a contract 'hit man' for a West Coast crime family. Wharton's permanent base was Las Vegas, where he worked as a blackjack dealer in a Fremont Street casino. He'd been given the assignment via a coded telephone call early yesterday morning, and left for Phoenix minutes after his evening shift ended. Driving his black 1997 Ferrari, he sped through star-drenched desert landscape of northwest Arizona, averaging 90 mph until the lights of the sprawling city showed on the horizon, Two hours before dawn, he entered the Terminal 4 parking garage at Sky Harbor Airport, followed the circular ramp to the nearly deserted rooftop level, and power-napped in his seat until 5:30 a.m.

He locked his sports car, made his way down to the arrivals level and took the shuttle bus to the central car rental complex. He chose a company at random, signed for a two-day rental, and was on the freeway heading for Allman's motel before most Valley of the Sun residents had sat down for breakfast. He'd been provided with Allman's physical description, his motel and unit number, and the color of his Jeep. He was expected to carry out the hit within 24 hours of his arrival in Phoenix.

The desk clerk, the owner's eighteen-year-old son, was still half asleep as he registered the early morning arrival. Wharton located Allman's room on the motel map and asked for a room nearby. He'd been driving all night from Los Angeles, he told the disinterested youth, and wanted to be as far away from the street as possible. He used a false name to register and paid cash. The drowsy teenager mumbled his thanks and shuffled back to the family living quarters behind the office. Wharton pretended to study the rack of tourist brochures until the youth was out of sight, then reached behind the counter and grabbed the spare key to Allman's unit.

THE ASSASSIN'S BRAIN WHIRLED INTO gear, much like a computer awakening from sleep mode. The rush, almost sexual in nature, was sparked by the crunching sound the Jeep made on the gravel as it came to a stop. The time to kill—the climax—was mere moments away. He'd slipped into Allman's room unseen, soon after his target had departed. He'd been swallowing mild 'uppers' every hour to stay awake. The drawn drapes kept the room in semi-darkness.

He moved swiftly to the corner beside the door, which hid him when Allman opened it. Two seconds after the lights flicked on, Wharton took one step, raised his pistol and fired twice into the back of his unsuspecting victim's head. The moment Allman's body thumped to the carpet, the assassin turned the lights off and closed the door.

He unscrewed the silencer, shoved it into his pants pocket, and tucked the pistol under his waistband. Before leaving the room, he peered around the edge of the drapes to check for signs of activity outside. There were none. He casually opened the door, stepped outside, and hung the 'Do Not Disturb' on sign on the doorknob.

Five minutes later, the blackjack dealer was on his way back to the airport. He dropped off the rental car, retrieved his Ferrari, and headed for the freeway. He'd only driven a few miles when a sudden thought hit him. There had only been one audible 'pop' from his silencer-equipped Glock. It must have jammed with the second pull of the trigger...

56

"I've found the chalet," Jacques Brunelle said, "and I think someone's staying in it. I'm going to check it out later tonight."

"Be extremely cautious, then, Jacques, don't play the hero. If it is Carlos, he's dangerous," his boss warned him.

BOUTIN HAD SENT BRUNELLE OFF yesterday with maps of the Bruelle Valley below the massif, plus a word of caution. "Don't ask questions about the chalet, find it yourself," Boutin advised. "If it's still in the Amaras' hands, someone local probably keeps an eye on it for them."

Posing as man and wife, Brunelle and Lise had checked into the small inn in Bois-sur-Mont Monday afternoon. He'd let on to the nosy innkeeper that they were down from Paris for a brief hiking trip to celebrate their first anniversary. The cover story was easy enough to pull off for the attractive young twosome: they were engaged and planned to marry next summer. But the main purpose of their trip wasn't to enjoy the fresh air and exercise. Brunelle was on a scouting mission to locate the chalet that Francoise Amara and her family had stayed when she was a youngster.

The cliffs were approximately five kilometers [three miles] in length with foot trails dotting the area below them. A switchback trail at the northern end lead hikers to the mostly level plateau and rewarded them with a 360 degree panorama of the countryside below. There were numerous cottages and chalets in the area and it wasn't until they were on their second walk of the day, after lunch, that Brunelle spotted the Amara chalet. The distinctive wrap-around balcony and three dormer windows on the upper level matched those in the old photograph. Brunelle scanned the terrain below the chalet with his binoculars, spotted the access road leading to it, and highlighted it on his Michelin map.

JACQUES TIPTOED DOWN THE STAIRS from their second floor room to the inn's lounge. The only light source was a dim lamp above the reception desk. He opened the main door, stepped outside, and peered around. There was no traffic, and the only indication of human activity was the muted sounds of laughter emanating from the bar and restaurant directly across from the inn.

He edged along the front and side of the building, and froze. A shaft of light from the full moon had pierced the broken layer of stratus cloud and lit up the grassy hillside between him and the narrow road leading up to the chalet. A minute later the landscape was abruptly plunged into darkness again, and Jacques, his heart rate having slowed again, started his climb.

It took him twenty minutes to clear the last of the houses lining the road. Satisfied that he had made it this far unnoticed, he stopped and pushed back the hood of his grey sweatshirt. In spite of the cold night air, Brunelle was sweating heavily, more from nervousness than effort. His night vision had peaked, and he had no difficulty following the road without having to use his flashlight. He swallowed some water and resumed his trek. He'd estimated that it would take him between about two hours to reach the chalet, poke around for signs of life, and return to the inn. A time frame that would see him back in his room well before any early riser stirred.

His departure had not gone unnoticed, however...

The barman nudged his old friend, the innkeeper. Did you see that, Jules?" The sudden shaft of light escaping from the inn's front door had caught their attention. Jules took another sip of Pernod before replying.

"Yes, Armand...that can only be the young man from Paris, if I'm not mistaken, who professes to be an avid hiker, yet shows up wearing brand new boots. And who goes walking at midnight?"

'Aha! Up to no good, is he? And he's heading towards our friend's lodge, n'est ce pas?"

Jules shrugged. "Exactement, mon ami. I'm not sure who's been staying at the chalet for the past few days, but, it isn't the old men."

"No, they always stop in if just to say hello, don't they? Must be one of the younger family members," the barman surmised. He was a second cousin to the senior Amara brothers. "Perhaps it's nothing, but I think a call to Marseille in the morning is in order..."

57

PHOENIX, TUESDAY, NOVEMBER 23

Don and Hank Gillette had been taking turns behind the wheel of the Texan's '98 Mustang for almost eleven hours when they got to *LUCKY STAR* motel. Their all-night dash began after Don was unable to contact Tom Allman yesterday. Allman hadn't called as expected, and there had been no replies to Don's calls to him. Don realized something must have gone wrong and the sooner they got to Phoenix the better. Using Gillette's helicopter wasn't an option: it was sitting at a general aviation airport near Amarillo awaiting a regular inspection. They arrived at 9:15 a.m. to find the *Do Not Disturb* sign on Allman's door. There was no response to Don's heavy pounding on it. He rushed into the motel office and confronted the manager.

"Mister Allman in 118, when did you see him last?" Don asked sharply.

"Uhh, two, three days ago, maybe," he stammered. "I'm not sure. The cleaning lady hasn't been in his room because he's had the sign out."

"Give me a key, then!"

The flustered Asian immigrant fumbled around under the counter. "It should be right here, but I don't—"

"Fuck it, Don! I'll break down the door," said Gillette, rushing outside with Don right behind him.

The lock to Allman's room gave way at Gillette's second swift kick. Don was only one step over the threshold when he saw the victim's feet.

"Ahh, Jeezus, you rotten bastards," he muttered, falling to his knees beside the body. He felt for a neck vein while trying not to touch the pool of dark, dried blood around his friend's head.

"Oh God, I think he's still alive! I'm feeling a faint pulse. Call 911 now!"

Four hours later, at the Sun Valley Regional Hospital, the two weary men almost knocked each other over struggling to their feet when a young doctor entered the emergency department waiting room and beckoned to them. "He should pull through, he offered. "The plate in his head saved him and the bullet didn't enter his skull."

The surgeon gave them a brief report on Allman's condition, including his opinion that it could be some time before he regained consciousness.

The gunman's bullet had hit the plate, dug a furrow along the exterior of the skull, tearing through numerous veins before exiting above the victim's right temple. "Good thing you found him when you did," the doctor said. "Another two or three hours and the shock from blood loss would have been fatal."

Thank god we left Texas when we did, thought Don.

Gillette told the doctor and Don that the plate must have been inserted in Allman's skull after he'd been seriously wounded by shrapnel during the first Gulf War. He'd been evacuated to an American military hospital in Germany for surgery, Gillette recalled, and by the time he'd been released, the conflict had ended and their unit was back in the States. When Allman rejoined them several weeks later, he'd never said anything about the plate.

Although it had saved his life, the sudden impact from the bullet had pushed the plate against his brain, causing potentially lethal swelling, and rendering him unconscious. The coma would last until the swelling—'edema' in medical terminology—subsided, according to the doctor.

AFTER THANKING THE DOCTOR, THE shaken men left the hospital and stopped at a nearby bar. "Here's to Tom," said Don, draining his shot glass of scotch whisky.

"Amen to that, let's hope he pulls through," replied Gillette, downing his glass and signaling for refills. They sipped the second round quietly, each lost in his own thoughts.

Eventually Gillette asked, "So what do we do now?"

"That's the million dollar question," sighed Don. "If we can't talk to Tom, we'll have to try and find out where Minh is ourselves."

"Yeah...and the doc didn't offer much hope that he'd come around soon, did he?"

"Well, we can't sit here drowning our sorrows all day," Don said, shoving his empty glass away. "Drink up, Razor, and let's head back to the motel. Might be something we can use there."

AFTER THE AMBULANCE CARRYING ALLMAN'S comatose form had sped away from the motel earlier, Don had cautioned the owner to stay out of the victim's room until they returned. The police would have to be called, Don knew, but he wanted to have a good look around the room first. The door to room 118 was still closed when they arrived a few minutes after half-past three.

Don left the heavy drapes closed, turned on the overhead light, and stepped around the pool of dried blood. He picked up the keys lying on the bed. One was obviously a room key.

"These'll be for his Jeep," he said, handing Gillette a ring with three keys on it. "Must of had them in his hand when he fell."

"What are you looking for now?" asked Gillette, as Carling continue his probing.

"This!" he smiled, thirty seconds later, handing him the small hunk of flattened metal he'd dug out of the closet door frame. "I figured it must be here somewhere when the doc said it hadn't penetrated his head. Looks like a small caliber to me."

Gillette studied the spent bullet briefly before handing it back to Don. "Yeah, I'd say it's a .22, maybe a .25. Could have been fired from any number of handguns."

They searched the floor for the shell casing, but came up empty-handed.

They found two cell phones when they searched Allman's Jeep, a Nokia and a Motorola model. "I'm guessing he's been using this one to call Archer or other local numbers," Don said, indicating the Motorola phone. "They're all in the 604 area code."

There were only two numbers on the contact list on the Nokia, and one was Don's. The 'missed call' list totaled eight. "I made three of these, but I wonder who the others were from?"

They had their answer almost immediately, when the phone in his hand rang.

"...Hello?"

There was a long pause from the caller's end. "...Who's this?"

"I'm a friend of Tom Allman. He's been hurt." Don put his hand over the speaker and passed the phone to Gillette, "I think it's Charlie Minh, but he's suspicious. Maybe he'll recognize your voice."

"This is Razor Gillette talkin' now. Is that you, Charlie?"

There was another pause before Minh replied. "What was our squad's call sign in Iraq?"

The question brought a chuckle from Gillette. "It was 'Satan', you oriental misfit!"

"Okay, okay, then I guess you really are the bigoted asshole from Texas I once knew," retorted Minh. "What happened to Trigger, Razor?"

Gillette quickly filled him on what they knew about the shooting that left their Army buddy in a coma. When Minh started to tell him where he was and what was happening, Gillette cut him off. "Let me put Trigger's boss back on, Charlie. Don's his name and he's legit, so you can talk freely to him."

Five minutes elapsed before Don was ready to hang up. "Okay, Charlie, call me as often as you can. I've got to call the local cops now, and then contact the FBI. We'll probably try and catch up to you sometime tomorrow, as soon as Razor can arrange for a chopper. We'll keep in touch on this phone."

MINH HAD FOLLOWED THE TERRORISTS' RV from Phoenix to Flagstaff yesterday afternoon. The first stop they made was at a shopping center where one of the men entered a supermarket and emerged with three bags of groceries. When they pulled into a nearby RV park, Minh checked into a motel directly across the highway from it. He was up early this morning and fell in behind the RV when it left the park shortly after 9 a.m. The RV headed north on Highway 180, the route which ultimately led to the South Rim of the Grand Canyon.

But the world-famous natural wonder wasn't their destination. Seven miles from Flagstaff the RV turned off 180 onto the access road leading to the Alpine Ski Resort. Three miles below the resort, Minh saw the camper turn off on to a fire service road. The unpaved road, closed during the winter, wound around the south side of the Humphreys Peak, the highest mountain in the state.

"Charlie's assuming they're going to camp somewhere along the isolated road, which dead ends about six miles from the highway," said Don. "He had to fall back for fear of being spotted. I guess it's pretty rough and winding terrain.

"Yeah, I've dry-camped on wilderness roads like that myself," said Razor. "And so do lots of other hardy souls who like to be alone. Maybe that's why they chose the location."

"Yes, and they're probably thinking the higher elevation will help if they're going to rely on satellite phone communications to activate their explosives. Anyway, Minh is still getting a good signal from the transponder hidden on the RV, and they'll have to pass his location to get back to the highway."

Don asked Razor to call the local cops while he questioned the motel's owner. *Had he or the cleaning staff seen anyone lurking around Allman's room on Sunday or Monday?* The owner produced a registration card and showed it to him.

"This man checked in early yesterday morning. The maid thinks he must have left the same afternoon. When she went to clean the room this morning, the bed hadn't been slept in."

Don studied the card. The name didn't mean anything, nor did the Los Angeles address. "Make sure you give this to the police when they show up," he told him. He was sure the information would prove to be fictitious, but that was for the police to find out.

The two Phoenix detectives, who responded to Gillette's call, were obviously pissed to learn that almost six hours had elapsed since they had broken into Allman's room. Most of their testiness stemmed from having to take the call only ten minutes before their shift was to end. They were both scheduled for five days off through the Thanksgiving weekend.

"Well, we weren't going to stand here watching him die while waiting for you to show up, or you'd probably been dealing with a homicide," Don explained, as diplomatically as he could. They were even more irked when Don gave them the bullet fragment. The older detective suggested that maybe he should charge Don with disturbing the crime scene.

Rather than argue any longer about why they took the actions they did, Don bluffed an end to the impasse. He told them he was an undercover agent investigating a terrorist plot and that's what had lead to the shooting. "We're due at the FBI office downtown in ten minutes, so that's where I'll be if you want to talk to me. Here's my cell number," he said, handing him a slip of paper.

Don and Razor drove away, leaving the detectives shaking their heads. The cops' mood did not improve when they arrived at the hospital. The ER surgeon who had treated Allman was in the operating theater and wouldn't be available for at least another two hours.

GILLETTE LET OUT A LONG chuckle once they were out of sight of the detectives. "Good move back there, Don! Left them stuck for an answer, didn't you?"

"Well, it wasn't really my intention to piss them off any further, but we had to get out of there. Only the FBI can help us now," Don replied. "Let's hope they've got someone on duty when we get there." They pulled in to the Bureau's almost-empty parking lot a few minutes after 6 p.m. and hurried towards the entrance.

The bullet-proof doors were locked, and Don hit the buzzer to get the attention of the security guard he could see sitting at a desk inside. Over the intercom, Don identified himself and briefly stated their business. The mention of a terrorist plot wasn't lost on the overweight ex-cop and after showing him their photo ID through the door, he let them in.

They were directed to the third floor where Special Agent John Briscoe, 31, met them as the elevator arrived. He ushered them into his office, a glass-walled cubicle with no windows. "Have a seat," he said, indicating two folding chairs in front of his desk. According to the framed certificate resting on the corner of his desk, Briscoe was a graduate of Yale University with a degree in behavioral science. Two other agents working in adjoining cubicles paid no attention to the after-hour visitors. "What's this about a terrorist plot?"

Where to begin? was the ongoing question Carling had wrestled with for days, pondering how best to explain everything to the FBI when the moment came. *How can I make a viable case, one with links in so many places, in a manner that this man will be able to comprehend and act on quickly?*

He would be starting from scratch, as Briscoe had already checked the office log book and informed him that there was no record of a call from anyone named Tom Allman.

Forty-five minutes later it was a moot point. Canadian private investigator Don Carling was handcuffed and on his way to jail...

HANK GILLETTE WAS SLUMPED IN an uncomfortable plastic chair outside his unconscious buddy's curtained-off cubicle. He was utterly exhausted. He took another sip of cold coffee as he tried to make sense of all that had happened since he and Don arrived in Phoenix twelve hours ago.

While agent Briscoe had been listening to Carling's story, he'd had another agent run the Canadian's passport through the federal data base. After his colleague had done that, he'd beckoned to Briscoe. The two had a short discussion outside his office before Briscoe returned, shaking his head.

"Well, in spite of what you may have been told, it appears the arrest warrant from France is still live," he informed Don. "Sorry, Mister Carling, but I have no choice but to place you under arrest."

Two hours later, Carling had been arraigned before a night court judge. The judge listened politely, but skeptically, to the Carling's story.

As he was unable to prove his assertion that the murder charge had been dropped, he ordered Carling held in lieu of bail of $100,000. Because of the time difference—it was 12:45 a.m. EST—any inquiries regarding the warrant would have to wait until tomorrow morning when official Washington began its work day.

The judge had granted Carling's request to make one call before he was locked up. While he'd been waiting to be brought before the judge, the PI had been thinking long and hard about how he might extricate himself from the dilemma facing him.

Now that he was basically as incapacitated as Tom Allman, chances were high that the terrorist plot might succeed. And even after the problem with the arrest warrant was cleared up, he might still be having a lot of explaining to do as to why they hadn't turned to the federal authorities sooner. He could only hope that Special Agent Briscoe had believed his account of the terrorist plot now unfolding right here in Arizona.

He concluded that his best option was to contact RCMP Inspector Brian Roberts. He was probably the only person that might have the necessary contacts to get him released quickly. He called Brian's office number and left a message explaining his predicament as concisely as he could. If he were allowed access to a phone in the morning, he would call again, he said. If that wasn't possible, he asked the inspector to take any calls from Hank Gillette. Before he was led away, he gave Gillette his cell phone and urged him to call Ottawa at six o'clock tomorrow morning, 9 a.m. eastern time.

"No change in your friend's condition. Why don't you go and get some sleep yourself," a nurse suggested to Hank when she saw him nodding off.

The Texan took her advice, dragged his weary body out to the parking lot, and headed for the nearest motel.

58

MARSEILLE, WEDNESDAY, NOVEMBER 24,

Nasir Amara, two days short of his seventieth birthday and racked with emphysema, listened to the caller's message without comment and thanked him when he finished. "No, you were right to call. I will look into it," he said.

"...A problem, Nasir?" asked his brother Jaabar.

They were sitting in their neighborhood café, taking their daily coffee and cognac. It was a ritual they'd started fifteen years ago after serving their prison sentences. Nasir nodded, struggling through a phlegm-induced coughing spell before he could reply. "Someone has been taking an interest in the chalet, it seems. A *'tourist'* who isn't acting like a tourist, according to our cousin."

The brothers sipped at their coffee, individually pondering the possible ramifications of this untimely revelation from Bois-sur-Mont.

Almost five minutes passed before Jabaar spoke. "Is that where your son is at the moment?"

"Perhaps. I haven't heard from Carlos for over a week," his brother answered. "I will try and contact him when I get home."

CARLOS WAS STILL ASLEEP WHEN the phone rang. He'd been up until almost four o'clock scanning television news channels via satellite. He'd been watching for any reference to the communique he'd emailed to major networks earlier yesterday. The Arabian network al-Jazeera was the first to mention it, but the report was short on specifics. It only mentioned that a previously unknown cell of al-Qaeda World had threatened *'to disrupt rail travel in the United States.'*

There were no mention of the communique on the BBC or the two American networks about the first explosion, which left him wondering if VET had been successful. Then again, maybe the US authorities were not taking the threat seriously. He'd decided to wait until the time frame for the second planned attack passed before attempting to find out.

"Why have you not called, my son?" Nasir asked when Carlos finally answered. "I thought you would still be in Paris."

"Yes, that was the plan, father. But there were indications that ... uhh ... our security might have been breeched there. It should not affect the operation in America, but as a precaution I felt it best to leave the city."

"But don't you have a back up plan in case the event VET has problems?"

"Yes, but I can manage it from here. And I haven't told anyone I'm here, also as a precaution."

"Well, that's why I called. You may still be at risk because—" Nasir broke off, fighting through another coughing fit.

"... Because what?" asked Carlos when his father's attack subsided.

Nasir told him about the suspicious visitor that his cousin and the inn keeper had spotted sneaking out of the inn late last night.

"Well, I haven't noticed anyone poking around the chalet since I arrived. Where is this man now?"

He and his companion left town an hour ago. They wanted to stay another night, but Jules lied and told them that he was booked up.

"I see. I'll check with Jules myself. Another twenty-four hours or so will see the fulfillment of our plot. After that I'm going away for a while. Just carry on as usual, father. There should be no reason for you or Uncle Jabaar to worry."

Carlos couldn't have been more wrong...

"Get this to Commandant Rheaume right away!" exclaimed the technician. He was waving a printed copy of the call made minutes ago between Nasir Amara and his son. "This is proof that the suspect they're after is definitely holed up at the chalet!"

The radio operator grabbed the slip of paper, scanned it quickly, and punched the buttons to connect him to the government jet carrying the commander to Marseille.

Rheaume had ordered the tap on the phone lines of both Amara brothers first thing Monday morning. Their residences in Marseille had been listed with the police when they were paroled years ago. Rheaume made his move after meeting with Paul Boutin and Inspector Monet on Sunday, and his subsequent interview with Francoise Amara. The evidence that connected Drouin, the prostitute's killer, to the senior Amaras, had been the key to obtaining permission for the phone taps. At the time there was no proof that they were involved with the terrorist plot, but Rheaume figured that Carlos might turn to his father for help now that he was on the run.

Rheaume had moved swiftly after learning from Boutin that the Amara chalet had been located and was thought to be occupied. Rheaume and a four-man commando team were now en route to Marseille to position themselves for a possible raid on the chalet. Now that they had confirmation that Carlos was indeed hiding there, it appeared that his plan was justified.

The team was poring over maps and photos of the Bruelle Valley as the twin-engined Dassault executive jet began its descent to the military airbase near Marseille...

OTTAWA, WEDNESDAY , NOVEMBER 24

Inspector Roberts liked to get to his office early, usually by 7:30, and today was no exception. The quiet 25 or 30 minutes before his staff began their work day gave him time to check phone and email messages.

The message from Don Carling caught his attention immediately. He hadn't heard from the private investigator for some time, and hoped he was calling with an update on his investigation of the suspected terrorists. The last time they spoke, Don had suggested they were about ready to turn it over to the American authorities.

According to the rather rushed message from Phoenix, however, that wasn't the case. He listened to the message a second time, making notes, and shaking his head.

Don, Don, what were you thinking? In the US using a false name, and now in custody because of the French warrant...

As soon as his secretary popped in with his first coffee of the day, he told her to expect a call from a man named Gillette.

"Put him through right away, Denise," he said, "and I'll want to talk to Agent March at DHS after Gillette calls. Please check with his office and give him a 'heads up'. Tell them it's urgent."

HANK GILLETTE CALLED AT 9:02, introduced himself, and explained his connection to Don Carling.

"Don is hoping you could sort out this arrest warrant problem. He got a call on Saturday night, you see, from his contact in France telling him he had been cleared of the charge," said Gillette. "That's why he gave the FBI his real identity."

"I see. Well, if the extradition request was only rescinded a few days ago, the paperwork is probably still in the mill. But I'll check it out at this end," Roberts said. "Now, am I to understand that although Allman has been shot, there is still someone tracking the suspects?"

"Oh yeah, an ex-Army buddy of ours, Charlie Minh, is up north watching them, and that's why we went to the FBI. Don told them all this, but I guess Briscoe thought arresting him was more important."

"What do you mean by 'up north'?" asked Roberts.

"Oh, these guys are on a mountain north of Flagstaff, about 150 miles from here. Probably went there because of the higher elevation. Allman figured that the charges are to be set off remotely by satellite phone, and by using the RV to move around, they're hoping to foil any attempts to pinpoint them electronically.

"But according to Don's the message, there's been no sign that this uhh...*cell*, has come to the attention of any US agency."

"That's right," replied Gillette. "And that's why he's counting on you to use your connections to convince the feds down here that they should go after this RV, or there's going to be fireworks on a large scale somewhere pretty soon."

Inspector Roberts took down the name and phone number of the police facility where Don Carling was being held. "I'll get back to you in a few hours, Hank," he sighed.

ROBERTS CALLED THE JUSTICE DEPARTMENT immediately and spoke with a senior staff lawyer on the international desk. It took all his powers of persuasion to convince the civil servant that he was facing an emergency situation vis-a-vis an imminent terrorist attack in the United States that precluded him from making an official request for the information. A slight exaggeration on his part, but it worked. Fifteen minutes later the lawyer called back, advised that the notice rescinding the request to extradite Don Carling had only been received yesterday, and a copy of the document was being faxed to him.

The fax was scrolling off his machine as he thanked the lawyer for his cooperation and hung up. He scanned through the two pages of legal verbiage before buzzing his secretary.

"How did you make out with DHS, Denise, did you reach Agent March?"

"Yes I did, sir. Actually he appeared to be chomping at the bit to speak to you. I'll connect you now."

"Morning Brian, you're just the man I need to talk to," said Bob March. "It appears your PI's information regarding a possible terrorist strike was accurate."

"Oh? What's happened?"

"We now believe that an incident yesterday in Wyoming may have been a terrorist act."

What was initially seen as an accidental derailment of seven or eight cars of a freight train was now believed to have been caused by an explosion. When company investigators reached the scene—in open country thirty miles east of Cheyenne— they found that a tank car of liquid fertilizer had been blown to pieces, tearing up thirty yards of track and derailing the cars behind it.

"Any casualties?" asked Roberts.

"No, the car was towards the end of the train. It might have been a lot worse if it had exploded while passing through a town, though."

Confirmation that terrorists were behind the explosion came via a communique sent to major news outlets on three continents two hours ago. The BBC, the Arabic network al-Jazeera, and CNN headquarters in Atlanta all reported receipt of the message, and CNN passed the information to Washington immediately. The message warned that yesterday's explosion was only the beginning: a similar explosion would occur somewhere in the American west at 2300 hours GMT today. The message was attributed to al-Qaeda World.

The balance of the lengthy communique was a rambling diatribe against the American voters and businesses for their ongoing support of the anti-Islamic administration in Washington.

"al-Qaeda World, eh?" said Roberts. "That's a new one to us. A spin off of Bin Laden's organization, maybe?"

"We think so, Brian. We've had the occasional mention of it recently from various sources. But this bombing is the first concrete evidence that it's for real and has apparently got to the operational stage. And that's why I need your help."

"Well, Bob, your timing is impeccable. I've just found out where Carling is at this very moment."

Roberts relayed the information Hank Gillette had given him from Arizona less than an hour ago. Roberts could offer no insight as to yesterday's explosion, or the warning March referred to about a second one that is supposedly set for 3 p.m. Pacific time today.

"And this operative of Carling's has been shot and can't speak? And Carling has been arrested?" March asked, incredulously. He checked the wall clocks displaying local times around the globe. "Jeezus, we've got less than eight hours before they strike again!" he fretted.

Agent March and Inspector Roberts formulated a short list of what needed to be done ASAP. Getting Carling released was the first item. "Fax me the paperwork canceling the extradition request, and I'll forward it immediately to DHS in Phoenix and instruct them to get it in front of a judge with the power to action it," vowed March. In the mean time, he would work on setting up a coordinated effort by law enforcement agencies in Arizona to apprehend the suspects.

"This couldn't have come at a worse time, Brian," he said. "Most of official Washington has already left town for the Thanksgiving holiday. My boss, Assistant Director Egan, is probably on his sailboat in the Bahamas. But I'll do my best to get the FBI and the National Security Agency up to speed right away," said March.

Roberts could almost visualize the sweat breaking out on March's brow. "I'm sure you'll make the right moves, Bob," he encouraged, "and I'll be available 24/7 if there's anything I can do from this end. The fax will be on the way in five minutes." Roberts refilled his coffee and returned to his office, wondering what, if anything, he could do to help the Americans with their looming crisis. He came up empty, but decided it wouldn't hurt to have a chat with his British colleague, DS Derek Houghton.

"YES, THE SITUATION IS CHANGING quite rapidly here as well, Brian. And after what you have just told me, I'm fairly certain it's connected to their situation," said Derek, after the RCMP officer apprised him of the latest developments in Arizona and Washington. "We're aware of that communique from al-Qaeda," Houghton continued. "The BBC alerted us to it an hour ago."

"Well, you can imagine the scene in Washington right now. This terrorist cell couldn't have picked a better time to act, what with the major holiday weekend ahead."

"Then what we have just might help..."

Last night Saahir Kayani had sent an email that was intercepted by his counterterrorism team, Houghton revealed. Ever since his hard drive had been rigged during Scotland Yard's investigation of his sister's murder—while Kayani himself was in Pakistan—the police had access to all his email traffic. The brief message, addressed to FARMER, advised him that he had been unable to contact BREEDER.

59

NORTHERN ARIZONA, WEDNESDAY, NOVEMBER 24

The phrase 'not a happy camper' definitely described Frank Archer's mood. And he'd felt that way since he and Omar had driven up the wilderness road in the RV yesterday. They were parked in a small clearing thirty yards off the rough access road with no facilities. Frank was becoming more upset by the hour. Yesterday the vehicle's toilet system quit working, and now the interior of the cramped camper smelled like an alley in a third world slum. The surrounding woods was their only option when nature called.

They were also running out of food, at least food Frank considered edible. Their third day on rice, beans, and now mostly stale bread was not helping his increasingly foul demeanor. The small generator they had barely supplied enough electricity for the VET's needs and he was using it sparingly. The overnight temperature had dropped below freezing, and Frank had been too cold to sleep for more than an hour at a time. He wanted to run the generator this morning to warm up the RV's interior, but Omar turned him down.

"I need it later," he said sternly when Frank objected. "And again tomorrow, so we will have to make do without power for now. You'll have to forego your incessant coffee drinking for the time being."

Omar also vetoed running the vehicle's engine to supply power, as it would be needed as back up in case the generator failed. "The mission comes first, and it will be completed tomorrow," he said. "Another explosion in a few hours, and then the climax when this greedy nation of infidels sits down for their pagan celebration tomorrow."

Omar had become increasingly edgy during the past 24 hours, both in speech and physically, Frank noticed. He never seemed to sit still for more than five minutes at a time, and most of Frank's questions about how the plot was to end and how they would make their getaway went answered.

He'd had a nightmare-ish thought at 3:30 this morning. *Was he was caught up in a suicide mission, with one of the switches on Omar's control panel designed to send them both to a fiery death when the last of the explosives had been detonated?*

OMAR HAD USED THE CONTROL panel for the first time yesterday to set off the first explosion. The Egyptian engineer had even gone to lengths to try and explain its workings to Frank, his pride in its innovative complexity obvious. Had it not been designed to abet terrorism, the device would win accolades from engineering associations world-wide, he boasted. He even had a name for it. "This is *'PETBE'*," he'd said. "The *'God of Revenge'* in Egyptian mythology."

The portable console contained twenty-four mini 'brains', each connected electronically to one of the explosive devices. A six-inch square LED screen displayed portions of the earth's surface, using a program similar to Google Earth, but downloaded from an orbiting European satellite. Omar had customized the unit to show the Western United States, from the Canadian border south to Mexico, and from the Mississippi River west to the Pacific Coast. An area as small as one square mile could be displayed. A flick of a switch for a given device activated a flashing red light to indicate its geographic location. By homing in on it, the operator could see precise details of its location.

Omar had chosen yesterday's target after checking all the circuits. Five of the devices did not emit a signal. This was not unexpected, and had been considered in the planning phase. The engineering did not provide the capability to determine if the loss of contact was temporary or permanent. Nor did he expect that all the target cars would be a suitable position on Thanksgiving Day. As few as five or six explosions in strategic locations should have the desired effect on the public.

FARMER had been working on a list of potential targets since Carlos had first conceived his plan to attack America. The list included refineries, airport fuel storage farms, and harbor facilities on the Gulf of Mexico and the West Coast.

When he checked the system yesterday, Omar had been elated to find that four rail cars were already in prime target areas, and two more were moving towards optimum locations. The plotters knew it wouldn't be the number of explosions , but the threat of more to come that would maximize the panic and uncertainty they were hoping to achieve.

Yesterday's bombing had been the first step in the three-day plan. The second step—the issuing of a communique taking credit for the bomb and giving notice of another—should have been circulated this morning by BREEDER. The third step was the one VET was working on now. He'd noted two choices for the next explosion when he'd checked *PETBE* earlier this morning. He would decide which of the two to use just before the deadline.

News broadcasts from the few radio stations they were able to pick up had made no mention of the yesterday's explosion in Wyoming. This did not come as a complete surprise to the terrorist. There were two possible reasons for the silence, he told Frank. One, perhaps the real cause hadn't been determined yet, and it was thought to have been an accident.

However, VET was leaning towards the second, more plausible reason. "They probably know it was caused by explosives, but the authorities are scrambling to decide how to handle it," he explained. "Even if they believe the communique is valid, they don't want to go public just yet. What would a blanket warning to the population accomplish now? Would they chance bringing transportation to a halt on one of the busiest travel days of the year?" Frank offered no reply to Omar's rhetorical questions. "No, nothing will be heard from Washington until after I move this switch here in..." Omar checked his watch. "...Exactly thirty-seven minutes."

"But what if they don't work? Don't you have a way of knowing what's happening?" asked Frank.

Omar nodded. "Yes, of course. And that's why FARMER will call us later today from New York with news, at exactly 6 p.m. I expect by then the second communique will have been circulated. And that's when this country will start to shut down...just as we planned."

60

THE WHEELS HAD TURNED REMARKABLY fast to get Don Carling released from custody, considering that it was the start of the holiday weekend. Agent March had reached his immediate superior, Assistant Director George Egan, on his yacht anchored off Freeport in the Bahamas. After March had convinced him that there was no doubt they were facing a burgeoning terrorist plot, Egan called the White House. The order that spurred a federal judge in the Arizona capital to order the Canadian's immediate release was signed by the vice-president himself.

Razor Gillette wasn't the only person waiting for Don as he signed the release for his personal effects. Among the items confiscated before he was locked up last night were his wallet, passport and the cell phone they'd found in Tom Allman's Jeep. FBI agent John Briscoe and his partner, agent Robin Weir, were also on hand. It was 12:45 p.m.

"Try and get a hold of your guy up Flagstaff way, will you? See if he still knows where the terrorists are," Briscoe urged Don. They were on their way back to the FBI building, with Briscoe's female partner behind the wheel and running red lights.

"WHAT THE FUCK'S GOING ON down there?" Minh asked. "I've been trying to call you guys since last night!"

"Sorry, Charlie, it's a long story. This phone ahh...hasn't been available to me for a while," apologized Don. "Anyway, we need an update on your situation."

After trailing the terrorists as far as he dared yesterday afternoon, Minh had parked his Subaru further down the road. Late last night he had trekked up the wilderness road and found where the RV was parked. He had retreated back down to his vehicle and curled up on the back seat.

"These guys are still up the road somewhere. I'm still getting a weak signal from the transponder. I think they must have gone further up the road. Probably while I was in Flagstaff early this morning," Minh said.

He had gone to town to for food and a sleeping bag, and rented a mountain bike, he explained. "It's not exactly tropical up here after dark, you know. I hope someone's paying for all this."

"'Oh yeah, no problem that way," Don assured him. "So the RV has disappeared? And what's with the bike?"

"This road ends at the ski resort parking lot. I'm gonna ride up there on the bike to see exactly where they are now."

"Okay, Charlie, call me again when you have a 'visual' on it. We're with the FBI, on our way to a meeting to decide how best to come after them. We'll relieve you as soon as possible."

Carling ended the call just as they reached the FBI building. Agent Briscoe's phone beeped while they were hurrying inside. Briscoe answered it while they waited for the elevator.

"Yes, sir, he's just been released. I'll put him on."

The Canadian gave him a questioning look. "For me?"

"Yes, Agent Bob March from the Department of Homeland Security wants to speak to you."

"...Carling here."

"Mister Carling, I'm glad to hear your ahh...*problem* there has been rectified. You can thank Inspector Roberts in Ottawa for that, by the way," March began. "I understand you had an agent working undercover with this cell, and I need any info he may have given you about them before he was shot."

Don did so, repeating what he'd told the FBI yesterday before he was arrested.

"So, let me see if I have it right," March said. "There are as many as two dozen freight cars fixed with explosives, and they could be anywhere now. The bombs are detonated remotely from this RV, using some sort of controls or phones in their possession."

"Yeah, that's it in a nutshell," Don agreed. "Tom Allman is still in a coma, unfortunately, so that's all I know about their set up." Razor had stopped by the hospital earlier and learned that there had been no change in their buddy's condition.

DON GRATEFULLY ACCEPTED BRISCOE'S OFFER of coffee and a sandwich before they entered the conference room. Three men summoned by Briscoe were already seated around the table. They represented three different agencies: the Highway Patrol [DPS], Alcohol, Tobacco and Firearms [ATF], and the Maricopa County Sheriff's Department.

Briscoe wasn't sure they would all be needed, but didn't want to leave anything to chance. The urgent call from the Bureau's number three man in Washington—placing him in charge of the local operation pending the arrival of a more senior agent from Los Angeles— had been explicit.

Don't screw up Briscoe. Your career hinges on your performance in the next six or eight hours.

After introducing Carling and Gillette, Briscoe briefed the local officers on the apparent terrorist plot. He was just about to take questions when a staffer entered the room, apologized for the interruption, and whispered into Briscoe's ear.

"Shit," he muttered to himself, before speaking to the men at the table. "Gentlemen, the authenticity of the threat is no longer an issue. Another train has just been blown up. There's no doubt now that we're dealing with a terrorist situation . That's the message just received from Washington. I'm to expect further information within the hour."

His statement was met with stunned silence. Eventually the Sheriff's Department representative asked, Do we know exactly where these bastards are right now? If we do, why don't we send a SWAT team to take them out?"

His suggestion sparked a flurry of comments and suggestions, none of which Agent Briscoe was prepared to authorize without first consulting with Washington.

WASHINGTON, 5:30 P.M.

Keeping news of the second explosion from the public was not an option. The car—loaded with liquid fertilizer—blew up twenty miles southeast of Lubbock, Texas. And there were fatalities. A State trooper on patrol along Highway 84 had witnessed the fireball. The train tracks ran parallel to the highway, roughly a mile to the east, and the trooper arrived at the scene five minutes later. The mangled remains of a Dodge pickup truck that had been waiting at the level crossing was visible amidst the jumbled pile of derailed and burning cars. The mangled remains of a man and a woman were inside the truck's cab.

Even before fire trucks and emergency vehicles arrived, news of the wreck was already being aired by a Lubbock TV station. A passerby had sent photos taken on his I-phone to the station's news room, hoping to win a cash prize for his 'breaking news' report.

THE SWITCHBOARD AT DHS HEADQUARTERS was aglow with flashing lights ten minutes after Fox News followed in minutes by CNN— interrupted their regular programming to report the Texas explosion. As soon as Agent Bob March heard the reporter refer to the explosion as a 'possible act of terrorism', and suggested it was similar to a suspicious bombing in Wyoming yesterday, he knew the skeleton staff on duty for the holiday weekend were about to be overwhelmed. The calls were from media all over the country seeking comments and requests for interviews. He dashed off a quick statement for the public information officer to circulate...

'DHS is aware of the two derailments that have occurred and are awaiting reports from experts as to possible causes. At this point in time, we have no evidence to suggest that the incidents are related, or have been other than unfortunate accidents. Although two people were killed in the Texas derailment, DHS does not feel there is any threat to the public at large.'

It was bit of a 'cop out', he knew, handing it to the waiting public information officer, but it would have to suffice for now.

It wasn't long, however, before his hastily written release was being derided by commentators. CNN went public with the communique sent to them yesterday—purportedly from al-Qaeda World—giving the exact time of today's explosion.

MARCH DIDN'T HAVE TIME TO fret over the reporter's reactions now that CNN had let the cat our of the bag. His boss, George Egan, called from his yacht. "Glad you called, sir. I was just about to try and reach you," he lied.

"March, what the hell is going on? I just got a call from the president's national security advisor. He was trying to tell me there had been a terrorist attack near the Texas White House. Is that right?

"No sir, that's not exactly what happened..."

March gave Egan a terse rundown of the facts as known so far. The acting director's only comments as he listened to March were a few muttered curses. When he finished, Egan said, "Hang on a moment, March, I've got another call coming in."

March turned his attention to the bank of TV monitors while he waited. All the news networks were now running with the terrorist threat story. He only recognized one of the commentators. Like most weekends and holidays, the regular anchors were off, replaced by lesser known personalities on most prime time news shows. But Larry King was large as life on CNN, hunched over his desk and wearing his disaster frown. March muted the veteran broadcaster when Egan spoke again.

"Okay, listen up, March. That was Washington again. They're sending a chopper to get me off my yacht. As soon they get me over to the mainland, the Air Force will fly me up to DC. I'll have full communication capability once I'm onboard the jet. Be ready with any updates as soon as I call. And check with the other agencies. See if they have anything on these attacks. Got it?"

"Yes, sir. Understood. I'll be standing by for your call. Over and out," he added facetiously. March had already made the calls, and representatives from the FBI, CIA, and NSC were en route.

"CHET! GOOD TO MEET YOU in person. Guess you got 'joe'd' with holiday duty, too," said March, greeting CIA agent Chet Holtz, the first to arrive.

Side by side, the two presented a 'Mutt & Jeff' image. The mustachioed Holtz, whose ID card listed his height at 6' 4", was a good eight inches taller than March. Neither man was carrying any extra weight. "Yep, the seniority system at work, right?" Holtz chuckled.

March nodded and smiled. "Well, with most of the top brass are out of town for the weekend, you and I and are 'it', at least for now. I'm sure we're going to be summoned to the White House soon, but until then we'd best cover as many bases as possible."

"Right on, Bob, and this might help." Holtz gave March a copy of the signal he'd received from the Agency's London office regarding a tip from the British. They had intercepted an email message in which two code words that various intelligence groups had been trying to put names to were used.

"Yeah, we received the same info, but I haven't had time to do anything about it," said March.

"No problem, we're ahead of the curve on that. When London contacted me with this," Holt said, tapping the print out, I got onto the FBI in New York. Fortunately I talked to a guy familiar with the investigation concerning the codes, and—"

"Didn't happen to be Dwight Ewing, did it?" interrupted March.

"Yeah, it was! Very cooperative, and on the ball, too," replied Holtz.

"I agree," replied March. "We consulted on the codes when they first came to light, but I haven't talked to him since."

FBI AGENT EWING HAD PULLED strings to find out to whom the email British Intelligence had intercepted was routed. According to a manager at the Internet Service Provider, he or she was an individual whose phone number and address were those of the Cote Verde mission to the United Nations.

When the FBI put two and two together, they were 99% sure that a member of the mission, Karim Ahmad Bakir, was FARMER. The Bureau's hands were tied, however, because Bakir had diplomatic immunity. Ewing was working on a 'sting' operation to get their hands on him, he'd told Holtz.

"Well, all indications we've had from various sources point to this cell having at least one operative entrenched in the New York area, and Bakir is the prime suspect in my mind," sighed March.

"Amen to that. The FBI has placed a 24/7 watch on the mission. As of two hours ago, the suspect was still inside. If and when he shows, their agents will put the operation in motion."

61

Omar was holding the satellite phone in his hand when FARMER finally got through. He'd been unable to reach them via Frank's cell phone as planned, he explained. "We are almost in the dark communication-wise," Omar told him. "Coverage in this area is extremely poor, and Internet use is impossible. But it is too late to move. What has been the reaction to the explosions?"

THE FIRST TWO EXPLOSIONS WERE successful, FARMER reported, and were now the major topic on news broadcasts across the country. "Our hoped for impact is a reality, and our second communique is being aired repeatedly. The government is definitely worried, and has issued a weak statement devoid of facts. But that is exactly what we expected. After you complete your task tomorrow, widespread panic will ensue. When the follow-up communique is released, threatening airline travel, the country will come to a standstill. And the government will be powerless to prevent it."

Omar was smiling when the call ended. It was a 'first', Frank was thinking.

IN WASHINGTON, THE PAST TWO hours had been a blur to Bob March. It was now 9:35 p.m., giving him a few minutes to check with Phoenix again before he left for the White House.

"Any change in the situation?" he asked FBI Agent Briscoe, who was still in charge there.

"No sir, we've moved a SWAT team up to Flagstaff to be closer if needed," he replied. "As far as we know, the two terrorists are still on the mountain. Communication with the 'civilian' agent near them has been patchy at best. Might be due to his location, we think."

"Understood. We don't expect any activity by the terrorists overnight, so do not—I repeat, DO NOT—make any move on the RV until it is authorized from this end."

The order from March was in response to Briscoe's earlier suggestion that they have a SWAT team take out the RV. They might only get one chance to take them by surprise, March reasoned, so the plan had to be foolproof. Carling's informant believed the terrorists had the capability to trigger all the charges simultaneously with just a flick of a switch. March feared that's exactly what would occur if they got wind of an impending attack on their RV, and to ensure that didn't happen, the take down had to built around the element of surprise.

"CAN YOU HEAR ME OKAY?" asked Minh.

"Yes, you're loud and clear now, Charlie," replied Don.

"Roger that. Just as I suspected, the RV is now parked in a corner of the ski resort parking lot."

The unpaved lot was relatively deserted, Minh explained, because the resort hadn't opened yet. Some snow was visible on the peak above the complex, but the ski runs were still bare. He had spotted hikers on the hills, and presumed the few other vehicles parked in the lot, two minivans and a jeep, belonged to them.

"Where are you now?" asked Don.

"Back where I'm parked, about two miles down the road. I rode up and back on the bike. Any instructions for me? I thought the cops were supposed to be taking over the surveillance."

"Still in the planning stages, Charlie. Should have relief for you in the morning. Can you hang in there until then?"

"Oh yeah, that's not a problem. How's Trigger doing?"

"No change, really. He's still unconscious, but stable. Call if the RV moves."

MINH'S CALL CAME JUST AS the meeting in the FBI building was ending. The representatives from the other agencies had just left, but Agent Briscoe had asked Don and Razor to stay behind until he heard from Washington again. Carling gave Briscoe the latest news regarding the terrorists' location. The FBI agent wondered why Minh was using a bike.

Razor Gillette had an explanation that made sense. "Charlie was a keen bike rider when he was in the army. He used to ride in marathon races, and maybe he still does. He probably jumped at the chance to do some serious uphill ridin'. I'll bet he figured a guy on a mountain bike wouldn't draw attention from these assholes, even if they did notice him."

An idea struck Don, one that might put Minh and his bike to good use...

62

DHS AGENT BOB MARCH ARRIVED at the White House at 10:15. He had never been inside before. His wife had been bugging him to take the public tour ever since they'd moved to DC three years ago, but he'd always come up with an excuse to put if off. And his appearance tonight certainly didn't qualify as a tour—he'd been whisked through a rear entrance never seen by the public.

He was escorted to a well-lit conference room where the acting director of the DHS and six grim-faced men were already seated around a highly-polished wooden table. His boss indicated the chair beside him without making any introductions. March recognized the man seated at the head of the table: Vice-President Dick Cheney. The others, he surmised, were probably advisors to the president or representatives from agencies responsible for national security.

Egan had checked with him after his flight from Florida landed at Andrews Air Force Base. His instructions were short and simple: be ready to give a full briefing on the terrorism plot.

March took a sip of ice water before he started speaking. Some of the grim-faced men took notes during his fifteen minute account, while others just shook their heads at times. When he finished, Egan surprised him by offering a quick and accurate recap before throwing the discussion open.

There were plenty of questions, and March did his best to answer them. His boss rescued him from having to explain one thorny issue.

"We really can't say yet exactly how the plotters got to this point, sir," he said, addressing the vice-president's question. "As I'm sure you know, we are inundated daily with tips and intelligence from many sources, and it's a very difficult task to prioritize what needs to be followed up, and when.

"In this case," he shrugged, "tying an investigation by this Canadian PI to what we're now facing would ahh... probably have required a few more pieces of the puzzle in our possession before we categorized it as a viable threat."

To his credit, the vice-president accepted Egan's explanation and silenced others who wanted to pursue the perceived failing. "Gentlemen, lets not dwell on the 'whys', 'what ifs', and 'who dropped the ball'. In my opinion there is no blame to be laid at this stage. Suffice to say—and I know I'm speaking for the president—we have full confidence in all the agencies in our ongoing battle with would-be terrorists. And that includes Acting Director Egan and his department. So let's get on with what's happening now. If I understood Agent March correctly, the aim of this terrorist cell is to panic our citizens, with the resulting damage to the economy, similar to what happened in the aftermath of 9/11."

Cheney looked to March for confirmation. "Yes, sir, that's our understanding," he answered. "I do not believe these explosions are designed to cause human casualties, although two people were killed by the explosion in Texas."

"Thank you, March. So the question, gentlemen, is what should we do now?"

The V-P's question sparked a spirited discussion, during which Bob March remained silent. When it was obvious to him that none of the suggestions being bandied about could be acted on without the help of those already on the scene in Arizona, he tried to catch the vice-president's eye.

"Yes, March?"

"Sir, may I suggest that we leave it up to the agencies in Arizona to formulate the take down options. They are in the best position to do so, and are working on them as we speak. I've given them a deadline of midnight Arizona time to come up with recommendations," March explained. "Of course they will need authorization from the White House to proceed, no matter what they decide," he added.

There was unanimous agreement from those present, which gave March the confidence to bring up another point. "I mentioned that there was a confirmed French connection to this plot. Their anti-terrorist forces are close to apprehending a key suspect in this previously unknown cell. Possibly the connection between al-Qaeda World, as they referred to themselves in the first two communiques, and these two individuals in Arizona."

"Does this cell have a name?" asked a senator sitting across from March.

"No sir, they haven't used one to date. The only references have been to al-Qaeda World." March didn't mention the use of code words to identify cell members.

The French authorities were planning to arrest the suspect early tomorrow morning, European time, according to the call March received from Paris minutes before he'd left his office for the White House. He'd asked them to delay any such action until after the meeting called by the vice-president because it might have repercussions vis-a-vis the current situation in Arizona.

"What don't you like about it, March?" asked his boss.

"Well, sir, we know these people are using satellite phones to communicate with each other. If this French suspect should learn that he was about to be arrested, he might have time to call the cell members here and—"

"And order them to set off the rest of the explosives immediately instead of sticking to their scheduled time frame," interrupted AD Egan.

"Exactly, sir," replied March.

"Scheduled time? What am I missing here?" queried the vice-president. March looked to his boss to see if he wanted to handle the question, but Egan nodded for him to continue.

"Sir, advance notice of the first two explosions were received from al-Qaeda World, and the information was accurate. We believe these explosions were just to get our attention, and the main attacks are yet to come. Probably multiple explosions in varied locations. And these, I have no doubt, will occur sometime tomorrow, designed to have the maximum impact on Thanksgiving Day."

His sober explanation elicited muttered curses and deep sighs around the table. "So far, however, there has not been a third communique. Perhaps there won't be one, and the terrorists will detonate more bombs without warning."

Discussion turned to what to tell the public. The media were already running with stories about the two communiques and the explosions the cell was claiming responsibility for. The only response to the hundreds of calls to the White House seeking comment had been a terse release from a staffer saying that there would be a press conference 'sometime tomorrow morning'.

"What's the alert status, George? Still at Orange?" frowned Cheney, removing his glasses and pinching his nose.

'Orange', on the color-coded alert system, meant the threat level was 'high' as perceived by DHS. There was only one level higher: 'Red', for severe.

"Yes, sir," answered Egan, "and I think we should leave it unchanged for now. I suggest we wait until morning before making any official statement. As Agent March has so succinctly expressed, there isn't a hope in hell of finding all these rail cars overnight, or even in the next 24 hours. Let's get a plan in place to take out the terrorists first, and go from there."

Another fruitless discussion broke out, which the vice-president abruptly put an end to. "Gentlemen, we'll reconvene at 0600 hours," he stated, and, addressing the DHS acting director, added, "George, if the situation out west changes dramatically before then, call me immediately. I'll be speaking to the president, update him as to the situation tonight. Rest assured he does not want another 9/11 debacle on his watch—with or without human casualties."

AFTER VICE-PRESIDENT CHENEY ADJOURNED THE meeting, and the others had left, Egan asked, "What didn't you tell us in there, March? I got the feeling you were holding something back."

"Sir, the FBI in New York are planning an operation that may have a positive effect regarding the situation facing us," he said, and outlined the Bureau's impending attempt to spook the suspected cell member operating there.

"Are you're referring to the so-called trade representative from the African country?"

"That's the one, sir ... Karim Ahmed Bakir. He's attached to the Cape Verde mission and has diplomatic immunity. German intelligence sources belatedly placed him in Hamburg at the same time as a few of the 9/11 suicide pilots. This would have been in '99 or 2000. He disappeared from Germany shortly after that, and didn't surface again until this Canadian PI came across him, and eventually the FBI got into the act. How he ended up in New York is unknown, and really isn't important at this point."

"Probably not," agreed the AD, frowning. "Well, let's hope they can somehow get their hands on him before too many more hours pass. Check with the Bureau for a status report. Tell them not to worry about diplomatic niceties. I'm not too concerned about some jerkwater African country raising a fuss at the UN."

63

LONDON, NOVEMBER 25, 0510 HOURS

DS Derek Houghton was in bed but not asleep when his mobile phone emitted its unique buzz. In fact he had been awake for the better part of an hour, the terrorist plot unfolding across the Atlantic on his mind. The communications supervisor at Scotland Yard HQ was calling. "My apologies for the ungodly hour, sir, but we've just received an urgent signal addressed to you from Washington."

Derek slipped out of bed, causing only a slight stirring from his soundly sleeping wife. He padded barefoot to the en suite bathroom, and quietly closed the door behind him.

"Right, understood, Jennings," he said after the supervisor read the signal. "Call the officers on my Alpha list. Tell them to report in at 0700. Leave messages for those you don't speak to directly."

THERE WAS A FULL COMPLEMENT of DS Houghton's counterterrorism squad on hand when he entered the room at ten past seven. He was late because the judge he called at 6:30 wasn't used to dealing with requests for arrest warrants before he'd eaten his daily breakfast fare of oatmeal and kippers. Houghton had to bite his tongue while the judge lectured him on the impropriety of his call. A request, he postulated, that the Americans should have made themselves via diplomatic channels. Eventually—and grudgingly—he gave in to Derek's polite but insistent argument that he needed to act immediately.

"Morning gentlemen, and Sergeant Norman. I have just been granted permission to apprehend Saahir Kayani under the Emergency Anti-terrorism Act."

His statement sparked a flurry of comments and questions. Kayani had been under round-the-clock surveillance for the past eight days, ever since he had been 'yellow carded' by Houghton's team. The suspected terrorist had gone about his normal routine during the period, and not met with or spoken to anyone outside his small circle of acquaintances, mostly co-workers.

Until he sent the email to FARMER that was intercepted by the Americans...

THE THREE-MAN TEAM SWOOPED ON the surprised Kayani at the bus stop near his house and bundled him into an unmarked panel van. He was still protesting and demanding a lawyer as he was hustled inside Paddington Green Police Station. After being read his rights—and informed that a public attorney was being arranged for him—the suspect was deposited in a holding cell.

By law, Kayani could be held for up to 72 hours without being charged. If, after the time limit passed without charges being laid, the police would have to release him. That didn't really concern DS Houghton now, though, and he dashed off a signal to DHS to say that Kayani was in custody.

A NIGHTMARE WOKE BOB MARCH abruptly at 4:30. In it, he was standing in chains, barefoot, dressed in old-time, striped prison garb, with an angry crowd pounding on his cell door and calling for his head. He shuddered and glanced around the dimly-lit cell. It wasn't a cell, although the confined and rectangular area reminded him of one. The small bedroom was a only few steps from the White House War Room. He had slumped onto the single bed well after midnight. He shook his head to clear the cobwebs and checked the time. He'd had less than three hours sleep, most of it in 20 to 25 minute stretches.

A steward popped into view seconds after he turned on the overhead light, a coffee pot in one hand and a cup and saucer in the other. March yawned, excused himself, and reached for the cup. After taking a few sips of the steaming brew, he moved to the wash basin, and held a hot cloth to his face. He rummaged through the amenity kit provided, gargled with the mint-flavored mouthwash, and brushed his teeth. Feeling better and almost fully awake, he slipped his shoes on, finished the coffee, and entered the now-busy room.

It was surprisingly quiet, considering the number of men and women moving about. There were at least a dozen, he figured, glancing around. He looked around for a familiar face.

"Over here, Bob," called Jane Bloom, stepping away from the two men she'd been talking with and waving a handful of paper. March was glad to see that she had responded to the voice mail message he'd left for her. The twenty-nine-year-old brunette held a commerce degree from Yale, and March had hired her shortly after he'd joined DHS. Jane Bloom was March's logistics expert.

"Sorry to spoil your Thanksgiving, Jane, but this thing is about to become a national emergency. Have you been here long enough to get up to speed?"

She fanned the reports she was carrying. "Yes I have, and you haven't spoiled anything. An afternoon with Jeremy's mother and his inquisitive aunts I can do without." Jane was 'semi-engaged', as she like to phrase it, and had been for two years. March was never sure exactly what that meant, but he wasn't expecting a wedding invitation any time soon. "You've got replies from London and Paris," she said, handing him two cables stamped 'Top Secret'.

Bloom had managed to latch onto an empty desk and pulled two folding chairs up to it. "Have there been any more warnings from the terrorists overnight?" asked March, sitting down.

"No, I checked with all the major media outlets twenty minutes ago. Nothing. Al Jazeera claims they haven't received anything, either," Bloom answered.

March swore under his breath. Not having a deadline—theoretical or not—was like watching a clock with no hands: just a steady 'tic tic tic' until it suddenly stopped, leaving the terrorists to celebrate.

MARCH READ THE CABLE FROM London first. "Okay, good. The London connection to this cell won't be able to contact anyone for a few days at least," he said, handing the message back to his aide. 'Let's see what the French have to say."

He had sent the French authorities a similar signal to the one the British had acted on: request that you do all possible to prevent suspected members of the cell from using any form of communication for the next 24 hours. Commandant Rheaume's reply arrived two hours ago.

BRUELLE VALLEY, NOVEMBER 25, 12:30 P.M.

Carlos Amara, aka BREEDER, was none the wiser as to what was about to befall him as he hurried out of Armand's restaurant and got back into his Peugeot 444. He'd wakened two hours ago to discover that the chalet's power was off, and the telephone not working. He'd tried to call down to the restaurant using his mobile phone to no avail. The abundance of tall evergreen trees surrounding the chalet and its distance from the nearest relay tower made reception spotty at best. And, with rain and fog cloaking the cliff side this morning, service was impossible. His satellite phone would work, but that was reserved for overseas calls he might need to make later. He'd stopped at Armand's to ask about the electrical outage.

Two other residents who lived on the same road as the Amara chalet had called Armand to say they were without power. "Still a common occurrence," Armand told him, "especially when it rains. Doesn't usually stay off for more than a few hours," he'd added.

The fog was even heavier as Carlos left town heading for Marseille, limiting his speed on the winding road to a cautious 50 KPH. He had to slow even further when he caught up to two large delivery trucks. There was no chance of passing them, as oncoming vehicles didn't appear until they were three or four car lengths away. The slow pace set his mind to thinking again about the unsettling developments of the past 24 hours. After his father called yesterday, Carlos had phoned down to the bar and spoken to Armand. He'd had him repeat his suspicions about the visitor from Paris who'd been staying at the inn. Armand couldn't say for sure that the man had been heading for the chalet the night before, but it spurred Carlos to check around outside for signs of an intruder. He hadn't found any, and there had been no sign that anyone had been tampering with his vehicle.

He'd then called Jules, the innkeeper, and asked him to check to see if the couple had moved to another hotel in the region, but none of them had rented a room to anyone fitting their description.

He was about to forget about the suspicious outsider when a warning bell went off in his head. The timing of the power outage may have been a coincidence, but not the loss of the land line phone. Armand had said that the two neighbors asking about the power interruption had *telephoned* him. *Maybe someone had cut his line … a ruse to get him to leave the chalet, perhaps?*

He didn't have long to wait for an answer. A few kilometers from the junction of the valley road and the main highway, the fog suddenly lifted. He was able to pass both trucks and speed up as he approached the intersection. But just as he got to it, a camouflaged armored vehicle pulled abruptly in front of him. As he hit the brakes, another police unit blocked him from behind. Within seconds he was surrounded by armed and helmeted men wearing face shields. Both front doors were wrenched open, and he was violently pulled out, slammed against the side of his car, and handcuffed. A hood was slipped over his head before he was half-dragged to a third vehicle and shoved into the back seat.

Forty minutes later, Carlos Amara was locked in a cell at a French army base outside the port city. Unknown to him, his father and uncle were similarly isolated in separate cells only yards away.

EGAN APPROACHED MARCH AS HE finished reading the classified cables. "Morning, sir, good news from Europe," he said. "Both the Brits and the French have done as we asked."

Egan scanned the cables and handed them back. "Excellent, March. What about here? Anything new from New York yet?"

'No, sir. The plan for Bakir is all set. They're just waiting for him to show his face this morning. Probably won't have anything from them for a few hours yet." Although Bakir had an apartment away from the Cape Verde mission, he occasionally spent the night inside. The surveillance team had followed him there last night.

"Let's hope he shows. You seem quite sure he's calling the shots, not the two out in Arizona." It was a question as much as a statement. "The Arab may be the one pulling the trigger, but he didn't surface here until a few weeks ago," replied March. "This plot wasn't put together that quickly. When we put all the bits of 'intel' together, an individual—maybe more than one—has been operating here for at least six months."

"And what is your assumption based on? Info from these private investigators, one of them supposedly working undercover with this cell?"

"Well not entirely. The Fed's have had him on their radar screen for some time as well."

"I see. How did this former Ranger manage to infiltrate this cell?"

"He was recruited by them back in early summer, in Toronto. He's the guy who was shot a few days ago. The PI's name is Don Carling, and I spoke to him last night. He's on the scene in Phoenix now, helping our people there."

"Well, perhaps they shouldn't have played a lone hand for so long. If it all turns to shit later today, they may have some serious questions to answer," said Egan.

March wasn't so sure the situation was as cut and dried as the AD pictured it. Don Carling had given a logical explanation as to why he had waited until now to contact the authorities. They had pressed on with their investigation hoping that Tom Allman would eventually find out exactly when and how the plot was to be executed.

"Well, let's hope that 'better late than never' applies here," March said. If not for Carling, he knew, the first explosion and communique might have come as a complete surprise to them.

64

FARMER MIGHT NOT HAVE SPOTTED the tail so easily if it had been a normal Thursday morning in America's largest city. Most weekdays saw the streets clogged with taxis, delivery vans and trucks of all sizes. It was 7:44 by the clock on the Bank of America building as he turned onto East River Drive, and he driven less than two miles before he became aware of the grey sedan. The car was still following him when he reached the ramp to the Manhattan Bridge. After descending onto Flatbush Avenue at the Brooklyn end, Bakir realized he had no choice but to abort his hastily arranged rendezvous with FOX. The need for the urgent meeting arose when he hadn't received the scheduled call from BREEDER in France at 6 a.m., a call to okay the release of the third and final communique and then authorize VET to detonate the rest of the explosives.

RATHER THAN CONTINUE TOWARDS JFK airport, he turned left at the first traffic light. Three lights further on, he turned right, keeping to the speed limit, and driving in the curb lane. The tail was still a conservative twenty or so yards behind when he turned into the Sunnyview Mall's large and mostly empty parking lot. The grey sedan turned into the next entrance fifty yards further on.

Still hoping to give the impression that he was just out for a casual drive, he entered the drive-thru lane at Starbucks, the only business that appeared to be open. He ordered an expresso coffee via the radio box and drove around the building to the pick up window. From this vantage point, he had a clear view of the parking lot while he waited for his coffee. The grey car was nowhere in sight.

Slightly relieved, he retraced his route back towards the airport expressway. *Could his pursuers have passed surveillance to another vehicle?* he wondered. *Or was he just being paranoid?*

The answer was delivered just minutes later via a sudden and frightening jolt when he stopped for a red light.

Seconds after he noticed the rapidly approaching vehicle in his rear view mirror, the dark SUV had rammed his rear bumper. The impact snapped him forward against his seatbelt, but wasn't enough to activate the air bag. As he straightened up, the grey sedan reappeared and screeched to a halt in front of him at a forty-five degree angle.

Before it fully registered in his mind that the 'accident' was staged, both his front doors were yanked open.

"Sir, get out! Your gas tank is leaking!" urged a man wearing a toque and heavy sweater as he reached across the stunned driver and released his seat belt. "It could blow up at any moment!"

As soon as the belt was free, the FBI agent literally dragged the shocked terrorist out of his seat. Another agent grabbed his other arm, and he was unceremoniously propelled towards a police cruiser that had miraculously appeared on the scene.

"My briefcase!" he moaned, the only words that he managed to get out of his cotton-filled mouth before he was shoved into the cruiser's rear seat.

WORD THAT BAKIR HAD BEEN apprehended reached Washington at 8:33. "We've got the bastard!" said an elated FBI Agent Dwight Ewing. "He had the draft of another message in his briefcase!"

"What does it say?" asked Bob March.

"Well, it looks like he was still working on it. He'd crossed out and changed some of the wording, and has question marks after others. It's a bit rambling in places, too. But there's some key info in it. I think he was probably on his way to consult with someone higher up."

"But you took him down before that happened?"

"Yeah, unfortunately, but it looked like he was on to us. So I decided to move up the operation," replied Ewing. "He was heading for the bridge back to Manhattan, probably back to the mission." "Then you obviously made the right call, Dwight. Good show!" lauded March. "Give me the gist of the message."

MARCH HAD LEFT THE WAR Room to take the call from New York, and when he returned he huddled with AD Egan and the vice-president. Since the pre-dawn meeting began shortly after six o'clock, the assemblage had been debating the pros and cons of the plan put together by those on the scene in Arizona, and when it should be carried out. After hearing March's report, the vice-president rapped the table to get everyone's attention.

"Gentlemen, listen up, please. We now have confirmed intelligence as to the next move planned the terrorists. They intend to detonate as many as twenty bombs at noon Arizona time. In other words, less than five hours from now. I'll give you fifteen minutes to consider how to handle this information, specifically whether or not to go public with it. In the mean time I need to speak privately with the president."

President Bush—after conferring with the vice-president and his other advisors last night—had decided not to return to Washington. His unplanned appearance would only lead to alarming and unhelpful conjecture by the media, they felt. Not only that, the president's personal physician was strongly opposed to him making the trip.

The president had come down with a severe chest cold two days before he and his family had flown to Texas. His condition had worsened, and he was now being treated for double pneumonia, and confined to bed.

After his call to Texas, the vice-president read the text of the press release that was to be distributed to the dozens of media representatives waiting in the White House briefing room.

Federal authorities continue to investigate the suspicious explosions in Wyoming and Texas. An unknown terrorist organization has claimed responsibility for the attacks. It is not known at this time if more bombings can be expected, but the president has been assured that concerted efforts are underway to locate and apprehend the perpetrators. The Department of Homeland Security urges all citizens to be vigilant and continue to report suspicious activity immediately.

March didn't envy the spokesperson who would have to deal with the barrage of questions and demands for details that the rather vague statement would draw.

The administration was between a rock and a hard place, of that March had no doubt. It just wasn't possible to bring rail traffic nationwide to a halt, let alone check every car. It would take weeks, even months, to search them all. Time they didn't have. With three suspected cell members now in custody, going after the two in Arizona was the only option that might prevent the plot from succeeding. The president, his advisors, and the representatives from the other agencies entrusted with the nation's security, had given unanimous assent to the plan put together last night in Phoenix. A bold and deadly attack on the terrorist's RV from the air, to be launched at first light this morning in Arizona.

THE PLAN WAS DEFINITELY DOABLE, according to the Operations Officer for the USAF A-10 Thunderbolt squadron. But the lack of a straight run to the target—the small recreational vehicle resting in the corner of the mountainside parking lot—would require some fancy flying by the pilots. That was the opinion of the squadron's CO when the request reached him. The pilots would need GPS coordinates for the target area, information they would use to position themselves for a visual attack. The A-10 attack aircraft was equipped with a rapid-fire Avenger Gatling-type cannon mounted in the nose and air-to-ground missiles. The straight-winged, subsonic jet was also known as the Warthog.

A three-man team of weapons specialists, plus a radio operator from the local Army National Guard unit, had left Phoenix at 1 a.m. to aid the air attack. They were equipped with laser guns and associated hardware. Although A-10 pilots were capable of manual attacks on a surface target—a tank, for instance—'lighting up' the RV with a laser would give the onboard tracking system a 'can't miss' focal point before the pilot depressed his firing button.

As soon as the Guard vehicle turned onto the mountain access road three and a half hours later, the Highway Patrol set up a manned road-block. Drivers planning to head up the mountain were told that an accident was blocking the road and it would probably be mid-afternoon before it was re-opened.

The camouflaged-clad team rendezvoused with a very hungry Charlie Minh—he'd finished his small store of supplies yesterday, figuring he would have been relieved long before now. He devoured the chicken sandwich a soldier offered him before they set out on foot for the parking lot, with Minh wheeling his bike. Once they reached the lot, Minh pointed out the darkened RV. The team assembled and tested their weapons and equipment, and by 0645 hours had hidden themselves in the woods below the RV. Sunrise would occur at 07:37, and the A-10 pilots were to make radio contact with the ground team by 07:30.

A surprise attack from the air might have succeeded, too, if the weather hadn't closed in...

"OH SHIT," MUTTERED THE NATIONAL Guard sergeant, "we're fucked." He was pointing at the cloud bank moving rapidly towards the parking lot from the west, just as the first rays of sunlight were striking the mountain peak.

The clouds and fog enveloped the parking lot and ski slopes just as the lead A-10 pilotcall sign Green One—called for a radio check. The two A-10s were thirty miles south at an altitude of 14,000 feet, he reported, but had no visual contact with the ground. He requested a weather check in the target area.

"Clouds have just moved in, Green One. Forward 'vis' less than a mile. Ceiling estimated at two to three hundred feet."

"Roger that," replied Green One. "It looks like it could be a temporary condition. Skies are clear to the west of the area."

The A-10s were carrying enough fuel to hold for an hour, make an attack run, and then return to base. They climbed to 28,000 feet to conserve fuel and wait until the weather improved. "Will standby this frequency. Check in every one-five minutes with an update," the pilot instructed.

"Roger. Will do," acknowledged the sergeant.

After the planes were in a holding pattern at the higher altitude, the leader radioed a situation report to the military radar controller tracking them, and requested it be passed on.

THE REPORT OF THE WEATHER problem was met with groans and curses when it was relayed to the White House.

"And if it doesn't improve? Is there a plan B?" Vice-President Cheney asked Acting Director Egan, who turned to Bob March for an answer.

"Yes, sir, there is. It was suggested by the PI, actually, and he ran it by me last night. I don't know if it got off the drawing board, but it wouldn't hurt to check with them.

"Do it, March," ordered Egan, checking the clock. "Time is running out, goddamn it! We're talking less than four hours now before we're faced with another 9/11. And that is not something I want to have to answer for!"

Don Carling and Hank 'Razor' Gillette were sitting at Tom All-man's bedside when an intern entered and picked up the still-unconscious man's chart. All his vital signs were stable, he assured them, but he wouldn't offer an opinion on how much longer his coma might last.

After the doctor left, Gillette leaned over his buddy. "Wake up, Trigger! Ya' goldbrickin' SOB!"

Don was still chuckling when his cell phone buzzed. Bob March was on the line. After he'd told Don about the bad weather, he had two questions for him. Were they still capable of carrying out the plan Don had spoken of last night? And if so, how long before they could be ready to go? Don asked him to hold, and put the questions to Gillette.

"Yeah, there's still time, but it's cuttin' it a bit fine. An hour, maybe a little more," shrugged the Texan. It was 8:40 a.m. in Arizona.

"Okay, we can do it. We made a start on it last night," Don said, and gave March the estimate.

"Thank God for that!" he replied. "I'll clear it with the Phoenix command center to make sure you get their full co-operation. If the A-10s can't make an attack, you'll be the primary element."

"Good thing we didn't listen to that prick last night when he basically told us to fold our tent and piss off," said Gillette. That wasn't exactly how Don had read the situation, but he'd come to realize that Gillette, like his buddy, Tom Allman, wasn't a big fan of government officials.

The senior FBI agent from Los Angeles, Charles Waite, had arrived yesterday to take over the operation. He'd quickly shot down their idea for a Plan B. If the air attack failed, he'd get the army team to take out the RV.

" That might negate the element of surprise, you know. They would only need a matter of seconds to detonate the explosives if they see they're about to be attacked," Don's had suggested, but Waite hadn't seen that as a problem.

As they were driving away from the FBI building, Gillette said, "Think I should call Chad Rich anyway, Don?"

"Damned right I do. There's too much on the line here, and Waite's overconfidence scares me. Having another alternative is a 'no brainer' in my mind."

In hindsight, it was a good call. Gillette's friend would be ready and waiting if needed.

65

"DIDN'T I SAY THAT WEATHER around the mountain was unpredictable in November? Those A-10s would need almost perfect visual conditions to make a successful attack up there," said Razor Gillette, pointing at the rising terrain in front of the Bell 407 helicopter. "And they sure as hell haven't got it with all this cloud. So much for the rosy forecast that 'fed' dummy put his faith in."

The helicopter's pilot, Captain Chad Rich, nodded. He and Hank Gillette had trained together at the Army's Flight School in Fort Rucker, Alabama, in 1988, and stayed in touch after their careers had taken them down different paths. Rich left the Army in '94 to join the Arizona Department of Public Safety [DPS] He'd been appointed head of the aviation detachment based in Phoenix three years ago. Rich hadn't needed any convincing after Gillette had filled him in on the terrorist plot. He'd readily agreed to help, and made a few calls of his own to set things up.

Rich had scheduled a 'routine training flight' for this morning. He donned his flying suit and was headed out the door five minutes after getting the call from Hank Gillette. His wife gave him a dirty look as he blew her a kiss. "Don't sweat it, sweetheart," he smiled, "I'll be back in time for the family festivities this afternoon."

The chopper's engine was idling smoothly and Rich had completed his pre-flight checks when Gillette and Don Carling climbed aboard at 9:45. Gillette had never flown the Bell 407, but after a quick briefing from Rich on the craft's avionics and radio set-up, he was ready to handle the co-pilot duties. After a short hop to Army National Guard base to pick up the weapon Gillette had requested, they were airborne again and heading north.

As the chopper disappeared from his view, the Guard unit's Senior NCO was still puzzling over the signal from Washington authorizing the immediate release of the army weaponry to civilians.

WHEN THEY OVERFLEW FLAGSTAFF AT 11:02, Gillette radioed their position and gave an ETA of 11:25 for the target area. They had been flying in clear skies, but visibility began to drop quickly as they neared the mountainous area. Rich slowed the chopper's forward speed to 60 knots per hour to deal with the worsening conditions. By the time the parking lot loomed into sight, forward visibility was a mile at the most. The outside air temperature had dropped to a few degrees above freezing, and Rich had activated the anti-icing systems for the helicopter's engine and rotor blades.

"OVER THERE!" GILLETTE SAID, POINTING to the man waving at them. Rich tilted towards the figure, and gently settled onto the wet gravel surface twenty yards away. It was now 11:42.

"Hurry up, I'm freezing my ass off out here!" shouted Charlie Minh to Hank Gillette, the first one out of the chopper.

Pretending to be an injured bike rider was Minh's role in Plan B. Details of the new plan had been radioed to army unit shortly after the A-10s—having burned through their holding fuel—headed back to base to refuel.

THE NOISE FROM THE APPROACHING helicopter had rattled the RV's windows as it swooped low overhead, adding to a tension-filled atmosphere inside.

"What do you suppose that is doing here?" wondered a nervous Omar.

Archer struggled up from the couch where he'd been dozing and joined him at the window. "...Looks like an emergency plane. It says 'rescue' on it," he said. "Must have been an accident...probably one of those bike riders we've been seeing."

Omar relaxed, but only a little. He checked the time again, something he'd been doing constantly while waiting for FARMER's call. A call that should have come two hours ago. Finally he had digressed from the plan and tried to call FARMER thirty minutes ago, but there was no answer.

What could have gone wrong? Should he wait until exactly noon to detonate the rest of the charges, even without the final okay?

His reluctant accomplice was no help. Archer's only suggestion was to abort the mission, head back to Phoenix, and leave the country. He was sure that something had gone wrong and they should get out while they were still able to. Omar's nerves had taken another hit when he had tried to reach Carlos via satellite phone: his number was no longer in service.

Omar had been monitoring the lone Flagstaff television channel the RV's small aerial pulled in. FARMER should have released the final communique by now, but there was no mention of it on the news broadcast, much to Omar's consternation.

How could the government ignore a warning that more bombs were going to be set off in two hours? The communique was also to have warned that the nation's air traffic system would be attacked over the weekend.

The rhetoric about air travel was a ruse to cause more chaos and panic. There were no plans to attack airplanes or terminals. But Washington wouldn't know that. Just issuing the threat should have the desired effect.

Omar feared that his inability to make contact with the cell members in France and New York spelled disaster, but he wasn't going to admit it to Archer. Nor was he going to abort the mission. With or without a call from FARMER, he had all but decided to carry out the last stage of the plot.

It was just a matter of when...

Should he go ahead and trigger devices now or wait until noon? He also harbored thoughts of setting off all the remaining charges, not just those in chosen locations. *Why not? Some might not cause much physical damage, but it would add to the panic and economic damage.*

He'd ordered Frank to stop whining, and an icy silence had ensued between them. When he wasn't pacing, Omar's attention was on his innovative control panel, *PETBE*

The key component in the satchel-like devices was a microchip designed to trigger various signals. One, of course, was to fire the detonator when a *PETBE*-activated satellite call was received. The chip also contained a data base of latitude and longitude coordinates for 30 prime targets. Omar had complied the information from maps and the Internet before the panel had been packed and shipped to Mexico. When a rail car's GPS coordinates placed it within a one-mile radius of a stored position, its corresponding light on *PETBE* lit up. It would remain ON unless the car moved outside the one-mile radius again.

As most of the prime targets were not singular structures—such as a building or a bridge—they did not have to be pinpointed to more exacting criteria. A blast in the middle of an oil tank farm, for instance, would definitely result in a conflagration of major proportions.

Just before the helicopter appeared, Omar had checked the five lights illuminated on *PETBE* against map locations. A surge of accomplishment washed over him. America was in for a massive shock—just as he'd predicted to Carlos when the plot was still in the planning stages.

Two of the lights corresponded to cars that were definitely situated in areas that fit the bill. They were in the midst of multiple refineries and storage tanks along the shores of Galveston Bay south of Houston, Texas. Fires started there could take days or even weeks to extinguish, with the resultant damage to the supply system.

On the West Coast, a tank car was sitting near a major petroleum facility south of Los Angeles. Another was slowly moving through the port area at Long Beach, California.

Further north in Seattle, Washington, a freight train was idling on the tracks that passed through the heart of the city. What the terrorist didn't know was that the tank car full of liquid gas and fitted with the explosive device was only twenty-five yards from the cavernous Qwest Stadium. And inside the stadium—home to the National Football League's Seattle Seahawks—over sixty thousand football fans were awaiting the kick-off of today's game.

BESIDE THE HELICOPTER, TWO SOLDIERS unloaded the stretcher and placed it beside the 'injured' biker, Charlie Minh. Captain Rich remained in his seat, with the engine at idle and the blades slowly rotating, hoping that anyone watching would view it as an emergency airlift of an accident victim.

While Minh was being attended to, Gillette readied the shoulder-mounted assault weapon [SMAW]. The rocket it contained was capable of destroying a tank 500 yards away. As soon as Washington gave the go ahead, moving five yards to his left would put him in front of the chopper with a clear field of fire to the target.

AGENT BOB MARCH YANKED HIS headset off and spoke to the vice-president. "Sir, the helicopter is on the ground and ready to take them out. All that's needed now is your authority to fire."

The noisy chatter in the War Room had lessened noticeably in the past hour as the helicopter neared the terrorists' location. It was apparent to everyone that they no longer had any 'wiggle room', a term the vice-president had used quite often while discussion raged over options to end the threat. The officers in the Phoenix command center were also on pins and needles.

"Thanks, March, give me a few minutes to talk with the president."

The V-P reached for the phone to consult with the still bed-ridden Commander-in-Chief, who had been following developments via a monitor positioned at his bedside.

Although the president had already ceded on-the-spot decision making to him, the V-P felt obliged to advise him of the order he was about to give. He knew that the president would ultimately bear the brunt of criticism if the terrorists succeeded, in spite of being incapacitated at the time.

MARCH AND AD EGAN WAITED anxiously for the vice-president to end his call with the president. An eerie silence had fallen over the room. March put his headset back on and glanced again at the wall clocks: the Arizona clock showed 11:51. To March, the numerals appeared to be turning over in 'fast forward' mode. The muted 'thump' of the chopper's blades he could hear in the headset matched his own heartbeat.

Hurry up! We can't wait much longer! What if the terrorists decide not to wait for the noon deadline? Why did he have to speak to the president now?

IN THE RV, OMAR CONTINUED to fiddle with the control panel. Archer abruptly stood up and opened the door. "I'm going over to the toilet. Maybe I can see what's happening around that airplane," he said, stepping outside without waiting for a response.

Archer spirits had risen temporarily when they had moved up to the parking lot yesterday and he'd spotted the portable toilets. He'd had enough of using the woods for his bodily functions. The 'Port-a-Pottys' were lined up on the far side of the parking lot near the helicopter. As he got close enough to see the activity around the aircraft clearly, he froze.

That guy's holding a weapon of some kind on his shoulder! And there are soldiers!

The confused Frenchman's first instinct was to keep going to distance himself from Omar. Instead, he made a fatal mistake. He did an about turn and started quickly back towards the RV ...

RICH HAD BEEN KEEPING AN anxious watch on the time as Archer approached. It was 11:54. When the startled man suddenly turned around he grabbed for the microphone.

"Washington, we've been blown! We need that okay to fire in ten seconds or it'll be too late!"

There was no doubt of the urgency in the pilot's voice. March glanced towards the vice-president, who was still on the phone. "...Jeezus," he muttered. "Hurry up!"

A caution his instructors had emphasized numerous times during his training flashed through his mind... *'In certain situations, he who hesitates might end up dead.'*

Before he knew what he was saying, the words were out of his mouth. "Go ahead! Take them out!"

Rich reacted immediately, rapping sharply on the craft's plexiglass bubble to get Gillette's attention. When he looked up, Rich gave him a 'thumbs up' and pointed at the RV. Gillette acknowledged, sidled clear of the chopper, and steadied the launcher on his shoulder. He trained the weapon's optical scope on the target and made a slight adjustment to focus the crosshairs squarely on RV's side.

In the RV, Omar—seeing the shocked look on Archer's face as he was quickly retracing his steps—reached for the master switch on *PETBE*. The time had come, he couldn't delay any longer. "Allah Akbar, Allah Akbar," he intoned reverently. The switch would detonate all the remaining charges.

Gillette braced himself for the expected kickback and squeezed the trigger. Milliseconds later, and before the Arab could flick the switch, the RV disintegrated in a yellow fireball.

"Fuckin' A!" shouted a soldier

"Amen to that, brother! Wow!" from another.

A third soldier remarked laconically, "Think their collision insurance will cover that?"

DON CARLING RAN TOWARDS THE downed figure of Frank Archer, lying motionless fifteen yards from the smoking wreck. What he saw, as he neared the body, stopped him dead in his tracks and caused him to gag. He managed to swallow the surge of bile as he gaped at the sight. The corpse was headless. He drew the back of his hand over his mouth and peered around. Archer's head, its eyes wide open, lay twenty feet away atop the jagged piece of metal siding that had sliced it cleanly off.

Carling swallowed again, stepped carefully around the body and approached the blackened depression holding the crumpled remnants of the RV. The largest identifiable parts were the engine block and an axle. He stared at what he first thought was a pile of fibreglass insulation and bloody rags. It took him a few seconds to realize exactly what he was seeing—body parts of the vehicle's lone occupant. A severed hand, its bloody fingers grotesquely curled around a toggle switch, lay at his feet.

Rich sat motionless in the cockpit, watching Carling. When he turned and started back towards the helicopter, Rich pressed the mic button. "Mission accomplished...target eliminated, over."

THE PILOT'S TERSE MESSAGE SPARKED an outburst of applause and handshakes at the White House. March joined in and exhaled a long sigh of relief . Seconds after he'd given the order to fire without permission, Vice-President Cheney had motioned to him. "Its up to us. Give them the green light," he'd ordered. March had turned away and faked a call. He would never have to tell the nation's Number Two that he had jumped the gun.

While the noisy chatter around him continued, March's throat suddenly felt as if he'd swallowed a handful of sand, and he reached for a bottle of water. *Are we celebrating too soon? Did the terrorists have time to set off more explosives?* He kept the thoughts to himself, though, and another anxious hour passed before he finally relaxed.

Two hours after the RV was destroyed, another Guard unit summoned from Flagstaff had sterilized the site. The wreckage was loaded onto a flatbed truck, covered with tarpaulins and hauled away to be examined by forensic experts. Frank Archer's corpse and the remains of the Arab terrorist were placed in body bags and flown back to Phoenix aboard an army helicopter.

Bob March was stuffing papers into his briefcase when the vice-president came over and extended his hand. "Well done, March, I believe most of the credit for the successful conclusion to our problem belongs to you. And that's exactly what I told the president."

March blushed. "Thank you, sir, but it really took a coordinated effort by a number of people to pull it off."

"You're too modest, March," smiled the V-P. "But before you make any plans for the rest of the weekend, I have another job for you."

66

FRIDAY, NOVEMBER 26

The Lear jet carrying Bob March landed in Phoenix at 11 a.m. A DHS agent met him and whisked him off to the federal building where Don Carling, Hank Gillette, and the local law enforcement officers involved in yesterday's action awaited him.

"The president has asked me to convey his sincere thanks for your timely and professional efforts," March told the gathering. "And I can now state with confidence that your efforts prevented a callous terrorist attack on our nation over this Thanksgiving weekend."

March then asked each of the officials to relate for the record the actions they or their organizations had taken in the hours leading up to yesterday's deadline. Their accounts would be included in a comprehensive report that he was to prepare for the president and all the agencies responsible for national security. When he had all the needed information, March threw the meeting open for questions. Hands shot up all around the table, and he quickly changed his mind.

"Tell you what, gentlemen, I think I know what you're going to ask," he smiled broadly. "So perhaps it might be better if I tell you as much as I can about this cell and its origins. The investigation has international ramifications and for obvious reasons there are certain aspects I can't talk about now. But I can tell you this..."

The terrorist cell, previously unknown to US intelligence agencies, was supposedly backed by al-Qaeda World. Only a few if its members were operating in the US. Two were now dead and a third was in custody in New York. March didn't know the identity of the terrorist killed in the RV. Neither he nor Archer had checked out of their motel rooms before their trip north. Archer had left his passports behind, hidden in the lining of a suitcase, but nothing to identify his accomplice was found in the other room. No passport, airline tickets, nothing with a name on it. Archer's name was on registration slips for both rooms. It was assumed that the unknown victim had his papers with him and they were destroyed along with the RV. One usable thumb print had been lifted from his mangled remains and had been forwarded to Interpol for possible identification.

"To sum up, then, my department believes that this cell and its plot was a 'one off' situation and will not be heard from again," stated March. "However, I'm sure you all realize there will be others and I urge you to remain vigilant every day on the job. Thanks again for your help."

MARCH HAD PURPOSELY BYPASSED DON Carling during the debriefing, but took him aside now.

"Don, I personally think my government owes you and your helpers a commendation of the highest order. But that isn't going to happen," shrugged March. "Because—"

Carling held up his hand. "It's okay, Bob, I understand completely. I know we pushed the envelope, and almost went too far before contacting you, but..."

"Hey, it wouldn't have been possible without you guys, and you won't be called on the carpet over anything you did or didn't do."

March revealed that arrests made in France and Britain—suspects initially identified by Carling's investigation of Archer/Amara—effectively derailed the cell's ability to communicate in the critical hours before their Thanksgiving Day deadline.

Carling shook the federal agent's hand and they exchanged business cards. "What do you think chances are of me getting a copy of your report? Slim to nil, right?" asked Don, half in jest.

March returned his smile. "Tell you what, your friend in Ottawa will receive a copy. I'll leave it up to him to decide whether or not to show it to you. Okay?"

Epilogue

TWO WEEKS LATER ...

Homeland Security had issued a press release late on Friday, November 26, the day after the terrorists were eliminated.

It read: *'The two explosions that occurred early this week are now thought to have been caused by a small group of eco-terrorists attempting to disrupt the rail system. There is no proof that they have any ties to al-Qaeda, in spite of the communiques that were purportedly attributed to that terrorist organization. The national transport system is subject to strict security and the public should not be hesitant about using it.'*

The timing of the release effectively defused public fear about the possibility of more attacks for two reasons.

First of all, Black Friday, as the day after Thanksgiving is known, was the busiest shopping day of the year in the US. Few among the millions of bargain-seekers were aware of it, and by Monday it was old news. And second, as there had been no further communiques, the media had nothing with which to contest the DHS assessment.

There was a very good reason for the silence: the surviving cell members were still incarcerated.

Karim Ahmad Bakir, the suspected ringleader masquerading as the Cote Verde trade attache, was the subject of a legal battle between his lawyers and the US Justice Department. Not surprisingly, his lawyers had agreed to conduct negotiations out of the public eye. Bakir did have diplomatic immunity, and the US did intend to deport him. They were delaying to give Germany time to put together a possible case against him in regard to his actions in Hamburg on behalf of the 9/11 attackers.

In France, Carlos Amara was not talking. He was being held incommunicado in a military prison and would eventually be charged with numerous offences, including membership in a terrorist organization and aiding and abetting murder. His father and uncle would also be charged after authorities determined exactly what role they had played in the younger man's plot. For her cooperation, Francoise Amara was allowed to go free.

The British link to the cell, Saahir Kayani, detained at the request of the Americans, was no longer in custody. However, he was once again under 24/7 surveillance, effectively neutralized from taking part in any subversive activity that British extremists might be planning.

In Washington, DHS agent Bob March was still working on his report about the terrorist plot that had been averted in dramatic fashion on Thanksgiving Day. The 'turkey without the trimmings' plot, as he referred to it, when discussing it with his aide, Jane Bloom. He'd made a thorough study of the intercepted email traffic, phone intercepts, and other intelligence data, looking for missed clues that might have brought the plot to their attention sooner.

Eventually he concluded that the plotters had been extremely clever in disguising their intentions. The code words, limited use of dates, shipment references, and innocent phrasing were all designed to mislead analysts who might have come across them. Without more definitive evidence with which to paint a cohesive picture of the cell, the data was given a low priority initially. Fortunately it all came together in time, thanks to intelligence received from the British and Canadian counterterrorism forces. Intelligence that they had strung together after information regarding the terrorists had first been brought to their attention by PI Don Carling.

March's report was to include an update on the search for unexploded devices rolling stock moving about the country. Experts had concluded that once their batteries died, it was highly unlikely they would explode. However, a monumental task to locate and disable them was underway and so far a dozen had been found. The first to be discovered was on the tank car that had been moving slowly past Qwest Stadium in Seattle, Washington, at exactly noon on Thanksgiving Day.

ALL THE CELL MEMBERS REFERRED to by a code name had been identified and were either dead or in custody except for one...

FOX had returned to work as usual at JFK airport on Monday after the Thanksgiving holiday weekend. To his co-workers and employer, Rene Amara was known as Roger Caron. He'd spent an anxious four days, at times expecting to be arrested at any moment. When Karim [FARMER] hadn't kept their rendezvous on Thanksgiving Day—and hadn't been heard from since—he knew they were in trouble. The misleading press release from Homeland Security only confirmed what he'd already realized: he would never hear from Francois [GROWER], Omar [VET] or Carlos [BREEDER] again.

He was left with no choice but to resume his role as a sleeper agent. A role that would have him show up twice a year—July 4 and New Year's Day—at the same location and same time in the arrivals area at JFK Airport to see if anyone contacted him with a new assignment.

IN TORONTO, DON CARLING WAS humming happily as he stepped off the elevator and into Danielle Clyde's office.

"Congratulations, Don!" she enthused, surprising him with a hug and a big smile. "And thank you for making time for me today of all days. I'm sure you and your fiancee have plenty to do before your wedding."

"Not really, we're fairly well ready to go. Yvonne is a great organizer, and I've left most of it to her. We fly to Barbados tomorrow and the wedding is the next day." Danielle indicated the large leather sofa beside her desk, and they both sat down. "And I did want to give you a full report on my investigation before we left."

"Well I can't thank you enough for your efforts, and I really appreciated your call from Arizona to tell me what happened to Francois."

He shrugged. "That was the least I could do. I didn't know when or even if the American authorities planned to contact you. So far they've managed to keep a lid on what really happened, but I'm sure the full story will come out some day courtesy of a keen investigative journalist."

"No doubt, but personally I'll be content if it doesn't, at least with regard to Frank's involvement."

Don gave her a sanitized version of the terrorist plot, focusing on her dead husband's role. The only name he mentioned was that of his cousin, Carlos Amara. "Carlos was the mastermind, and why Frank went along with him we'll probably never know."

"I had no idea that's what he was up to, no idea at all," said Danielle, her amazement showing.

Why would you, given your 'non-marriage' all these years? Don kept the thought to himself. "I promised you some good news, too, didn't I?"

He told her what Paul Boutin had discovered about Frank's illicit art dealings, transactions in which he acquired paintings that were never delivered to Canada. Two gallery owners in Paris, and one in Geneva, admitted having prepared false invoices at Archer's behest. Basically, Archer would purchase more paintings than were shipped to Toronto. But the invoice submitted to Danielle's company would show a total price of all the works he'd bought.

"Frank had the others, ten in all, delivered to either the Amara chalet or his sister's condo in Paris," Don explained. "According to her, he planned to open a gallery of his own after he moved back to France for good. My colleague is arranging for them to be shipped to you."

"So that's why you wanted those invoices... well done!"

DON ONLY HAD ONE MORE item on his 'To Do' list before he and Yvonne left for Barbados.

Tom Allman had emerged from his coma ten days after he'd been shot, and was recuperating at Razor Gillette's ranch. Don had left it to Razor to give Allman the full story of what had happened after he'd been gunned down. He poured a glass of wine for Yvonne and a scotch on the rocks for himself before he called Texas.

"Hey, pard, how're ya doin? Razor told me you're gettin' married. Who's the unlucky gal?"

"It's the wonderful Yvonne, and she's right here beside me. We've got you on speaker phone so watch your language," chuckled Don. At the other end, Gillette was also listening in.

"Don't do it, Yvonne!" Allman urged, "you're resignin' yourself to a life of misery and all that twangin' and bangin' stuff he considers music!"

"Well, I was hoping that whack to your brain might have shaken loose some unused smart cells," countered Don, "but obviously that didn't happen, *Trigger.*"

The emphasis wasn't lost on Allman. "Ahh, somebody's been tellin' stories, hasn't he?"

A FEW DAYS INTO OPERATION Desert Storm in 1991, American forces were poised to drive the Iraqi army from Kuwait. An army helicopter made an end run from Saudi Arabia and deposited Allman's Ranger squad in a remote area a few miles inside the Iraqi border. They had landed under a moonless sky at 0100 hours, and hunkered down in a depression between two sand dunes. Their mission was to take out a nearby artillery battery at dawn. With a few hours to kill, the four-man team settled down to grab some shut-eye. As leader, Allman took the first watch, and moved halfway up one of the dunes.

"I was just nicely into dreamland when he's rousting us, telling us we've got company," said Razor, chuckling. "'I nailed one of 'em!' he yells." With their adrenalin surging, the team had donned night vision goggles and quickly set up a defensive box between the dunes. "So, we lie there for thirty minutes, all puckered up, waitin' for a horde of 'I-raquis' to—"

"Yeah, yeah, just get on with it, Razor," muttered Allman.

"Want to guess what our fearless leader's itchy trigger finger had wasted, Don?" Without waiting for an answer, the Texan blurted, "A big old curious camel! Emptied a whole magazine into the poor thing! Seems it didn't know the password!"

CPSIA information can be obtained at www.ICGtesting.com
Printed in the USA
239708LV00002B/14/P